i

Beaton Again

By the same author

John Beaton Series
The Beaton Path
Beaton Back

Children's story
Moonbly Moonjuice

Stage Play/Dinner Theater
The Duck Hunt

Beaton Again

The Third John Beaton Adventure

Alan Searle

To grandchildren everywhere

John Beaton had never liked February. Why would he? No one else in the Pacific Northwest did. It was unpredictable. It would be cold, just above freezing, with horizontal rain. Then, when you thought of giving it all up and moving to southern California, it teased you with a sunny day and a little color returned to the earth. Of course, the color was likely to be gone just as quickly, browned by frost, covered by snow, or, in the case of the decapitated crocuses he was frowning at, eaten by deer.

The only thing February had in its favor was it was short, but not short enough. It didn't help that he was recovering from a cold and couldn't summon the courage to get out of the house, go to the gym and try to pretend he was bicycling along leafy summer lanes instead of pedaling a static machine in a testosterone sweat-shop. He was standing on his front porch, protected from the rain, if not the wind, looking and coughing at the suburban deer-damage and wishing he lived in the country again. Then he could have had his revenge, filled the freezer with venison and no one would have noticed. He couldn't do that in suburbia. His neighbors would object and there would be "consequences."

Or perhaps there wouldn't? Maybe they'd join in with a deer-kill – he thought the neighbors were unlikely to have been spared the assault on their flower beds.

There was one minor obstacle to the fantasy slaughter; the home owners' association regulations forbade hunting (but did they say anything about just killing?) There was also one major obstacle – he had never killed a deer in his life and doubted that the only weapon he possessed, a sharp kitchen knife, would get the job done. He was much more likely to murder more crocuses, or himself, than any doe-eyed bucks. Or was it buck-eyed does? He shrugged, took off his boots and moved them far away from the grasping reaches of the weather, opened the door, stepped inside the warm house, put on what he hoped were deer-skin slippers (maybe there was some justice in the world) and took the mail to his armchair.

"The deer ate the crocuses," he announced.

"I know," Ann replied, immersed in her book.

"Oh."

"I noticed it yesterday." She looked up. "Is that the mail?"

"Yes. There's not much — a couple of bank statements, a few charity requests, and a job-offer for you on a postcard." He handed her the mail, sat back in his chair in front of the pseudo-log gas fire and picked up The Economist.

Ann looked over the job offer, the requests for urgent money, and with the envelopes from the bank statements placed the paper in the recycle pile by her feet, and returned to her book.

"It says here that the degree of global warming we are likely to get may postpone one or two ice ages," John said, glancing up from his magazine.

"Oh, yeah?"

"Yeah. Unfortunately, it doesn't say if that's going to be bad or good."

"Mm."

"It probably means we won't need our woolen underwear for at least another thirty-thousand years."

"That's good."

"It could be hard on clothes moths. They might go extinct if there's no wool for them to chew on for all that time … on the other hand maybe they'll be quite happy chewing the woolen underwear which humans are storing in boxes under their beds."

"Maybe."

"So, you agree then. We might as well get rid of the woolen underwear we don't have?"

"Of course."

"Did you hear what I said?" John asked.

"Of course." She turned a page.

"Yeah?"

"You said how wonderful I would look in woolen underwear, so you are going to buy some so you can sell it, and just keep me in silk underwear for the rest of my life. I think that's sweet. That's what you said, didn't you?" She looked up.

John hesitated, smiled at Ann and said, "You were listening. You are quite correct."

They both returned to their reading.

The afternoon wore on, the rain persisted, but they were warm.

A game of Scrabble after dinner broke the monotony of the evening, but by 10:30 they were in bed, had cuddled, wished each other good-night, and by 10:35 they were both asleep.

His cell-phone rang.

John looked at his watch. It was 4:00 am.

He blinked himself awake, picked up the phone and answered. "John Beaton."

"Oh, Mr. Beaton, I hope we didn't get you up too early?" It was a woman.

"Well…"

"Only we waited to twelve o'clock, you see, and Janet said it's five hours time difference between us and New York, so we thought we'd wait until it was seven with you. That's OK isn't it? I mean we 'aven't got you up too early 'ave we? I mean what time is it with you?"

"It's … it's four o'clock."

"Four o'clock! We're sorry. We can ring back later if you'd like."

"No, please don't do that. I'm awake now anyway."

John recognized the lilting Welsh accent on the phone and added, "What is it then?"

"Well, my name is Gwyneth Morgan and I'm a nurse at Glan Clwyd Hospital and I believe you are the next of kin of Mrs. Olwen Lewis?"

"Yes." John was now wide awake.

"Well, she's all right. She 'ad a turn and she was admitted 'ere yesterday. It looks like she's got a bladder infection and it's made 'er confused. She should be sent home in a couple of days though."

3

"Good. You know her memory hasn't been good these last few years, and she's been getting a lot of help at home?"

"Oh, yes. We know about that. But she seems 'appy enough and we should be able to send 'er home in a couple of days. We'll let you know what's going on. Do you 'ave any questions?"

"No, I can't think of any. Please let me know if anything changes.'

"Oh, we will. Sorry to wake you." She rang off.

John turned onto his back, sighed and looked up into the blackness of the room.

Ann asked, "Was that a call from Wales? Auntie Olly?"

"Yes."

"She OK?"

"I don't know. That was the hospital; probably a UTI caused her to get more confused and she's been there a couple of days. They said they plan to release her home in a couple more days, but I don't think that's going to happen. This is probably it."

"What are you going to do?"

"I don't know. I'll have to think about it." He paused and let out a sigh. "I hate being woken at this time in the morning. I don't think I can get back to sleep just now. I'll have a think about it," he repeated.

He gave Ann a quick kiss and got out of bed, closed the bedroom door behind him, then reconsidered. He opened the door again and asked, "If I go over do you want to come?"

"To Wales?"

"Yeah."

"For how long?"

"Maybe about a week."

"Will you be OK by yourself?"

"Oh … yeah."

"Well, I am working tomorrow. Sorry, I am working this morning, and the rest of the week, so it would be easier if I didn't come."

"So, you work and I get to jet-set around the world."

"Someone has to do it."

"Work, or jet-set?"

4

"You figure it out. I want to get back to sleep if there's a chance."

"Good idea."

John reclosed the door and switched on the lights in the corridor. He squinted against the sudden brightness and made his way to his computer. He turned it on and let it do its thing while he poured himself a cup of cold tea and heated it in the microwave. He peeled a banana and took it with his tea to his computer chair.

He'd known this day would arrive sooner or later. Why it hadn't happened sooner was the miracle. Auntie Olly, the last surviving member of his father's siblings, was his father's step-sister. She was born Olwen Gladys Williams and had married John Evans Lewis at the end of the Second World War. Her marriage to John Lewis had not been without its trials and tribulations. She had stuck it out for thirty years, but eventually she could no longer ignore, or support, his drinking and philandering. He had left her, for the "love of his life", one too many times and, with John's father's encouragement she had refused to take him back again. He had begged and claimed Auntie Olly was really the "love of his life", but for once she remained adamant.

Unfortunately, it turned out that, despite his behavior, she probably was the love of his life, and maybe he was the love of hers. When he died six months later she entered two years of grief, guilt, and mourning.

John's father must have felt some responsibility for Olly's condition (although maybe his Welsh Baptist upbringing encouraged him to always feel guilty about something). He took on the task of moving her to live closer to him and ministering to her needs. She became passive and needy and John, if he didn't go out of his way to avoid her, at least didn't spend much energy connecting with her.

All changed when John's father died. She suddenly seemed released from the yoke of being passive and needy, and started to enjoy life more. She joined a choir and a professional women's lunch organization. She resurrected her golf clubs and found new friends to play with. She even jumped on flights to Seattle and dragged companions to visit John.

At her age it could never last. She'd had a good ten years of her new life when a series of small strokes took its toll. They slowed her down, and although outwardly she made a good recovery, her thinking changed. Her judgment failed. She would let any caller into the house during the day, but at night insisted on locking doors with a combination of bolts, locks and chains. If there had been a fire she would never have escaped in time.

And there had been a fire, or at least a pan left on the stove, a smoke-filled house, and the fire department arriving with flashing lights. So, the local authorities cut off the gas to her cook-top with the simple addition of a shut-off valve in a cupboard. The helpful ladies who came to clean the house, chat, and heat a meal for her knew how to turn it on, but Olly never figured it out.

John had visited her whenever he could. He painted her house, cleaned the gutters, pruned the fruit trees and did his best to make sure the house didn't appear neglected, or looked like a little old lady lived there

When it was discovered she was still driving, her license was taken away and she became more isolated and home-bound. John had tried to convince her to move somewhere where she could have had more help and companionship, but she stubbornly refused. Maybe she knew she wouldn't last long anywhere else.

This was what John was concerned about now. Last year he had taken her to the family reunion which had been held at a hotel on the outskirts of Chester. He'd taken care to put her in an adjoining room and left the connecting door open. He'd made sure the family knew her limitations. She seemed to enjoy herself, but two days later, when she was back in her own home, she had no memory of the weekend.

Her continued survival in her own house had been hanging by a thread. She might have recovered from one night, maybe two, in a hospital, but after that the likelihood of her safely returning home diminished by the hour.

John sat at his computer and logged on to his favored airline website. He winced at the cost of flights at such short notice, but booked one for the next day going through Paris to London. He had to get to Colwyn Bay, in North Wales. He considered Manchester; it was closer, but no quicker, considerably more expensive, and he'd have to go through Chicago.

He booked a Virgin train from London to Colwyn Bay, leaving three hours after his arrival at London's Heathrow airport. He hoped that would be enough time to get to the center of London and Euston train station. As it was he wouldn't be getting in to Colwyn Bay much before 8:30 pm. He groaned inwardly at the planned lack of sleep, apprehension, anxiety and jet-lag he had just purchased.

At least he could stay at Auntie Olly's house. It would be strange to be there without her. She had always been there, bustling around in her small kitchen, making cups of tea and coffee, even when she no longer had any way of baking or cooking.

He had to remember to make a note of the code for the key-safe, hidden behind the drain-pipe in the side yard, or he'd be looking for a hotel room. He decided to make a list of things-to-do and things-to-take and wrote 'key' at the top.

Next, he wrote 'Gore-tex'. After all, he was going to Wales in February. He wondered if he would be the only American in Colwyn Bay at that time of year. Maybe he'd be the only American in Wales. He'd have to remember to take dark clothes – he didn't want to stand out any more than he had to. He'd realized years ago he couldn't get by as being British any more. What sounded like a British accent in Port Orchard, Washington State, became as obvious as a Texan drawl to a New Yorker in Wales. He opened his mouth and was instantly recognized as a foreigner, and it seemed the more he tried to speak with an English or Welsh accent the more American he became.

He wrote 'passports', 'money', on his list and looked at the clock. It was already 5:30. He thought about going back to bed to see if he could catch up on some sleep, but knew it would be futile.

7

He brewed himself a fresh cup of tea, and sat at his desk again looking through his diary to see if there were any appointments or meetings he had to cancel for the seven days he would be away, and the four days of brain-fuzz he would experience on his return.

There were none.

Not only would he not be missed, he didn't even have an excuse to pretend to not want to go. Although, it would hardly be pretending – he really had no interest in going to Wales in February.

He let out another sigh and realized he was feeling sorry for himself. In the circumstances he thought that was quite reasonable. He'd do the responsible thing; he'd do what had to be done, and he'd be home, and back into hibernation, in no time at all.

He was pouring Cheerios into his breakfast bowl when Ann appeared in the kitchen, uniformed and ready for work. At five feet and six inches she was only three inches shorter than John, and only one and a half inches shorter when she was wearing her work shoes and he was barefoot, as he was now.

"Good morning, doctor," she said.

"Good morning, nurse," he replied, looked into her blue eyes, smiled, put his arms around her and added, "I might as well get in as many hugs as I can. I won't get many in the next week."

"So, you arranged everything?"

"Yes, out of Seatac tomorrow evening, arrive Thursday, stay a week and then back Thursday of next week."

"You won't have time to get jet-lagged. You'll be gone and back too quickly."

"Maybe. More likely it'll be that I just get over it one way, then have to get over it again when I get back."

"I think if you assume it will be miserable, it will be." She added, "Do you have anything you need to cancel?"

"No, and that doesn't help. No one is going to miss me. There was nothing to cancel.'

"I'll miss you."

"I bet you're only saying that because you're supposed to."

"Damn! You've seen through me again." She squeezed him a little harder, pecked him on the cheek and they broke apart to pursue the business of breakfast.

Thirty minutes later Ann left for work. John picked up his pen and added to his list. He unearthed his small backpack and a rolling duffel-bag from the back of the under-stair closet.

He padded around the house slowly collecting anything he might need. He worked on the principle of getting it all together then winnowing stuff down until he had space. He didn't need a lot of clothing, since he could always do laundry at Auntie Olly's. He'd watched a Rick Steves show once and remembered the aphorism, "There are those who pack light, and those who wished they had packed light."

It was a goal he was working towards, but would probably never achieve. This time he had an excuse. He had to bring back packets of good tea, McVitie's Chocolate Digestive Biscuits, a pound of Cheshire cheese, and Branston Pickle. Maybe he'd find a few treasures from his childhood at Auntie Olly's house to help stuff the bag on his return trip.

He'd once managed three weeks in Mexico in winter with only a regulation-size carry-on bag, but for Wales he would need more protection from the elements – it wouldn't be seventy-five Fahrenheit during the day. He wondered what it was going to be and spent a depressing ten minutes online finding out that no matter how cold, wet and windy it was in Port Orchard, Washington State, the forecast for Colwyn Bay, North Wales, was colder, wetter, and windier

He had also learnt the lesson to not rely on airlines to get both him and his luggage to his destination at the same time. He'd once spent three cold days in Milan in November surviving with one shirt, one light jacket, one pair of hiking trousers, and one pair of underwear while the airline located his checked bag. Since then he'd made sure his carry-on would at least keep him warm, dry, and not underwear-challenged.

By 3:00 he had packed his bags, retrieved a jumbled pile of clothing, which he returned to their hangers and drawers, and was ready to go. He wondered if he should have planned to leave that evening instead of the next day, but that would not be his style. He was tired, wrapped himself in a comforter and lay down on the bed for a brief nap.

He was woken by a kiss from Ann.

Startled, he asked, "What time is it?"

"5:45" She replied.

"I've been asleep for over two hours!"

"Well, you obviously needed it."

"I won't be able to sleep tonight now."

"Yes, you will. I'll make sure you will." She gave him another kiss and lay down on the bed next to him.

Dinner was late again.

The next morning John managed to find a dry spell between rain showers and went for a two-hour walk. He was back by noon, and when the taxi came to pick him up to take him to the Kitsap Airporter shuttle at 2:30 it was 40 Fahrenheit, windy and raining hard.

2

Twenty-one hours and seventeen minutes later Dales Taxi Service dropped John off at Auntie Olly's house in Colwyn Bay. It was 4 degrees centigrade, windy and raining hard.

He stood in the rain and struggled to open the lock-box to access the key. Eventually he had to use the light from his cell-phone to illuminate the numbers. He regretted not wearing his hat, as it became hard to see through his rain-spattered glasses and he felt cold rain creeping down the back of his neck. He had forgotten how quickly his fingers could become stiff in the cold rain, but finally he retrieved the keys, opened the door to the house and stepped inside.

It was completely silent. The sound of the wind and beating rain couldn't penetrate the brick and stone walls of the small semi-detached bungalow where Auntie Olly lived.

Or, John wondered, used to live.

He switched on a light, put down his bags, took off his jacket and walked to the kitchen at the back of the house. He picked up a towel, cleaned his glasses and dried his hair. There was a click as the small refrigerator snapped on and started to hum. Absentmindedly, he opened its door. He found two cartons of milk nearing their expiry date, an unopened package of Cheshire cheese, a half dozen shriveled apples, a partially eaten, but still wrapped, loaf of sliced white bread, but little else. Curious, he opened the freezer compartment and found it stuffed with frozen meals. At least he wouldn't go hungry.

He wandered back into the hallway and noticed a neatly-stacked pile of letters on the shelf. One of the neighbors had probably popped in and organized the mail, but it would have to wait – he wasn't sure his brain could cope. Next to the mail he noticed the telephone. He checked his watch. It was nearly 9:00 pm. Back in Port Orchard it was 1:00 pm. He picked up the handset and dialed. Ann was at work so he just left a short message to say he'd arrived and already missed her.

The house was not cold, but not particularly warm. He checked the thermostat in the hallway and it was set for 13 centigrade. He remembered 16 centigrade was 61 Fahrenheit. He turned up the thermostat to 21 and was rewarded by hearing the gas furnace in the kitchen kick on. It would take an hour or two for the radiators to warm the house, and for the time being he decided to leave his wet jacket on.

He felt exhausted. He was exhausted, but wasn't sure he could sleep. After all, his internal clock thought it was still in Port Orchard, some time shortly after lunch, and he should be reading a novel, working in the yard, or tackling a Sudoku.

He stuck his head around the door to Auntie Olly's bedroom and switched on the light. For a moment he almost expected to see her. The room had been tidied, the bed made, and the assorted clothes she hung over the backs of the three easy chairs in her room had been put away. He turned off the light and quietly closed the door.

The closet-sized spare bedroom was at the back of the house. He picked up his bags and opened the door. Immediately he could feel the cold and see his breath in the light from the forty-watt bulb as he inched his way around the unmade single bed. He felt the radiator. It was stone cold. He knew why. Why bother to heat a room that wasn't being used? He would have done the same. He bent down and turned the radiator knob counter-clockwise and a few seconds later felt a surge of warm water at the top of the radiator.

He smiled to himself. Now this radiator was working he should probably turn off the one in Auntie Olly's room – she'd expect it of him.

He decided to make the bed first, and in order to make this a little easier, and gain some maneuverability; he had to put his bags back in the hallway. At least there was plenty of bedding, although it had that slightly damp feeling from not being used and stored in a cold closet for too long. It also had a lingering odor of moth-balls and mold, but he was too tired to care. Since it was warmer in the hallway than in the bedroom he left the door open when he finished.

He returned to the kitchen and rewarded himself with a cup of hot chocolate. As well as cocoa he'd found tea, a solid lump of something which may have been coffee crystals in the bottom of an unmarked jar, and a collection of full jam jars labeled with Auntie Olly's spidery penmanship. None of these was less than five years old, most were over ten. A little more searching revealed two boxes of bran flakes, a package of prunes and, in an old Quality Street Chocolate Assortment tin, a reliable supply of McVitie's Digestive Biscuits – he would survive.

John took off his jacket, put it over half the radiator and sat at the small kitchen table with his back as close to the rest of the radiator's warmth as he could tolerate.

He dunked a McVitie's Digestive Biscuit in his hot chocolate and looked around at the cluttered kitchen. There were a few refrigerator magnets he recognized from the Pacific Northwest – a plastic refrigerator slug and a plastic Orca whale, but most of the bric-a-brac predated refrigerator magnets – if that were possible. There was a miniature brass bell from Cornwall, a pottery trivet with a Greek inscription, and a three-inch-high doll in Welsh costume. He picked up a small lidded tankard from Edinburgh and inside found a rusty sewing needle, a postage stamp, and a used band-aid. Everything was slightly dusty and greasy.

He sighed, closed his dry and gritty eyes, pushed back against the radiator and rested the back of his head on the wall.

It was all a little depressing. He had vague recollections of some of the significance of the kitchen-cluttering items, but for the most part they had no meaning for him at all. He doubted if Auntie Olly could remember much about them now. He also knew that there were hundreds of similar kitchens, each with dozens of mementoes in the same town, accumulating layers of chip fat and grime once their novelty had faded – they just became joggers-of-memories and things to move when you dusted.

He realized thoughts like that would get him nowhere but even more sorry for himself. He was here and had to make the best of it. He needed to get out of the clothes he had worn for

13

almost twenty-four hours, have a shower, go to bed and see if he could at least get in a few hours sleep before his biological clock interfered again.

Then he remembered the shower and groaned.

For some reason, lost in the archives of building codes in all the municipalities of the whole of Great Britain, British houses had a dual pressure system. Cold water came into the house and supplied the cold taps with pressure, and also filled an open water tank in the attic. This supplied water to a hot water tank somewhere else in the house. The problem was the pressure in the hot water system was solely dependent on the height of the attic tank above whatever tap was being turned on. In a single story building, like Auntie Olly's, this meant there was very low pressure in the hot water system. The British got around this by only having bathtubs with separate faucets, and accepting that four or five times as much water came out of a cold tap as a hot tap. If you wanted a shower you had to have a completely different system which heated cold water at the shower head (far too expensive for Auntie Olly to consider) or you could take the poor man's solution.

This was rubber tubing, available in most fine hardware stores, which fitted over the end of the two taps in the bath and then joined at a shower-head attached to the wall above the bath. If you turned on the cold tap you got a normal shower flow. If you turned on the hot one you got a trickle of water which got less as you raised the shower head. The answer was to keep the shower-head as low as possible, turn the hot fully on and then add a miniscule flow of cold to regulate the temperature. Getting to the point where there was a reasonable temperature meant jumping in and out of the flow as it intermittently froze or scalded any part of your body it could get its hands on.

John realized he couldn't face the shower head. Damn global warming. For once he'd have a bath.

It was amazing. He didn't know why he hadn't had one before. Lying in the hot water with his ears just above the surface was as close as he felt he would ever get to a warm, weightless nirvana. Of course, that's probably why you were only allowed one per week. Any more than that and a good Welsh Baptist could risk his mortal soul if he started to enjoy it.

Eventually, all good things had to come to an end. The water started to cool and the hot tap only produced tepid water, so John thought he should get out of the bath before he felt so relaxed and sleepy he'd never want to get out. Or, more likely, the water cooled so much he'd get hypothermia and never be able to get out.

He sat up, and then stood slowly to get over feeling lightheaded until his body realized what was expected of it. He toweled himself dry and put on a T-shirt and shorts. He cleaned his teeth, reminding himself next time to do that before he laid in the bath. He checked the thermostat temperature, which had soared to 16 centigrade, and reset it to 17. The Welsh part of him wouldn't be able to sleep if it was any warmer than that.

He left his bags outside the spare bedroom, slipped into bed and fell asleep.

3

Ella resisted the urge to look around. She knew Stefan would be close, but she couldn't be sure there weren't other eyes watching her.

It was Stefan's job, not hers, to watch for them.

She wondered again if she wasn't being a little more paranoid than usual. After all, she was just there to meet her brother, Kamal. After seventeen years of silence, and not even a birthday card, he'd contacted her a week ago and asked her to meet him in Istanbul. He said he had a villa on the coast in the town of Avcilar and would arrange for a car to pick her up at the airport.

It had been good to talk to him after all those years and after that argument. With both their parents dead he had assumed that she would bow to his choice for her lifestyle. After all that is what she was expected to do, and that is what her parents would have wanted, or so he had liked to keep reminding her. The final straw was when he found a marriage match for her – a senior attorney from the firm he had recently joined, thirty, no nearly forty years older than she and by her brother's standards quite a 'catch'.

He'd cajoled, flattered, and implored. "I'm only thinking of you. He has money. He has a reputation. He says if you are worried about whether or not you'd have children to tell you his … what did he call it? Oh, yes, his sexual prowess. I was to tell you it was still working perfectly. Come on. I'm sure you'd get to like him. You know it's what our parents would have wanted."

He added that it was irrelevant that such a marriage would have improved his career prospects too – he was just thinking of her. She objected. She had just received her degree in business management from Istanbul University, had started work for a security company, was living in an apartment in Besiktas, and had her own set of friends.

Her last words before she left were, "I have no interest in the attentions of some lecher old enough to be my grandfather. Tell him where he can stick his sexual prowess." They hadn't talked since.

But time made a difference, and perhaps people changed. Now, she could see his perspective, even if she couldn't agree with it. Maybe they should have talked before. They say blood is thicker than water, or so he'd reminded her when he'd called. They only talked for ten minutes, but it hadn't taken her long to recognize he needed her now more than she needed him. He seemed frightened – of what she didn't know, but she suspected he was calling as much for her services as he was hoping for reconciliation, and maybe even forgiveness. She came away from the conversation still not sure who was supposed to be forgiving whom, and for what.

However, Kamal was her brother and, no matter how narcissistic and narrow-minded his view of the world, they still came from the same womb. She felt if she could help she must. She had no idea what her brother had got himself into – she'd find out soon. She hoped it was not illegal, or not too illegal. Dispassionately, she knew it was the fact he needed the help of the company she now owned, not the joy of reconnecting with his little sister. In Turkey the company was still called TPSI (Total Personal Security International), but for its international activities it went by the catchier name of SIGNAK. Most of the company's clients did not realize this was a contraction of 'siginak', the Turkish word for haven or refuge.

She was a little surprised at herself for still mulling over the mixed reasons and emotions she had for being there. She had flown from Rome two hours earlier and was now waiting for the carousel to deliver her bag. She was usually poised, confident and perceptive. She was also successful – very successful. Back when she'd been in her twenties she had bought out the small company she worked for and built it into one that was recognized around the Mediterranean as one of the best in the business. SIGNAK provided protection from attacks – physical or cyber. It could move, evacuate, conceal, and protect you anywhere on the planet. Its services were not cheap, but they came with a 'lifetime' guarantee.

Whose lifetime? Yours.

If SIGNAK failed to guard you from the evils of the world and you succumbed, you, or your designated heir, got your money back. It was an unusual business strategy, but it worked. Clients appreciated being told that SIGNAK hated to give up good money, and would use every resource available to keep them safe. Then they were told of the other option – should the unthinkable happen you could choose to use the money to hasten the demise of the company, government, or entity that harmed you. You could not choose to harm any human physically in any way – that would be illegal.

Over half her clients chose this option.

Her single, plain, black roll-along appeared and she pulled it behind her towards customs. At five feet and four inches she was not distinguishable from the other women around her. She chose to wear a brown headscarf, in hijab style, over her black hair, and loose, dark, poorly-fitting clothing. Although she was not married she wore a modest wedding ring on her left hand over a pair of thin brown gloves. Dark-rimmed glasses completed the picture of dowdiness she hoped to achieve. She had noticed long ago that the film-star airport garb of large floppy hat and reflective designer sun glasses only increased attention – clearly achieving its goal. Instead, Ella chose anonymity.

She was waved through customs and emerged into the glaring sun, dust, demands, and din of Istanbul airport. She ignored the demanders and dealers, turned to her left, and walked slowly, with her shoulders slightly hunched, to where she had been told to meet her brother's driver. She noticed, but did not acknowledge, Stefan, who strode past her to a waiting SIGNAK Mercedes. It felt reassuring to have him close. Her brother had wanted her to come alone. She said she would, but she hadn't made her money from naivety. She and Stefan had discussed the closer security presence she usually traveled with, which Stefan preferred, but she had prevailed. She wanted to feel like a sister visiting a brother, not a meeting with a corporate client. The only concession she had agreed to was for the driver of the Mercedes to give Stefan a package. If he couldn't be close, he could at least be armed.

She found the car her brother had sent for her – another black Mercedes, chatted briefly with the driver, made sure she was the only passenger, opened the rear passenger door, sat down and fastened her seat belt. She knew the vehicle she was in was being tailed by a GPS tracker which Stefan's driver had attached under a rear wheel arch.

They set off towards Avcilar. She maintained small talk with her driver – yes, the roads were awful, the drivers were awful and, of course, the police were awful. Life in Istanbul, or maybe drivers, hadn't changed much since she'd been a student.

She had never been to Avcilar before and wondered what it would have been like before industry and cheap housing had blighted its coastline. There were a few older houses among the chimneys, brick warehouses and wire fencing and the driver pulled into the circular driveway of one. The building had a tired, grey look with echoes of former grandeur in the Corinthian columns flanking the main entrance, but the windows were dusty and the dark paint was flaking off the front door.

Her driver carried her bags to the door and rang the bell. She heard bolts and locks being moved and then the door was opened cautiously by her brother.

She hoped her expression didn't reveal her feelings, but she was shocked. Kamal was only four years older but his once-dark hair was now completely white, his complexion grey, like the peeling paint on the building, and he was fifty pounds heavier than she remembered. She was spared further embarrassment when he opened his arms and gave her a brief smile, revealing yellowed teeth, and hugged her. She reciprocated, although she almost recoiled from his odor of grease and stale cigarettes. She reminded herself, yet again, he was her brother, not a client, and that was what mattered.

The driver put her single piece of luggage in the lobby and went back to his car. Her brother closed the door after him and indicated to Ella to follow him.

"Follow me, Fatima, or should I call you Ella now?"

"My name is Ella," she replied sharply.

After all this time he was still playing games. He knew she'd never liked the name, Fatima. She understood her parents would have chosen it after the daughter of the Prophet, but there was also the Fatima of Portugal – the Moorish princess who was captured by a Portuguese knight, allegedly fell in love with him, and converted to Christianity so she could marry him. Ella considered this medieval legend a prime example of the Stockholm syndrome and didn't want a name associated with it. She had picked the more anonymous Ella in college – as far as she was aware it was not associated with any international disputes or religious practices.

She followed her brother and could feel herself getting angry. He led, knowing she would follow. He didn't look back, didn't ask after her, and clearly seemed to think he was doing her a favor. She resisted the urge to goad him – he may not have changed, but she could show she had.

He took her along a corridor which opened into a small shaded courtyard. It was quiet there away from the industrial ugliness of the drive from the airport.

"Please sit," he indicated a chair.

She was curious and asked, "So, this is your house, Kamal?"

"No. It is a friend's," he replied. "I'll make tea."

He turned and disappeared into another room off the courtyard. She could hear kitchen noises, but no other sounds in the house. She began to relax and took off the wedding ring and her gloves. The soft chair she was sitting in was old and worn, and the small wooden table and dresser close to her were covered in a fine layer of grey dust. She assumed he was living alone. She realized she should find out if he was married, if she was an aunt to any children, or how he'd been living for the last fourteen years.

She never got to ask.

As Kamal emerged from the kitchen carrying a tray with two slices of baklava and two glasses of tea the bullet hit him in the middle of his forehead.

21

The sounds of the gun, the glasses and tray smashing on the stone courtyard, and Kamal falling backward, revealing red on the wall where no color had been before, seemed simultaneous.

She turned her head and twisted in her chair. There were two of them. They emerged from the same passageway she had taken from the entrance. She started to stand but the shorter of the two men stepped forward and shoved her down. She could see them now. Both had guns – one was pointing his weapon at her and the other had a gun tucked in his belt – they looked like 9mm Berettas, but she couldn't be sure. It didn't matter anyway.

They had guns and she didn't.

They were also not wearing masks. Either they didn't expect any witnesses, or there weren't going to be any. Both were clean-shaven, probably in their mid-twenties, dressed in T-shirts and blue jeans. They could have passed for students from Turkey, or any eastern Mediterranean country, and they looked enough alike to be brothers. The shorter man, who was still standing close to her, seemed to be in charge. They were talking, but she couldn't quite understand the language. Her native tongue was Turkish and she recognized some Turkish words, but she didn't need to understand to realize they were deciding what to do with her. In the circumstances there was only one thing they could do. The younger, taller man, seemed to be having qualms about killing her – maybe this was his first kill – but she knew the older would prevail. It was logical and just a matter of time. As he discussed the plan, talking to his brother over his shoulder, she noticed he allowed the gun he was holding in his left hand to drop and move to her left. It was no longer pointing directly at her.

She had one chance and took it. With her left hand she grabbed the hand holding the weapon and yanked it towards her. Using the momentum to pull herself to a standing position she punched hard with her right fist at the front of his larynx. The blow was not quite centered but she felt a crack as it landed. The man dropped the gun and clutched his throat.

She turned towards the other man and stopped. She was one second too slow. He had pulled out his gun before she could get around the man she had punched. That man was now on his knees – his breath harsh and raspy. She also knew that any doubts about the plan of action the younger man may have had disappeared when she'd broken the larynx of the man she presumed was his brother. His hand was shaking so much he pulled up his other to steady the gun and aimed it at her.

There were two gunshots in rapid succession, and she felt a bullet pass by her right ear. The man who had been standing at her pointing the Beretta was on the floor with blood staining the right side of his T-shirt. Stefan emerged from the passage holding a revolver in front of him, and checked the courtyard.

"Are there any more?" he asked.

"I don't think so," she replied. "I think they came in the front door behind us."

"They did, and they killed the driver before coming in here. I only saw the two of them."

Stefan walked towards the man he had just shot and kicked his gun away. It wasn't necessary. He was unconscious and would be dead in a couple of minutes. He turned his attention to the other gunman who was losing the struggle to breathe and was barely conscious. He left him, glanced around the courtyard again, then went over to where Kamal lay.

"Is this your brother?"

"Yes," Ella replied and sat abruptly in the chair again.

"I'm sorry about that. I know you were hoping for a better relationship with him."

"I was, but I don't know if it would have been possible and… oh, I …" She found herself shaking and crying. She leaned forward and buried her face in her hands. "I feel awful."

"You are supposed to feel like shit." Stefan said. He walked over to her, crouched and placed both hands on her shoulders. "If you didn't there would be something wrong with you. You've just lost your brother, you were nearly shot, but your training worked. You avoided being shot."

Stefan gently rocked her as she continued to sob.

They had worked together for over five years. If SIGNAK had any labels for its higher management she would be called the

23

chief financial officer and Stefan the chief executive officer, but this didn't fully explain how well the company had thrived with both their talents.

At one time they had tried being lovers – they were both dark, slim, attractive and intelligent and would have seemed a good match, but after a short affair they realized they were better off remaining just colleagues.

Stefan pulled Ella to her feet and hugged her.

"We have to get out of here." He spoke quietly to her. "Let me deal with this."

She pushed back a little, raised her head and said, "No. Let's do this together."

"OK, but stay here for a minute. Don't move. Do you know where the kitchen might be?"

"I think it's probably in there." She pointed to the room where her brother made the tea.

Stefan left and came back a minute later with a handful of plastic bags.

"Put these over your feet and if you touch anything do it with one of these over your hands. I couldn't find any gloves, so these will have to do. Did you touch anything when you came in?"

"Just my bag, and this chair." She sat in the cloth-covered chair and began to tie the plastic grocery bags around her ankles. "What about you?" she added .

"The front door was open, so I just used my shoulder to get in. I don't think I touched anything," he replied.

"Good. Now what?" She was regaining her composure.

"We check these guys out." He pointed to the two dead men. "And we check out your brother," he added.

"OK."

"Don't step in any blood."

"OK. And … could you check Kamal for me?"

"Of course."

For the next ten minutes they searched the bodies and the courtyard. They couldn't get close to the man Stefan had shot because of the blood pooling around him. On the other man they found a wallet with a driving license, Turkish lira, a cell phone, car keys and very little else. Stefan kept the cell phone, photographed the remaining items and and replaced them. He found little on Kamal, but in the kitchen he found another cell phone. He tried to access its call records, but it was password-protected. He put it in his pocket. Ella searched the other rooms in the house looking for anything that would explain why Kamal had wanted to see her, or why he had been killed.

She found very little. No ornaments, paintings or photographs were on display. There were two bedrooms, each with a double bed, but only one looked slept in. She found male clothing, but nothing female – she assumed this meant she had no sister-in-law nor nieces nor nephews, but Kamal had said this wasn't his house, so she still couldn't be sure.

In the television room she found a large sofa almost submerged in dried, unwashed plates, pizza boxes and discarded underwear. There was just enough room for two persons to sit. It reminded her of a college dorm room too close to the end of the semester. The only relatively tidy item in the whole room was a computer desk, but even then she had to push the full ashtray and packet of Turkish cigarettes away from her when she sat down.

Starting with the bottom drawers she removed all the documents she could find and photographed them with her cell phone. She paid no attention to the written contents – she didn't have time. However, when she opened the top drawer she stopped. It held no documents but was full of photographs of her family from twenty years ago. In one her brother and her parents were happy and smiling for the camera in front of the Blue Mosque. She wasn't in the photo, so maybe she was the one who had taken it, but she couldn't remember being there or using a camera. She was tempted to keep it, but that could prove risky. She photographed it and closed the drawer. She decided to try the desk-top computer. She touched the mouse and the screen came alive and asked for a password. She tried her brother's birth date, then her parents'. It was when she put in her own birth date that the welcome screen appeared.

She paused for a moment and wondered if there was any significance to that, took a breath, then refocused her attention and started to look over the files, but there were too many to analyze. She walked to her luggage by the front door and retrieved a thumb drive, returned to the computer and started to transfer as many files as she could. While this was running she examined the bookmark file and deleted the link she found to SIGNAK. She then deleted the computer's browsing history and logged out.

She was working on the theory that she had a couple of choices.

One: Do what she was doing now and make sure there was no evidence of her being in recent contact with her brother, and make sure there was no evidence of her being in this house.

Two: Sit and wait for the police to come and explain what she had seen – her brother being killed after he put up a gallant fight against insuperable odds. She would have to weave a tale to keep Stefan's presence out of it.

Of the two choices the first seemed the more palatable, if only because she couldn't be certain who had been the target. She doubted it, but it was possible someone had asked Kamal to lure her there with the promise of reconciliation. Then again, maybe it was the government he was afraid of. In that case she would not want to deliver herself to the police. The one major drawback with the first option was she couldn't be certain she had not been filmed at the airport getting into the Mercedes. It was a risk she would have to take.

She met Stefan in the hallway.

He said, "Have you found any surveillance in here?"

"No. You?"

"No, that's good. We need to go."

"Agreed. What about the … bodies?" Ella asked.

"My gun is now next to your brother's hand. Any fingerprints on the gun, or on the bullet casings are his. The gun is untraceable to us. There is only one piece of baklava on the floor and one broken tea glass. It's not perfect, but it's the best I can do. Basically, your brother fought bravely and killed his attackers.

26

If they look closer it won't hold water. We have to hope that they won't look closer." He shrugged.

"Thank you. Time to go?"

"Yes. But before we go outside you need to know what is out there. There are three cars. There is the Mercedes you came in. Did you touch anything in the car?"

"Yes, but I still had my gloves on."

"Good. Kamal's driver is dead, lying across the front seat. There is an older car out there which belongs to the gunmen. Then there is our car. I trust our driver completely. You walk out of here with your luggage and sit in the back of our car. I will close the door behind me and be a couple of seconds behind you. OK?"

"Yes."

"Let's take these bags off our feet now."

They took the plastic bags off their feet and hands. Stefan collected them and stuffed them into a spare bag.

Ella put on her brown gloves and said, "You go out first. I've got gloves on. I'll be right behind you."

Stefan considered this briefly, then nodded."OK," he said.

He left, Ella took her bag, locked and closed the door behind her and walked to the SIGNAK car. She walked past Kemal's car and stopped. Something had caught her attention. A small thin metal outline of a hand and forearm had been left on the hood of the car. It was about twelve centimeters by five. She took a photo of it, moved on and sat in the back seat of the SIGNAK car.

"What kept you?" Stefan asked as the car moved out into the light traffic.

"This." She leaned forward and showed him the image of the hand. "I suppose the gunmen left it there. I don't know what it means – maybe a calling card or something?"

"I don't know – one more mystery we'll have to work on, but for now we need to upload the photos we took and then delete them from our phones."

"OK, and I have a thumb drive to upload too, then I think we both need to get out of Turkey as soon as possible."

27

"Agreed. What about our rooms at the Sheraton? Should we cancel?" Stefan asked.

"I think we should. I'll get dropped off there now – it's on the way to the airport. I'll tell them my business was concluded earlier than I thought, cancel in person, get to the airport and take a flight out of there later this evening. I think there's an Air France to Paris around seven or eight and I'll stay there. You stay in this car, go to the airport, pick a different flight, and I'll see you back at base Tuesday afternoon. Do you think we covered everything?"

"I think so. Time will tell."

"Then, I apologize. You were right," said Ella.

"I was?"

"I should have listened to you. Next time, more security. We made it, but we almost didn't."

"You're right. Let's hope that there won't be any more times like this." He hesitated, "But, does that mean I missed a 'told you so'?"

"Oh, I'm sure there will be other times."

"Which I will probably miss too."

"Not if I keep reminding you."

They both allowed themselves brief smiles and felt the tension ease a little.

"I'll catch the earlier plane, but ... well ... it doesn't seem right leaving you like that at the airport, in Turkey."

"It does to me. My Turkish is a lot better than yours, and you don't have to always be the white knight." She nodded at him in the mirror and added, "Sometimes I like to carry the lance and sword instead."

At 6:15 Stefan's flight to Rome left Istanbul Airport.

Later that evening Ella tilted back her seat in the first class section of the Air France Airbus. She kicked off her shoes and allowed the foot rest to lift her legs. She had the row to herself. She closed her eyes and let the tears come. Quietly, she grieved and sobbed for the family and opportunities she had lost, or had been taken from her. She was the only one of her family left, and

the only one who had the resources and knowledge to find out …
and then what? She had always thought revenge was a poor
motive for any action. She had seen how wasteful it could be, but
now she wondered.

4

The wording of Paris's Rue du Faubourg Poissonniere doesn't translate well into English – Fishwife Suburb Road sounds like the sort of name which might be ascribed to an alley in London, or maybe a road where the residents would petition to have the name changed. It runs north between the ninth and tenth arrondissemonts (districts) until somewhere between Sacre-Coeur and Gare du Nord it becomes the Rue des Poissonniers (Fishmonger Street). Going south it stops where the old city walls would have been, and another route continues the short distance to the River Seine. It has resisted the worst of the blight of the tourist areas along the river, and of Montmartre to its northwest, and has retained much of its Parisian charm. Its restaurants and cafes are frequented more by Parisians than by tourists.

This is where SIGNAK had its headquarters. It occupied all four floors of a mid-nineteenth century apartment building. Admission was through the courtyard to its rear, but access to the courtyard was strictly limited and constantly monitored. Clients of SIGNAK were usually seen at their home or place of work, or anywhere in the world and never directed to the building. Those who were seen in Paris were directed to the Café d'Oc opposite where they were told it was possible to have a more private conversation. Nothing could have been further from the truth. The café was a thriving business. It was featured in the Michelin guide, the chefs were well-paid, tables intruded onto the sidewalk, and chairs were paired and faced the street in true Parisian fashion. However, it was owned by SIGNAK. Every table, every waiter, the street, the headquarters opposite, even 'les toilettes' were wired or discreetly videoed.

Stefan and Ella were meeting in the second floor of the headquarters that overlooked the Café d'Oc. They were the only two occupying the small boardroom which had once been the ornate sitting room of an apartment rumored to have been used by the mistress of one of France's presidents. Ella had no idea if this was true, or whether everyone selling any Victorian apartment in Paris claimed a similar amorous reputation, but she had preserved the mild opulence of the room when she refurnished with eighteenth and nineteenth century antiques. It served as a softer refuge from the stresses and pressure of her business, and the strictly functional rooms of the rest of the SIGNAK headquarters. They were sitting on a restored Louis XVI sofa.

Stefan said, "It's been ten days now and there's been nothing in the newspapers, television, or online. There have been no rumors we have been able to pick up on either."

"So, there are four violent deaths and four corpses all in one place. In most places in the world, even in totalitarian regimes, there would have been some murmurs somewhere, or some media input," said Ella.

"Agreed."

"So, we're in the clear?"

"I think so, but I don't know. Normally ... well, you know what to expect."

"Of course, but no one has notified me of Kamal's death either, but there again does anyone know if he had a sister who might want to be contacted, or how to contact her, or if she still exists? This makes me wonder if it's the Turkish authorities who have kept this quiet."

"I agree, but what authorities? If it had been the police it would not have been kept quiet. We would have had some hint of something, but there's been nothing. One of our people drove by the next day and there was no car outside. Yesterday, he reported the house had a 'For Sale' sign outside," said Stefan, leaning forward towards Ella. "Assuming the police were not involved, then the staging of the bodies so it looked like Kamal killed those two brothers worked, and ... we should be in the clear."

"But if it was not the police it was someone, or some organization, with some clout. Any idea who or what? Who killed my brother?" Ella asked.

"We don't know yet, but there may be more than one question there. Who did the killing? And who wanted him killed? They may not be the same."

"Any thoughts?" She looked into his eyes and, not for the first time, wondered if they had been hasty at agreeing to a strictly platonic, business relationship. She dismissed the thought – it could cause complications.

"Let me bring in Danilo." Stefan stood. "He may give us some answers, or at least he can tell us what he's working on."

Stefan left the room and Ella also stood, took a deep breath, stretched her back and walked over to the window. She looked down on the Café d'Oc opposite and noticed a slight drizzle had driven patrons back to the shelter of the restaurant. The door to the boardroom opened and Stefan returned with Danilo. Ella joined them at the table.

Danilo, not his real name, was an Italian who had been recruited to SIGNAK when his online hacking activities had been noted by an organization which, allegedly, once had ties to the Italian Prime Minister, Silvio Berlusconi. The organization didn't take kindly to someone being interested in their finance and personnel files. SIGNAK had whisked him out of Italy one step ahead of his being arrested and jailed for an unrelated trumped-up offence – Danilo knew he would never have made it to court. As an additional bonus for his rescue he brought some of those finance and personnel files with him and later established "back door" access to the organization's computers – this time making sure there could be no tracing any intrusion back to him. He was in his late twenties, pale-skinned, with black curly hair and Roman good looks, but was already developing the Italian male pasta-paunch. He loved everything about Paris, especially his job.

He spoke in English with a mild Italian accent. "The driving license you brought me is Turkish, but it is fake. The records associated with this number belong to a retired teacher in Antalya. However, the other documents indicate the man was Azerbaijani." He looked at Ella. "I believe you said you didn't recognize the language, but some of the words he spoke sounded Turkish?"

Ella nodded.

"That would fit with Azerbaijani, and probably an Azerbaijani dialect, but not sure it helps us much. He was probably just a hired gun. The fact that he shot your brother in the middle of his forehead is probably not a lucky shot. He may have been hired to kill before. We just don't know. However, we do have an idea of what your brother was up to and what led him to be a target." Danilo paused. He had been told he was not the most tactful person to deliver bad news and was doing his best to seem diplomatic.

Ella let him off the hook and said, "Go on. Tell me the worst."

"We think he was involved in money laundering and may have either helped himself once too often to whatever funds he was dealing with, or it's possible he was an innocent victim of someone else's greed, or someone just didn't like him, or someone was getting at the organization he worked for by bump ... er... having him killed."

"Which is the more likely?" asked Ella.

"The first and last. He was definitely helping launder money."

"For whom?"

"We don't know, but we're working on it."

Stefan added. "We don't know exactly. We know who his main contact was from the files we downloaded from his computer. We also have telephone numbers from his cell phone. It's more likely his contact was a member of an organization, and so your brother was probably working for an organization rather than an individual. He was also a lawyer and it seems he was on leave from his law firm. They have no idea he is dead, and the records we have been able to access there are apparently completely benign – nothing like what was on his computer."

"So, how do we narrow this down?" asked Ella.

"The contact lives in Ankara. We are going to have to go there and have a talk with him," said Stefan.

"When?"

"Friday morning."

She never asked the question, and that was one more reason John knew she was not going to go home – it would never work out.

He'd dreaded the question, because he didn't want to lie to her, and he'd rehearsed the answer if she'd asked, "When am I going home?"

He'd planned to say, "When you get better," which was only half a lie, but it turned out he didn't have to.

He could have probably said, "When it stops raining," or "When the government says you can." Any appropriate sounding answer would have done, since he would have to repeat it again in a few minutes, but Auntie Olly just sat in bed talking about her neighbors, her dog, which had died ten years ago, and the red roses on a nearby table. Any remaining grasp of reality had been undone by her hospitalization.

The room was light, airy, and warm. It held another ten beds, all of which were occupied. It reminded John of the sanitariums you saw in romantic movies of the 1920's.

Auntie Olly had no idea where she was, how she'd got there, or how long she'd been there, so she never wondered about going home. She never wondered about home.

John had tracked her down. He'd been trying to work out how to catch a bus to the acute care hospital ten miles away, but fortunately had called first and found she'd been moved to the local cottage hospital for 'recuperation'. In reality she was just waiting for the mental health evaluation, the visit from the social worker, a blessing from the nurse, or maybe a doctor, and a nursing home placement.

He'd woken at 6:00am, surprised to have slept so long. He'd eaten a breakfast of cereal, toast smeared with antique jam, watched the morning news on BBC Wales, and at 10:00, when he'd felt his energy flagging (2:00 am back in Port Orchard he reminded himself) had ventured out into the Welsh winter. It was windy, but the rain had stopped and the cold revived his spirits as he walked the mile to the cottage hospital. He enjoyed seeing the double-decker buses and their strange advertisements, and he paid careful attention at intersections to the wrong-side-of-the-road driving. He stopped to look in some of the windows of the second-hand shops and see what amazing bargains were being offered to the public in North Wales. There weren't many. The town had too many thrift stores, 'value' stores, and boarded-up stores. It had never recovered from losing the beach-and-beer crowd to Spain in the 1960's. The presence of the older rail line and the construction of the A55 freeway in the 80's, between the town center and the beach, had walled off most of the community from the Irish Sea. The new road had made Colwyn Bay's better parts into bedroom communities for the major English cities of Liverpool, Manchester and Chester. In return, the unemployed had taken their benefits from the inner cities to the sea air and cheaper accommodation around the middle of Colwyn Bay.

There were lots of things John loved about Wales. Colwyn Bay wasn't one of them.

Now, sitting in the hospital, John felt his spirits sagging again and the warmth of the room was making him drowsy.

At the best of times it was tiring trying to maintain a conversation with Auntie Olly. It was hard to make it more than two parallel monologues. She seemed to have some spark of recognition of John, and if he was careful he could avoid the traps of mentioning the government, a dead brother-in-law and his unwanted attentions, and her own parents. But the effort to do this couldn't be sustained and she would replay the same parts of the broken record of her memories until John picked up a newspaper and showed her the front page, or pulled out his driving license to distract her. The repetition was depressing, but from her point of view it was only by reviewing these chunks of memory that she could hang on to any sense of reality. He wondered if he took her to her house would she know where she was. He briefly considered the idea until he realized that he really needed to consider her illness and hospitalization as a gift.

It could have been a lot worse; now it was out of both Olly's and John's hands.

The system would take it from here.

An aide came with lunch and John excused himself, promising to return to see her the next day. He made a note of the timing of lunch, so he could escape again if necessary, and walked to the exit. On the way out he paused at a room holding three uniformed nurses. He was relieved to see they were talking to each other and not one was looking at the computer screens behind them. Using his best diction he confessed to being an American.

They nodded knowingly.

He asked about Auntie Olly and what they expected.

They explained, using their best diction, that she would probably be there a few more days, the social worker would see her that afternoon, and it would be John's responsibility to find a nursing home.

Did they have any suggestions?

Well, they gave him a list, but they really couldn't make any recommendations. It would really be up to John to find out.

In some ways it was reassuring to know the medical culture was the same in North Wales as in the Pacific Northwest – some things you only shared with your colleagues. *We could let you know, but let's see how you get on by yourself to begin with.*

John smiled and left with the list.

He didn't feel rejuvenated by the wind as he left the antiseptic comfort of the hospital and started on his way back to Auntie Olly's house. He just felt cold.

He stopped at a supermarket to buy apples to replace those from Olly's refrigerator, which he had relegated to the compost pile in her small garden, and he bought lettuce, tomatoes, vegetables and a few essentials to help him survive the next five days. It was Friday and John wondered if anything happened at the weekends in the National Health Service.

He made it back to the silence of Auntie Olly's house.

He found it depressing just being there and witnessing how small and lonely her life had been. Logically, he knew she hadn't been able to get out of the house for a while, and when he'd called her she always seemed reluctant to hang up the phone, but standing in her hallway he understood a little of the solitude of her existence. Maybe now she'd be better off in a nursing home with some company, but it was probably too late to make a difference wherever she went. He could understand why she'd wanted to stay in her house, surrounded by her memories, but the isolation hastened the effects of the disintegration of dementia which had been creeping up on her.

He shook the thoughts out of his head, picked up the pile of mail, and with his supermarket purchases walked to the kitchen – the warmest and brightest room in the house.

He thought about microwaving one of the sodium-filled frozen meals he'd found, but couldn't face it, and opened the mail while eating his own Cheshire cheese and tomato sandwich and a fresh Cox's apple.

The mail was inconsequential. John had arranged direct payments years ago and there were no outstanding bills in the handful of statements, magazines and flyers in front of him. There was nothing for him to do. He leaned back against the wall in the kitchen and closed his eyes.

The phone rang.

He walked the twenty feet back to the hallway and picked it up.

"John Beaton," he answered.

"Mr. Beaton, I believe you're the next of kin of Olwen Lewis. Is that correct?" It was a woman with a soft Welsh accent.

"Yes, that is correct."

"My name is Gwyneth Nelson. I'm the social worker. I must have just missed you at the hospital. The nurses there said you asked about a nursing home for Mrs. Lewis?"

"Yes, they said it was really my responsibility to find a nursing home for her, and I asked what they recommended. They gave me a list of the possibilities."

"Well, it makes a difference how much money she has. Do you know what her finances are like?"

"Yes."

"Well, do you know if she has more than thirteen thousand, five hundred pounds to her name?"

John thought for a few seconds. Auntie Olly probably had about twice that, and then there was the value of her house.

"She has about twenty-five thousand and then she has money in this house too," he replied.

"Then she is going to be self-pay, at least for a while. That makes a difference where she can go."

"Yeah?"

"Yes, it means she can look, or rather you can, at more places than if the local health authority had to pay for it."

"Oh."

"In fact, you don't have to look at them all. There aren't many vacancies at present. If you have a pen I'll let you know which ones have beds available."

John picked up a pen from the phone table. It didn't work. Nor did the second, but the pencil stub he found was just functional. He wrote down the three nursing homes which had beds available. He was told to expect they would cost Auntie Olly 500 to 600 British pounds weekly. John translated this mentally into a lot of money or, in US terms, 750 to 900 dollars every week. It probably wouldn't help Auntie Olly to know it would have been even more in the US. Her pension would cover some, but she'd have to sell her house.

No, he realized – he would have to sell it for her.

John thanked the social worker and hung up.

It was tempting to lie down and take a nap, but he knew this would make it even harder to get a good night's sleep. He glanced outside and noted it was windy, but not raining, steeled himself, and wrapped in scarf and hat strode out onto the frozen tundra of the sidewalks of Colwyn Bay.

The first nursing home he visited was less than a mile away in a quiet residential area. It had probably started as a six bedroom, mini-mansion, constructed in grey stone and red brick sometime around the beginning of the 1900's. It was set in two acres of landscaped lawns and gardens.

In the ensuing century it had acquired, in fits and starts, another forty bedrooms. There was the first addition, probably around the time of the Second World War, which was architecturally compatible with the original. Then there was the cheap, tired and decaying, two storey extension with single-pane metal windows from the sixties. The most recent red-brick addition, probably built in the last twenty years, was sturdy, had vinyl double-paned windows and since it was separated from the original building by the sixties addition, looked almost architecturally appropriate. There were hotchpotch buildings like this all over the United Kingdom; most seemed to be nursing homes or government offices.

The staff was friendly and pleasant, both to him and to the residents. And, yes, there was a vacant room that he could look over. He checked; it was a small, but adequate, room with a single bed, a sink and a view of trees. It was clean.

John made the decision. He knew there was no way he could evaluate any nursing home in the few minutes he was able to spend in each one – so, this was going to be it. This was the one. He would look no further.

He signed the paperwork, wrote the check, shook the hands, and it was done. He asked to use the phone, called the social worker he had talked to earlier and, all being well, Auntie Olly would be transferred on Monday.

Maybe he was done too?

His flight home was in six days.

As he walked back to Auntie Olly's house he wondered if he should get on the next train to London and see if he could catch an earlier plane back to civilization.

It was tempting, but it was not a John Beaton thing to do. He had responsibilities and he would be responsible.

Responsible could have even been his middle name.

He would stay and help and occupy himself, and he would start now. He stopped, looked around, carried on walking and took the next left turn and headed away from Colwyn Bay and towards the promenade and the Irish Sea. It was still not raining. It wasn't dry – there were plenty of puddles around, but the normal state of the February weather – rain – was absent. He would enjoy it while he could.

He was still two blocks away when he heard the water. The closer he got the louder it became. It was high tide and the brisk northwest wind was picking up waves and pebbles and dropping them with a roar onto the promenade. Beyond the churning waves the grey sea was scattered with white caps. Gulls screeched and soared over the water. He could taste the salt of the sea on his lips and his glasses fogged with salt spray.

It was magnificent. It was the perfect antidote to the claustrophobia of air travel, jet-lag, hospitals and nursing homes. He smiled and stood watching the waves for ten minutes.

However, he was who he was. He had a few choices. He could go back to Auntie Olly's house; he could take a right turn and run the gauntlet of the crashing waves, or he could turn left, avoid the worst of the waves, take the safe way along the promenade and the long way home.

John turned left.

It was almost 6:00 by the time he made it back to Auntie Olly's house.

He thought about phoning Ann, but she would be at work, so he made a mental note to call her over the weekend. Then, he thought twice and made a real note and put it on the phone.

He heated one of the Tesco frozen-fish dinners in the microwave and complemented it with a salad, an apple, and a Greek yogurt which he ate sitting watching BBC Wales in Auntie Olly's chair in her sitting room. The meal seemed filling enough and he then channel-surfed through a dreary medley of reality and game shows – apart from the accents he could have been back in the US. He stopped looking when he arrived at a western he thought he'd never seen before. He just needed to be kept awake. He didn't need to think or be outraged.

By 9:00 he was asleep.

6

The jet-lag faded each day. John made a list of the items at Auntie Olly's house which needed fixing, and started to repair what he could with the few tools he found in the small, dark shed at the bottom of her overgrown back yard.

Olly was transferred, as planned, on the Monday and John took some of her clothing to the nursing home. He found a couple of framed photos of her family and a few pictures to hang on the bare walls of her room. He visited her and had the same conversation with her each day. She didn't ask when she was going home, but she did seem to recognize him, even if she couldn't remember his name.

In between squalls and rain John managed to walk as much as he could along the narrow lanes of the surrounding countryside, and began to appreciate that living in Colwyn Bay might not be so bad after all.

But it was an isolated existence. He woke to a silent house in the morning and ate his breakfast half-listening to the news on the radio. After he visited Auntie Olly he returned to the stillness of the house, or postponed it for the solitude of his walks. In the evenings he read or watched television. He felt lonely and dull.

He wasn't ready to become a dementing, single, old-age-pensioner. If he'd planned on being there longer he would have joined something or volunteered somewhere. He thought about going to a restaurant or a cinema, but he couldn't face the prospect of eating out, or watching, alone. If you believed beer advertisements then heaps of good-looking and friendly company could be yours just by visiting a local pub. If you were an introverted family doctor with an American accent it wouldn't work. Either you would be totally, but civilly ignored, or worse, you would become an object of curiosity and questioning.

But by Wednesday evening he couldn't stand it anymore.

He'd packed his bags ready for the journey back to Port Orchard the next day. The egg sandwiches he'd made for lunch were in the refrigerator along with the apples, bananas and the last slice of malt loaf. He had enough food for breakfast and had taken a frozen meal out of the freezer for his evening meal. He made the mistake of looking at the ingredients label, sighed, and placed it back in the freezer for future damage. He would go out for dinner and he knew just the place.

The fish and chip shop was a quarter-mile away.

Like most of the thousands of the take-away fish and chip shops around Britain this was brightly lit with fluorescent strips, had a high, white-tiled counter, and its walls were painted a light institutional green. John had noticed this particular shop on his travels to visit Auntie Olly at the nursing home. It was also one which had managed to squeeze a couple of tables into the limited space between the counter and the steamed-up shop-front window.

John lowered the umbrella, which was mainly ineffective against the rain and wind, and stepped into the heat of the shop. There had been no one on the street, and even the cars had seemed reluctant to go out into the cold rain, so he was a little surprised to find he was fifth in line to order.

The first was a slim man in his thirties, who received his cod and chips and sat at one table with his back to the wall, facing the door. Next was a family of three – two obese parents and an apprentice obese ten year-old son. They took their fish and chips and occupied the second table.

John had listened to the pattern of ordering. He knew there was a difference between "two cod and chips" and "cod and chips twice", but could never be quite sure if he'd get it right. He wasn't sure if he got it right this time. There was a moment's hesitation, two seconds of silence from the family, and a glance from the single man when John opened his mouth, but he was used to it by then. Something must have worked because his order of fish and chips came. He asked for a little salt, no vinegar and looked for a place to sit.

He wasn't sure of the seating protocol, but he wasn't going to go back out in the miserable weather without his fish and chips inside his stomach, so he asked the single man, "Is this seat taken?" Obviously, it wasn't, but it was polite to ask.

The man turned to look at John and with a nod indicated the seat was available. For a second John hesitated. Most of the man's face was hidden by the hood of his jacket and a full black beard, but what caught John's attention was how pale and thin his face looked. His brown eyes looked tired and he glanced at the door as John took his seat.

John took off his hat, picked up his plastic fork and began dissecting his generous portion of battered fish and munching the chips. He noticed the man was not eating and looked up. The brown eyes were staring at John. John smiled and returned to his task, then looked up again.

The man said, "American?"

John nodded, swallowed, and said, "Is it that obvious?"

"Maybe." The man replied. "The accent clinched it, but your anorak is a little unusual around here. It has an REI logo. Your haircut isn't local, but it would pass, and you were using an umbrella – that's not usual in this weather, since it's not very effective, as you no doubt found out. Also, you're wearing hiking boots. Very sensible in this weather, but it would be more likely to be wellies, you know rubber boots, around here. Then there's the baseball-style hat with flaps to keep the rain off your neck. To me it all screams American."

"Couldn't I just like dressing this way in weather like this?" John asked.

"Maybe, but then the accent…?"

"And I thought I was blending in, being anonymous you know."

"Do you want to be anonymous?"

"Not really, but I don't want to be noticed as obviously foreign."

"Oh, you're not obvious."

"You noticed."

"I am good at noticing things like that."

The man picked up a chip and nibbled it. John noticed most of the man's meal was untouched, and returned to his own fish and chips.

The man asked, "Where do you come from in America?"

45

Before John could answer the man added, "Wait, don't tell me. I'm going to guess West Coast. Maybe Oregon or Washington ... am I right?"

"Pretty good. How did you get that close?"

"REI I believe is a Seattle store, and your clothing is not new, so you probably bought it in a part of America where it's wet."

"Very good." John replied, "And I do live near Seattle."

"Never been there, but I hear it's nice."

"It is."

A tingle of caution entered John's mind. He couldn't see where this conversation was leading, but the last person he thought he'd encounter in a fish and chip shop in North Wales in February was someone with observational skills and geographical knowledge like this. The man may have picked up some of John's concern and said.

"Maybe you're wondering what a stranger in a fish and chip shop in Colwyn Bay knows about America."

John nodded.

"Well, let me show you."

The man reached with his right hand into his jacket. John noticed he winced a little and hesitated as he did this, leaving his hand inside his jacket.

"Are you OK?" John asked.

The man took a few shallow breaths and answered, "I banged up my ribs a couple of hours ago, and it still hurts, but ... I think I'll be OK. I just wanted to show you this." He pulled out a thick paperback and placed it on the table. He seemed to be able to breathe more easily and John looked at the title – 'Reamde' by Neal Stephenson.

The man asked, "Have you read any of his books?"

"I've read 'Cryptonomicon', but I haven't read that one."

"He lives in Seattle. At least that's what it says on the cover, and I've read all his books. So, that's how I got to know about Seattle. Then I looked it up on Wikipedia."

"And one day you'll get there?" John asked.

"I doubt it, but who knows?"

John nodded and returned to the remains of his fish and chips. Behind him Mr. Obesity leaned back and asked for another order of chips for his family. For a second John wondered if they were training for a polar expedition, but it was more likely they were anticipating getting home to their couch, ice cream, and their favorite TV show. The thought made John leave the last of his food on the table. He picked up his gloves, planning to leave, wiped the condensation off the glass and looked outside. It seemed to be snowing. He let out an unguarded groan.

The man opposite asked, "What's wrong?"

"It's starting to snow."

"That's North Wales in February. It won't last … Does it snow in Seattle?"

"Sometimes, but not much. It snows in the mountains, which is where we want it to stay."

"Are you going back there soon?"

"Tomorrow morning."

"Been here long?"

"Just about a week. I was looking in on an aunt who's now in a nursing home."

The man nodded and thought for a moment before saying.

"It's a long flight?"

"Ten hours."

"Well, I won't be needing this book any more. Why don't you take it? It'll help get you through the flight." The man pushed the book towards John.

John hesitated.

The man looked at the book and pulled it back. John thought the offer of the book had been withdrawn, but the man picked it up, pulled out a pen, scribbled something on the first page, put it in the plastic bag that once held his food and handed the package to John.

John thanked the man and accepted the gift.

He replaced his hat, stood, opened the door and stepped outside.

He was glad to be wearing his REI jacket and Goretex lined boots. The rain had turned to a miserable soaking sleet. A few cars were collecting snow on their roofs and a wet slush was gathering at the edge of the road. He tried his umbrella but the wind made it useless.

He made it back to Auntie Olly's in ten minutes and finished his packing. He held the paperback package in his hand and wondered what to do with it. He had reading for the flight and he knew he'd be back in Colwyn Bay sooner rather than later – he'd read it then. He looked for somewhere to put it. The phone rang. He put the book down and talked to Ann on the phone for ten minutes – she said she planned to be at SeaTac to take him home. He wasn't going to argue about that.

At 5:15 the next morning he was about to leave the house for the waiting taxi when he noticed the bag containing the book was where he'd left it the previous evening on the kitchen table. He picked it up, opened the door to the small bedroom and threw the package onto the bed. It bounced, the book slid out of the bag and over the far edge of the bed. John hesitated. So what? – he'd know where the book was next time. He picked up his bags and left the house.

At 5:42 it was still raining and trying to snow as John stepped from Colwyn Bay's platform two onto the Virgin train to London Euston. He arrived there exactly three hours later and took the London Underground Piccadilly Line to Heathrow Airport. By 13:45 he was flying over the Irish Sea and at 23:22 he touched down at SeaTac airport where the local time was 15:22 in the afternoon.

He was glad to be home.

7

The black Ford Mondeo pulled to a stop at the curb on the opposite side of the road from the fish and chip shop.

The car idled, the wipers swept away the sleet from the windshield, and the heater did its best to blow away condensation.

There were three men inside the vehicle. The driver was nineteen year-old Evan Williams. He was feeling nervous and doing his best not to show it. His mind was flying in different directions. He wasn't sure he wanted to be there. It'd seemed an easy job when the man sitting next to him, his older step-brother, Gareth had told him all he had to do was drive and drive carefully. The money was good, and he needed it for his habits. You didn't get much with unemployment benefits – it was barely enough for his beer and cigarettes, and last week Megan had told him her period was late. He'd thought back and maybe it was that time they were both amped on cocaine and they'd screwed like rabbits, or maybe it was that time when they … he couldn't remember. He couldn't remember if he'd used a condom then or not. He felt like a lot of shit was coming down on him. He needed money, but he didn't want to get caught, or worse, or to go to prison for whatever his brother was up to. He wondered again if he should be there. He'd done things for his brother before, but nothing like this. He thought he knew what his brother did for money. Of course, he knew better than to ask, but as for money … well, his brother always had plenty of it and Evan wanted some too, and if he had to … well, he'd have to. At least he thought he could.

He was sitting at the wheel of his brother's car. He liked cars, and he liked driving. It was hot in the car and he found himself sweating – maybe more than he should be. He really wanted to take a couple of hits of the joint he had in the pocket of his jacket, but he knew he couldn't. Smoking, of any sort, was not allowed in Gareth's car.

Gareth Williams was ten years older than Evan, and was totally calm. Both brothers had been raised in a small house, on a small street, in the small town of Abergavenny in South Wales. As best she could their mother had loved and cared for them and their older sister, Janice, who was now married and settled in the small town of Ludlow on the Wales-England border. The only cloud over-shadowing their upbringing was every two to four years there was a change in the father figures in their lives. Despite the years between them, and their different fathers, Gareth and Evan looked remarkably alike. This may have been because of their mother's predilection for curly-haired, dark-complexioned partners, but they both looked a little like the South Wales and Las Vegas entertainer, Tom Jones. At least that's what they were told during their local high-school careers. Evan had to live in the shadow of Gareth who had been academically gifted enough to move on to Goldsmiths College in London, and was athletically gifted enough to play for the school rugby team at scrum-half. At six feet he was a little tall for the average high-school player in this position, but he was fast, tough and coordinated.

However, Gareth was a psychopath.

Most of his teachers didn't know this. His class-mates may have done, but none of them could find the right words to describe why they kept him at a distance, or just didn't feel comfortable around him.

After all, he masked it well. He'd observed people from an early age and learned that showing empathy and concern for fellow humans was a trait expected and admired by others. He was incapable of such feelings, but he was capable of acting. He was a chameleon. Not in the sense that he changed his appearance to fit in with the background, but emotionally he could be anyone he thought you wanted him to be. He could fit in anywhere. He could be your best friend – at least for a time – and he could manipulate you as he wanted. Those who thought they got to know him ended up hating or loving him, and never quite knowing why. He was a little different for everyone he met.

And how did he feel about this? Well, most of the time he didn't feel anything. He may have felt alienated, but didn't know what the feeling was. He knew he didn't fit in, although most of the time he made it look like he did. It didn't bother him. He could pick up, entertain, and discard people whenever he wanted to.

However, like most psychopaths, he was partial to violence. It seemed to provide him a satisfaction he couldn't find elsewhere. At high school he had managed to channel his aggressive tendencies on to the sports' field, but at college this was more difficult. There was an incident with a female Chinese student that would have brought Gareth to the attention of the law had it not been for the third man sitting in the rear seat of the Ford Mondeo.

Huw Jones had been on the faculty of Goldsmiths College. Purely by chance he had been born in Cardiff and, despite his Welsh-sounding name, which he had chosen later in life, he had no other ties to Wales. He taught Arabic and Arabic studies. His parents had worked for the British Foreign Office so he spent his teens, and a couple of college years, around the British embassies of numerous Middle-East countries. He was thirty-eight years old, lanky, brown-eyed, lightly tanned, and completely bald. He didn't smoke and he rarely drank. He was single, projected the persona of a frail professor and appeared dedicated to his work.

He was dedicated to his work, but his chosen profession was not that of a self-absorbed academic.

His real occupation was the practice of criminality. He was a resourceful criminal, and he worked hard at it.

He had acquired a reasonable inheritance when his parents died, and had expanded his wealth by developing a reputation and skills in what could be described as a "niche" criminal sub-specialty. As far as those who dealt with him in these activities could tell he was more of a consultant. His fees were high, but fair. Of course, those he dealt with were also criminals, and some mistakenly thought they could get away with deceiving him, so

51

he was sometimes the victim of lies, deceit and potential violence.

However, he was still around; his double-crossing clients were not.

But that was not how he met Gareth.

It had been a wet November Friday and Huw Jones had taken a late train home. He walked the five minutes from the College to New Cross Gate Station and took the train to Forest Hill. There he raised his umbrella and made his way to his house. He had never liked walking alone at night. One of the problems of looking like an absent-minded professor is you also looked like a victim to certain members of the criminal classes – of course, not the class Jones belonged to.

He walked along Woolstone Road, turned left into Elsinore Road and stopped abruptly as a man stepped in front of him. The man was masked and was holding a short knife in his right hand. He extended his left arm, palm up, and spoke in a cockney accent.

"Come on, 'and it over," he said, signaling with his left hand.

Jones instinctively stepped back and felt a hand grip his right shoulder. Another man's voice spoke into his left ear.

"Do loik 'e says, mate. You don't need no trouble do yer?"

Jones had no time to react before he heard a thump, a grunt from the man behind him and the grip on his shoulder was released. Jones half turned to see a man, now at his side, holding a three-foot length of iron piping. Jones jumped aside alarmed, and then looked down to see an unconscious man lying on the sidewalk behind him.

The man with the knife hesitated a fraction of a second and then lunged forward with his knife hand extended. The descending arc of the pipe shattered his right arm. His scream was cut short as the pipe hit him again in the left temple and he crumpled to the ground. The man holding the pipe looked at both unconscious bodies and placed the pipe in the grip of the man who had held Jones from behind. Jones's criminal mind noted the man on the ground was not wearing gloves, the man who had just arranged the pipe was. He looked up into the expressionless face of Gareth Williams.

The attempted mugging and rescue had taken less than thirty seconds.

"I think we'd better get going," said Gareth looking around. He began to walk up Elsinore Street.

Jones nodded, looked down at the two unconscious men, noticing even in the darkness the blood creeping from under their hoods mixing with the rain in the gutters. He walked quickly and caught up with Gareth. He realized he was still holding his umbrella against the rain.

"Do I know you? " He asked.

"That depends," replied Gareth, picking up his pace.

"On what?"

"What are you going to do about it?"

"About what?"

"About what happened back there."

"I wasn't going to do anything. Someone tried to mug me, or maybe worse, and you … you saved me. Thank you."

"So, you're not … I'm going to cross the road. You should do the same and lower your umbrella."

Jones looked up to see a group of three men approaching on the sidewalk. They were less than a hundred yards away. Gareth stepped between the rows of parked cars, moved to the other sidewalk without breaking his pace and Jones followed. There were no pedestrians on this side of the road. Jones angled his umbrella to obscure their identities as the group passed them on the other side of the road.

"We need to get off the street." Jones said.

Gareth gave him a brief, curious glance and said, "I agree. Do you live around here?"

"Yes, near the junction with Vancouver Street."

"Are there any CCTV cameras around?"

"No. I haven't seen any."

"Good."

"Then may I suggest we spend the next hour at my place."

"Good idea," replied Gareth, glancing behind.

"It's thirty seconds away."

Jones's place turned out to be an anonymous, slightly decrepit, semi-detached, 1930's house with an overgrown privet hedge shielding it from the street. There were hundreds like it in south-east London. They entered the house, but didn't turn on a light until Jones had led them along the narrow corridor to the back of the house and the kitchen.

Over hot chocolate and digestive biscuits Jones found out that Gareth was a student at Goldsmiths. He'd been on the same train to Forest Hill, had recognized Jones from the College, and had taken the same route from the train station. He said he lived nearby. Jones asked if anyone had followed him from the station.

Gareth said he hadn't noticed anyone until just before Jones turned into Elsinore Street. He said he'd stopped to tie a shoe in the shelter of overhanging plastic sheeting at a house remodel. A van stopped and a man got out; he looked around, but didn't see Gareth, pulled a ski mask over his head, then headed after Jones. Gareth had picked the iron pipe out of the construction trash and followed. He assumed the other man, the one who confronted Jones, had also been in the van. Jones asked if he'd noticed anyone else in the van. Gareth said he hadn't, but couldn't be sure.

Once again, Jones thanked Gareth for his help, and emphasized if Gareth ever needed anything he had just to ask.

But he knew he'd have to check. He had no choice. He didn't want to move house, but if this was anything but a random mugging, he'd have to make alternative arrangements.

Two hours later Gareth slipped out of the still dark house into the continuing rain.

Jones checked. He contacted someone who could find out things and would let him know.

He received the report two days later.

Gareth passed, but Jones waited to make sure.

As for the muggers he couldn't tell. A week later his discreet enquiries found that one was recovering in a nursing home and the other was still unconscious. Both were from the London district of Hackney, and both had a history of violence.

Jones debated whether he should make further enquiries. It would cost him more money, and might bring more police attention to the two muggers if they discovered someone was snooping around. On the other hand, it would be good to know if his cover had been compromised.

He thought about arranging the deaths of the muggers, but that was risky. He wouldn't do it himself so it would mean involving other contacts. He'd prefer to restrict those contacts, and their peculiar talents, to business, not personal activities. And, of course, to business activities well away from Britain.

He decided to let it go. He'd increase the already formidable security measures in his house, take a cab home from the railway station, or from college, and only sleep in his safe room.

It seemed he made the right decision – nothing else happened and he heard of no threats from his personal grapevine.

Four months later when the Chinese student incident threatened to derail Gareth's college plans Jones came up with the twenty-thousand pounds necessary to make the problem go away. He considered it a good investment. He probably didn't need to, but he had bought Gareth's silence and loyalty. He required three other things from Gareth.

Gareth was to register for Arabic and Arabic studies his last two years of college, and he was to enroll in a martial arts school, preferably one based in an inner city area of east London. The third requirement was not to acknowledge any relationship between himself and Jones. If he complied with these there would be a job waiting for him on his graduation. Jones could see Gareth's potential, but unless he learned to control his violence he would be no use to Jones.

Ten years later they were both sitting in the Ford Mondeo watching the fish and chip shop in Colwyn Bay.

Jones wiped away the condensation from the side window above the driver's side rear seat.

"He's still in there?" he asked.

"As far as I know," replied Gareth.

"Then I don't think we have a choice."

"It's not how we usually do things. This is not two arms' length – it's not even one."

"I know, but what choice do we have?" repeated Jones.

"I agree."

"We also have to get on it. We can't wait. He may have called for help."

"We don't know that," said Gareth. "But I suppose we … we could wait for him to come out."

"We haven't got the luxury of waiting. We have to act."

"OK. So, how many do you think? There'll be two behind the counter. I can see some movement in there, so there could be another three or four."

"I agree. Let's plan for six. Ski masks and Arabic like we planned?"

"Yes."

"Cameras?"

"There are two, but they don't cover the entrance to the shop and there aren't any on the side streets. There may be one in the shop."

"Are we on one now?"

"No."

"Evan," Jones addressed the driver, "Drive on and take the first left. Drive around the block and come back on the other side of the road. Then take the first left after the fish and chip shop."

Evan put the vehicle in gear, but before he could move Jones added, "Wait … the door's opening."

Evan disengaged the clutch and the three men in the car looked across the road.

"It's not him," said Gareth.

They watched as a man stepped out of the fish and chip shop and tried to put up his umbrella against the sleet and wind. He gave up, pulled his hat brim lower and clutching an object to his chest wrapped in a plastic bag in one hand, and holding the umbrella in the other, walked with a cautious gait away from the shop.

Jones stared after him for a few seconds before turning back to Evan and saying, "Let's get going then."

"Wait a second," Gareth said. "I'd hate to miss him while we drive around the block. Let me get out. I'll cross the road and check in the fish and chip shop. I'll join you when you park."

He got out of the car and stood back while Evan drove off. He crossed the road and walked slowly and evenly past the fish and chip shop giving the appearance that his total concentration was on preventing slipping on the sidewalk. He couldn't be sure what the CCTV cameras were watching. With the sleet he thought he wouldn't have to be too concerned, but there was no point in arousing suspicion.

He turned left onto a side street. The Ford Mondeo pulled to the curb in front of him and he slipped into the front passenger seat.

"He's in there. He's sitting to the right, near the window," said Gareth.

"Let's do it then," said Jones.

Both men knew exactly what to do. They put on black ski masks and black beanie hats.

"Keep the car running, Evan. No lights inside the car. We'll be back in ten minutes," Gareth said and got out of the car.

They walked the short distance back to the fish and chip shop and, with no hesitation, opened the door and stepped inside. Gareth entered first and pulled a short, stout oak club from his jacket. He took two paces from the door to the man at the table. The man started to rise but Gareth brought the club down across his skull, and in another two paces reached up and knocked the CCTV camera onto the floor. Then he pushed open the half door to get behind the counter. There were two women there. The older started for the phone, but stopped when Gareth smashed the club across the receiver and tore it from the wall. While looking at the terrified woman he said something in Arabic to Jones.

Jones stood at the door and translated. "He says if you try anything like that again he will break your arm and push your

57

face into the chip fat. He usually means what he says. Now, come out here."

The two women scuttled to the front of the shop. The older was middle-aged, plump and grey-haired, the other was skinny, in her twenties, with tattooed arms and purple spiky hair. She started crying.

Gareth followed and examined his handiwork. The man was slumped over the table, bleeding profusely from a cut over the left temple. Gareth tapped him on the head with his stick and got no reaction. He looked at Jones and shrugged, then searched the jacket of the man. He found a cell phone and wallet. He looked briefly at the cell phone screen before pocketing it and the wallet. He moved to stand at Jones's right. He held the club loosely in his left hand.

Jones addressed the women and the family at the table, "The man at the table is one of our associates and he let us down. We believe he may have given information to someone here. Tell me what you know."

Silence.

"I appreciate you are frightened, but unless you start talking, I will leave you in here when I burn this place down. Do you understand? Nod if you understand."

They all nodded.

Jones changed tactics.

"You!" Jones pointed at the obese father. "You give me your driving license."

The obese father reached into his coat and with a shaky hand pulled his driving license out of his wallet. Jones took it from him and read out the name and address.

"Robert Holte, 97 Rhodfa'r Grug. Not a common Welsh name," he commented.

"Where's your license ... Mary?" he asked the older server, reading her name badge.

"In my 'andbag," she replied indicating the back of the shop.

"And yours ... Sandy?" he asked the younger one.

"It's there too."

58

In Arabic he told Gareth to go and find both women's coats and bags. Gareth brought them back, emptied the contents of the bags on the table and gave the driving licenses to Jones.

"Mary Williams, Abergele Road. Sandy Evans, Conway Road. Now we know where you live." Jones read out the details and pocketed the licenses.

He continued, "I'll ask you one more time. Mary, Sandy, Robert, I won't ask again. I want to know what happened here." He looked directly at Robert.

Gareth took a step forward towards the group.

"Well, 'e was in front of me, and 'e ordered fish and chips," Robert started. "Then 'e sat down there at the table and started to eat them. Then the other man sat down with 'im. In't that right?" he asked his family and the two serving women. They all nodded in agreement.

"What man?" asked Jones.

"The man 'oo came in after us," said Robert.

"Tell me about him," said Jones.

"Well, I don't know," Robert replied with anxiety creeping into his voice.

Gareth brought the wooden stick down across the table. The two women and the family jerked away startled.

"But, I don't know," repeated Robert.

"'E was American," said a squeaky voice. It was Robert's son.

"American?" asked Jones. "How do you know?"

"I 'eard 'im talking, and 'e wasn't from around 'ere, so I listened to what 'e said and 'e was American. The man over there at that table – well, 'e called 'im American. I could 'ear them talking. 'E said 'e was from Seattle."

"Seattle?"

"It's in America. We did it in geography."

"What did they talk about?"

"I don't remember … oh, yes, they talked about a book and 'e gave 'im the one 'e'd been reading."

"Who gave who a book?"

"The man at the table there gave the American a book."

"What was the name of the book?"

"I dunno."

"You don't know?"

"No, I dunno."

"Do you remember anything else about him?" Jones asked the boy and the rest of the captives. They all shook their heads.

"Did he say what he was doing here?" Jones looked at the boy.

"No... oh, yes. 'E was visiting his auntie."

"Auntie?"

"Yes. I think she lives around 'ere.

"Where?" Jones demanded.

"I dunno. 'E didn't say."

"Do you remember what he looked like?"

"'E wore glasses," said the older woman

"'E had an 'at," said Mr. Obesity.

"It was an American 'at," said the boy.

"American hat?" asked Jones.

"It was like one of those, you know, baseball caps, with flaps to keep off the rain."

Jones realized the man he had seen leaving the fish and chip shop was the 'American'. He made a decision.

"All of you can leave. It is by the grace of Allah I have spared your lives. Now get out of here. The police will want to talk to you, but remember, I know where you live. If you talk to them you will have to answer to me. May all perish like him," he indicated the man slumped over the table, "if they take the name of Allah in vain. Allahu Akbar."

"Allahu Akbar," shouted Gareth.

He stood aside as the captives ran out in to the sleet and away from the fish and chip shop.

"Flash-bang? It should go well with the chip fat," stated Gareth.

"Good." Jones nodded. "Let's go ... and leave a Hand."

"Are you sure? I thought we weren't going to do that."

"It fits with the Arabic, and it should help distract any investigation."

"OK, you're the boss," said Gareth and pulled a small thin metal outline of a hand from an inside pocket. He placed it on the table near the unconscious man.

Jones dropped the licenses he'd confiscated onto the floor and left the shop. Gareth went behind the counter to the pans holding the heated chip oil. He picked up a handful of wrapping paper, dipped the sheets in the fat and dropped them on the counter and in the pans, then picked up the rest of the paper pile and spread it over the floor.

From his coat pocket he brought out a flash-bang – a device which produces brief intense heat, light and sound. He pulled the activating pin and dropped the device onto the greasy paper behind the counter. He walked towards the door, counted two seconds, closed his eyes and covered his ears for another two seconds to mask most of the flash-bang's effects, then followed Jones to the car.

Gareth used the mobile phone he'd taken from the fish and chip shop to send a text. Then, with the help of a screwdriver, he removed the battery and threw it, and the phone, out of the car window as they left Colwyn Bay.

Evan changed the number plates on the car on a side street on the outskirts of Chester, and at midnight they reached the M25 ring road around London.

By 2:00 am both Jones and Gareth were asleep and Evan was waiting for a charter flight out of Gatwick to a package holiday in Orlando, Florida.

8

Mustafa Okyar's business was on the fifth floor of a nondescript office complex close to the castle and citadel of Ankara. The logo on the door was a simple intertwining of three capital 'I's over the name of his company written in English (Izmir International Investments), in Turkish, and in Arabic.

Stefan and Ella had asked for the last appointment before lunch – implying, if their business went as planned, they would like to take Okyar to lunch. Stefan opened the door and walked in without knocking. Ella followed him. She was wearing a head scarf, or hijab, loose-fitting, plain, conservative clothing and the veil, the niqab. They found themselves in a simple outer office with a woman, presumably an administrative assistant, who was sitting at a computer desk also wearing both the hijab and the niqab.

"Mr. Smith to see Mr. Okyar," said Stefan in English. "We have a twelve o'clock appointment."

He didn't add that he and Ella were about to ruin Okyar's day.

The woman nodded, rose, knocked on an inner door and directed them into the opulent office of Mustafa Okyar.

It was a marked contrast to the functional outer office. It was almost as if an interior designer had intentionally taken cues for furnishing the room from Hollywood's silent-movie portrayals of a Bedouin chief's tent, or a sultan's harem. There were elaborate, colorful carpets everywhere, embroidered couches, and heavy draperies obscured most of the windows. On the walls there were multiple paintings of harem scenes with well-endowed, slightly obese women lounging on furniture in the same style and colors as the office. The overall effect, in any culture, was amazingly tasteless.

However, that was clearly not the opinion of the owner, Mustafa Okyar, who rose, smiling, from behind his large rosewood desk and indicated they should seat opposite him. He was short, fat, sported a small mustache, and was wearing an open embroidered vest. He looked like a character in the paintings surrounding him.

"Welcome, Mr. Smith," he said in English. "My name is Mustafa Okyar, but please call me Mustafa. And this is … ?"

"My sister, Fatima."

Ella acknowledged the introduction by lowering her head a little. She waited for Stefan to sit before allowing herself a seat in a chair a little to the side of, and behind, Stefan.

Stefan continued. "Thank you for agreeing to see me at such short notice."

"No. Not at all, not at all. It is I who should be thanking you. Before we start, would you like something to drink?"

"Do you have any tea? My sister would like some water."

Mustafa clapped his hands. His assistant must have been outside the door, waiting for his signal, and entered promptly.

"Tea for me and for Mr. Smith. Water for his sister."

The assistant left the room.

"I see you like the room?" Mustafa said, almost as a question.

"It's certainly different," said Stefan. "Who designed it?" he asked, knowing the answer before it came.

"I did," said Mustafa, beaming. "I wanted to portray both a bygone era and a modern one and came up with this. I have several clients from Arabic countries and they like it, just like you. And … er … where are you from?"

"We flew in from Istanbul today."

They hadn't, but Mustafa didn't need to know anything else about them apart from the fact they were sitting in his office.

The tea arrived promptly. The assistant brought in an ornate silver platter on which she had placed two glasses of hot tea and sugar cubes. There was also a plastic bottle of water. Stefan leaned forward, added a single sugar cube to his tea and stirred it slowly. He took a sip of tea, picked up the bottle of water and handed it backwards to Ella without looking at her.

Ella thought he was playing his part well, or was he beginning to enjoy treating her this way? How was she supposed to discreetly drink from the bottle with this veil over her face and no glass?

64

Stefan opened and looked into the black leather briefcase he had brought with him, made a show of shuffling the papers and carefully brought out a red file cover from which he removed five sheets of paper. He handed the papers to Mustafa.

The effect was not immediate, but as Mustafa scanned the numbers and names he became visibly more agitated.

The conversation was predictable.

"Where did you get these?" he asked aggressively.

"I'm sure you know," replied Stefan.

"They are, of course, fake. They are complete lies." He placed the papers on the desk in front of him and pushed them away with a dismissive gesture.

"They are not fakes. They are not lies."

"Of course they are. They have nothing to do with me. I run a legitimate business here. I don't know where you got those, but they are a complete fabrication." Mustafa remained indignant.

"They are not fakes," repeated Stefan in an even voice.

"Who are you anyway?" Mustafa asked.

"We are not the police. We are not the authorities. We could be. We could give these papers, and some of the others I have here, to the police." He tapped his briefcase. "But, that won't be necessary. We may turn out to be the best friends you could have."

Mustafa eyed the briefcase wondering what else it contained. "What do you want?" he asked defensively.

"Information."

Mustafa relaxed a little.

Stefan continued. "You have an associate in Istanbul. Let's call him … Kamal. This is where we got these records. You have not heard from him in the last couple of weeks. Is that correct?"

"It may be."

"According to our records he normally contacts you every week. He has not done so for a week or two. Is that correct."

"It may be."

Mustafa was feeling a little more confident. It was time for Stefan to deliver the really bad news. He fished into his briefcase

65

and brought out a photograph which he passed across the desk to Mustafa.

"He hasn't been in touch with you because he is dead."

Stefan and Ella watched Mustafa's face as he finally recognized the face with the bullet wound. Mustafa seemed to crumple and shake in front of them. Stefan added a little more salt to the wounds. He passed two more photos of Kamal's dead assassins to Mustafa. He waited until Mustafa looked up.

"We didn't kill Kamal. The other two photos are of the men who did. Do you know them?"

Mustafa looked down again and shook his head.

"We don't know who they are either, but we'll find out."

"Who are you?" Mustafa asked again.

Stefan replied in an even, quiet tone. "It doesn't matter to you who we are except you are lucky we are not the police, and we have nothing to do with them or any other authorities. On the other hand, if you prefer to take your chances with the police we could arrange for them to have the same information."

In reply Mustafa shook his head slowly.

"So, tell us about your relationship with Kamal."

"What do you want to know?"

"Everything. Start at the beginning and tell us about it."

"Why should I tell you?" Mustafa almost pouted. He was still resisting.

"I'd have thought that was obvious. We have something in common."

"What?"

"We both knew Kamal. Kamal was shot to death by someone or some organization. Agree?"

"Yes."

"How do we know the same organization isn't going to be coming after us if they find out our links to Kamal?"

It was a few seconds before Mustafa understood the full implication of Stefan's statement. He became visibly paler and more agitated.

"You mean ... how do I know it's not you?" he blurted out.

"It's not us. If it were us you would be dead by now. We are as concerned as you are. And, before you ask, we have links to Kamal, and we don't want them advertized, and you don't need to know what they are."

"I heard he had a sister," said Mustafa looking directly at Ella.

Ella's face was hidden by the veil and Stefan's expression didn't change when he added, "Interesting. We hadn't heard of that. It's something we may have to look in to. Can you give us any details?"

"No, it's just something he mentioned once," Mustafa said and looked back at Stefan.

"So, tell us about your relationship with Kamal," Stefan asked again.

Mustafa hesitated then seemed to make up his mind. "We met about three years ago. I met him at a meeting, here in Ankara. I had given a short talk at a workshop for lawyers. It was one of their annual meetings and my talk was about international investing and Turkish regulations. I met a couple of people after the talk and one was Kamal. He told me he was an attorney and had a client who was interested in investing through my company. He invited me out to dinner to talk a little more, and he said his client was particularly interested in currency conversion. He had money in one currency and wanted to invest it in other currencies. That isn't necessarily an easy thing to do in Turkey, or any country, but there are ways around it. Some are …" Mustafa hesitated, "… some are more legal than others. There are lots of areas of the law and regulations which are not exactly black and white, and some are frankly contradictory, but that's how we do business and what we have to live with here. "

Stefan nodded in understanding.

Mustafa continued. "After the workshop Kamal contacted me. He said he had a client who wanted to invest on a regular basis and had no need of immediate cash, but if he wanted cash he wanted it in US dollars. He sent the first monthly check to me and after that I received 5,000 Turkish lire every month. That's about 1,000 euros. I thought it a little strange, but didn't really think much more about it." He paused.

"Why was it strange?" asked Stefan. Ella watched him as he took a sip of his tea.

"The sums were small. If you want to get some dollars of small amounts like that you can buy them at the bank. You will have to fill out forms, but it should be no big deal. If you want to just convert lire to dollars, avoiding any scrutiny, there are ways of doing that too. The commission on something like that could be 20-40% so if you have time, especially with larger sums, you buy something in one currency and sell it in another. It's easy with property. For example, you buy an apartment in a resort on the Black Sea in lire and you sell it to someone in dollars. Or, maybe you buy gold in lire and sell it in dollars. The problem with apartments is they can burn down, or lose their value, and gold can disappear. But, I didn't think anything more about it until a year ago. Kamal came to see me here in this office and he brought a client with him – the client who had been investing through him and me."

He paused again and Stefan waited.

Mustafa continued. "I could see when Kamal arrived all was not well. He looked nervous – anxious. The client, who just called himself Ali, told us he had good news for us. He said we had passed the test and had successfully invested over 100,000 lire with us. Now he was going to give us even better news – he was going to invest 250,000 lire every month with us. The currency would not always be in lire, some would be in other currencies, but he expected it to be available to him with thirty days notice in US dollars.

"Naturally, we objected. What we had done up till this time was skirting the legal/illegal border, but this was clearly illegal. He smiled and told us he didn't want us to do anything illegal, but he had records of the financial exchanges we had already arranged for him. Since he was a model citizen he would take them to the police to see what they thought of them, unless we cooperated with him. He also told us that if the police arrested us he would make sure that we would never leave jail alive. He had us … how do you say … over a barrel?"

"So, he threatened you?" asked Stefan.

"Yes. We both knew what he meant."

"Do you know who he was, apart from Ali? Did he say who he represented?"

"I know that he represented something I'd rather not be involved in. He was an Arab and he implied he worked for an organization. He didn't say which one. Kamal and I discussed it afterwards. We didn't think it was a local criminal group, but it could be the Kurds, the Taliban, or Al-Qaeda, Daesh, or any of another dozen groups who need financing, and any faction within those groups."

"Then what happened?"

"The money arrived. For some reason it still came through Kamal and he brought it to me each month. We were worried. What had worked for small sums wasn't going to work for the money we were being sent. We had to pay off more people and pay bigger percentage commissions. Kamal told me Ali didn't like that, but we told him we were doing our best. Then, about a month ago it all stopped. We didn't get any more money and we hadn't heard from Ali. As time went on I thought we were out of the loop and wouldn't have to deal with Ali any more, but now you've brought me this." He indicated the photos on the desk in front of him.

Stefan asked. "Tell me what you think of Kamal. Was he skimming money off the top?"

"You mean was he cheating Ali?"

"Yes."

"No. He was scared. I suspect he knew more about Ali and his connections than I did, and perhaps I should have thanked him for that. Ali wanted details of where his money went and it would have been difficult to fool him."

Stefan remained silent for a moment then fished into his briefcase again and brought out a photo of the metal hand and forearm outline Ella had noticed on the hood of her brother's car. He passed it to Mustafa.

"Do you know what this is?" he asked.

Mustafa looked at it briefly, then looked again and held it closer to his desk light. Ella thought a brief expression of concern, or even alarm, crossed his face.

"Interesting. It looks like a copy of the Hand of Hamsa, or Khamsah. Where did you get it?"

"It was found near the body of Kamal," said Stefan.

Mustafa looked again. He seemed to lose interest in the photo, but asked.

"Was there anything written on it?"

"No. That photo is all I have."

Mustafa shrugged, but glanced at the photo one more time.

"Have you seen anything like this before?" said Stefan.

"No, it's a common symbol in many Mediterranean countries. I have no idea what it means." He looked Stefan in the eyes for a fraction of a second too long.

Stefan thought for a moment. He would have liked to confer with Ella, but that would have changed the dynamics of the conversation. Instead he asked, "The money that Ali gave to you. How much is there?"

Mustafa turned to his computer and entered a few key strokes, then looked back to Stefan.

"There is about a half a million dollars worth still in it. That's about half of the total that was there. Ali took the rest out about a month ago."

"Can he take it out himself, or do you have to do it for him?"

"He let me know he wanted the money in dollars, and a week later he took it out. If he'd wanted it in lire he could have taken it out himself almost immediately."

"Sooner or later he, or maybe someone else, is going to want that money. Do you agree?" said Stefan.

"Yes."

"You can buy a lot of death for half a million dollars and whichever organization Ali belongs to will want that money. If we can find you I think they will too."

Mustafa's confidence disappeared again. He asked, "What makes you think that?"

Stefan leaned forward. "A couple of things make me concerned. I have a theory and it goes like this. You and Kamal were laundering money for an organization, maybe a terrorist organization. You told us as much, but if a terrorist organization arranges to assassinate someone it doesn't keep it quiet. If they had killed Kamal they would have announced it to the world, but that hasn't happened. I think Ali was freelancing. He was diverting funds for his own use and someone was about to find out. He arranged for Kamal to be killed, but he couldn't use his organization, so he hired a third party. He also arranged for the clean-up of Kamal's place afterwards. I think the metal hand was the equivalent of a calling card. It was to be left to show that the work had been done, but the work wasn't done. Kamal fought bravely and both his attackers were killed too. Logically, you would have been the next one to disappear, and maybe the killers would have been on their way here if Kamal hadn't killed them. I wonder if Ali is still alive too. This may explain why you haven't heard from him. You can hope that no one got their hands on the same files we have, but you could be literally staking your life on that." He paused. "Anyway, that's my theory. What do you think?"

"I ... I don't know. I don't know what to think."

"Well, you could look at this optimistically and hope that whoever cleaned up the mess at the house where Kamal was killed also destroyed any links to you. Since no one has got in touch you could be in the clear. In fact, if you wait long enough the rest of the money which Ali gave to you could be yours." Stefan could see Mustafa's mind working through that scenario and the glimmer of opportunity it presented. Stefan continued. "On the other hand someone could walk through your door this afternoon and demand the money you hold for Ali. You would, of course, have no choice but to give it to them. If you are lucky that is all they would do. If not they could arrange for a painful death." Stefan let that sink in for a few seconds then added. "There is also the problem of the two dead assassins. I'm assuming they didn't work directly with Ali. They may have colleagues, relatives, friends who would really like to know what

71

happened to them and who might be responsible. They may come looking for you."

"What can I do?" Mustafa moaned.

Stefan started to pick up the photographs and files he had passed to Mustafa and answered. "I have a couple of suggestions. First, you go back to your wife in Sincan."

Mustafa looked surprised.

Stefan nodded and said, "Yes, we know where you live. You go to your wife and you tell her that you are going on a business trip, or you can tell her you are both going on a vacation. I suggest you leave town for a few weeks. You can rent a house in Antalya and enjoy the spring weather, or you could go to the Canary Islands, or anywhere it would take a little more effort to find you. You leave your assistant here and pay her to come in every day you are away. You can contact her every few days to check on business. If someone has come looking for you you'll soon know. Then, it's up to you what you do next."

"But what about my business?" Mustafa whined.

"What about your life? You could, of course, hire security to protect you 24 hours every day, but that is expensive, far from perfect and then it may make you look guilty. Spend the money on a trip. Relax. Enjoy yourself."

Stefan rose and put out his hand which Mustafa shook reflexively.

"I suggest you don't wait too long to make a decision," said Stefan.

"And who did you say you are?" Mustafa asked.

Stefan turned and without replying left the room. Ella followed him with the unopened bottle of water still in her hand.

"You noticed, I hope, that I did not offer him the services of SIGNAK," Stefan said as he and Ella sat in the Honda Civic. He had taken the driver's seat and Ella sat next to him.

"I did notice, and I also noticed you enjoyed playing the male superior part in his office."

"Good. I think I did that rather well. I thought you'd appreciate it." He smiled and moved the car into the stream of traffic.

"Don't make it a habit." Ella replied curtly.

"I thought you looked good with the hajib and the niqab."

"How would you know? You had your back to me all the time. It's like wearing a tent. On the other hand it's sort of comforting – I appreciate the anonymity it gives me. Maybe I'll get to like it."

"I think you should keep it all on for a little longer," said Stefan, checking the mirror. "I don't think we have a tail, but let's be sure. What did you think of him?"

"Mustafa? He could be telling the truth – at least part of what he said seemed to ring true. However, I wouldn't be surprised if Ali didn't exist, or he may be Ali himself. I also think he agreed to your unlikely crime scene interpretation a little too easily. You noticed he feigned lack of interest in the photo of the hand?"

"Yes. I wonder what that was about. Well, we are going to monitor him, and his phone calls, for the rest of the day – I hope it doesn't take any longer. The story that he was only a middle man doesn't seem right. I think he'll make a move, or contact someone very quickly. I'm going to circle the block and join our man in the car park opposite his office."

Stefan's cell phone rang. He answered it, spoke briefly, and then said to Ella.

"Change of plan. He's on the move. I suggest we follow him. He's being tracked. Apparently, he made a phone call to someone and they invited him right over."

Stefan concentrated on his driving in the midday Ankara traffic while Ella monitored Mustafa's route on Stefan's cell phone. They headed north, out of the city. At times they came within fifty meters of Mustafa's vehicle, a dusty, red Peugeot, but as the traffic thinned they hung back further until they were on a minor road in open, barren countryside with little traffic. Here, they stayed a half kilometer behind, always trying to make sure there was more than one vehicle between them and Mustafa. It was reassuring to know that another SIGNAK car was following them.

"He's turned off to the right," said Ella. She looked at her watch. They had followed him for two hours and twenty minutes.

As they closed the distance they could see the dust rising from Mustafa's vehicle as he climbed a short slope off the asphalted road. They passed the exit he had taken and drove on for another two minutes before Stefan U-turned and returned to the same exit. By now Mustafa's car was out of sight over the low ridge and the grey dust he'd thrown up was drifting to their right. Stefan pulled onto the shoulder near the beginning of the dirt road.

"I think we should wait a while," he said.

"I agree. How far does the tracker signal go out here?" asked Ella, her eyes on the cell phone screen.

"I'm not sure. Theoretically, it could follow anyone anywhere in the world."

"Does it require a cell phone connection?"

"Yes, the way we are using it. Why?"

"We probably don't have coverage out here. There is no signal – it just disappeared."

"Let's move then before anyone else uses this road, so we can follow his dust. I think that's all we can do."

"Agreed. What about the SIGNAK car following us?"

"They're tracking us and their system is direct – it doesn't need a cell phone."

They pulled onto the dirt road and sped towards the brow of the hill. As they crested the hill Stefan slowed. The road dipped a little then carried straight on to another low rise. The dust from Mustafa's car indicated he was still on the road. Again, they accelerated towards the top of the rise and then slowed to make sure they were far enough back to minimize the risk of being seen. For over five miles they continued the pattern of speed and stealth following the road and the dust cloud.

"That's interesting. I'm getting coverage again," said Ella. "It's only one bar so far, but it wasn't there a few minutes ago."

"Maybe we're getting close"

"Close to what though?"

Stefan slowed the car as he drove over a short rise, then stopped. In front of them, a half-mile away in a low valley the road ended in a collection of small buildings. The surrounding area looked liked someone had once made an attempt at farming. There were small fields of dirt outlined by the ghosts of stone walls, and stunted trees. It was impossible to tell if they had been abandoned in the last six months, or when Marco Polo passed by six centuries earlier.

Mustafa's car was parked outside the largest of the buildings – an intact, tall, white-washed villa. They could see no other vehicles or people.

"Let's give him fifteen minutes and then we join him," said Ella.

"Are you sure? It could be dangerous." Stefan sounded concerned.

"It may be, but it will be less dangerous for you if I am along. Also, let's give them some truth if it comes up. Tell them I am Kamal's sister."

"OK, but in that case you'd better be my wife. I can object profusely if they start harassing you in any way."

"You mean you wouldn't object normally?" Ella smiled.

"Of course I would, but maybe profusely isn't the word. How about dramatically?"

"OK, you can be my husband, but don't overdo the drama."

It was Stefan's turn to smile. He changed the subject, turned to Ella and said. "We'll play it like before. You remain mute, inscrutable and apparently subservient. You wear the hajib and niqab. I do the talking but you …"

Ella interrupted, "I'll have you covered." She tapped her left forearm under the bulky sleeve. "It's still here, and I'm wearing the wire."

"I'm sorry. No matter how many times we've done this I always get a little nervous," Stefan admitted.

"So do I and I think it's good that we do. And, this isn't like any other time. We're more stretched and we don't know what we are getting in to." She squeezed his hand gently. "I don't want anything bad to happen to either of us."

9

Ella checked to make sure her microphone and receiver were functioning. Their conversation would be monitored by the SIGNAK employees following in the back-up vehicle – the ear piece was concealed under her hajib. She replaced the niqab over her face, nodded she was ready, and Stefan drove the last two-hundred meters at a conservative twenty kilometers per hour. He didn't want to create any more surprises than he had to.

He parked close to Mustafa's car, but on the side away from the villa. The cloud of grey dust from the car's passage swirled around the vehicle then drifted away. Stefan waited for the air to clear before getting out of his car. He stood up tall, stretched his arms above his head, and slowly turned around. There was no one to be seen, but he noticed at least two security cameras on the villa pointed his way, and another on a ramshackle house fifty meters away. He started to walk around the back of his car, but apparently noticed an untied shoelace, put his foot on the top of the rear wheel of Mustafa's car, attended to the lace and removed the tracking device from under its wheel arch. He sauntered around to the other side of his car and opened the passenger door for Ella. He didn't help her out – he didn't think it appropriate for the role he was playing. With his back to her he reattached the tracker under the rear wheel arch of his car – it was less likely to be found there if either of the cars was searched. He indicated to Ella to follow him and walked towards the nearby villa.

It was still a few months before summer, but he felt hot and was beginning to sweat in the cloudless afternoon sun. He and Ella climbed the rough concrete steps to the only visible door into the villa. It was solid and made of grey wood and iron bars. There was no knocker or bell, so Stefan rapped his knuckles on the door. There was no answer. He waited thirty seconds and knocked a second time. Again, no response. He was beginning to feel exposed and vulnerable standing there with Ella close by and that, he realized, was the purpose. He knocked one more time and a few seconds later heard the whirring and click of an electronic lock. The door opened inwards and a man wearing worn army fatigues waved them into an ante-room.

The room was ten degrees cooler than the outside of the villa and illuminated by bright, bare fluorescent bulbs. It was occupied by another two men, in the same fatigues, but also wearing side arms. These were clearly guards and watched silently as Stefan's briefcase was opened and he was patted down by the first man. Satisfied there were no threats the man approached Ella. Ella stepped back and crossed her arms defensively across her chest. The man hesitated and looked towards the taller guard for orders.

"Carry on," the guard said in Turkish. The man moved towards Ella, but she recoiled again.

Stefan half turned and said, in English, "My wife doesn't want to be searched. I do not want her to be searched."

The taller guard pushed forward and came within half a meter of Ella's face. She could smell his lunch of garlic and cheap cigarettes on his breath. She visualized what it would be like to kick him in his balls – a trick she had learned to help her at times like these, but instead continued to look down at an imaginary spot five meters in front of her.

Apparently satisfied she presented no threat, he spat on the floor, turned around, headed up a stairway leading off the ante-room and indicated for Stefan and Ella to follow. Stefan went first; Ella uncrossed her arms and followed. The other guards brought up the rear.

The stairway led to an open arched balcony which overlooked a leafy courtyard in the middle of which was a low, gurgling marble fountain. The balcony ended at another heavy wooden door which was slightly ajar. Without knocking the guard led them into the room.

The first thing Ella noticed was a huge gilt-edged mirror almost completely covering the wall opposite her. She could see in the reflection the two armed guards take up station by the door behind her. Next, she noticed the three armchairs. Two were occupied; one by Mustafa who was sitting on the edge of the cushion looking angry or embarrassed – she wasn't sure which, and the other by a bearded man wearing a white caftan. She judged him to be in his mid fifties. He wore no head covering, and had graying hair in his beard and temples. He was slim with a smooth, dark complexion. His grey eyes were magnified by his rimless glasses. He was sitting, relaxed in his armchair, and with legs crossed. He also appeared slightly amused.

"Please sit," he said in perfect English, indicating the remaining armchair to Stefan. He then added, "Bring a chair," in Turkish. He indicated to one of the guards to find a seat for Ella. Stefan sat in the armchair and Ella looked behind and accepted the wooden stool one of the guards pushed towards her. For the second time that day she found herself a little to the side and behind Stefan. She continued to keep her eyes lowered but as she sat noted that with the help of the mirror she could see all the people in the room. She was two meters from one armed guard and three from the other.

The bearded man spoke. "Allow me to introduce myself. My name is Ali. I believe you have met my colleague, Mustafa."

Mustafa looked uncomfortable and ignored Stefan's nod towards him.

Stefan replied, "My name is Stefan and this is Fatima." He waved his hand in Ella's direction and introduced her without looking at her directly, but he caught her eye briefly in the mirror.

"Allow me to offer you tea." Ali said in English and then in Turkish, "Tea for all, Ishmael."

The unarmed guard nodded and left the room.

"How can I help you?"

"We are seeking the killers of Kamal Demir."

"Really? Why? Who was he to you?"

"He was my wife's brother," Stefan answered.

"He was known to me, but why are you here? Why do you think I had anything to do with his death? I, myself, only found out about it a few minutes ago."

"I am sure Mr. Okyar has told you we visited him this morning." Stefan looked at Mustafa.

"He has, but I still wonder why you apparently followed him here. He told me no one followed him."

"His red car is easy to follow. As to why we followed him? Well he did say that you, or someone named Ali, basically blackmailed him to launder money. Is that correct?"

Ali laughed. "Mustafa has a vivid imagination. However, I suspect you didn't believe everything he told you, or you wouldn't be here, so I can see why you want more information. But I will start by saying I did not kill, nor arrange to have killed, your brother." He looked directly at Ella, who gave a small nod of acknowledgement then lowered her eyes again. "I am pretty sure I know who arranged to have him killed, and I know who killed him."

"Who?"

"Before we get to that I feel I may have been unjustly portrayed by my colleague here." He indicated Mustafa, who looked a little more uncomfortable, but not as much as Ella thought he should.

Ali continued. "I am, for the most part, a legitimate business man. I buy things and I sell things, mainly in Turkey and the Middle East. In order for someone to buy my goods I sometimes help them facilitate the changing of money from one currency to another. This is where Kamal came in. He was very good at arranging transfers of money and did so with the help of Mustafa here. I work for myself. There are no other entities involved, but the nature of my business is such that there are competitors, sometimes quite nasty and vindictive ones. I am not on any terrorist list, but some of my competitors are. I believe it is one of these competitors who arranged for Kamal to be killed. However, what is interesting is I believe that Kamal's killers were not part of my usual competition. I suspect, from what Mustafa has told me, that someone hired the killers. If I am correct he spent a lot of money to arrange this kill. Now, please tell me –"

He was distracted by the door opening and the guard returned with a small samovar and traditional small, glass teacups. He poured hot tea into three of these and handed them to the seated men. Ella would have been left out had not Ali ordered, "And for the lady," in Turkish. The guard seemed a little uncomfortable but complied. Ella noted there was a small side table for the glasses of the men, but not for her.

Ali spoke to Ella in English, "Some of my men come from what is sometimes called in the West 'traditional backgrounds'. I apologize for their lack of courtesy."

Ella nodded and accepted his apology. She looked around for a table for her hot glass.

"And a table for her," Ali added sharply in Turkish, then in English said, "Again, I apologize." He shook his head and turned back to Stefan while a table was found for Ella.

There was knock on the door. The unarmed guard answered it and was handed a sheaf of papers which he took to Ali and whispered in his ear. Ali perused them for a full minute. Stefan recognized the papers as his car rental agreement. He'd paid with his SIGNAK credit card. He hoped that wasn't a mistake.

"You see what I have here?" Ali asked.

"You have paperwork you took from my car." Stefan spoke evenly.

"We have only borrowed it and only to see if you are going to tell us the truth."

"I had no intention of doing otherwise. You can see that I am usually employed by SIGNAK, or TPSI, Total Personal Security International, as it is known here, but I am not working directly for that company at this time. We normally protect people. However, that is not why I am here. My wife wishes to find out what happened to Kamal Demir, and who killed him. We have no interest in any other activities."

Ali waited before saying, "But how do I know you are not here to undermine or damage my businesses?"

Stefan shrugged and replied, "You don't, and maybe you can never be sure, but we are not interested in you, just who killed Kamal Demir."

Again, Ali waited a short time before saying, "I understand from Mustafa that you have photographs and other documents. I would like to see them."

Stefan opened his briefcase and handed the information he had previously shown Mustafa to Ali, except he held back the photograph of the hand.

Ali ignored the financial information but looked closely at the photographs. "Did you take these photographs?" he asked Stefan looking at him directly across the small table and tea glasses.

Stefan sipped his tea, placed it on the table, and answered, "I did."

"Did you kill these men?"

"I didn't. I can't be quite certain, but I think Kamal killed them, and was killed by them. I arrived too late to know exactly what happened."

"Why were you there?"

"Kamal enquired about SIGNAK services. I am not sure why, and I never found out."

"Did you call the police?"

"No."

The next question could have been, "Why didn't you call the police?" but both knew the answer would have been obvious, for multiple reasons, in Turkey.

Instead, Ali said, "I believe there is one more photo?"

Stefan handed over the photograph of the hand. Ali stared at it for a long time before looking up and saying, "I haven't seen one of these for a long time. Do you know what this is?"

"Mustafa told us it is a replica of the Hand of Hamsa."

"Mustafa wasn't being quite truthful. It looks like the Hand of Hamsa, or Khamsah, but it also includes part of the forearm, not just the wrist, and the middle finger is longer than usual ... I wonder if that isn't significant." He looked closer. "There's the beginning of an inscription on it. It looks like the letters J and A, but then the light reflection hides the rest. It also looks like it was photographed on the top of a car. Where did you get it?"

"It was found near the body of Kamal," said Stefan.

"I wonder if it wasn't inscribed in Arabic on the other side. That might have helped identify it, but the inscription we are looking at probably says, 'Jaafer' or 'Ja'far'. It is from 'Ja'far Ibn Talib'."

Stefan looked expectant.

Ali added, "Ja'far was a cousin, I believe, of The Prophet. He was famous because he lost one arm in a battle, I can't remember which one, carried on fighting, and then lost his other, but fought on holding the banner under his chin until he was finally killed. You can find out all about it in a history of Islam."

"So you have seen something like this before?" said Stefan.

"Unfortunately, I have." Ali hesitated, swallowed hard, reached for his tea glass and added. "I found one of these by the side of my dead brother and sister."

Stefan leaned forward a little, but remained quiet. One of the guards fidgeted and coughed. Ali sat still and stared unfocussed at the small table in front of him. Finally, he added, "I still see them in my dreams as I found them. I suppose I always will … I have tried over the years to find out who killed them. I found out who ordered the killing, but it was a time of increased turmoil in Jordan, and that man was killed before I could find out any more. And then I never found out who killed him. For many years I have tried to discover who he paid to kill my family. I failed until recently. I now know there is an organization which will 'disappear' people for a fee. If you disappear it is almost like you never existed. One day you are there, the next you are gone and never heard of again. No one knows what happened to you. The police can't find out – the police are rarely informed, or maybe they are bribed. However, sometimes you are not disappeared, you are just killed. In those circumstances there may be a metal hand left behind. I suspect when the hand is left behind it is a message, or a warning. It was to me."

He paused, leaned forward and took another sip of his tea. "Metal hands like these have been found next to dead people around the Middle East and Europe over the last, maybe ten years. It is impossible for me to review all the newspapers in all these countries, but I have done my best to make a note of when the main media reports a metal hand, or forearm and hand associated with a crime. I am sure I am missing many reports, but once a year or so I discover some report in some media outlet about a metal hand like this. Have you noted anything like this?" He looked directly at Stefan.

"No. I checked with our files and sources at SIGNAK and found nothing."

"Then, may I suggest you look again, or look harder, or look differently. From what I have told you it would seem that you should have an interest in this organization."

"I agree. Have you found any name associated with it?"

"No. No name, no creed, no religion, no associations with any so-called 'terrorist' organization."

"And, I assume, no way of knowing how to contact them."

"Exactly. I am not sure how their services are procured, but now I think I may have a way of doing this."

"Which is?" asked Stefan.

"Like I said before, I know who wanted to kill Kamal, but that person does not know I know. I will ask him for the information."

Stefan was about to ask how Ali was going to 'ask', but thought he probably didn't want to know. Instead, Ali gave him another piece of information.

"I don't know if you follow the British newspapers, but a few weeks ago The Guardian reported on a crime scene in North Wales, of all places. A man was killed, there was a fire in a restaurant and, according to the press, a metal hand was found at the crime scene. Whether the hand left in the restaurant had anything to do with the crime is unknown, but it's something you may want to look into. Oh, and I should warn you the man who died may have had something to do with the British security services – that's what the Guardian story suggested."

"Thank you. I will do that, but isn't that something you would be interested in too?" said Stefan.

Ali gave a slight smile and said, "Of course, but the climate there is a little too severe for my constitution. I prefer to stay away from Britain, and the British probably prefer I stay away from there too."

Stefan nodded and asked, "And what now?"

"You go back to where you came from, and I will find out what I find out. I assume I can keep these." He indicated the documents on the table. He picked up the car rental information and handed it to Stefan, leaving the photographs and financial files.

"Of course. I will also begin to make enquiries. Will you let me know what you find out?

"Do you want to know?"

Stefan hesitated for only a second. "Of course." He reached into his briefcase again and presented Ali with his card. "Call me any time. Let me know if we can help in any way. I will also find out what I can about the incident in North Wales. How can I get hold of you?"

Ali hesitated, then said, "You know how to reach Mustafa. Let him know if you find anything."

He rose and so did Stefan. The interview was clearly over. Ella and Mustafa also stood, neither having contributed to the conversation. Ella left her full glass of lukewarm tea on the table. Ali indicated to the guards to follow and the group walked out of the building to Stefan's rental car. Ali shook Stefan's hand and gave a slight bow to Ella. Ella sat in the front of the car as Stefan lowered himself into the driver's seat.

Ali leaned forward and said. "It could have been foolish for you to come here today. How did you know I didn't kill Kamal? I could have killed you at any time. We know you were followed here and we have immobilized your backup vehicle and team. Don't worry," he said as a look of concern flashed across Stefan's face. "No one has been injured, but next time I suggest you be more careful."

Stefan started the car, rolled down the window, leaned towards Ali and said, "Kamal has been killed and until you know better I suggest you increase your own security. You and Mustafa may be on someone's list. You have my card if you need SIGNAK help."

He was about to put the car in gear when Ella put her hand on his and said, "Stop. I think he needs to be told."

85

She opened her door, got out of the car and walked around to its other side where Ali and his guards stood. For five seconds she stood in front of the guard who had attempted to search her and looked into his eyes. He looked away, uncertain of how to react. Then she turned to Ali and said, in Turkish, so the guards would also understand, "We always travel with extra backup. And, by the way, another SIGNAK suggestion – always search the woman. This time you were lucky."

She winked at Ali, who hesitated then broke into a broad grin. She sat back in the car. Stefan rolled up his window and drove away.

"I needed that," was all Ella said as she reclined her seat, reached for a bottle of water, pushed up the niqab and finally got to drink something.

Over the first rise they came across their first backup team. Two SIGNAK employees were sitting in their car with the doors wide open to keep the inside of the vehicle cool. They acknowledged Stefan with a wave, then started the car, closed the doors and followed him. Nearby, two men wearing the same uniform as Ali's house guards were seated on the ground back to back. Their hands and feet were tied and they looked unhappy. Stefan and Ella slowed and waited until the backup car caught up with them. After a half kilometer Stefan checked his rear-view mirror and saw the vehicle stop behind him. The trunk opened, one of his men got out of the car and emptied the contents of the trunk, the guards' weapons, by the roadside.

Stefan smiled. Their other backup team was nowhere to be seen.

This time things had gone to plan.

10

..The three men and one woman watched the video in silence. They were meeting on the third floor of Thames House on Millbank in London – the headquarters of the British Security Service.

The screen showed a camera recording of a snowy street scene at night. The falling snow obscured most of the detail, but a couple of parked cars and a row of small shops, their lights seeming strangely bright, could be made out on one side of a road junction. A man appeared and they watched him walk cautiously along the sidewalk across the back of their view. He wore a peaked hat, walked slowly to avoid falling on what must have been a slippery sidewalk, and may have been carrying something in his hand. He was concentrating on making his way and there was no good view of his face.

There was a brief pause while the video blacked out then the same scene reappeared. A few cars drove by slowly, and the snow continued to fall. Nothing happened for a few more seconds until a man, a woman, and a boy half ran, half walked across the lower half of the screen. This was followed by a minute of more snow. Suddenly, a bright flash obscured further details for a few seconds. Less than a minute later two men walked along the corner of the camera's view, but only their lower two-thirds were visible. One may have had a slight limp, but that could have been from negotiating the slush which had been gathering on the sidewalk. Then the scene slowly became brighter with light coming from the left.

The screening of both videos lasted less than two minutes.

"That's it?" asked the woman. Georgina Southport was the most senior officer present. At age 61, five-foot-two, thin, and with a full head of curly grey hair, she was the shortest, but the most senior in years and intimidation. She was single and apparently liked it that way.

"That's it," replied Jonathan Tibbs – his voice as neutral of emotion as possible. He hoped his Liverpool accent wasn't too distracting – he'd been doing his best to smooth out the edges in the two years he'd been in London. At twenty-six he was the youngest present, and was doing his best to not feel intimidated by The Witch, as she was unaffectionately known. He noticed one of the two other men in the room, his immediate superior, William Burns, avoided eye contact with her. The other seemed slightly amused by her questioning.

He carried on, "We checked with the North Wales Police. They have videos of other parts of Colwyn Bay and the A55, but the weather made any surveillance tapes useless. There is no way of identifying any vehicle which may have been involved in the incident."

The Witch grunted. Tibbs hesitated then continued.

"It's all in my report, but I thought I would go over the pertinent pieces again." He looked up expectantly at the others in the room. Getting no signal to stop he carried on.

"Our man, Jeremy Ellis, called for backup at 17:21. We can trace his mobile phone, but only when he calls or texts. We don't routinely track phones of our people ... we, uh ... we don't have the manpower." He hesitated briefly. "We don't know how he got to Colwyn Bay. We checked the cameras on the ferries from Ireland. We checked all the station cameras, only some of the bus cameras, and found no evidence of his travelling on any of them. Of course, the cameras, as you can see are not perfect, and nor is the coverage.

"So, we have to assume he arrived there in some other way, possibly by car, and he probably wasn't driving because no stray cars have been found by the police. The call for backup was the coded alarm text, and no other message was left. We started tracking him immediately after he called, and for the next fifteen minutes he was on the move until he got to the fish and chip shop. Our backup left Manchester at 17:35. At 17:40 the duty officer decided that it would take too long to get to Colwyn Bay in a reasonable time and contacted the North Wales police. They were busy dealing with multiple accidents on the A55 and it wasn't until 18:15 that they managed to get a single male officer to the scene, or about four minutes after the fish and chip shop was set on fire. He had no way of knowing if there was anyone inside the building. The fire department arrived only three minutes later – they had been called out for another reason and were diverted to the fish and chip shop. Unfortunately, they were unable to save Jeremy Ellis. His body was found later. A post-mortem showed he died from burns and smoke inhalation, but may have been unconscious since he had a fractured skull and two broken ribs on the left." He paused.

"Did you know Jeremy Ellis?" The Witch asked.

Tibbs shook his head. She looked at the other two men. They shook their heads too.

"I knew him quite well." The Witch said. "He joined us after University. He went to Cambridge … same as me … and he was very committed to his job. He … uh …" She tailed off, looked away for a few seconds and then seemed to remember her reputation. "Any more?" she asked abruptly.

"Yes, ma'am," said Tibbs. "The police interviewed the people who had been in the fish and chip shop at the time. Apparently, the two men had very successfully intimidated them, so there was some reluctance to come forward until the police told them their driving licenses, which had been taken from them, were found partly melted, on the floor of the fish and chip shop. Two shop assistants, the parents of a twelve year-old boy, and the boy had been present when Ellis was there too. They couldn't say much about the two men. The police told me they thought the men spoke Arabic to each other, but since none of the witnesses speaks Arabic they can't be certain. They may have shouted out Allah, something or other, before they left and the one who spoke English said something about infidels. The police told me the best witness was apparently the boy who said he thought both of the men understood English, although only one spoke it.

"There had been one other customer in the shop, and he had left a few minutes before the two men entered the shop. He's the man in the first video clip. Apparently, he sat at the same table as Ellis. He had an American accent, which the others picked up on, but it was the boy who listened to their conversation and heard the American say he was from Seattle and had been visiting his aunt here. It seems Ellis gave him a book, and that could be what the man in the video is carrying. It's impossible to be certain though."

"That's interesting. How old was this man; the American?" The question came from the man to Tibbs's right. He had a guest ID badge with no name on it, but had an American accent that Tibbs was not expecting. Otherwise, he could have been mistaken for a slightly disheveled, middle-aged, Cornish farmer with a ruddy complexion and grey beard.

"I apologize, Tibbs," said The Witch. "When I introduced Mr. Ethan McKeen I forgot to mention he was FBI. He's here today because I asked him, and to see if he could help us with this – especially identifying this American."

Tibbs had the presence of mind to nod at McKeen and answer his question.

"The witnesses placed him at an age between fifty and seventy, sir."

"OK. Let's assume he is sixty then. So, his aunt is likely to be between seventy and ninety. Agree?"

"Yes, sir," agreed Tibbs. The others nodded too.

"Well, I have never been to Colwyn Bay, but it's not high on my February tourist site list. Maybe that's the only time this guy can visit his aunt, but maybe he had to visit then. Maybe it was an emergency. I suggest we check with hospitals and maybe nursing homes to see if any recent admissions have any relationship to hospitals."

"Do you think this American is important?" asked The Witch.

"I don't know, Georgina. He may be, but it would be nice to rule him in or out. However, if we take it a little further it's possible our two friends who torched the fish and chip shop may also want to find him. In that case we need to find him first. He may know something, but I doubt it. What do you think Tibbs?"

Tibbs was surprised to be asked for an opinion, not a fact, but he hadn't been a government employee long enough to know not to stick out his neck.

"I think that's a good point, sir. The two men in the shop were interested in the American too. They may try to find him."

"Why do you think they'd bother?" asked McKeen.

"Well, I don't think we know why they followed Ellis to the fish and chip shop. There must have been something he found out that made them follow him and kill him. Maybe they just wanted to silence him. It may be he passed on some information before he was killed. They would want to know that."

"I suppose that's possible, but no one has contacted us here or in the US yet, so that makes it less likely that any information was passed on. Don't you agree?"

Tibbs hesitated. "Possibly, but no one knows we haven't been contacted."

"So, it would be nice to find this American?" said McKeen.

"Yes, sir."

"And…?"

"It's easier said than done, sir. We've done some checking. If we assume this American left the UK and headed back to the US in the three days after the incident, and if we narrow it down to flights which could connect to Seattle, leaving from Manchester or London, we still have over two hundred and fifty single potential individuals. The database has birthdates and gender, and including only males between the ages of fifty and seventy gives us just under two hundred. It's probable most of those would be business travelers. These represent those we think were traveling alone, but there is no way to be certain of that, and we don't know if our American was traveling alone. We also have only included American nationals. If someone was resident in the US, but not a citizen, we may not be able to identify them. And, the real problem is that these people are now back in the US where we have no jurisdiction."

McKeen said, "So, the proverbial needle in a haystack, Tibbs?"

"Yes, sir. And we can't even get close to the haystack."

McKeen smiled. "Any other thoughts?'

"I think your idea of checking out hospitals and nursing homes should be explored, sir. We will get on to that."

"When? It's Friday now."

"I'll call the North Wales Police after this meeting and discuss it with them. I think they would have more chance of finding anything than non-locals like us."

"And especially Americans," stated McKeen.

"Yes, sir."

"Thank you, Tibbs. You seem to know what you're doing," McKeen added.

"Thank you, sir," Tibbs nodded, wondering if he was off the hook yet. He wasn't.

"Tell us about the forensic findings." It was The Witch who was looking down at the report in front of her.

"The fire limited our findings, but we have identified the source of the bright flash you saw on the video as an M84 stun grenade. It's also known as a flash-bang grenade."

"I thought they didn't cause fires – just a bright light and a very loud bang."

"That's correct, ma'am," Tibbs replied. "However, if there is anything volatile around, or there is a good source of flammable material, it can cause a fire. In this case the hot fish and chip fat and the wrapping paper seemed to have caught fire after the grenade was activated."

"Bill," The Witch addressed the fourth person in the room. "Any thoughts on that?"

William Burns, a thirty-year civil service veteran was a little startled to be asked a question. He was hoping the meeting would end with his underling, Tibbs, being the only one in the hot seat. He should have known better, but that was one of Burns's problems – he should have always known better.

"It's in the report, ma'am," he answered weakly.

"I know. I've read it, but what it doesn't say is why an M84 was used."

"It was a good choice in the circumstances."

"I agree, but why an M84? Are they in common use in situations like this? Tibbs, what do you think?"

Tibbs knew he was screwed. He could answer like his boss, William Burns, and not rock the boat. On the other hand if Burns felt as if the rug was being pulled from under him, it might not go well for Tibbs back in the office.

He tried a compromise. "I think, although it worked, it was an unusual choice. Maybe there's another side to this. Maybe it was meant to send a signal."

"Why was it an unusual choice?" asked McKeen.

"Our police and Special Forces have access to stun grenades for extreme circumstances, but we don't use the M84 version."

"So, what signal was being sent?"

"I think it needs to be considered with the claim." Tibbs wasn't doing a good job of compromise. If he wasn't careful he'd end up with both his boss and The Witch putting spells on him.

"You mean the claim that was phoned in?"

"Yes, sir," replied Tibbs. "It was texted in on Ellis's mobile phone. It was tracked for a short distance away from Colwyn Bay, but then the signal stopped. We haven't found the phone. We assume it's been destroyed."

"What do we know about this claim?" asked McKeen.

Tibbs looked at Burns and said, "I think Mr. Burns can help you with that. He has extensive knowledge of that." He hoped he sounded deferential, not flattering.

McKeen and The Witch looked at Burns.

This time Burns was pleased to answer. Unfortunately, his eagerness contrasted with his earlier replies. "It was a text and sent to the same number as Ellis had texted his emergency to." He looked at his notes. "The text read 'so perish any infidels who dare to cross the Hand of Khamsah'." He looked up and smiled. "Now, the Hand of Khamsa is a middle-eastern symbol and can be found across many countries and cultures. It's probably been around for a couple of thousand years or so. It's a sign of protection, and maybe power and strength. Khamsah is Arabic for five – like the five fingers of the hand. Now, we've heard similar claims in the past, but we didn't know it was the same group this time. However, the same evening as these events the Daily Telegraph in London received a similar claim. Again it was texted in. Now, it seems the Telegraph confirms that this claim came from the same source. The first time they received one, about six years ago, the source indicated a code, more like a password, they would use every time they texted the paper. Now, apart from that…" He looked down again. "Um…the text this time said, 'may all traitors of Islam perish as he did in Colwyn Bay. The Hand of Khamsah'." Burns stopped.

"Thank you," said McKeen. "Do we know who The Hand of Khamsah are?"

The Witch answered. "We have had similar communications in the past following apparent assassinations in Spain and the Middle East. However, we have no idea who they are. More to the point, we don't know why Jeremy Ellis came to be killed by them. Jeremy was investigating an apparent resurgence of the Free Wales Army, or the Welsh Republican Army, or whatever it may call itself now. It was, or is, a paramilitary organization which in the past has gone as far as burning cottages owned by absent English, but more commonly has just spray-painted road signs and issued threats. Jeremy was acting on a tip that they had grander ideas. He told me – I talked to him about three weeks ago – he thought this meant they were going to use bigger spray cans for their graffiti. Whatever they were working on ended up with Jeremy losing his life. Our Cardiff office has no idea what happened in the two days he was missing before we found him in Colwyn Bay."

"So, is this an Islamist terror organization?" asked McKeen.

"Maybe. We aren't sure."

McKeen raised an eyebrow.

The Witch continued. "In some ways it behaves like one. Just like this case there is often an Arabic component to their activities. However, our sources in other Islamist organizations have indicated they know little or nothing of this organization. The little they know is there may have been a meeting, or meetings, between The Hand of Khamsah, sometimes known as The Hand of Hamsa, and other Islamist terror groups, but that is about all. Of course, our sources are not always high enough up, or reliable. One source said there was resentment in some of the groups about the claims of the Hand of Khamsah, which I thought was interesting. It may be that this group has nothing to do with Islamist terrorism."

McKeen said, "The press considers them an Islamist terror group."

"Maybe that's what they want them to think."

"Well, that's an interesting idea," said McKeen. He turned to Burns and Tibbs and asked, "Do you have any thoughts on this?"

Again, Burns looked surprised and turned to his junior for support.

"I have been wondering who the call to us, and the message to the Telegraph, were aimed at," began Tibbs, avoiding looking at Burns. "If you throw in the use of the M84 to start the fire, then it looks like they were trying to be seen as a terror organization. I wonder if this was outside their usual pattern of activity. Jeremy Ellis may have stumbled on their activities by accident and they had to do something about it quickly. I haven't had a chance to look at their previous claims, but it might be interesting to go over them again."

"Interesting. So, Tibbs," The Witch started, "Maybe this was a clean-up operation which resulted in Jeremy's death, but you think this maybe swings the pendulum towards this being a domestic group, not necessarily Islamist?"

"Yes, ma'am. I agree with you that this is what they want us to think. It wasn't really necessary to give any claim to this incident if it was a clean-up."

"I'm not sure that gets us anywhere," said McKeen. "It may help to keep it in mind though … Now, is there anything else? I have a plane to catch at Heathrow in just over two hours – I have to get moving. Mr. Tibbs, could you get me that list of passengers. I will see what I can do at the US end of this. I will start with direct flights to Seattle – maybe we'll get lucky."

"I'll get those to you, sir."

"And then, Tibbs, why don't you go ahead and contact the North Wales Police and see if they can help us identify the American's relative," The Witch added.

"Yes, ma'am."

"And Bill, have a look at the previous claims by The Hand of Hamsa. Oh, and let's call it Hamsa – it's easier."

"Yes, ma'am."

"And get someone to help you look into Jeremy Ellis's background a little more. Who knows? Maybe he recognized someone when he shouldn't have."

"Yes, ma'am."

"And let's get moving on this. If we have figured this out, and that's still an 'if', then there's no reason why they haven't done the same."

The meeting ended.

"That man of yours – Tibbs – he seems intelligent," said McKeen.

"He is. I just hope he doesn't turn into another short-time civil servant like Burns," sighed The Witch.

She was driving McKeen to Paddington Railway Station and the Heathrow Express – the only chance he had of making his plane on a Friday afternoon. Even so, he was cutting it close.

"What happened to him?" asked McKeen.

"A year ago there was the question of leaked information in the department. He was interrogated a little forcefully and objected, probably quite reasonably, and has not been the same since. He only has another three months and then he can retire to his flower garden in Surrey. It's a pity – he was one of the sharpest minds in the department at one time."

"What happened about the leak?"

"It was a relatively minor problem about a leak to the press, but it shouldn't have happened. We never quite figured out where it came from and..." She braked suddenly as a black London taxi pulled in front of her at a stop light.

"Well, there's been nothing since then ... and by the way you'd be proud of me – I stopped smoking."

"I don't believe it. What about your reputation Georgina? It will be trashed. No one will fear you any more!" McKeen joked.

"Oh, they still call me The Witch, Ethan. I even heard a rumor the other day that I am known to eat my partners after mating, which was a new one to me. And now I am gaining the added reputation of being tough enough to break the nicotine habit. Don't tell anyone but I haven't actually inhaled a cigarette for twenty years. I used to go outside, or walk around, to clear my head. Suddenly, this February I wondered what the hell I was doing standing outside in the cold by myself pretending to smoke."

"Has it affected your reputation?"

"I work hard to make sure it doesn't."

McKeen laughed. The Witch pulled up at the curb.

"OK, we're here. You'd better get moving. Next time in London– dinner on me."

"And dinner on me when you're next in DC. Bye, Georgina."

"Bye, Ethan."

Georgina pulled away from the curb into the traffic crawl outside Paddington Station.

She wondered if McKeen believed her about the leak.

The text was sent at 16:36 by a man walking over Lambeth Bridge in London away from Thames House on Millbank.

It was brief. It said, "re col bay looking for aunt and american." It was sent to the number he'd been given. From there it was automatically forwarded to a cell phone in Paris. The recipient wrote out the message, then re-typed it on a phone and passed it on to a number in Morocco. From there it made its way to its intended ultimate destination.

The man on Lambeth Bridge thought about dropping the phone in the Thames, but it was crowded, it was a crime to litter and he didn't want attention to be drawn to him. He replaced his gloves, wiped the phone over his jacket to remove any fingerprints, walked over the bridge and dropped it in the nearest trash bin.

Overall he thought it had been a good day. He was meeting a couple of friends at a pub near St. Thomas's Hospital and who knew what would happen after that?

11

Gareth parked his rental car on Oak Drive, a few blocks up from the center of Colwyn Bay, and away from any prying CCTV cameras. He was about to step out of the vehicle when the text came through on his mobile phone. He hesitated, considered its implications, then locked the car and started to walk the short distance to the public library in the light drizzle. He would have to get moving. He had twenty-four hours at most to accomplish his task before the authorities got in his way. It was Friday evening and maybe he'd be lucky and they wouldn't start looking until after the weekend, but he couldn't assume that.

Most information Gareth found online, but sometimes he just had to be there, and sometimes he needed a public library. The trouble with libraries was most had CCTV cameras monitoring their entrances. He knew how to deal with those, but he was later than expected getting to Colwyn Bay. He checked his watch and picked up his pace a little, but when he did that he noticed it made his limp a little more obvious. If he was careful, and walked slowly, he could hide the limp.

The fracture of his left femur had healed well. There had been no shortening of the bone, only a little external rotation that was enough to give him a painless limp.

He'd stuck to his agreement with Jones and had been attending the karate classes in Stepney for six months when the attack occurred. It was dark and raining, he had taken a shortcut across the park, and was not paying attention. He ran, but the three cornered him, and although they were masked he recognized them. Their leader was a black belt at the dojo who liked to be called Zero. He was a little older and taller than Gareth and had been initially welcoming, but he was a bully and liked his position of authority which he thought was being threatened. He was right. It was obvious to all the other students that after only six months, Gareth's dedication and natural abilities would eventually surpass his.

Zero could not allow that.

The first blow from the crowbar had broken Gareth's left femur and put him on the ground. For some reason they gave up after he was down – maybe they'd heard someone coming, or they thought they'd done all they needed to, but they left with only a few parting kicks to his ribs. They assumed they hadn't been recognized.

Jones came to see Gareth in the hospital. After all, what could be more natural? – The academic concerned about the welfare of an injured student. He told him he would make arrangements to handle the bully, but the other two would be Gareth's responsibility.

The police had interviewed Gareth when he was initially hospitalized, and came to talk to him again as he was about to leave. It seemed that one other student from the dojo, a black belt, had been attacked while Gareth was in the hospital. Both his legs and his arms had been broken. Did Gareth know anything about this? Did he know of anyone who might have a grudge against the dojo? Gareth, of course, knew nothing.

When he returned to the dojo three months later he was still using his crutches. He took aside both of the other students who had participated in his mugging and told them they had a choice. They could leave the dojo and never be seen again, or they could all go back to the park and Gareth would see if they could finish what they had started. And, he wondered, "How was Zero doing?" Wisely, they chose to quit the dojo. Had they known anything about healing of fractures they would have realized Gareth hadn't needed crutches for the last six weeks – he had spent much of the time finding out how useful a crutch could be as a lethal weapon.

It was nearly 5:00 pm when Gareth reached the library. He had thirty minutes before it closed. He kept his umbrella up a few seconds longer than most of the customers and avoided the CCTV surveillance.

He found his way upstairs to the newspaper section and The North Wales Pioneer – a free newspaper that was either posted

100

through your letter-box, or ended up in the library. Since it was free you couldn't get hold of its details in any other way, including online. News of the fire in the fish and chip shop had missed the previous week's publication, but the editor had made up for it in the following edition. There were front page photographs showing the shop looking forlorn with ply-wooded windows, barricades of yellow police tape, and the covering of a light snowfall.

Gareth ignored the headlines but found what he wanted. One of the witnesses was named. He remembered Robert Holte as the fat man who had sat in the corner. It seemed he had suddenly become brave and given an interview to the newspaper. Gareth checked the local phone book and found Holte's address. At 5:20 Gareth left the library and headed back to his car.

He wasn't sure he'd need the information, but over the years he'd found he could never be sure. If he was going to potentially expose himself to the attention of the police it paid to have backup plans.

He'd discussed it with Jones before he left London earlier that morning. Jones was unhappy with the plan, but both decided there was no alternative. He didn't like it when he or Gareth had to take matters into their own hands. Usually, he arranged for a colleague, or a colleague of a colleague, to carry out his wishes, but sometimes, he and Gareth agreed, you just had to do it yourself. Gareth understood the risk involved when this happened, and maybe he wouldn't get away with it forever, but risk was what he lived for.

After all, life without risk wouldn't be life for Gareth.

The hours could be erratic, but the money was good, and so were the women when he had a chance to get away to Prague or Bangkok, but that wasn't why he liked this life. It was the adrenaline, the excitement of the chase, and the reactions of his fellow humans when he took something from them. That's what made him feel alive.

He'd only arrived back in London the previous day. He'd known when he employed his half-brother, Evan that it might be a mistake and something he would have to deal with later.

It was a mistake and he'd had to fix it – after all, it was just business.

12

Gareth had flown to Miami using a British passport in the name of John Roberts, rented a mid-size car using a German driving license and credit card, and driven three hours towards Orlando. He stopped short of the city and checked into a Holiday Inn using another credit card.

Evan had wanted to go to Spain, but Gareth pointed out the weather in February in Orlando was warmer than the Costa del Sol.

There were a couple of other reasons for suggesting Florida which he hadn't mentioned to Evan.

In Spain it was the quiet season, but in Florida it was a busy time of year and there were more people around – it would be easier for Gareth to hide in a crowd. And then there was the drinking age in Florida of twenty-one. This meant it would be harder for Evan, who had yet to turn twenty, to satisfy his alcohol dependence. Of course he might find a way around that, but more likely he'd have to use one of the other drugs he was fond of to keep the shakes and the sweats away.

Gareth had no trouble finding Evan. He already knew he was staying at the Columbus Hotel and his white legs, cheap blue polyester shorts, bad haircut and red 'Wales Rugby' shirt, made him easy to identify among the other tourists in their pastel-hued Florida outfits. Evan was there with his girlfriend, Megan, from Blaina. She was showing just a little too much cleavage in her lime green halter top. Her shoulders were sunburned and her black spandex shorts squeezed up a thick roll of fat around her bare midriff and oozed out smaller rolls on the upper parts of both legs. Maybe Evan liked her that way. Gareth didn't.

Gareth watched as they entered the hotel lobby. The concierge politely asked them to put out their cigarettes and they complied.

It was the end of a long day. They'd gone to Disneyworld, or Epcot, or maybe nowhere, and they really needed that drink. Except they couldn't get one, so they would have to substitute something else for the next hour or two until Santa could help out. And Santa intended to help.

At 6:30 Gareth placed the bottle on the floor outside Evan's room and knocked on the door. He walked around the corner of the closest stairwell and waited. He heard the door being opened and Evan saying, "Whoa, look what we got!" He heard Evan's voice fade a little as he talked to Megan and walked back into the room with the bottle.

Gareth reached the door in four strides. He placed a pencil-top eraser in the jam and prevented it from closing by a quarter of an inch. He retreated to the stairwell and waited for one minute. The door did not reopen – Evan had not noticed. Gareth headed down the stairs to dinner at a local Arby's.

Santa had visited.

Three hours later the hotel was still busy enough for Gareth to be inconspicuous. He walked the five flights of stairs to Evan's hotel room and knocked on the door. He didn't expect a response, but there was no point in not being careful. To make sure he'd not be noticed he'd taken care of redirecting the CCTV cameras on this floor and in six other areas of the hotel. He moved them just enough so that they weren't quite right. He assumed, correctly, that the cameras were not closely monitored. They were there for intimidation purposes only.

There was no response to his knock. Gareth pushed the door open and found what he expected; Evan and Megan flat on their backs, naked, passed-out and lying on the bed.

The rum had masked what little bitterness the lorazepam had added to its taste. Gareth was a little surprised to find the bottle nearly empty. With the alcohol they had ingested nearly twenty milligrams of lorazepam between them, and God knows what else. Gareth nudged them to see if there was a reaction. There was none, so he tried a little harder, and even with a hard slap there was no response. He checked – both were still breathing. There were two empty syringes with attached needles on the nightstand beside Megan. This would make Gareth's job easier. He picked up one and holding it carefully by the needle pressed it into Megan's hand and pushed her fingers onto the plastic barrel of the syringe. Her hand was sticky from the rum and it was easy for Gareth to see the fingerprints she made. He placed the syringe back on the stand.

Gareth looked at Evan's arms and found more than one recent needle track. He took his own syringe from inside his jacket, tied a tourniquet around Evan's upper arm, and found a large vein which he had no trouble entering with his 18 gauge needle. He released the tourniquet and rapidly injected the potassium chloride. He kept pressure on the wound for two minutes – by that time Evan's heart had stopped and he was dead.

He swapped the bottle of rum and lorazepam with a nearly empty bottle of only rum. He put the rum and lorazepam bottle in his jacket pocket with the syringe and needle. He made sure Evan's and Megan's finger prints were on the new bottle, then scattered a few 2mg lorazepam tablets on the nightstand.

He walked towards the door, hesitated, and walked back into the room.

Maybe Megan wouldn't be able to recall how they'd got hold of the bottle of rum, but if she did would the police believe her? And what about the lorazepam? Gareth had told Evan to never mention anything about Colwyn Bay, or where the money for the trip to Florida had come from. Could he trust Evan? Would he have talked to Megan? He looked at the bodies in front of him and sighed.

The problem was he had no more potassium chloride. He thought about this – he could inject air, but he had no idea of how much he would need for it to be fatal, or if it could be discovered at autopsy. Although he still had his syringes he had no more lorazepam solution to inject – it had all been mixed with the rum. He wanted to avoid any evidence of violence, so he couldn't cut her, or strangle her. There seemed to be no alternative to using a pillow – not ideal, but effective, and maybe the coroner would still blame Evan for her death. He reached for a pillow then had another idea. Her breathing was so shallow he wondered if just a nudge would be all she would need. He moved to her side of the bed and knelt beside her. Using his gloved hands he pinched her nose with his left hand and with his right covered her mouth. He wasn't sure if it would work. Initially, he didn't get a good seal with his hand, but with a little care and readjustment he was able to make sure she was taking in no air at all. For the first few minutes her chest had heaved as she'd tried to breathe, but with each passing minute the efforts to breathe became weaker. Five minutes later he took his hands away then watched her mottled face and dark lips for another two minutes. There was no breathing. She was dead – the nudge had worked.

He stood and looked around the room. It looked like just another double death from drug and alcohol abuse, but maybe there was one more thing he could do. He pulled Megan towards the side of the bed and then rolled her onto her side burying her face, especially her mouth and lips, in a pillow. He adjusted the pillow and her body until he thought it looked "natural."

He stepped back and gave the room one more glance before going to the door.

He checked the corridor and the CCTV camera. Standing close to the camera, but out of its view he repositioned it using the "selfie-stick" he had designed for this purpose. He repositioned two other cameras as he left the hotel.

He drove south towards his hotel, taking care to stick to the speed limit. On the way he stopped at a rest area and emptied the remainder of the bottle down an outside drain. He cleaned and wiped the bottle, then dropped it in a convenient rest-area recycle bin which the State of Florida had provided for him. The syringe went in the regular trash.

After a good night's sleep he spent the next morning driving south past Miami to Highway 1 and onto Big Pine Key. He spent two days there relaxing on a beach and swimming in the warm waters of Little Pine Island.

He gave no thought to killing Megan. If he gave a thought to the killing of his step-brother, it was because it would be a hassle – he'd feel obliged to go to a funeral or memorial service. It would probably be in Abergavenny, where his mother still lived. He really didn't want to go, but he would be expected to be there and say the right things. Sometimes he just had to appear to be like normal people.

On the Wednesday he drove back north to Miami International Airport and took a noon flight to Baltimore. From there he took a shuttle bus into DC and another back out to Dulles International. By that evening he was on a 6:35 Continental Airlines flight, and at 7:00 am the next morning had cleared customs and was on the Heathrow Express into central London. He met with Jones and the next day he headed north to Colwyn Bay.

He sat in his car in the town of Colwyn Bay and realized he'd been busy and it had been fun. He smiled to himself – a lot of fun. Once he'd sorted out this loose end it would be time to take a rest. Perhaps he'd head back to Florida and spend more time in the Keys; maybe go down to Key West and see why Hemingway liked the place so much.

He started the car and drove through the small roads of Colwyn Bay to the A55 highway and headed east until he reached the motel where he was staying. He'd asked for ground floor so he could come and go as he wanted.

He went to bed early; he had another busy weekend in front of him. He was looking forward to it.

13

Stefan said, "You are going to have to call her. I can't see any way around it."

"I know" agreed Ella. "It's just I know she'll want to meet somewhere when I tell her what it's about."

"So, she'll want to meet in Paris or London. That's not too difficult is it?"

"No, it's … it's more of a territorial problem. I can share what we have, but she may not tell me anything about what she has."

"Is there anything else? You seem hesitant to meet her."

"No more reluctant than I would be meeting anyone like her who is the head of a section of a country's security service."

"I thought she had invited you to contact her if you had any questions or concerns."

"That was a while ago when I met her at that reception, here in Paris."

"I know."

It was a week after their trip to Istanbul and Ella and Stefan were discussing their next steps. One of which was to approach the British Security Service, and particularly, Georgina Southport, whom a contact in the DGSI once told Ella was called 'The Witch' by her co-workers. Ella had met her, and didn't find her at all witch-like, but Stefan was suggesting Ella renew the contact and use the meeting to find out more about what had happened in Colwyn Bay. According to the newspaper reports they had read, a male security officer had been killed. Ella seemed reluctant to call and arrange a meeting.

Ella, who had been looking through the window, walked across the conference room and sat on the chaise-long across from Stefan and continued, "It's probably just me, but I have had my fill of international travel for a while. I thought we could just sit here in Paris and pull the strings of our organization from here for a while longer. I also think I am missing Kamal more than I thought I would. That's completely strange, since I hadn't seen him for years, but I have been dreaming about him since we got back."

"Good or bad dreams?"

"Mainly bad. I keep seeing him being killed." Her eyes began to moisten.

Stefan stood and crossed the room to sit by Ella on the couch. He took her right hand in his, looked into her eyes and said, "I'm sorry, and I can see how it could affect you. You nearly died that day. I'm sure the psychologists have a name for it, but it's normal, not abnormal to feel like this. It's happened to me too. It's probably happened to everyone under fire, or who went through what happened to you. It's part of being human. It'll fade. It may never go away completely, and you probably wouldn't want it too, but time is a great healer with this." He added, "And ... I am here for you if you need me."

Ella held his gaze for a second longer, then looked away and stood again.

Now was not the time, and they both knew that, but Ella was feeling vulnerable and didn't want to start anything they might have to back away from.

She turned to face Stefan and said, "Thank you. When this is over you can take me out to dinner and we can discuss whatever we need to discuss then, and not before." She smiled.

Stefan grinned back at her, "At least I seem to have made you smile."

He stood, walked to the desk, pushed a button and said, "Please could you ask Danilo to come in." He turned to Ella and added, "Back to business."

Danilo knocked and entered the room.

He sat in the middle of the chaise-long, which they had just relinquished, and presented both Ella and Stefan with three-ring binders, which they opened while they looked for open seats elsewhere in the room.

Danilo started, "We have found four occasions when a metal hand was left at the scene of a crime, always a murder, in addition to the ones you know about in Wales and in Istanbul. Although the one in Istanbul is really an odd one out – we know about it, but there have been no press reports and no internet activity mentioning it. The other times the hand was mentioned in the press. Of course, there may be other times when a hand was left, but was not found by the police, or maybe the intended finder-of-the-hand found it before the police and took possession of it. The cases we have found all took place in the Middle East, or North Africa. I have included Turkey in the Middle East definition here." He paused.

Stefan asked, "Any pattern, or anything you have found out that the press didn't know about?"

"No, the only pattern is the leaving of the metal hand. Otherwise the modus operandi would indicate there is no link between these murders – at least in the press reports."

Ella asked, "Is there a way we can figure out who gained from these murders, or maybe the question is what would the killer gain by leaving a metal hand at the place of the killing?"

"We've talked about both of those. We can't tell from the police reports who gained by the murders, but each of the victims we have found was well-connected. There were a couple of business men and the other was, if you believe the press reports, skating close to the margins of legal activity, but none of them seemed to be overt criminals. The one in Wales seems to be an exception too. However, we think it's likely all the victims had rivals of some sort, so the appearance of the hand could have two ... um ... benefits. One – it's a way of letting the contractor know who did the job. Two – it's just advertising."

"Advertising?"

"Yes. It's a little like getting a flyer when someone has been working in your neighborhood."

"It is?"

"Yes. You know. Someone does some gardening or fencing, or something like that in your neighborhood and leaves you a card, or a flyer, so you can contact them for more work."

"I suppose that's logical," murmured Ella. "After all, it's not a line of work you could look up online, or in the yellow pages."

Stefan asked, "And all that information is in these folders?"

111

"The information from the newspapers and the killing in Istanbul is in them, but the possible causes have been left out. It is, after all, just speculation at the moment."

Stefan said, "Thank you, Danilo. Once again you have been a great help. We'll let you know how we are going to proceed from here." He stood and opened the door.

It took Danilo a couple of seconds to realize he was being dismissed. He said, "Thank you," to both Ella and Stefan and returned to his desk. Stefan closed the door.

Ella skipped through the contents of the binder and said, "I'll take this with me to London. I'll see if I can get an appointment to see Georgina tomorrow or the day after."

"I'll arrange one of our people to go with you. After Istanbul it's not worth going it alone."

"I suppose I agree, but let's make sure he doesn't make it too obvious," said Ella.

"He? It'll be a she this time and I'll make sure she is close, but not too close."

"Thank you. What will you be doing?"

"Someone has to run this business," he said, wiping imaginary sweat off his forehead.

Ella responded by rolling her eyes.

Stefan smiled and continued, "I'll stay here. I have a pile of paperwork and other chores to deal with. I am also meeting a new client tomorrow, but I will be with you in spirit, if not in person."

"I appreciate that. I'll make the phone call."

14

The Reverend David Jenkins, a new curate at All Saints Christ Church, pushed the door bell at Ridgemont Nursing Home. He looked very much the part of a budding Church-of-England-in-Wales minister. He was in his mid-thirties, clean-shaven, wore no hat over his blond curly hair, and was taking advantage of the miniscule porch to shelter, as best he could, from the incessant rain. He was dressed in an open rain coat over a tweed sports jacket. A black shirt with a white clerical collar completed the outfit. He was not using an umbrella, but held a wooden walking cane in his left hand.

Irene Morgan bustled as quickly as she could to open the door. She was in charge on the weekend and took her responsibilities seriously. She would not want a man of the cloth to wait outside in this weather. She smiled at Reverend Jenkins through the glass, opened the door and invited him into the lobby.

"'Ow can I 'elp you Reverend?" she asked looking at his bespectacled face, blue eyes, and ... was that a suntan?

For the third time that morning the Reverend David Jenkins gave his most disarming smile and said, "Maybe you can't." He had a gentle mid-Wales accent, and she noted he needed the cane for support when he'd entered the building. He added, "I'm Reverend Jenkins, the curate at All Saints church and I'm looking for a parishioner of ours. The Reverend Thomas ... perhaps you know him?"

Irene Morgan shook her head.

The Reverend Jenkins continued, "Well, the Reverend Thomas asked me to look in on a parishioner. He told me she had recently been admitted to this care centre, maybe two to three weeks ago and he just wanted me to see if she was doing well. The trouble is I wrote down her name on this piece of paper." He produced a wet, disintegrating wad of paper. "It blew out of my hand and landed in the gutter. By the time I retrieved it the ink had run so much I couldn't read it." He put the paper back in his coat pocket. "I tried to phone the Reverend Thomas, but he isn't answering just now. All I can remember is she came here about two to three weeks ago … and … oh, yes, I believe she has a relative, maybe a nephew in America who visits her every now and again. I think I'll have to go back to the church office to see if I can identify her. I'm sorry to bother you." He turned to leave.

"Oh, you must mean Olwen Lewis," said Irene.

Bingo, thought Gareth, but the Reverend Jenkins just said, "Olwen Lewis … Lewis? Yes, I think that must be her name. Is she doing well?"

"Oh, yes. Let me take you to see her."

"Thank you. I hope it's not too much trouble."

She noticed how much he needed the cane for support.

"War wound." He said when he noticed her looking.

"I'm sorry. I didn't mean to pry," said Irene.

"Think nothing of it. It is a little obvious I know. I call it my 'war wound'. I got it in the Congo from a spider bite when I was a missionary there."

"Oh, dear." She said, feeling sorry for this poor man.

She led him along a corridor to a well-lit sitting room. It contained about twenty padded wing-back chairs, most of which were occupied by senior citizens in various stages of disrepair. It was tea-time and a couple of women in pink outfits were distributing cups of vitamin T to the residents. Irene led him to a corner chair and introduced him.

"Olwen. This is the Reverend Jenkins. E's come to talk to you." She pulled up a chair which the Reverend Jenkins accepted and asked him, "Would you like a cuppa tea dear?"

"Yes, if it wouldn't be too much trouble," he replied.

"Sugar?"

"No thank you."

She scooted away and came back with an institutional-green cup of milky tea, rearranged the cushions around the back of Auntie Olly, gave him a quick smile and left with a "let us know if you need any 'elp won't you?"

The Reverend Jenkins nodded his thanks and found himself facing a grey-haired wrinkled woman who was eyeing him suspiciously over her glasses, which had slid down to the tip of her nose. She was sipping tea from another green cup and had crumbs from her last meal sticking to both her chin and the chunky red woolen sweater she was wearing.

"My name is the Reverend Jenkins," he said.

"Pleased to meet you," she replied. She placed the cup of tea on a short table on her right.

"How do you like it here?" he asked.

"His name was Harold and he made advances to me you know," she said.

"Harold?"

"My sister should have never married him."

"Oh … what was the name of your sister?" he asked.

"Mildred. You know her don't you?"

"I don't know if we've ever met." He changed the topic. "I believe you have a relative who lives in America. Is that right?"

"America? I went there. I liked it. There are big mountains there."

"Do remember the name of anyone in America?" he asked.

"George Bush. That was the name of the man I met there. It wasn't Harold."

"Do you remember the names of anyone else in America?" he asked.

There was no reply.

"Let me help you with your tea," he suggested.

It was really far too easy. He reached for the cup and, despite the multiple watchers in the room, no one noticed as he palmed the vial and emptied it into her cup. He picked the teaspoon out of the saucer, stirred the tea, and handed the cup to Olly. She sipped a little, smacked her lips, and for a second Gareth wondered if she was going to stop, but then she continued drinking and emptied the cup. Gareth took the cup from her and looked in the bottom. There was minimal residue. He splashed some tea from his cup into hers to hide the bottom. He finished the rest of his cup and asked, "So Harold was your lover?"

"I didn't have any brothers," she said.

"But you knew George Bush?"

"The president?"

"Yes."

"No, I didn't know the president. Don't be silly." She laughed. "But I do know John."

"John who?"

"Harold was John's father."

"But who is John?"

"You know who he is." She laughed.

Gareth knew this conversation, or two monologues, was going nowhere. He stood, shook Olly's hand gently, just as a good priest should, and left in search of Irene. He found her sitting at a desk in a room off the exit corridor.

"Finished already?" She asked when he poked his head around the door.

"Well, conversation is a little difficult, and I hadn't left myself a lot of time," he said.

"I know, but at least she's still trying. Sometimes she seems to 'ave moments of clarity, but not often. Still, she's a lot better than most of them in 'ere."

"I can see that," Gareth said. "One last thing. I don't know if you can help me here, but Reverend Thomas wondered if I could drive by her house and give it a quick once-over. I think he was concerned about if it was being looked after. The only problem is, just like her name, the address was rained out."

"No problem. I think I 'ave it 'ere somewhere." She leaned to her right and pulled a file out of a cabinet. "She lived at 98 Sebastopol Terrace. That's in Old Colwyn, off the Conway Road." She pointed in a vague northerly direction. "But don't worry about 'er house. 'Er nephew was 'ere recently, and 'e's been looking after it. 'E told me 'e thought 'ed 'ave to sell it."

"Is that the one who lives in America?" Gareth risked a leading question.

"Yes."

"Big place, America. I've never been there though. Have you?"

"No. My 'usband wants to go to Florida, but I 'ere it's too 'ot there in the summer."

"I wouldn't know. Do you know where the nephew lives in America?"

"I think it's near Washington, but I don't know any more than that." She looked down and read the address. "It says PO Box 9561, Port Orchard, 98366 ... whatever that means." She shrugged and put the file away.

Gareth recognized his cue. "Well thank you so much for your help," he said. "I'll make sure Reverend Thomas knows about this, and one of us will be back to visit her in the next week or two. I can see myself out."

"Oh, no you can't," she said. "You 'ave to know the code. You know – it stops the residents going out." She smiled, stood and led Gareth to the door.

It was still raining as he limped to his car. He started the engine, turned the heat on high, and pulled out into traffic. As he left a police car passed him on the opposite side of the road. He looked in his mirror and noticed it pull into the nursing home parking lot.

He'd give himself thirty minutes – no more.

It was cold in the house, but at least it was quiet and Gareth was out of the rain. It was as he expected – the home of a little old lady who was now dementing in a nearby nursing home, uncertain why Harold was bothering her, and who was about to become very sick.

He didn't find anything – that would have been too easy, but he had to check.

Anyway, it probably didn't matter – the other plan was in motion. It would mean another trip back to Colwyn Bay, but that couldn't be avoided.

He made sure no one was watching him, or the house, closed the front door and walked the hundred yards to where he left his car. With his collar pulled up, his umbrella as low as possible, and a beanie to cover his head he was unidentifiable and unremarkable.

Back at his motel he restored his hair color to its usual dark brown and wiped the room for any fingerprints. He was careful about this. He always limited what he touched with his bare hands and only wiped there. After all there would be dozens of fingerprints in any motel room. Wiping the whole room would be suspicious. He paid for his room in cash – it was the sort of motel that preferred cash to credit card – returned to his car and headed south towards London.

At the edge of a parking lot in a service area off the M6 he removed the false number plate appliqué. He filled the tank with petrol and was back in London by late afternoon.

Now, all he had to do was wait.

15

Detective Cynthia Hayes of Florida's Orange County Sheriff's Department didn't really want to know what she was hearing in the phone call. She was planning to spend the weekend on a boat in Charlotte Harbor, maybe get in a little fishing, a little swimming, and maybe get in some other more personal recreational activities with her husband, but now all that was in jeopardy.

"Are you sure?" she snapped.

"As sure as I can be, Detective," came the reply.

"Damn, damn, damn," she said.

"Planning a weekend of fun?"

"I had been, but I don't know what's going to happen now. It's really too bad. Shit."

"Well, I have to tell it like I see it," said the voice on the other end of the line – Dr Nathan Klein of the Orlando Medical Examiner's Office.

"Well, Doc," she sighed. "Give me the details. I'm in shock. I mean, to me it looked like a classic accidental overdose. These two kids shoot up, take a little too much booze and whatever and end up killing themselves. They're from out of town … well … out of country, and it's sad, but if you play with fire you end up getting burnt."

"OK, and maybe that's all it is, but it may be something else."

"OK. Well, give it to me." She picked up her pen.

"A couple of things. I checked their blood and both had levels of lorazepam and alcohol which would put them to sleep for hours, maybe permanently. They also had opiates in their blood which were not as high, but the combination with the alcohol and lorazepam could be lethal. Now, they had very high levels of lorazepam, but all I saw in the reports were a few 2mg tablets you found at the scene. Is that right?"

"Yeah. I think there were three or four around."

"Any container they could have come from?"

"No."

"Well, I wondered how they could get such a high level. I checked their stomach contents. It looks like they had pizza, but that was probably 3-4 hours before they died. There was fluid in both their stomachs which also demonstrated high levels of lorazepam and alcohol. But, and here's the kicker, with those sorts of levels I would expect to find tablet residue in their stomachs and I didn't find any. I checked the bottle of booze they had and that had no lorazepam either. I find this all a little strange. They could have shot up the lorazepam, but then I wouldn't expect to find such high levels in their stomach."

"Could they have taken the lorazepam earlier, say with the pizza?"

"Maybe, but they would have had to take such a big dose I doubt they'd have made it back to their hotel room."

"Could they have shot it up earlier?"

"Again, I doubt they could have made it back, and I assume you only found those couple of syringes?"

"Yes."

"Well, they checked out for opiate only, no lorazepam, so they didn't get it that way."

"So, how do you think they got it?"

"Not sure, but it's likely they ingested it and if it wasn't in tablet form it was in liquid form. You can get lorazepam injectable, so that's a possibility."

"But you're not sure," asked Detective Hayes

"True. I don't know how they got it, but it seems unusual."

Hayes thought for a few seconds.

"What was the other reason you were concerned?"

"Again, it might be nothing, but I don't think so. It's about the girl. I've looked at the photos and it looks like she self-asphyxiated. She seems to have most of her face in a pillow. Well, that's unusual in itself. She wouldn't have become suddenly unconscious with these drugs. She would have laid down first and would still have enough faculties to not put her face half into a pillow. However, given that she may have done this then I would expect to find pink, frothy bubbles in her lungs. It's common in suffocation and is caused by the negative pressure of trying to breathe. And, indeed, she had this in her lungs and throat, but when I look at the photo, especially of the pillow, and when I look at the pillow case you sent us, there is no froth on it, or anything much else. So, she was certainly killed by suffocation, or maybe you can say from the drugs inside her that caused her to suffocate, but I have to think it's likely she became unconscious on her back, like the male, and was turned onto the pillow after she was dead. Based on the levels of lorazepam I think both were unconscious before they died. There was no evidence of a struggle by either of them. It may not have taken much to finish them off – just pinching her nose and putting a gag over her mouth could have done it. I really didn't find any evidence around her mouth to indicate any force or gag was used, but in the circumstances I wouldn't necessarily expect to."

"Could the male have killed her?"

"I doubt it. Their body temperatures were the same. They both had rigor, so that doesn't tell us much, and the appearance of the bodies and a few other factors makes it likely they died around the same time, which was about twelve hours before they were found. However, the drug levels, while different, really mean these two would have been unconscious about the same time too."

"Did you find anything on the male to indicate anything suspicious?" She asked.

"No. He wasn't asphyxiated. He had evidence of shooting up in the past, but there wasn't much else."

"But why would anyone want to kill these two?" Hayes asked.

"That's your job, Detective."

"Well … thanks. I'll have to think about this."

"Well, I hope I haven't ruined your weekend. There's a few more findings in both reports. I'll post them, fax them over, and I'll let you know if anything comes up." He hung up the phone.

"What the hell!" Hayes said out loud and thumped her desk with her hand. It had seemed a pretty straightforward double overdose, and now this. And if what the medical examiner was saying was true then it could be one, maybe two, murders. The trouble was it was going to be hard to prove, and then if it was

121

murder someone had gone to a lot of work to make it seem it wasn't. Maybe someone who'd done this before? Who would want to do this? Well, she hadn't a clue who could have done it, or who could have done it to make it look "natural".

So, look at the victims. Who would want them dead?

For God's sake they didn't even live in the USA, let alone Florida or Orlando. Did they piss off some American with a grudge? There were plenty of Americans with grudges, but most wouldn't kill someone. Did they piss off someone in … where was it they came from?

She opened the file on her computer and checked the addresses of the victims.

Wales.

Well, she'd heard of it. Her husband's grandmother's family had come from there.

Abergavenny.

She looked up 'Abergavenny police' and found it was part of Gwent Police in Wales. She hesitated. It was nearly 5:00 pm in Florida. That meant it was – what 10:00 or 11:00 in Wales? On a Friday night they would probably have other things on their minds than dealing with a phone call from America, so why didn't she get back here early Monday morning, around 5:00 am and give them a call then. It seemed like the best plan. Maybe she was rationalizing but she really needed this weekend. She'd be refreshed for whatever the next week would throw at her. She'd even call on the way back to be ahead of the game.

An hour later Hayes lay back in the passenger seat of her VW Polo as her husband drove southwest on Interstate 4 to their weekend in Punta Gorda. She was planning on enjoying herself. She needed to put everything out of her mind and enjoy herself.

But, why would anyone want to kill those two?

16

Irene Morgan had never had so many visitors in one morning, and they were all interested in the same resident.

First there had been that very pleasant minister. What was his name? Reverend Thomas? No, that was who he was helping … Jenkins? That was it – Reverend David Jenkins.

Then a policeman had come along and asked all the same questions about Olwen. She'd mentioned the minister had just been to see Olwen, but didn't say he'd asked the same questions. Perhaps she should have. But she gave the policeman the address and the phone number of Olwen's nephew in America and he seemed pleased with that. He had asked to talk to Olwen, but Irene had said he wouldn't get any useful information and it would be wasted effort. It was also time to make sure the lunches were being served.

She bustled to the sitting room where she found the two aides who should have been serving lunch were leaning over a resident. Irene saw immediately it was Olwen.

"What's going on?" she asked.

"She's thrown up and we can't get 'er to respond," said one of the aides. Both stood back to let Irene see her.

The sharp smell and the sight of yellow fluid on Olwen's cardigan confirmed the vomiting, but Olwen was sweaty, barely conscious and when Irene felt her pulse it was slow and irregular.

"I think she's 'ad an 'art attack," was Irene's pronouncement. "Call for an ambulance," she said to one of the aides.

A minute later, when the aide returned, Irene added, "You two get on with lunch. I'll look after 'er."

She stayed with Olwen until the ambulance left then sat down in her office wondering what had invaded her usually quiet world.

She made herself a cup of tea – it helped.

The ambulance took Olwen to Glan Clwyd Hospital's Accident and Emergency department.

There she was placed on oxygen and the i.v. started by the paramedics was stabilized. The monitor showed intermittent complete heart block with a pulse of 38 and a blood pressure of 85/40. An EKG was ordered as well as the usual lab work for evaluating a possible heart attack.

Dr Anwar Reddy, a consultant in emergency medicine, looked at the EKG. It wasn't what he'd expected. There were changes, but not the ones definitely confirming a heart attack. In fact the scooped ST segments were more reminiscent of digoxin toxicity – not something he saw as much of nowadays. He scanned the note from the nursing home. There was no mention of her taking digoxin, but that didn't mean she wasn't taking it – nursing home records were notoriously incorrect, and of course there may be others at the nursing home who were taking digoxin. Maybe she had got into their supplies. He hesitated for a second, and then asked for another blood draw and a digoxin level. He called the house officer in charge of medical admissions and arranged for her to be admitted to the coronary care unit.

He moved on to his next patient.

17

Detective Cynthia Hayes stuck to the promise she made to herself. Her husband wasn't entirely happy with leaving Punta Gorda at 4:00am, but they'd had a good time over the weekend and it was time to return to reality. Cynthia had managed to keep her questions about the double deaths compartmentalized at the back of her brain while they had fished, relaxed, dined, and romped their way through the weekend. It had been fun, but duty called.

She dialed the number she had written down. It took a couple of attempts before she heard the double ring tones of a British phone. It was answered.

"Bore da, Heddlu Gwent."

"What?" she said.

"Good morning, Gwent Police."

"What did you say before that?" She couldn't help herself.

"Oh. Good morning, Gwent Police, but in Welsh. We answer in Welsh and then continue in whatever language the caller is using."

"Oh."

"Well, how can I help you madam?" the voice said. It was a man, speaking in universal police polite-talk. He had an accent she didn't recognize, but at least she understood what he was saying.

"I hope you can give me a little more information. My name is Detective Cynthia Hayes. I'm with the Orange County Sheriff's Department in Florida, and I am investigating the death of two people who lived in your area."

"Oh, you must mean Evan Williams and Megan Price. I believe someone called us from Orlando last week to let us know about their deaths."

Hayes realized she should have read the files more closely.

"I'm not sure who that was. I'm on my way into work at the moment, so I can't check." She said apologetically.

"It wasn't your office. I took the call and it was from the British Consulate in Orlando. I expect you notified them."

"Maybe. I think someone notifies the embassy or consulate in these circumstances … but … but if you know about these deaths do you know anything about the two of them?"

"Not really, but one of my colleagues would be able to help you. I'll put you through to him. His name is Inspector Rhys Owen. He knows a lot about the community."

The call was redirected.

"Rhys Owen speaking." Well, at least they didn't have to switch languages with internal calls Hayes thought.

She repeated her interest in the two deaths and waited.

"So, why are you calling us?" Owen asked. "It's early in the morning with you."

As if that was a suspicious act thought Hayes – maybe it was.

"It seemed to me that it was a simple, or," she corrected herself, "maybe straightforward case of double overdose." She paused. "Then I talked to the medical examiner on Friday evening and he has some concerns it might not be so simple."

"Really?" said Owen; his interest aroused.

"Yes. He's not certain, but it's possible they were murdered." Hayes hoped she wasn't giving away any state secrets.

"What makes him think that?"

"A coupla things. One is the very high levels of drugs in their blood and lack of tablet residue in their stomachs, and the other was the position of the bodies when they were found didn't quite add up to some of his findings."

"So, what you are saying is you have a crime scene which seemed to be an obvious case of double overdose, but when you looked closer things didn't add up."

"That is correct," said Hayes.

"And…?"

"And I can find no motive for anyone wanting to kill them here, especially anyone who seems to know how to make it look like overdoses. So, I wondered about the victims and called you. Can you think of any reason why anyone would want to kill these two?"

126

She could hear Owen sigh before he replied. "The short answer is, 'no I can't', but the longer answer is … maybe. You've brought up something interesting there."

Hayes waited for Owen to continue.

"The short answer is they were two kids, known to be into the drug scene around here. They went to Florida for a holiday; although how they could afford it I don't know. They took more drugs than was good for them and they died.

"The girl, Megan, has never been involved with the police. That may be she just hadn't been caught, but I suspect she was just caught up in whatever was going on.

"Evan Williams is different. He was first caught when he was sixteen dealing marijuana. He was arrested when he was seventeen for possession of cocaine, but after that has managed to steer clear of the law. He was not very bright. I'm not sure if he ever had a job, but he always seemed to have some money, but not a lot. It's probably more than he would have got from unemployment alone; enough to be able to run an old used car, and enough to be able to satisfy his habits most of the time."

Owen hesitated.

"You seem to know a lot about him," Hayes commented.

"I do, and this is the abbreviated version. But the reason I know so much about him is not that this is a small community. It is, but not that small. It's because I went to school with his brother, Gareth. We were in the same year. He went off to London. I can't remember the name of the University he went to, and I stayed around here and started a career in the police. We played rugby together at school and he was a good tough player. The trouble was, and I only realize this now – I suppose my training helps – Gareth is a sociopath. Not everyone realized that, and at the time I thought he was just odd, but there was something about him which made me keep my distance. Now, I haven't seen him for years, but there are rumors in town … well, if you know Wales there are always rumors in town." He chuckled. "Anyway, I suppose you could say 'the word on the street' is that he is involved in some form of organized crime in London. What sort of crime I haven't a clue. And then I have to

127

think about where these rumors come from. They may have come from Evan, who was about ten years younger than Gareth, and I know some of my other school chums met up with him when they were in London, but I don't know how long ago that was. His mother still lives here, but I don't think he visits her.

"So, to answer your question; I would say that anything that happened to Evan has to be looked at in terms of his older brother, Gareth. Did someone have a grudge against Gareth they took out on Evan? Maybe Evan was involved in activities we weren't aware of? I don't know if that helps you."

Hayes replied, "I don't know if it helps either, but thanks for the background information. I'll have to give this some thought and I may call you back."

"Feel free to phone me anytime, well anytime my time. I'm pretty much around 9-5 most days and if I'm not in they can get a message to me. What time is it with you now?"

"4:45"

"So, that's five hours difference... you are up bright and early. Is that standard for American police?"

"Only those who've had a weekend away and have to get back. I'm still over an hour from my office."

"And, dare I ask what the temperature is there?" Owen asked.

"Well, right now, according to the display in front of me, it's 65 outside, but yesterday it was 84 on the coast."

"So, that's Fahrenheit; so about 18 centigrade now and ... 26 yesterday. I'm jealous. Here it's 3 centigrade, I suppose about 35 Fahrenheit, windy and raining. One day I must get to Florida."

"If you do, drop in to see us. I'll show you around."

"Thanks. Bye for now."

"Bye."

Her husband drove and Hayes watched the flat Florida landscape slide by.

She thought another visit to the hotel would be appropriate. She'd been shown the position of the security cameras on that first day, but she'd found out that no recording of events had occurred. Also, they weren't monitored, so there wasn't any neat evidence available. The manager had said someone had repositioned some cameras the evening before the bodies were found. This wasn't unusual, especially around Spring Break, but that was still a month off. Some of the cameras were easily accessed because they were mounted low enough to be reached by a cane, or an umbrella. They had got around to moving them back a couple of days later. Clearly, the cameras were there for effect, not for monitoring. On the other hand it just added to the suspicion that this could have been a double murder, and a clever murderer could have moved the cameras.

It looked like it was going to be a busy week.

18

"Twelve-point five."

"What!"

"Twelve-point five, sir."

"Jesus!" exclaimed Dr Reddy shaking his head and taking the lab report from the nursing aide. He looked at the lab report and said, "Jesus" again. It had once seemed strange for a doctor, obviously from the Indian sub-continent, to be cursing in good old Christian ways, but he had been there long enough that neither he, nor the staff, gave it a second thought.

He looked again at the lab report. Her potassium was a little high and so was her creatinine. They weren't going to get better any time soon, and probably a lot worse.

He called the house officer who was admitting her in the CCU.

"She needs that Digibind stuff as soon as possible. She may also benefit from magnesium and phenytoin. Don't forget to keep an eye on her potassium."

That would be enough to make the house officer leap for the books. Reddy was surprised he'd remembered how to treat digoxin toxicity – he hadn't treated one for years. Maybe he wasn't getting so old after all. He smiled to himself and began to walk away, but then thought a little more about the case.

He wandered over and spoke to the admissions assistant, a bald, pale, tattooed man called Terry. Terry's extensive tattoos were all in Welsh; at least the visible ones on his arms were, and that's what Terry told him when Reddy had asked. He'd helped interpret for Reddy on more than one occasion and they worked well together – both respecting each others' contributions to their patients' care. It was enough for Reddy to have learned a second language – English. He'd never bothered to learn a third – Welsh.

"Terry, could you phone that nursing home where that patient who came in about an hour ago came from. Name of Olwen Lewis. Tell them it looks like she has digoxin toxicity and they may want to look into how she came to have taken it."

"Right you are, Dr Reddy," said Terry and picked up the phone.

Reddy nodded his thanks. He felt he had done the right thing.

"Where next?" he asked.

"Room 5," a nurse replied.

"What is it?"

"Vaginal bleeding."

Reddy paused at the door, took a breath, knocked, and entered the room.

19

Detective Cynthia Hayes removed her weekend outfit of shorts and T shirt and slipped into her grey workday pantsuit. Slipped may not be the word she would have chosen as she struggled to tighten the belt. She noticed the belt buckle was at a looser fitting, or should have been, but it felt just as tight. She looked in the mirror and wondered when she was going to lose those ten pounds, or was it fifteen now? Certainly, not this week.

By 7:00 am she was sitting by the swimming pool talking to Walt, the night manager at the Columbus Hotel. His shift had just ended and he seemed in no hurry to leave but eager to talk. Hayes wondered if he was bored working nights – who wouldn't be?

She discovered that most of his European guests visited the area as part of a package which included flights, ground transportation, maybe a few days of tickets to the area attractions, and usually breakfast and dinner. They were more common in the summer months when they came in droves, seeking the warmth of Florida, after Americans had fled back to their northern climates. Usually, they found oppressive heat and humidity, but enough of them must have liked it because they kept coming back year after year. Hayes nodded in understanding –she hated the mosquitoes and sweat of August. For a second she wondered if it would help if she lost a few of those pounds, but then dismissed the thought. She'd worry about that in August.

She steered the conversation around to the two deaths, not mentioning the possibility of murder. She enquired about the security cameras and confirmed they were essentially for show and were unmonitored. They couldn't afford the staff. When the hotel was built, in the 80's it had been one of the biggest around. It had 320 rooms, and at one time had parking spaces for all of them, but since most of the guests nowadays were shuttled around by bus, the next hotel, the Orange Residencies, had bought up some of the parking lot for the construction of its 450 rooms. Walt lamented that this made it difficult to park at the Columbus Hotel, but the Orange Residencies had also managed to get permission to reclaim an acre or two of land behind it. (Walt just knew someone had greased someone's palm). Now, it had plenty of parking. In those days land was cheap and no one thought about underground parking.

It was a long shot but Hayes asked if he knew if the Orange Residencies had any security cameras.

This gave Walt another opportunity to express his grudging envy of the neighboring hotel. It seemed they had more money (and you know where that came from) and had the sort of recording system the Columbus Hotel could only dream about.

Hayes left Walt with the realization that it was better for Walt and the world that he worked nights and strolled over to the lobby of the Orange Residencies hotel.

She was in luck.

The hotel manager showed her the video room and the collection of discs. He also told her she was the first person from law enforcement who had ever requested access to the system in the five years since it had been installed. It was not an active system – no personnel monitored the cameras, but it had faithfully recorded events both in and outside the hotel for all those years. There were multiple shelves of neatly cataloged DVD discs. Hayes asked for the disc for the relevant day, was shown how to use the disc-player, and was left alone.

It took her a while to find out how to move quickly through the images. After a few minutes she decided to concentrate on the parking lot – she had to focus her investigations as best she thought able. She was working on a long shot. It had occurred to her that if someone wanted to kill someone in the Columbus Hotel they would probably not park at that hotel, but they still might park close enough to get back to the car in a hurry if they needed to.

It was tiring work, but she could see her theory might be correct as soon as she started reviewing the images. On that day neither the parking lot at the Columbus nor at the Orange

Residencies was full. Most cars were clustered close to the buildings. On the disc she could just see the edge of the Columbus parking lot and a few cars were parked at the edge of both lots. She asked the manager about this and found that both hotels required their staff to use the peripheral parking spaces. She started by looking at these areas and seeing if anyone parked at the edge of the Orange Residencies lot and then walked across to the Columbus. After fifteen minutes of speeding up, slowing down and reviewing the images she realized she was looking at this from the wrong perspective. She put herself in the shoes of a potential killer. If he had been so careful about not leaving any evidence at the crime scene he wouldn't park at the edge of the parking lot, where, for all he knew the surveillance cameras of the Columbus might identify him. Maybe he would park closer to the Orange Residencies and try to avoid the cameras of both hotels. At least it was a place to begin; if it didn't work out she'd try other nearby hotels.

This made the search more difficult. She had to replay the discs several times when the video showed the hotel becoming busy in the late afternoon. She was thinking her whole theory was off base when she noticed a white car park about half way between the Orange Residencies perimeter and the building. This was a little unusual because there were closer parking spots. She watched a man get out of the car and stroll towards the camera and the building. He wore dark glasses and a baseball hat, so it was impossible to identify him, but one thing noticeable was a very slight limp. In itself this was not unusual, and it might have been caused by the bag he was carrying over his left shoulder, so she initially dismissed his visit.

She almost missed it. Her wide screen view included a little-used sidewalk on the top left of her screen which paralleled the road between the Orange Residencies and the Columbus. Occasionally, a pedestrian walked across this.

Then she saw him. The man who had parked the car at the Orange Residencies was walking towards the Columbus along the sidewalk. She recognized his limp. In five seconds he had disappeared. She reviewed the video and confirmed this. She tried zooming in on him and his vehicle, but details were blurred and she couldn't make out the car's registration number or any further details about the man. She noted the time this had happened 16:44. She sat back and thought. What she needed to do now was find out when he came back to the car. Maybe he just preferred staying at the Columbus. She fast-forwarded the video until she noticed the parking space was empty. Then she backed up for five minutes and waited. Initially she watched the top left of her screen. If her theory was right … and there he was on the sidewalk. Three minutes later she watched his back as he walked to his car. He opened it and drove away. She noted the time 18:03.

That was a problem. This man probably had nothing to do with the death of the couple. The medical examiner had put their time of death between 21:00 and 22:00 that evening.

She sighed and looked at her watch. It was already nearly noon. She could take a break for a sandwich or burger, or she could carry on. She remembered the struggle with the belt a few hours ago and soldiered on.

And there it was! It had taken another hour of DVD scanning but she saw it.

The man with the slight limp had come back. He'd parked in a different area. As before he was close to the building, although he could have parked a little closer, and again he reversed into the parking space.

Hayes watched him walk towards the camera. She held her breath and paid attention to the top of the screen. There he was again! He walked along the sidewalk towards the Columbus Hotel. She noted the time – it was 20.53. She fast-forwarded the disc until the car space emptied, then reversed and watched him walking on the sidewalk, then towards his car. He opened the door and drove away. Except this time, instead of driving away from the camera and exiting the lot, he made a mistake. He drove toward the camera, turned right and had to pause for a couple of seconds when his exit was temporarily blocked by a hyped-up pickup truck. As he turned she got a brief glance at the license plate. She couldn't see it all, but she could make out the last three symbols –OPD. The time was 21:52.

She gave a little whoop of joy, ejected the disc and left to find the manager. No, she couldn't keep the disc, but he'd give her a copy. She impressed upon him the importance of keeping the original safe, resisted giving him a hug, and walked out into the bright afternoon sunshine. She hadn't missed that burger and fries after all.

Now, the hard work would begin.

20

The first meeting in London had ended at 9:15 (the same morning Cynthia Hayes was poring over DVD recordings in Florida, five time zones away) but at 3:00 in the afternoon, Georgina Southport, "The Witch", reconvened the meeting.

Present again were Jonathan Tibbs and his superior, William Burns. Rudolph Mukherjee and Elaine Souza, two other operatives in the British Secret Service, were brought in at the last moment for the afternoon meeting.

The Witch began. "I thought it necessary to get back together this afternoon. Tibbs, get us up to speed about this morning's meeting for Mukherjee and Souza's sake."

Tibbs nodded and said, "We met this morning to discuss the next steps in trying to figure out why our man, Jeremy Ellis, died in the fish and chip shop fire in Colwyn Bay. There was one potential witness who met with Ellis in the fish and chip shop. We hadn't been able to locate him, but it was thought he was an American. On a long shot we asked the police in Colwyn Bay to ask around the nursing homes there. It was thought he might have visited a relative in a nursing home – one who had recently been admitted. Over the weekend they left us a message here to say they had probably found someone who fitted what we were looking for." Tibbs looked down at his notes from the morning. "A woman, called Olwen Lewis, had been admitted to a nursing home there. She has a nephew, a John Beaton, who lives in America and had recently visited Olwen Lewis. The police took the details and, as I said, contacted us. We discussed what to do next at this morning's meeting and decided to contact the FBI and see if they could help us contact this John Beaton." He stopped and looked at Burns.

Burns said. "About an hour ago I called the FBI in DC and asked them if they could help locate John Beaton. The address and telephone number were both in the Seattle area and they suggested we contact the Seattle office to see what they could do. It's just after 7:00 am in Seattle, so I can call after this meeting."

Tibbs continued. "Well, that's where we were this morning, but things have changed. The North Wales Police tell us that Olwen Lewis was admitted to hospital over the weekend. In fact, it was just after their officer visited the nursing home that she was found to be sick. This might not be unusual, after all these are old people, but the hospital discovered she had apparently taken an overdose of digoxin. The hospital checked with the nursing home and it was not a medication she had been prescribed. The nursing home keeps all drugs away from its residents except when they are being handed out. They checked again. They have one resident who takes digoxin but the pill count indicated there was nothing missing. So, the only way she could have digoxin in her is it was brought in from outside."

"You mean ... in other words she was poisoned?" asked Souza.

"Correct," replied Tibbs and continued. "The police found out about this late this morning and made some more enquiries at the nursing home. They talked to the weekend supervisor. Over the weekend Olwen Lewis had one other visitor. Apparently, he was a minister of religion who made the same enquiries about Olwen Lewis, and who also wanted to know about any American relatives. He left the nursing home just before the police arrived there. He also spent a few minutes with Olwen Lewis. He did find out where she and, it turns out an American nephew, live. Further enquiries revealed that the church he said he was associated with had no knowledge of him. We have a description of him, and the police are checking cc television, but ... well, we don't know yet."

"Thank you, Tibbs," said The Witch. "So, why do you think she was poisoned?" She looked across the room at the two newcomers.

"To silence her?" said Mukherjee. His accent was pure Yorkshire. He was third generation of Indian heritage and had never got closer to India than a skiing trip to Italy. He had been with the Service for three years.

"Maybe, but she was demented. She really hadn't a clue about what was going on. Going to this effort to silence someone in her condition doesn't seem right."

Souza asked, "Could there be an insurance policy someone could claim?"

"I don't know. We haven't got that far, but that's a possibility. On the other hand it probably isn't fair to ask you without giving you more background information, and you weren't at Friday's meeting either." The Witch paused. "No, I think the reason she was poisoned was to get her nephew back from the US. At least that's what I think fits."

"So, someone poisons this demented old woman to make her sick and bring a relative rushing to her side?" Souza said.

"I'm afraid so."

"That's awful. Makes me want to wish it's just insurance fraud!" Souza pushed herself back in her chair. She was the complete opposite of Mukerjee in some ways. She had spiked blond hair, blue eyes, freckles, and the hint of a chest tattoo on the nape of her neck poked above her white T shirt. She spoke with a mild London accent. The only things she and Mukerjee had in common is they were the same height, 5' 9", weighed within a pound or two of each other, and for the last six months they had slept in the same bed. They didn't talk about it, didn't advertise it, but the least any intelligence community can do is know what relationships are fostering, or maybe festering, under its wings. For the time being it was tolerated. The Witch knew about it, and waited to see if it would be to the advantage or detriment of the couple and the Service.

The Witch said, "I agree it's bad, but that's the conclusion I came to when I heard about the poisoning. I also understand she is likely to die?" She asked Tibbs.

"Yes, Ma'am. She hasn't regained consciousness and her kidneys were damaged by the digoxin. We haven't talked to anyone up there directly – we've always gone through the police, but they tell me that it is likely she will die."

"So, what are we going to do? Burns, what could we ask the FBI to do?"

Burns replied brusquely. "Well, like I said I asked if they might confirm the information we have on the nephew, John Beaton. Assuming John Beaton is an American citizen there is going to be a limit to what we can ask them to do. He isn't a suspect, he's just a witness, and he may, or may not, have some useful information."

"What do you think we should ask them to do then?" The Witch looked around the faces in the room.

Souza replied. "I suppose the two extremes are: one – we ask them to do nothing and, two – we ask them to talk to him and tell him what we are interested in."

"Good points, but put yourself in their shoes and turn it around. Say they ask us to talk to a British citizen whom they say may be a witness; well … would we go along with it unless we knew a lot more?"

She looked around the room again. "You see what I mean," she added. "And then we have the other point. If we tell the FBI all about it, and he comes over here, is he going to be in danger? Now, we can promise the Americans we will meet him at the airport and keep him under guard until he leaves the country. But, assuming he is an unsuspecting upright citizen, he will have to be warned and have to go along with the plan. If that happens we can get to talk to him and see if he knows anything. He gets to visit his aunt and maybe attend her funeral. It's nice and safe, but the one thing we won't have is the bastard who killed Ellis."

Burns said, "You're right. It would be impossible to keep him under protection without it being noticed. Assuming the same person, or same organization, who killed Ellis, is involved in the poisoning of Olwen Lewis, then they want him back here. We could ask the FBI to see when Beaton books a flight to come back here."

"We can get that information from here. We don't have to ask the FBI," said Mukerjee. "We can easily find out when he plans to get back here. The airlines and border control have that information."

"How many people do you think have access to that information?" asked The Witch.

"It's probably in the hundreds, maybe thousands," replied Mukerjee.

"In that case we can assume that whoever wants him back here has the same information."

"That's probably a reasonable assumption."

"So, we wait?" asked Souza.

"Yes. I think we wait," said The Witch. "And let's see what happens." She turned to Tibbs. "I assume that the hospital has let the nephew know about her condition?"

"I don't know, Ma'am. I'll check," replied Tibbs.

"Souza, Mukerjee, I want you to be able to get to Colwyn Bay with short notice. It could be as little as twelve hours, but I think it will most likely be a little later in the week. I think I may arrange another team to be there with you. Watch the flights from Seattle, and ... and this time save the department a little money and only book one room." She looked unsmilingly at both of them.

Souza blushed. Mukerjee may have blushed too, but his complexion hid it and he maintained the poker face that Souza lost.

"OK. You have work to do. Keep in touch with each other and me. You may go."

They all stood to leave. As Burns was about to exit she called him back.

"Oh, Burns, I need to have a word with you about our FBI contacts. The rest of you may go."

William Burns closed the door to the conference room and took the closest chair.

"Bill," she began, "I see you are still playing the disaffected employee. Is it working?"

"Georgina," Burns replied, "I'm not sure. It helps in some ways. I'm sort of ostracized so I can get on with my work. People keep away from me. When I walk into a room the conversation stops. You know how it is. I don't really like it, and I don't think it's working. No one has approached me with offers I can't refuse."

"Maybe we should increase the degree of suspicion around you? Maybe we could see if we could get you compromised. How about a gay lover?"

Burns snorted. "That may have worked fifty years ago, but not now. If we overdo it no one will want to even sit in the same building as me. No, I think I should just go back to being me – maybe not immediately, but over the next couple of months."

"So, the investigation isn't going anywhere?"

"The cell phone I retrieved from the rubbish bin had called one number in France. There was no record of anything else on the phone. It was purchased legally and that's about it. I didn't call the phone number, but we asked the French to look it up. They got back to me and told me it's a message-forwarding service they're aware of, but are unable to do anything about – something to do with their laws the man said."

"So?"

"Well, that's not going to go anywhere. As far as we know there are no regular contacts from him to anywhere or anyone else. I'm going to monitor him closely for the next two weeks and see what we find."

Georgina, The Witch, pushed her chair back, looked at the ceiling and exhaled slowly. "I agree with you and that plan. We have no alternative. I am not taking this any further up the chain at the moment. Do you agree?"

"Yes."

"OK. Let's talk about the Americans. Let's not call the FBI. Why don't we see if the nephew makes it back here without being contacted?"

"All right, but if we change our minds we should discuss this with the Seattle office only. The politics of the FBI HQ in DC can be quite cut-throat and I don't trust them. I know someone I can call in Seattle. We could emphasize this is about the Hand of Khamsah, sorry Hamsa – I'll have to get used to that – not about a murder of one of ours in Wales. I think they'd be more than happy to help us out."

"OK. I agree. There's one other thing I have in mind. Do you fancy some field work?" Georgina asked.

"Well, yes, of course. Where?"

"North Wales."

"Oh … you want me in Colwyn Bay?"

"You can be the other team."

"OK. And who will be my partner?"

"You can take him with you."

"You mean? … Oh." It was Burns turn to smile.

"Yes. Take him with you. It may help with your investigation.'

"Machiavelli would be proud of you." Burns smile widened.

"I hope so, Bill. I certainly hope so."

21

Detective Cynthia Hayes was discouraged. Life wasn't fair. She'd managed to skip lunch a couple of days ago (or was it just yesterday?) but when she weighed this morning it wasn't just the ten pounds of extra weight that had registered on the scale – it was fifteen! Of course her husband said the right thing and told her he would love her whatever her weight, and she thought she might even believe him, but the point was she didn't love herself. She had no choice – she'd have to go back to Weight Watchers – perhaps she should sign up for lifetime membership?

And then there was the video and the number plate. After the elation of finding a partial number plate on the car in the hotel parking lot video she had called the Department of Motor Vehicle Licensing and was told there were over 20 million vehicles licensed in Florida and the numbers she had provided only narrowed it down to about 4,000.

So, she tried another tack, assumed they were looking for a rental car, and with a couple of other detectives had spent the previous afternoon phoning car rental businesses in the Orlando area with no joy. It even seemed that while the rest of the world identified vehicles by their number plates some car rental companies categorized them by scanning windshield stickers. One of the agents at Avis had told her this made it easier because it involved no writing and less confusion, especially with number plates from other states. Hayes and the other detectives had reviewed the video and couldn't be sure the number plate in question was on a Florida registered car. They discounted expanding the search any further. They hadn't even covered companies in Orlando – they had nowhere near enough staff, or perseverance, to cover Tampa and Miami too. At 6:30 the previous evening they had given up and gone for a pizza and beer before heading home for the evening.

Hayes was regretting that pizza too.

The drive to work had been frustratingly slow and now, at 7:10 what was she going to do? There had been a shooting outside The Epcot Center the previous evening and someone would have to deal with that. Fortunately, no one had been seriously injured, the shooter had been arrested, and it was just a matter of interviewing the witnesses.

She sighed, resisted the call from the chocolate bar in her desk's bottom drawer and decided to call Wales. She would update Rhys Owen and express her apologies and annoyance of being stuck and unable to progress any further with the case. She dialed.

"Bore da. Heddlu Gwent," was the answer to her call.

This time she was ready. "Please can you put me through to Rhys Owen."

"I'm sorry," came the reply in English. "The Chief Inspector is out. Can I take a message?"

"Well, this is Detective Cynthia Hayes. I'm calling from Florida. We talked a couple of days ago. I'd like to talk to him again. I think he'll know what it's about. Do you know when he'll be back in?"

"I think he's gone to a funeral. He'll probably be back in before he goes home. Shall I get him to call you?"

"If you would, I'd be grateful," Hayes replied, and gave her number. She hung up. So, Owen wasn't just an inspector – he was a chief inspector – just like all those superb, but flawed, sleuths in the British PBS Mystery series her husband loved to watch. They had watched a few episodes of different detectives wrestling with, and always overcoming, impossible odds, but it was a little close to home for her. She didn't need to be reminded of her job when she was off duty. She looked on the screen at the reports from the shooting the previous night, called the detective in charge of the investigation and agreed to meet him at 11:00.

They met at the crime scene and were joined by a member of Disney Global Security. Disney World, Orlando, and Florida were averse to any suggestions that visitors to the Magic Kingdom, or its satellite realms, could be touched by any criminal activities. Fortunately, it seemed the shooter from the previous evening was known to the police and had not been inside any Disney facility for years. He was still on probation from his last offence, and was now facing firearm possession and assault charges.

He'd shot his own brother in the leg when they had started arguing over the price of marijuana. The brother had been treated at a local emergency room and had been discharged the same evening with his wound covered in a large Band-aid. The brother was unlikely to press charges, but he didn't have to – the police would do it for him and the person responsible for his injury would be kept away from society for another four or five years. Based on his previous history he was just as likely to repeat the crime next time he was released.

It was all straightforward and at 2:30, after the detectives had shared lunch (Hayes had insisted on a salad – so far, so good) she was walking back to her car when her phone rang. She didn't recognize the number.

"Hayes here," she answered.

"Rhys Owen here."

"Ah … Chief Inspector – thanks for calling me back."

"I had a message you called. How can I help you?" He asked.

"I just thought I would let you know what was happening here with our investigation of the deaths of Evan Williams and Megan Price."

"Thank you, and what is happening?"

"Well, not much to tell you the truth. We reviewed the videos from the parking lot of a nearby hotel around the time of the murders. Based on his behavior we thought we had one possible suspect, but couldn't identify him. We also had a partial number plate of the vehicle he was driving. We spent all the afternoon yesterday trying to narrow down the vehicle with no success, and we just don't have the personnel or time to take this any further."

"I can sympathize with that. I think in the same circumstances we'd have the same limitations," said Owen.

"Well, that's it then. I'm sorry we couldn't get any closer with this one. I hope you have a good evening." She moved the phone away from her face.

"Wait a sec!" Owen half shouted.

Hayes had been about to hang up.

"I'm still here," she said.

"Good. I wanted to check a couple more things."

"OK?"

"So, you told the family it was just a drug overdose and nothing about any possibility of foul play?"

"Yes."

"Are you going to change that? I mean will there be an inquest?"

"Well, I have to talk it over with my senior officers, and probably the local prosecutor, but in circumstances like this there is always an inquest, even if we had no suspicion of murder. Florida State law demands it." Hayes said.

"But until that time you are going to leave the provisional cause of death as being drug overdoses?"

"Yes. The medical examiner definitely thinks it was murder. If pressed that there was the possibility of it just being overdose deaths he might say there is a slim possibility, and that's all it is, but I'd have to talk to him about that. Why are you asking?"

"Well, you couldn't get hold of me this afternoon because I was at the funeral of Evan Williams."

"Really! I didn't know the bodies had been released."

"Well, maybe I should say memorial service. It was held in a church here in Abergavenny. There was a good turnout. His mother was there and so was his brother, Gareth. I mention this because after we talked last time I started thinking more about who would want either Evan or Megan dead? Like I told you Evan liked his drugs and most of the time kept his mouth shut about where the money came from, but now and again it seemed he let a little information slip about his brother's line of work. It was all innuendo, and maybe a little bragging, so I asked around my colleagues here. I didn't learn much more apart from the older brother was supposed to be some mafia gangster, but that just seemed like local Welsh exaggeration. I checked a little further and he has no record here, or in London, of ever coming to the attention of the law. However, I have to say that if anyone wanted Evan out of the way it would be Gareth."

"His brother!"

"Yes, I'm afraid so."

"But that's awful." Hayes thought of the wonderful relationship she had with her brother.

"I agree it's awful, and it's probably a stretch, but I can't think of anyone else who might have a reason to do this. And, of course, that pre-supposes that the rumors of Mafia involvement are true."

"Which you said there was no evidence for?"

"That's correct. However, I think I told you I was at school with Gareth, so I made a point of offering my condolences to him yesterday. We chatted for a few minutes and he seemed suitably sad about the occasion. On the other hand there were another couple of observations I made about him. The first was he had a bit of a sun tan – he didn't get that around here at this time of year, and the other, which I am sure he didn't have when he was in school, was a slight limp."

"A limp!" Hayes said.

"Yes, a limp. Not much, more of a slight roll to his gait, but it was a change from the days when I knew him before. I didn't ask him about it – it didn't seem appropriate, and I only noticed it after he was leaving, but it was there. You seem surprised."

"Well, I know it's not much, but the person we noticed on the video had a slight limp too."

"Oh …" Owen was momentarily lost for words. "But you said the person on your tape couldn't be recognized otherwise?"

"Yes, he was wearing sunglasses and a baseball hat and the resolution of the recording is not good. Even without the glasses and hat it would be difficult to recognize anyone. But, that's food for thought. If someone – maybe your Gareth – came into the country just for this, well maybe we would have other ways of pinning it down. We could go through airline lists, maybe check airport videos too."

"That sounds like a lot of work," said Owen.

"It would be."

"I could check my end too, but it's also likely he traveled under a false name, and maybe flew from another European city, not directly from the UK. I think there are all sorts of possibilities, so why don't I start with sending you a photo of Gareth. One of my colleagues took a couple of shots today – I'll check with her to see how they turned out. If that doesn't work I think I have one from my rugby days, and he hasn't changed much since then. Oh, and could you send me the video? You can send it to this phone and we can take it from there."

"I will go back to the station and arrange that now. Thank you, Chief Inspector."

"Thank you, Detective."

"We'll be in touch."

Hayes hung up. For once she wasn't hungry.

22

The phone rang.

It was shortly after 9:00 a.m. and John Beaton was attempting to multi-task. He'd just got home from the gym, and as he listened to the latest news on NPR he spooned his breakfast bran-flakes into his mouth, and worked on his daily crossword puzzle. Had he been asked he would have failed to recall any details of the news, apart from the fact it was going to rain, and he didn't really need a news program to tell him that.

He left his cereal, turned down the volume on the radio, and answered the phone.

"Hello, John Beaton here."

"Mr. Beaton? Mr. John Beaton, the nephew of Olwen Lewis?"

The Welsh accent and the official sounding question gave John a brief déjà-vu moment before he answered, "Yes, that's me."

"Well, this is Elizabeth Probert. I'm a nurse at Glan Clwyd hospital, and I've been caring for your aunt, Olwen Lewis."

"I didn't know she was in hospital."

John switched off the radio.

"She was admitted over the weekend. She got very poorly and the nursing home sent her here."

"What's wrong with her?"

"She came in here with vomiting and diarrhea and she became unconscious."

"That's strange. What caused it?" John asked with rising concern.

There was a pause. "I'll let you speak to the doctor," was the reply.

That was unusual. Doctors didn't usually participate in these conversations. A male voice came on the phone.

"Mr. Beaton?"

"Yes."

"My name is Dr. Kumar and I have been looking after your aunt since she came into hospital." He spoke slowly with a north

153

Wales accent. "She is very ill. It seems she has taken a big dose of a medication we call digoxin and it is affecting many organs of her body."

"Digoxin ... digoxin? I didn't think she was taking that. How come she took that?" John asked. He had always been pleased that his aunt was taking so little medication, and there was no reason he knew of why anyone would want to give her digoxin – a medication derived initially from foxglove and used for controlling irregular heart rhythms.

"We don't know. We are looking into it, but in the meantime your aunt is in intensive care here and we are doing everything we can for her."

"Thank you..." Then the medical part of John's brain kicked in. "What was the digoxin level when she was admitted?"

The voice on the other end of the phone hesitated before saying, "I think it was a little over twelve."

"I seem to remember that is a very high level. Is that correct?"

Again, the hesitation. "Yes."

John played the trump card cautiously. "I'm a GP here in the US, so please feel free to let me know what's going on." It worked.

"Oh, I didn't know. Well, she presented with a bradyarrhythmia, dehydration from vomiting, and her electrolytes and renal function tests reflected that. She was unconscious. She is now on a respirator, a temporary pacemaker, and is still unconscious. It's highly likely she had an arrhythmia which caused brain damage. We don't know how she came to take the digoxin. We have asked the nursing home to look into it, and it looks like the police are involved too."

"The police?" John said softly.

"Yes. The nursing home accounted for the supply of their one patient taking digoxin and there was no discrepancy. It sounded suspicious, so the police were called in."

"So, you don't know where she got the digoxin or how it got into her?"

"Exactly."

"Well ... I ... um." John was at a loss for words.

"It's a lot to take in … I know. We have been wondering here what could have happened."

"Well, it doesn't sound good. Is she going to make it?" John asked.

"I'm not sure, Doctor … well … I suppose I am. She had dementia before this and if she wakes up it is going to be a lot worse. However, her renal function is declining, we seem to have stabilized her heart rhythm, but we are barely managing to support her cardiac output. As I am sure you know that also comes at the risk of further jeopardizing her renal function. To be honest, she is unlikely to make it. I doubt she will last beyond the next couple of days."

John took a deep breath before answering, "Thank you, Doctor. I appreciate your being candid. Thank you for what you're doing for her. Please let me know if anything happens. I'll see if I can get over to see her, but the earliest I could get there would be almost twenty-four hours from now."

"To be honest, I think that would be too late, but that's up to you of course."

"I appreciate your honesty. I'll think it over. Thank you, Doctor."

John ended the call and returned to his breakfast. He picked up the spoon and finished his cereal on auto-pilot.

He had no reason to doubt what he'd been told. Whether he'd been told the whole story was another thing. He couldn't imagine how Auntie Olly had ended up with digoxin inside her. Well, there were only two ways – by mouth and by injection, and it was hard to see how either could have happened. He thought over what Dr. Kumar had told him. Her level was 12.5. He decided to look it up after he remembered that Britain and the rest of the world, apart from the USA, had long ago changed the units in which lab tests were reported. Maybe it wasn't as bad as he thought.

He was disappointed. Therapeutic levels of the drug by both measurements were in the 1 to 2 range. She must have had a massive dose to get a level that high. Digoxin was one of those drugs where the therapeutic window was quite narrow. If you

155

got much above that range you ended up with worse problems than those you were trying to treat.

He already knew he'd have to make a trip back to Wales soon – he just didn't want it to be this soon, and certainly not in these circumstances.

It seemed he had just got back from there, finally got over jet-lag, and now he was looking at another ten-hour-flight, eight-hour-time-change, and a week of jet-lag both ways.

He pulled himself out of the reverie, cleared the dishes away, called Ann who was at work and told her about Auntie Olly.

"Let's leave Thursday," she said. "And let's make it three weeks. We can go somewhere warm when we're over there. Oh, I know, let's go and visit Laura. She's in Italy at Bologna University. We could meet up with her and check out this new boyfriend of hers."

"That's great, but what about your work?" John wondered, pleased they would be going together and at the thought they might visit Italy and his daughter, but surprised Ann had made such a quick decision.

"The census is down. They were going to lay off one of the temps. I'll be a hero if I tell them I'll be away for a month. Let's do it."

"OK. Let's do it. I'll book Delta out of here on Thursday. Hey, we won't be able to plan anything else until we know what's happening to Auntie Olly."

"When we know what's happening to Olly we can figure out what to do. We can always go into one of those high street travel agents and book a last-minute package tour. What do you think?"

"Leave it to me. When are you going to get home?"

"I should be there by 4:30. Bye. Love you."

"Bye. Love you too."

By 4:15 John had booked two seats on Delta. The plane left just before 8:00 p.m. and arrived at London's Heathrow Airport at 1:00 p.m. the next day. John toyed with the idea of traveling in business class, and being able to lie flat for most of the flight, but couldn't bring himself to fork out the extra thousands of dollars this would incur. He settled for Delta's 'Comfort Plus' – a little extra leg room and a few more degrees towards horizontality. At least it looked like the flight wasn't going to be full.

At 4:25, just as Ann was pulling into the driveway the phone rang again.

It was the hospital. They informed him that Olwen Lewis had passed away just after midnight.

23

Chief Inspector Rhys Owen finished his call to Detective Cynthia Hayes and sat still for a few moments. It was after dinner and he was reclining on his living room sofa warming his feet in front of the artificial coals of the radiant gas fire. His wife was out at a Women's Institute committee meeting and he was enjoying a quiet dry sherry. At least he would have been enjoying the sherry a little more had it not been for the call he had just made to the USA. The policeman in him worried that two young people from his neck of the woods had died in Florida, and it was possible the brother of one of them had killed them. At times like this he called his own brother.

Assistant Chief Constable Clive Owen (not the actor, but one of the thousands in Wales with the same name) of the North Wales Police looked at the ID on his phone and answered the call.

"Hello, little brother. What can I do for you?"

"Well, bigger brother, I thought I would call and chat with you. You know – pass the time, discuss rugby and all those other sports you love."

Rhys Owen was quite aware that his older brother was the only living person in Wales who had an aversion to the national sport. This was not a well-known fact, except among family members, otherwise it could have been fatal for a career in the Welsh police force, and at 39 years of age Clive Owen had done well. He was likely to become Chief Constable within the next few years. He also knew that his younger brother did not like to be called 'little brother'.

"On introductory greetings our score is now even. Do you agree?" Rhys asked.

"I agree, Rhys. We're even. I think you won last time, and I thought I was ready for you, but things have been hectic here. I'm still at the station, I have the usual mound of paperwork to go through, and I've another meeting to go to in about fifteen minutes."

"At this time of night! What's happening?"

"Well, in a nutshell we've had two murders in the last month, both in Colwyn Bay, and maybe carried out by the same person. It's bizarre. You remember the case we talked about, oh … maybe two weeks ago."

"The man killed in the fish and chip shop fire?"

"Yes. Well, that turned out to be a murder. We thought it was, but it took a little longer for forensics to verify it because of the fire. Now, it seems the same man may be responsible for poisoning a woman in a nursing home here."

"Nursing home?"

"Well, it's a little bizarre. The woman was killed by an overdose of digoxin. Apparently, it used to be a common drug used in nursing homes, but newer medications have superseded it and the only likely source would have come from outside the nursing home. It may have also been given to the woman by someone disguised as a minister of religion. I tell you, these are outside the normal crimes we see up here and we don't like it."

"I wouldn't like it either."

"And the other thing is MI5 is involved, or whatever they call themselves nowadays – I think it's just the intelligence service. We tried to keep it from the press, and for the most part succeeded, but the man who died in the chip shop fire was with them. They were pretty pissed about it, but now they're back here again, and I believe the expression I heard once on one of those American cop shows is they are 'loaded for bear'."

"But those sound like two entirely different ways of killing. Why do you think it's the same person?" Rhys asked.

"Well, you're right there, but they may be linked. The intelligence boys from London seem to think the reason for the second, in the nursing home, is even odder. They think it was done to bring back from the USA the nephew of the woman who was killed."

"What! You mean kill someone so their relative has to show up for a funeral?"

"Basically, that's it. I'm not sure I agree with that theory, or want to agree with that, but they seem pretty convinced."

"So, what's happening with it? What're your plans?"

"That's what the meeting is about. We're expecting the killer to contact the nephew somehow and we hope to be there when he shows up. I am not sure what they've told the nephew, if anything. It's their show and we'll be providing back-up to the intelligence boys."

"I still can't see why they're involved. I mean I can see why they're upset about losing one of their men – who wouldn't be? But, why get involved with something which should just be a police matter?" Rhys wondered.

There was a slight hesitation before Clive Owen replied, almost apologetically.

"Well, it's all hush-hush, and I am not supposed to talk about it, but it looks like it has something to do with international terrorism."

"International terrorism! In Colwyn Bay?" Rhys was surprised.

"That's what I thought. It's a long way from our usual copper work."

"You're not kidding! Well, I'd better let you get to your meeting."

"Wait a sec," Clive said. "I've still got a couple of minutes. Any other reason you called me?"

"Well, there is as a matter of fact. I've had this troubling case, well, I don't even know if it's a case yet. I don't know if it made it to the newspapers up there – it was on BBC Wales one evening, but we had a couple of our teenagers die on holiday in Florida."

"I saw something about that. They overdosed didn't they?" Clive asked.

"Perhaps, but I've been talking to a detective in Florida and there were a couple of suspicious findings at the post mortem which makes her think it could be murder, or homicide as they say there. The question which worried her, and worries me, is why would anyone want to kill a couple in Florida and try to make it look like just an overdose. In fact, they did a good job of making it look like an overdose. It wasn't picked up until the post mortem."

"Is she getting anywhere with it?"

161

"Not really. She's been looking at surveillance tapes and sent me one this evening. It doesn't show much. But, here's the strange thing. The boy who was killed was called Evan. He was a druggie through and through, and probably so was his girlfriend. The boy's brother, however, was Gareth Williams. I don't know if you remember him, but he and I played rugby together for King Henry when we were there."

"Did he play scrum-half? Was he tall, pretty strong and black curly hair?"

"Yes, that's probably him, but I thought you didn't know anything about rugby."

"I don't, except I remember your playing, and it was good to come back as an old boy and watch you playing the game. Didn't you win some championship or something?"

"Yes, we did, but … but, the thing with Gareth is he wasn't one of the boys. He knew how to look like one of the boys, but he really wasn't. Looking back I realize now he was a psychopath, and we've seen enough of people like that over the years, but he managed to hide it from most people. I don't know what he's been up to for the last ten years or so. There were rumors that he was mixed up in something in London, but there's no evidence of the Metropolitan Police, or us, having anything on him. But, then I have to think about the source of those rumors and I wonder if they didn't come from his brother."

"The one who died?"

"Yes," Rhys confirmed.

"So, what are you thinking?" Clive asked.

"I am wondering if Evan didn't get in too far over his head in something, and couldn't be relied upon to keep his mouth shut, so it was shut for him. And … and I know you think this is strange, but I wonder if it wasn't his brother who did for him."

"His brother? Now, that is strange. Unless, or course, you're a medieval British king, when I think you were supposed to kill your brothers. On the other hand they were all psychopaths anyway, so maybe your man could have done it?'

"So, we should consider ourselves safe then?"

"What?"

162

"Well, we are not British, or even Welsh royalty, and you don't strike me as being a psychopath, so can I continue to sleep without a long sword by my side?"

"I think there were times in my childhood I'd thought about killing my little brother, especially after some of the tricks he pulled, but I'd leave your long sword in the garden shed if I were you."

"You know – every trick I know I learned from you."

"Well, thank you – I think. So, how close are you to proving it – the case?"

"Nowhere near," replied Rhys. "It's just policeman's intuition. I was at the memorial service for the brother today and Gareth was there. He seemed suitably grieving, but that doesn't mean a thing. The tape I got from the USA showed someone with a slight limp, and Gareth now has a slight limp too, but that's the extent of the proof we have so far. I'm not sure where to take it next."

"That's a difficult one, especially with the international issues. You can pass it up to the Home Office, but they won't do anything with it, especially with no definite suspects. They may pass it on to the Foreign Office, or maybe the intelligence services. If you know anyone in London you should try calling them. That's often the best approach."

"So, it's not what you know, it's who you know."

"Things don't change much do they?" Clive commented.

"No. Well, just a thought though – you don't think your guy and mine could be the same do you?"

"No, but ... oh, I have to go. Part of me says Wales doesn't need two killers like this, so I hope it's the same guy, but realistically it's very unlikely. On the other hand this is all very strange anyway. Do you have a photo of him?"

"Yes, took one today."

"Text it to me and we can keep a ... yes, I'm coming. Look, I've got to go. I'll call you later this week."

"Bye, Clive."

"Bye, Rhys. Keep the faith."

24

"He gets in at about one on Friday afternoon. I assume he'll hire a car and will be in Colwyn Bay by the evening. It's also likely he'll be staying at his aunt's place."

"Then I'll be in Colwyn Bay too," replied Gareth from the comfort of his chair. He had his feet propped up on the bed.

"Be careful. My source says there could be one or two teams monitoring him," said Jones.

"I always am."

"This time be extra careful. We need to get out of this whole Welsh screw-up and, as far as I am concerned, never go back there."

"I've no problem with that. Is there any more to do in South Wales?" asked Gareth.

"No. Everything's squared away there. I arranged for the contact we met in Llandudno to disappear. He won't be talking to anyone, and his absence should dampen any ideas anyone else may have of Welsh revolution. And … guess what? I even heard a rumor that the security services may have had a hand in it. It helps that the man we dealt with in Colwyn Bay was associated with them, so that end is tied up."

Jones moved away from the window where he had been standing, poured himself a glass of water, and sat at the desk

Gareth nodded and smiled. He appreciated Jones's attention to detail.

Jones continued. "Once we deal with Colwyn Bay we can concentrate on our Mediterranean enterprises again. I have a contact in Tunisia, likes to be called Raki – God knows why – I think you've met him?" Gareth nodded. "Well, he's interested in directing some work our way. I'm flying out to meet him tomorrow in Madrid. I'm also meeting a man I've had legitimate dealings with in the past. I'll tell you about both later and, in future, no more favors for any of our clients in our back yard. We'll stick to what we do best and not get distracted – nothing in the British Isles – even if the Queen herself asks us." He raised his glass in a mock toast and took a sip of the water.

It was always water only with Jones. There was never any alcohol.

It was Tuesday and he and Gareth were holding a business meeting over lunch. They were in a room on the fourth floor of the Hampton Inn at Gatwick Airport. This was Jones's choice. He was careful, almost paranoid, hated using cell phones, and chose a different hotel around London and its outskirts for each of their meetings. These were held on different days of the week and not on a regular basis. The only definite protocol they had established was meeting before either of them took a flight out of the country, and arriving at the meeting in different ways. Jones had taken the Gatwick Express train from Victoria and Gareth had driven a rental car to the hotel.

They could have met closer to London, where both still lived. Jones had maintained a rule of changing his residence every two to three years and was living in a superficially decrepit house in Forest Green – he no longer worked at Goldsmiths. Gareth had lived in a ground floor flat in a nameless development in Battersea for four years. He had thought about moving to somewhere a little more upscale, but he preferred the anonymity of his current address. It was very London-like – none of his neighbors knew or bothered him, and in return he ignored them.

Both men preferred to separate business from their domestic arrangements. Neither was married nor had any long-term relationships, they both knew where each other lived, but neither had visited the other's home. They liked it this way.

They had worked together for over ten years. In other circumstances a relationship like theirs could have matured over time, but in many ways they interacted as if they were still in the academic hierarchy of Goldsmiths.

Jones was obsessive, punctilious, calculating and demanding. He had noticed some of these traits in Gareth, but he also saw behaviors he would like to have, but could never comfortably pursue. Gareth had a careful lawlessness that Jones admired, but had never acquired.

Jones knew Gareth liked the lifestyle their association had brought. Gareth was an intelligent psychopath. He knew on which side his bread was buttered, gave his opinion when Jones asked for it, but usually accepted the lead Jones provided. The money was good and when the urge took him he could fly to countries that allowed him to realize fantasies that would have been illegal in Britain.

This was why the problem in Wales had become more than just a clean-up job – it had changed their relationship.

It had started as a simple request. A wealthy client from a Gulf state had asked Jones for a favor. Could he assist a friend of his to get his hands on something that could be "disruptive"?

This was not how Jones usually operated and he hesitated when he found out the friend lived in Cardiff, but the client intimated he would pay well for the favor, and for future business. Jones calculated the risk was marginally worth the benefit, but this was one job he felt he could not delegate and picked the seaside town of Llandudno to meet with the friend. Despite being told to be alone the friend had brought along another man to the meeting.

That man was Jeremy Ellis.

It took a few seconds after Jones and Gareth had entered the motel room for Jones and Ellis to recognize each other. Ellis had been at Goldsmiths University and had taken a class taught by Jones.

Ellis reacted first and almost made it to the door of the hotel room before Gareth caught him, rabbit-punched the back of his neck, and brought him to the floor. A kick to the ribs had brought no reaction, so he turned and found Jones sitting on the floor with a hand over his left eye. The other man had panicked and lashed out with the nearest thing he could find – a bedside lamp which he now held in both hands. He swung it wildly from side to side shouting abuse in Welsh. Gareth tried to pull Jones away but the man came at him. Gareth backed up for a second, feinted to the right, and as the man drew his arm back to strike, Gareth darted in close and punched him hard in the abdomen. Instantly, the man dropped the lamp and crumpled on to the floor. Gareth kicked him in the groin and he stayed down gasping for breath.

Gareth helped Jones up, and examined his face. He would have a black eye, but it could have been worse. He looked around.

Ellis was missing.

While they were distracted he'd regained consciousness and slipped away.

Gareth made a phone call to his brother, Evan, instructing him to follow Ellis while he and Jones dealt with the man in the hotel room.

Briefly they discussed the immediate fate of the man on the floor – they'd let him live. Gareth rifled his pockets and found a driving license which matched his face, credit cards in the same name, car keys, and a hundred pounds in twenties. Gareth pocketed the cash and gave the license to Jones. Gareth gave the man a passing kick to his kidneys, and then they left the hotel room.

They had not caught up with Ellis until the fish and chip shop. He wouldn't have made it to the next town, Colwyn Bay, if their driver, Evan, Gareth's half-brother, had stayed where he'd been told.

And then Evan ended up knowing too much and things had to be dealt with. Jones knew there could be no witnesses. Ellis died in the fish and chip shop fire and Evan, who had been given a trip to Florida for his labors, died in his hotel room. Both had died at Gareth's hand. The death of Evan's girlfriend in Florida and Olwen Lewis in Colwyn Bay had been collateral casualties.

It was essential to get back in control, but Jones had given Gareth more leeway than usual and was troubled by the carnage which followed him. Having let the cat out of the bag (or was it the genie out of the bottle?) would he be able to put it back in? Was Gareth indispensible? Jones considered no one indispensible, but finding a replacement for Gareth would be difficult, especially since Jones no longer had access to impressionable or venal students. He was a little surprised to find he was even thinking about it. He also found he was irritated by Gareth's feet resting on the bed in his hotel room.

So, Jones had decided to cover all his bets and update his plans to leave the country if all his schemes went to hell. He was close to getting back to their comfortable business. This had been so successful for the last ten years that this one slip was so frustrating, so unbalancing, that Jones found himself second guessing all his plans to see if he was making the right decisions.

And what was their business? Basically, Jones fixed things and Gareth helped. You wanted a shipment of something a government wouldn't want you to have? Big or small that could be arranged.

You wanted to neutralize a rival? It could be done.

You would like someone to disappear in another country? Well, that could be arranged, but maybe there are alternatives you might like to consider? Where would you like the blame to fall?

But Jones and Gareth had maintained their distance. Rarely did they see the contents of the container units they moved around the world. They were never in the country when the car bomb exploded, the business man's warehouse burnt down, or the politician disappeared. Jones's agents talked to other agents, who talked to drivers, sailors, and fanatics who took the risks.

Jones was the spider controlling his enterprises from the center of the web, but no one else in the web knew who was at the center.

Except Gareth – maybe that's why Jones was uneasy now.

The Hand of Hamsa rarely claimed responsibility for their work. They only used it when they needed to impress certain groups that they were good, probably the best at what they did, and nobody should consider messing with them. Jones was annoyed that the Hand had been associated with the killing of the man in the fish and chip shop in Colwyn Bay. In retrospect it would have been better to have just driven back to London that night. It was a night of errors and that had been just one more. He hoped he could work with the clients he was meeting in Madrid in thirty-six hours. He wanted his focus back.

169

Both had brought their own lunches to the meeting. For Jones it was a Greek salad and raspberry yogurt. For Gareth it was a pork pie, a pickle, and a Cox's apple. They ate in silence; Jones sat at the small desk spooning the last of his yogurt from its plastic recesses while Gareth munched the apple and rocked back on his chair.

Gareth finished the apple, stood and strolled to the window. "I'm going to a funeral in Abergavenny on Thursday – my brother's." He spoke without any trace of emotion. "I'll spend tonight at the Angel Hotel there and I can be in Colwyn Bay by midday on Thursday. If things go as planned I'll be back in London by the weekend and I will probably never have to visit Wales again. When shall we meet again?"

"My meeting is Wednesday morning in Madrid. I should be back by the weekend too. I'll contact you and let you know where we can meet. If I need you any sooner I'll let you know. I would have preferred you came with me to Madrid, but that couldn't be arranged," said Jones.

"You could always come with me to Wales," suggested Gareth with the hint of a smile.

"No thanks. You stick to what you do well and I'll stick to what I do well. We have a great partnership as long as we remember that."

Jones raised his glass again and took a sip.

Gareth nodded, left his apple core on the window sill and left the room with a brief, "Wish me luck and I'll wish you luck too."

For a few minutes after Gareth left Jones didn't move from his chair. He stared at the apple core on the window sill. He had a couple of choices. The easiest would be to stay in Madrid until he knew all was clear, but maybe that would be too passive. Instead of waiting for things to happen, maybe he should make them happen. Perhaps it was time for him to separate from Gareth. Gareth was good, but mistakes had been made – not necessarily by Gareth, but Jones wanted a clean, complete, closure. Should he wait until after the weekend, or should he act now? With a quick burst of energy Jones stood, swept the apple core into the trash bin and picked up his phone.

Gareth eased his Ford into the surprisingly light traffic on the M25 motorway and headed to the west side of London. Something didn't feel right and this concerned him. Jones wasn't his usual self. It was hard to put his finger on it, but it seemed he was trying too hard to be his usual self. Perhaps there was no meeting in Madrid; perhaps Jones was going to sit in his house, bags, money and passport packed until he heard from Gareth. There was of course one other possibility, but that wouldn't happen until he knew Gareth had succeeded or completely failed.

That's when Gareth knew he'd have to be careful.

25

The Eurostar train arrived at St. Pancras station in London at 10:40 am. Ella always found the two-and-a-half hour journey from Paris more relaxing and quicker than flying and sitting in taxis going to and from airports. She had skimmed through the information Danilo had given her one more time, but felt unsettled. She had taken a Dan Brown novel from her overnight bag and found reading it the distraction she wanted. It was also not entirely fantastic or predictable. Or maybe it was, but she didn't care. She wondered if any authors had used Islam, like he used the Catholic Church, as the bête noir of their books.

She left St. Pancras and headed west the short distance to Euston Station. She preferred the walk, even though the noise of the traffic on Euston Road made it less enjoyable every time she visited London. However, it was still preferable to her next form of transport – The Northern Line. This subway line, bisecting London into east and west halves always seemed to have the noisiest, hottest, and dirtiest trains. On maps of London's subway, 'The Tube' as it was called locally, the various lines were ascribed different colors. The Northern line had been given black, which she thought was quite appropriate.

She used her Oyster Card to access the subway and a merciful four stops and ten minutes later emerged at Leicester Square. She turned left and strolled along Charing Cross Road towards Trafalgar Square. She walked along the side of the National Gallery but at St. Martin-in-the-Fields walked up the steps to the front entrance and looked out over Trafalgar Square. Even at this time of the year there were dozens of tourists and hundreds of pigeons. Later in the year there would be thousands of both.

The other reason she wandered up the steps was to see who was watching her, or watching after her. It was a man. She had wondered if Stefan would do that – change the sex of her guardian without telling her. The man had been in front of her on the train. He seemed a little restless, used the bathroom a little more than the journey time dictated, and each time had glanced her way more than she thought usual. She knew she was attractive to men, but not that much. However, he was otherwise good at the job. He looked totally anonymous. He wore plain clothes. He had no beard and no mustache. He had brown eyes, brown hair and was of average height, but he was carrying a brown leather shoulder bag, and she noticed that again as, at that moment, he strolled in front of her on the sidewalk. She waited a few seconds then turned and entered the building. Inside she walked rapidly towards another building entrance but instead of making an exit, turned to her right, just inside the doorway and took the stone stairs down to the crypt.

Whenever she took these stairs she couldn't help remind herself of the tongue-twister, 'The cat crept into the crypt, crapped, and crept out again'. She shook her head. The more she tried to not remember it the more fixed it had become, because one of her joys of visiting London was a lunch-time concert in the church of St. Martins-in-the-Fields, followed by lunch in the crypt. On this occasion she would try reversing the order – lunch, then listening, if she had time.

This was a functional crypt. The church was no longer surrounded by fields, as its name once suggested, but its crypt had survived the London Blitz in the 40's and was now a busy restaurant with seating for over a hundred.

She reached the brick arches and smooth stone floor of the crypt, turned right, and slipped into an alcove she had visited before. She paused to glance to her right at one of her favorite London artifacts – the eighteenth century wooden whipping post just inside the room.

"I think it's a useful reminder that alternative forms of physical punishment have not been abandoned very long ago," said a voice to her left. "It was not until 1791 that it was abandoned for use on women. If you were a man you had to wait until 1837 before it was stopped." Georgina rose, smiled, and extended a hand to Ella. Ella shook her hand and turned to look at the wooden post.

"I've seen it before, but I'd always assumed it dated from a much earlier time," Ella said. She found a chair and sat next to

Georgina at the small table. She checked to make sure she couldn't be seen unless someone walked directly into the room, and pulled a file out of her bag. There was one other person present whom Georgina addressed.

"Jack, please put the sign up and then get us some lunch, and for yourself." She handed him a credit card. "Jack is my driver today. Actually, we took a taxi here since there is no convenient parking, but I trust him to select appropriate food and anything we don't eat Jack will finish off. Is that OK?"

"Fine with me," said Ella.

Jack grinned. He was in his early thirties and was clearly not just a driver. His build and presence indicated he was more likely one of the British security service officers who worked for Georgina. He moved a "No Entry. Private Party" sign across the entrance to the room and left them alone.

Georgina began, "It's good to see you again. I checked with my people before we left and they were impressed by what they found. You seem to have developed a very successful international security company – congratulations. It can't have been easy."

"Thank you. It has been rewarding work. It helped having the right people in place, and I think a lot of luck, and hard work, has paid off." Ella paused before adding, "Of course, my people checked you out too. You've done very well." Ella smiled.

"Well, thank you. How good is your research? Did you find out my nickname?"

Ella hesitated. "We found a nickname. It might not be your nickname, and I am not sure that finding your nickname should necessarily be a way of judging our research."

"And it was?"

"Well … let me just say it has to do with Halloween and broomsticks."

It was Georgina's turn to smile. "Very good. I hope that's the only one they have for me, but you never know. Now … I'm going to have to make this meeting as quick as possible. I'm involved in running an operation and it needs my full attention, but I'm taking time out from that because I was intrigued to follow up on our brief conversation. Basically, what do you want from me and what can you offer me? And, of course, our conversation is private and I don't want to see my face in the newspapers over this."

"You won't see your name in the papers," Ella asserted. "According to the British press you lost a man in Colwyn Bay recently. A metal hand was left at the site of a restaurant burning down and your man was inside. I assume the press reports were true?"

Georgina nodded and said, "Basically they were true."

"A few weeks ago I was in Istanbul. I was to meet my brother there for reconciliation after nearly twenty years. While I was there he was murdered and a metal hand was left at the site." Ella opened the file and showed Georgina the photographs of her brother and his assassins, and the metal hand she had photographed. She continued, "Is this metal hand the same as the one left in Colwyn Bay?"

"Yes, it looks like the hand from Colwyn Bay, but these other photographs? Who are they?"

"This one is my brother." Ella pointed, "And these two are his assassins. Apparently, my brother killed them, but was fatally wounded himself."

"What did the police have to say about this?" asked Georgina who had been planning an uneventful lunch.

"The police were not involved, and nothing came out in the media either."

Georgina said, "I see ... so ... that must be hard on you. You lost a brother – your only brother?"

"Yes, my only sibling. As I said, we weren't close, but he was still my brother and it's hit me harder than I thought."

"I'm sorry. I know how you feel, well ... I don't know how you feel I suppose, but I lost a sister once and it was hard; still is in some ways. I'm sorry."

"Thank you."

Both were quiet for a few seconds – privately recalling their losses.

"So, tell me what else you know about these hands," Georgina said, picking up the photos.

"Well, they aren't hands. Well, they are, but they also include part of the forearm as you can see from the photos. Superficially, they look like the Hand of Hamsa, but the inclusion of the forearm is unusual. Also, the middle finger is longer than usual and we were wondering if that is on purpose – a little like 'giving the finger' to someone. The inscription on the metal attributes it to Ja'far Ibn Talib. He was a cousin of the prophet who was killed in battle, but lost his arms first."

Georgina looked at the photo of the hand and said, "I can't see any inscription on this one."

"There is the beginning of a J and A, but you are right there is no inscription apart from that."

"So, where does this theory come from? How do you know about it?" Georgina put down the photo and looked at Ella.

Ella smiled, "Now I see why you have the reputation you have. I have one more photo to show you. It's a long distance shot taken a week or two ago in Turkey. It was taken by one of my staff at a meeting I had with someone who called himself Ali. I don't know if that's his real name, or not." She handed the photograph to Georgina. "He was someone we traced as a contact of my brother's. I showed him the same photo and he had seen one like it before – when his brother and sister were murdered. He told us the story about the hand, and that it was not quite the Hand of Hamsa."

"Did you believe him?"

"I did. I am not sure about his relationship to my brother, and he also hinted he might not be welcome in Britain, but I was pretty sure he told the truth about his brother and sister. He also suspects who may be behind my brother's murder. It may be that contract killers did the actual killing. Nothing has appeared in the press and, as I said, the police were not involved, so he would not have known my brother was dead unless I told him."

"And what are you going to do now with this information?" asked Georgina.

"I am going to give you what I have about these cases we unearthed. I am sure some are not new to you, but you would not have known anything about my brother and Ali. I would be grateful for anything you can do to get to the bottom of this. Ali has told us he will question the person whom he thinks was responsible for my brother's death."

"Thank you. This is new information and it may help our investigations." Georgina paused. "As you can imagine, I can't tell you everything about Colwyn Bay, but there was a fire in a fish and chip shop there. One of my staff was killed. We aren't sure why. He was working underground on Welsh nationalist issues, and may have been recognized, but, bizarre as some of the Welsh nationalists can be, they have never murdered anyone before, so we basically don't know. We don't know why the hand was left there. If there is a pattern to murders where the hand has been found before it would be that none have occurred in the UK, and the victims had some prominence."

"Ali thought that sometimes people are just 'disappeared', or if the body remains the presence of the hand is just like a calling card – it is a strange form of advertising."

"We have had similar theories proposed in our discussions. However, the murder in Colwyn Bay seems to have been unrelated to any pattern. There were two men involved and they probably spoke Arabic to each other, and spoke with thick accents when talking to anyone else. We wondered if they were trying to make it look like this was a killing by some Middle-East group, because we now believe at least one of the killers is home-grown. They left a couple of loose ends in Colwyn Bay and have been working to clean these up." Georgina stopped and wondered if she should continue. Ella waited – she could see Georgina was making a decision.

Georgina continued, "Of course, anything else I tell you is in strict confidence. If you were British I could threaten you with the Official Secrets Act, but I doubt that would impress you."

"I have no intention of telling anyone about the nature of this conversation, and I would probably be more impressed if you threatened to tie me to the whipping post," Ella replied.

Georgina smiled and continued, "We have a team in Colwyn Bay at the moment – that's the current operation I mentioned earlier. We hope to apprehend one of the killers, but he's very clever and has so far eluded us. We are working with the local police too. We don't know who he is though. If we catch him I hope he will lead us to his accomplice. I promise to let you know what happens and will let you know who these people are."

She thought that was enough information for the moment. There was no point in giving all the details and mentioning her suspicions about one of her staff. That was an internal matter and she hoped it stayed that way.

Lunch arrived. Jack brought a heaped tray of food and the three of them sat around the small table enjoying their meal.

If Ella thought she had not been told the whole story she didn't pursue it. If Georgina thought Ella was withholding information she decided not to mention it either. This was a preliminary meeting – they'd find out later if they could trust each other. They talked shop – if they weren't in exactly the same business they were in parallel organizations. Maybe they could help each other sometime in the future.

The meeting ended. Ella invited Georgina to lunch next time she was in Paris. Georgina and Jack shook hands with Ella, apologized for having so short a meeting, and left her in the alcove. Jack was about to move the "No Entry" sign, but Ella said she would replace it when she left. She sat, sipped her water, and wondered about the meeting and her next steps.

Her cell phone rang.

26

"Stefan, what can I do for you?" Ella answered her phone.

"Did I catch you at the meeting?"

"No."

"That's good because I think this is something we need to deal with, and we need to act quickly. It seems Ali has come through for us. I had a call from him about ten minutes ago, which in itself was strange – I thought he was going to communicate with us through Mustafa. It seems he asked the person whom he thought had Kamal killed how he did it and who he employed. He said that was last week. Ali implied it took a couple of days for him to get the whole story, but when he did he found out it was someone already known to him – someone he's done business with before."

"Known to whom?"

"To Ali. So, Ali sets up a meeting with this man in Madrid, and they meet yesterday evening. Ali makes up some story about a new deal he has in mind, but also tells him he has been having problems with a rival business group. He doesn't say anything else. They part and plan to meet again in a month or two. Before he goes he tells Ali he was planning to spend a few more days in Spain before heading to Munich. Ali has the man followed and he is staying at an inconspicuous hotel near the airport. Ali stays in town too and gets a phone call later that evening from the man saying if Ali is interested he knows of someone who can help with business problems. Are you following me so far?"

"Yes."

"Ali says he's interested and will discuss it when they next meet. The man says he could meet in the morning before his flight, but Ali declines – says he already has a commitment. But, Ali still has a tail on him and the next morning, this morning in fact, the man checks out of his hotel, goes to the airport and jumps on a plane, not to Munich, but to Gatwick. Ali is now stuck. His man cannot follow our guy on the plane. His man can buy a plane ticket, but when he gets to London he's likely to be arrested. I am not sure why – but I can guess. So, we get called."

"And what do we do?" asked Ella.

"We meet the plane at Gatwick."

"When?" asked Ella, gathering her bag and standing.

"It's a direct easyJet flight from Madrid. It lands in exactly sixty-seven minutes. You'd better get moving."

"How do I get there?" she walked into the main restaurant and headed for the stairs.

"You are booked on the Gatwick Express out of Victoria. It's a thirty minute journey and it leaves in thirty-five minutes."

"I'll never make it on The Tube – one too many changes."

"I agree. There'll be one of our cabs waiting for you at the top of Whitehall – we were lucky. We had one in the area."

Ella took the steps two at a time and found herself back outside in the bustle of midday London. She turned left and said, "I'll need help. Why don't you get whoever is covering me to make contact with me?"

"I have done. I wanted to check with you too. Get to that cab."

Ella looked at her watch. It was going to be tight. There were three sets of traffic lights between her and Whitehall. The first was green and she crossed in the middle of the gaggle of tourists, but the second and third were against her. She hurried by being on the flank of the gaggles, but by the time she reached the black cab in Whitehall there were just a little over twenty-five minutes left. The cab driver was standing outside his cab on the sidewalk holding up a small SIGNAK sign. Ella showed her ID – he showed her his. The driver opened the rear door for her. She was about to get in, but paused and stepped back in surprise. There were already two other people in the cab – a man and a woman. They leaned towards her and showed their ID's. Ella almost broke protocol by sitting in the cab, but her training took over. She accepted the cards, stepped back for a second so the driver and both the other occupants were in her line of sight. Both ID's checked out. She handed her ID to the other occupants. They examined it and returned it to Ella who slipped into the cab. The driver closed the door and started towards Victoria.

Trafalgar Square to Victoria is a journey which could be a pleasant forty-five minutes walk, taking in the sights and passing the centers of power in the British establishment. It could take fifteen to sixty minutes by car or taxi, or thirty to seventy minutes by bus. Ella had once lived in London and could have made the trip in twenty-two minutes by bicycle, which was the time it took the three of them to reach Victoria Train Station, emerge from the cab and stride to the waiting Gatwick Express. They had been booked first class seats, to assure some privacy, and thirty seconds after taking them the train began its southward race towards Gatwick Airport.

Ella had been pleased the man she had spotted before entering St. Martins had been following/watching her. His name was George and he'd been with SIGNAK for six months. This was his first field assignment and he had been working with Marie. Marie, like George was totally inconspicuous. She was in her mid-thirties, or it could have been mid-forties, had light brown hair, wore slightly tinted glasses, and like most Londoners around her wore no hat. Her clothing was dark, covering most of her pale skin. She was average height, and average in nearly everything. She wouldn't stand out anywhere in a northern European country. She'd been teamed with George, who had been picked to be the slightly more obvious follower – he told Ella he would not usually have chosen to carry his shoulder bag, but by focusing on him it was hoped that anyone would fail to spot the other tail. In this case, Ella admitted, it had worked. She congratulated them on a job well-done. They also assured her that they noticed no one else who had been tailing Ella. But now, what they had considered just a training mission, had changed.

The train rattled through Clapham Junction and picked up speed.

Their three cell-phones beeped almost simultaneously. They looked at their screens and each opened emails containing three photographs, taken at long range, of the man they were after. They were not great photographs – one was a little blurred and the other two were of low resolution, but the man they were looking at, although they didn't know his name, was Jones.

183

Ella called Stefan, "Do you have a team near Gatwick."

"No," he replied. "You will get there before any of them. The nearest is about an hour away. You got the photos?"

"Yes. Do we know who he is?"

"No. He doesn't come up on any of our usual screens. We haven't a clue who he is, although Ali said he spoke good Arabic. Not sure if that helps or not. So, the three of you are on your own for a while. Keep in touch … and look after yourself, Ella. Be careful."

"Thank you. I will." She hung up.

Ella said to the others, "We can expect no backup at the airport. This is what I suggest. He's coming in from Spain and will land at the south terminal, but he'll have to go through passport and customs. We can't get to the gate, so we are stuck with waiting for him on this side. We need to be close to the exit from customs, so I suggest George, you make a SIGNAK sign and hold it in front of you as if you were a driver looking for the correct customer. That way you can get close to the barrier and it's unlikely anyone not expecting a ride will look at you. Let's look at these photos again."

They each pulled up the photos of Jones on their cell phones.

Ella commented, "In all these photos his head is a little bent and it looks like he's half-looking the other way. He has a hat on with the peak low in one of the photos. I think he is used to avoiding surveillance – it's probably second nature to him. When he comes out from customs he is going to be going the same pace as those around him. He will probably come out with a lot of people around him, and he is likely to stay away from the barrier side and keep as many people between him and any observers. What do you think?"

George said, "Sounds reasonable. Do we know what he was wearing when he got on the plane in Madrid? That might help."

"Good point. I'll ask. Marie, any suggestions?"

"That could be useful, but if he was wearing a bright red sweater in Madrid you could almost guarantee he won't be wearing that when he gets through customs. We have to concentrate on looking for the face, not the clothes."

184

Ella texted Stefan. The reply, a minute later said simply, 'green jacket'.

Ella smiled and said, "For what it's worth he was wearing a green jacket, so it's reasonable to assume it's no longer green, or is just reversible. We need to bear that in mind." She continued, "There are multiple ways in and out of the airport. He may have a car there, he can catch a train, a bus, or he could fly on to some other destination. I don't think we can cover all of those. One of us will rent a car, and it looks like it will be me because I am not dressed for anonymity like you two. I will rent it at the south terminal so if he has a car there I should be positioned to follow him. If he takes a bus, or the train, then you two will have to follow him and I will do my best to keep up and support you. Any questions, suggestions?"

Both George and Marie shook their heads and said, "No." This was one of those situations when planning was of limited benefit. The only preparation was to be ready for anything.

They spent the last five minutes of the journey in silence. The train came to stop and they were among the first onto the platform. They walked into the terminal trying not to give the appearance of haste. Ella left the other two and headed for Hertz car rental.

27

Jones was sitting in the plane wondering if he shouldn't have gone to Madrid and just stayed at home and monitored the events in Colwyn Bay. He'd come back from Spain with the promise of more lucrative work from both his contacts, but they were just promises. Ali had come through in the past – he'd always seemed to be straightforward and focused. This time it seemed he had begun to enquire about the other services Jones could provide, but at the last moment he seemed to withdraw his interest and commitment. That wasn't unusual, but Ali had never been indecisive before – he always knew what he wanted and had gone for it. This time the connection between them seemed a little strange, and he wondered what that was about. Jones considered he had only survived in his line of work because of his paranoia, and he questioned if this time he hadn't turned up the paranoia dial a little too much – maybe he was worrying unnecessarily.

It didn't help that Gareth was somewhere in North Wales sorting out loose ends. Jones needed to get back to his base as quickly as he could. He'd always lived with the possibility that he might have to get out of town in a hurry, but he wasn't quite ready for that. He'd been distracted over the last week or so and his escape plan was out of date. He'd need at least three hours to get that ready, just in case the news from North Wales was not good.

The row in front of him stood and moved into the aisle. Jones stood and followed the line out of the plane. He matched his pace to his fellow passengers walking the long corridors of Gatwick to passport control. He held up his British passport, it was inspected briefly, and he was waved through and into the customs hall. He was not stopped when he walked through the 'Nothing to Declare' aisle. He slowed his pace a little to allow a family group to pass him then he walked through the left side of the double glass doors and into the terminal. His plan didn't quite work – one of the family was a little delayed and the rest slowed, so he ended up coming out by himself. He half-looked away, allowed the family to catch up and made his way across the main part of the terminal.

He'd arrived in the south terminal but had left his car in the north terminal. To Jones it was a simple precaution. Ten seconds after he stepped onto the shuttle to the north terminal the doors closed. He held onto a grab-bar and looked around the occupants of the rail car. He didn't recognize anyone who had been on the same flight, and he noticed no one glancing away when he looked in their direction. So far, so good.

The train came to a stop. Jones stepped onto the platform and headed for an elevator. He reached it just as the door was opening. He stepped inside and pushed the button to go down a floor, the elevator doors began to close, but the tired father of a family of four ran up and pushed against the door closure; the door stopped and retracted. The rest of the family – two toddlers and a harried wife, entered the elevator, the doors closed and the car descended to street level. Jones was the first out and he headed towards the parking garage. He stopped in front of a bank of three elevators, pushed the button turned around and waited. There were two men approaching the elevators. One seemed to be in his seventies and was pulling a wheeled carry-on size suitcase with a green "Thomson's Holidays" label. The other was in his early thirties and was carrying a leather shoulder bag.

A beep announced the arrival of the elevator car. Jones stepped in and pushed the button for the top floor, the sixth. The elder man pushed the button for the fourth floor, the younger man also pushed the top floor button. The door closed and the elevator started to rise. It stopped at the fourth floor to let the one man off, no one else got on and the elevator continued to the top floor. Jones exited first and turned to his left, the younger man turned to the right and walked away from Jones. Jones stopped and watched the back of the retreating man. He returned to the elevator and pushed the call button. The door was about to close when a woman rushed up and managed to get in the car with Jones. The woman looked at her watch and pushed the ground floor button. The door closed. She looked at her watch again and impatiently pushed the ground floor button. Jones looked at her briefly, but made no eye contact. She was in her mid-thirties, and was wearing dowdy clothing and flat shoes. She looked like what Jones imagined a school teacher would look like. Jones pushed the button for the third floor. He left the elevator as the woman leaned forward and pushed the 'close door' button and looked at her watch one more time. He walked indirectly to his car, making sure there was no one following him.

He felt he had arrived back in London without being noticed. He allowed himself a small smile, started his black Mini and headed for the exit.

28

"Where are you?" asked George.

"Second floor. Where now?" Marie replied into her cell phone.

"I'm on my way outside. There's only one exit and he'll have to go through that. Let's hope we can identify him then. I think he's driving a black car, but I was too far away to see what make."

"We need to keep back. He'll be onto us if he sees us again."

"I know. Ella, are you there?"

"Yes, I'm outside. I can see the exit from the car park. It looks like there's a pay booth and a barrier, so we have to assume he'll go through that. I'm about fifty meters back and there is one other vehicle between me and the exit. I am parked on a double-yellow line, so I can't stay here too long. I've got a white Opel Insignia. Try and get to me ASAP. If I see him I'll have to take off."

Ella scanned the cars exiting the car park. It wasn't easy. She only got a glimpse of most faces as drivers looked to their right before taking the compulsory left turn away from the car park. It didn't really help to know that Jones might be driving a black car, since it was the most common car color in Britain, and it seemed to her to be almost the exclusive choice of car park users at Gatwick.

Ella was distracted for a second as George, then Marie, slipped in to the rear seats of her rental car. She looked up to see a black MINI move to the edge of the street, then pause to let a vehicle pass before it pulled out of the car park. This time she had a better look – it was Jones. Ella pulled away from the curb and followed.

It was not easy. Keeping at least one vehicle between her car and Jones would have been easier on a freeway, but with the multiple roundabouts and traffic lights around Gatwick Ella had difficulty both keeping up, and avoiding catching up, without being noticed. Fortunately, as soon as Jones cleared the airport he headed north on the M23 motorway towards the middle of

London. At least it wasn't raining and she thought she had about an hour of good daylight ahead – she hoped that would be enough.

George called for backup from SIGNAK and was told help was about ten minutes away. Ella gave him the rental information receipt so he could let SIGNAK know the license plate number of her car, and the license plate number of Jones's. Now, all they could do was follow.

Jones continued north along the M23, crossed over the busy M25 ring road around London, and slowed when the motorway ended and became the A23 – still heading towards central London. They were north of Croydon, approaching Thornton Heath before George's phone rang.

"They're behind us," he said, glancing at his watch. "That took just over twenty minutes."

Ella looked in her mirror at a black car with a driver and a passenger. The passenger waved briefly. At the next opportunity Ella slowed, allowed the following car to pass, and then accelerated to catch up, but stayed further back trying to keep at least five vehicles between her and the SIGNAK car.

They continued past Crystal Palace Park until the A205 when Jones took a right towards Forest Hill, crossed the railway bridge and took another right onto a quieter residential street.

The SIGNAK car pulled back to allow Ella to close on Jones. Jones slowed and pulled to a stop towards the end of a nondescript road outside a Victorian era row house. Ella passed him, took the next left and stopped to allow George out of the car. George ran back to the end of the street in time to see Jones close a front door behind him. Ella drove around the block and parked fifty yards from Jones's vehicle and house. George walked around the block and joined Marie and Ella in the car.

"Now what?" asked Marie.

"I call a friend in the security services and let them take it from here. We watch him until someone tells us not to. We have basically no jurisdiction here, so we are limited in what we can do," replied Ella.

"What if he doesn't stay put until help arrives?"

"Then we follow him again, but let's see if we can make it a little easier. I don't have a tracker, but our other car might. George, give them a call and find out."

George called the SIGNAK car which had parked on a parallel street and found they had a tracker.

"Tell them we'll all wait a half hour then it will be dark enough for them to change places with us here. They can get some food in the meantime. When they take over they can put the tracker on his car, and remind them to switch their dome lights off."

George relayed the message and reported that they had already switched off their dome lights and said they offered a couple of spare blankets since it didn't look like the day was going to get any warmer.

"Tell them we'll accept the blankets but we hope it won't come to that. We expect to be relieved before much longer."

George passed on the message.

After the tension of following the car it was an anticlimax to just sit and wait quietly, but that was all they could do. Thirty minutes later the inside of the car was already feeling colder than was comfortable. Then the SIGNAK car called and said they would swap places in five minutes. Ella started the car, waited until the SIGNAK car was behind them and pulled out turned left and circled the block, eventually finding a parking space a hundred yards behind the SIGNAK vehicle. George got out of Ella's car and walked forward to talk to his colleagues in the other vehicle. He was back in five minutes with an armful of blankets.

"They're used to this, so I took what they offered. They will attach a tracker and said there was a pub offering warmth and food about a mile away. I thanked them and said we should be back in about 45 minutes."

They found the last space in the pub's parking lot. George and Marie went into the pub and ordered while Ella stayed in the car and made a call. It was answered immediately.

"Georgina Southport," was the terse reply.

"It's Ella – we had lunch together today."

"Oh, yes." The voice softened a little. "How can I help you?"

"After lunch today I received a call telling me that one of the men who may be responsible for my brother's murder, and maybe the killing in Colwyn Bay, was on his way to Gatwick from Spain."

"Who gave you that information?"

"It came via a colleague in France. He received it from Ali, the man I talked to in Turkey."

"So, it's reliable?"

"Maybe. I don't really know, but the point is we followed him from Gatwick to a house in south London. We are watching the house now and wondered what to do next. We have no jurisdiction here. All we can do is wait, watch, and follow if he moves. I'd like some help."

There was a pause before Georgina replied.

"That could be a problem. If I were in town I could help, but I am in a car on its way to Colwyn Bay – I have to help deal with what is going on up there and I don't know how long it will take. Most of my team is up there too, so they can't help. I hope we are all back in London tomorrow."

"Could you ask the local police here to see if they could help?" asked Ella,

"That could be a little difficult, because it's expensive in terms of personnel and money. If I request surveillance it has to be organized at a level where I know questions would be asked about the reliability of the sources, and I would have to be there to convince them."

"So, what should I do?"

"Can you maintain surveillance until tomorrow?"

"I don't know. I don't really like that prospect. Tomorrow morning or afternoon?"

"Probably afternoon, but I'll try to make it sooner if I can."

This time Ella hesitated. "I suppose that's the best we can do. We'll hang on and watch and let you know if things change. OK?"

"Well, yes. I realize it's not ideal, but I am limited with what I can do. Let me know if things change."

She hung up.

Ella slumped in her seat. This was supposed to be a day trip to London and she had hoped to be back in Paris by now. She didn't want to be playing MI5, or was it MI6? What had happened to the much vaunted British security services? She got out of the car and pushed the door a little harder than she needed to, attracting a startled glance from a couple leaving the pub. She calmed herself, nodded apologetically at the couple and joined the other two inside.

They took it remarkably well. Ella wasn't sure if that is because she was there – the head of the organization they worked for, or they were being paid overtime, or they liked the prospect of sharing a night in a small unheated car. Whatever it was she knew she would welcome the company.

Three plates of fish and chips arrived and they tucked in to their meal. George was about to order another beer when Marie pointed out that it might not be the best choice if he was going to spend the next twelve hours stuck in a car with them.

They discussed what to do and wondered how long the other SIGNAK car would be available. George walked outside and called them. He came back with the information that they could spend another hour in the pub, which would only take them to 9:00 pm, but after that their colleagues in the SIGNAK car had another responsibility and they were on their own. George also reported it was starting to drizzle. The only good thing he had to report was the tracking device had an alarm which would let them know if the subject's car started moving. Unfortunately, they couldn't be sure the subject would use his car so they had to cover all options if he decided to leave his house.

Ella made the brave suggestion that she could take them to a Tube station and they could wend their way back to St. Pancras railway station, find a hotel for the night, and be back in Paris for lunch the next day. George and Marie would have nothing of it. They insisted on staying. However, waiting another hour in the pub on a Friday night without a drink just wouldn't be right so they opted to challenge their bladders and worry about that when the time came.

195

At 8:50 they had one last trip to the pub toilets, walked through the drizzle to Ella's car and drove back to their parking place watching Jones's house. George retrieved the tracking monitor from the SIGNAK car and they settled down as best they could for the night. They agreed to change seats every two hours. It was the responsibility of whoever was sitting behind the steering wheel to keep the windshield clear of condensation and watch the house. The other two would try to sleep in the remaining seats. They flipped coins and George ended up with the first shift, Marie the second and Ella the third.

Ella called Stefan to keep him aware of the situation and assured him all was well.

Initially, none of them could sleep and they left the radio on, but boredom soon settled in. It had been a long day for all of them, but finding a comfortable position to sleep, or just rest, was difficult. Ella realized she must have dozed off because she awoke, startled, at 11:00 when George announced his shift was over and he needed to relieve himself of the burden of the beers, and was glad he hadn't ordered that third one. He stepped out of the car into the persistent drizzle, looked along the street, which by then was completely deserted, and found an appropriate space between a couple of parked vans. Without any other choice, and with the same problem, Ella and Marie decided to follow his example.

The night dragged on.

It was midnight on Marie's shift. Ella occupied the passenger seat and George had wedged himself into a corner of the back seat behind the driver, but none of them could sleep – they were all too cold. Ella found herself shivering uncontrollably and realized that with eight hours of darkness in front of them they were only going to find it harder to function if they had to follow Jones. They discussed this briefly and decided to run the car for ten minutes every hour. They understood the risk of the noise of the car starting and idling, but they couldn't see an alternative. There was still a light on in Jones's house.

"Maybe he'll turn it off when he goes to sleep or decides to leave. What do you think?" George asked.

The other two agreed if the light went off they would immediately stop the car engine.

They settled back to silence and the cold.

29

Once again John found himself landing at London's Heathrow airport. This time it was at 11 am on Delta flight 4349 operated by Virgin Atlantic from Seattle. Or was it a Virgin Flight operated by Delta? He really didn't care. He hadn't wanted to be here two weeks ago, or was it three?

And now he was back again.

He was feeling distinctly sorry for himself. The only difference was this time he had company and was doing his best to hide his disgruntlement. Once again he went through passport control and customs and he and Ann made their way to The Tube, London's subway. They presented their Oyster Cards at the barrier, and remembering to touch the pads with the cards this time, not just royally wave them, found seats to Euston Station where they arrived with plenty of time to catch the 14:10 to Colwyn Bay. Unfortunately, they were booked on the 15:10. They resigned themselves to the whims of the travel gods – if you leave yourself plenty of time you won't need it; if you don't leave yourself plenty of time you will miss the train/plane/bus.

Overriding his discomfort, and the taste of the tea he was sipping in the station restaurant, was his concern about Auntie Olly's death. He'd talked it over with Ann, but what was there to talk over? They didn't know what had happened. They could only speculate based on the limited information they received when John talked to the police in North Wales the day before they left. After a while they found themselves repeating their thoughts and conversations. This didn't give them any comfort and both were feeling ragged from the little sleep they'd managed on the flight from Seattle.

John had a niggling suspicion that the police were holding something back from him. He hoped he'd find out quickly enough when they got to Colwyn Bay.

They boarded the train, ten minutes before it left, and slumped down in their seats, but neither could sleep. They had to change trains in Chester, and not wanting to miss their connection they felt it would be too risky to try to nod off before then. So, they did what they could to amuse and keep themselves awake as they headed north into the deepening gloom of dusk.

It was dark and windy, with the threat of rain in the air, when they reached Colwyn Bay and took a Hales Taxi from the station to Auntie Olly's small house.

Ann held the cell phone, using it as a flashlight, while John opened the lockbox and retrieved the key to Auntie Olly's front door.

Sidestepping the few items of mail they found on the inside doormat John and Ann carried their luggage over the threshold and closed the door behind them. They paused in the hallway to take in the silence of the house. John had noticed this when he'd last visited the house and it stopped him this time too. He sighed, opened the door to his left into the sitting room and put his and Ann's bags on the sofa. He turned up the heat on the thermostat and walked to the kitchen where he put on the kettle for a cup of tea. Neither he nor Ann removed their coats – it would take another hour or two before they could comfortably do that. It wouldn't take as long for the hot water to be ready for a bath, or an adventurous shower, and the electric blanket would make the bed quite toasty in less than thirty minutes.

They both sat in the hard plastic kitchen chairs and found themselves relaxing. It was going to be difficult to stay awake and go to bed at a normal time. John wondered if he should contact the police now or in the morning. He favored the morning, after at least some sleep. The kettle boiled, he added the hot water to the tea bags in the pot and thought he should at least try to deal with Auntie Olly's mail. He walked back to the front door and stooped to pick up the mail. That was when he noticed something a little strange.

He and Ann had made the effort to not tread on the mail when they came in, but just at the edge of two pieces of mail there was the faint, but distinct, outline of a footprint. Someone must have been in the house since he last visited. Maybe it was the police? He looked at the postmarks on the envelopes and worked out that they had been posted locally on the previous Thursday. This meant they should have been delivered on the Friday or Saturday. Another clean envelope lay over both the marked ones, and this had a postmark from the Saturday, so it was probably delivered on Monday – the day Auntie Olly died. Even if it had been delivered the next day he doubted the police would have been in the house before the mail arrived, and he thought they would have told him. Perhaps it was jet lag – maybe they had, but he reminded himself to ask about this, and the dozen other questions he had in mind when he spoke with them. In the meantime he needed that cup of tea. He walked back to the kitchen touching the hallway radiator as he passed and noticed the first stirring of warmth as it came alive.

Ann was opening drawers and cupboards, as John had done less than three weeks earlier, and making a mental note of their contents. She opened the freezer.

"Have you seen all these frozen meals?" she asked.

"Yes. I've even tried some of them. They are not for the faint of heart." John replied and glanced into the freezer. It wasn't quite how he had left it. "Did you just open this?" he asked.

"Yes."

"That's odd. When I was here there wasn't much to do, so after I had thrown some of the older meals out, and rearranged the rest, I separated the remainder into fish, meat and others. They seem a little mixed up now."

"They are." Ann reached in and sorted the boxes of food into some sort of order. "You don't think you were jet-lagged when you did it?"

"No, I don't think so – not then. My thinking is certainly like molasses now." John poured the tea. "Did you find any digestive biscuits in your searches? They used to be in a tin down there." John pointed at a cupboard near Ann's feet. She reached down and brought out the ancient "Quality Street" chocolate tin box, opened it and offered John two of his favorite cookies.

Ann smiled and said. "Even jet-lagged I remembered that these cookies always come in pairs."

201

"We'll make you into a Brit yet." John returned the smile and carefully dunked a McVities Digestive biscuit in his tea. "These are the reason the sun never set on the British Empire," he added.

"I thought it was because God couldn't trust an Englishman in the dark."

"Oh ye of no faith," said John, closed his eyes, and savored the texture and flavor of the dunked cookie.

"You seem to be enjoying that cookie far too much."

"Does it show?"

"Yes."

"Oh, dear. Please don't let anyone in Wales know. By the way, it's a biscuit here, not a cookie. In private you can call it a cookie, but in public it's a no-no."

"But if I call it a biscuit, in my best American accent, won't they think I am trying too hard to fit in?" asked Ann.

"Good point. It's probably better for you to never say anything in public."

"At the moment that seems like a good idea since my brain can rest, but getting back to where we are now – we need to stay awake for another couple of hours. Any suggestions?"

"Well, I'm going to go through this mail." John indicated the small pile in front of him. "Oh, and yes, I forgot to mention it. It looks like someone has been in the house over the weekend."

"What makes you think that?" Ann asked.

John explained his conclusions and showed her the foot marks on the mail.

"Are you sure about that?" Ann asked again. "That's pretty smart deducing from someone as sleep deprived as you."

"I am pretty sure. I don't know why I thought it out, but I did. And, then there's the freezer. Things weren't quite like I left them. I wonder if someone came in the house and had a look around."

"Why would anyone want to do that?"

"I don't know."

"That's creepy. You don't think there's anyone here now do you?"

"I don't think so, but I hadn't thought about it. We should have a look around."

"Let's do it together." Ann suggested.

"Great idea."

In the sixty seconds it took them to check the whole house they found nothing suspicious. John put the chain across the front door. He couldn't find the key to the back door, but noted it was locked. He turned on the electric blanket. They retreated to the kitchen – the warmest room, but still not warm enough to make them shed their coats. They sat again in the plastic chairs. John topped up the tea in their mugs and reached for another digestive biscuit.

"It felt strange being here last time when she wasn't here and I was. It feels even stranger this time when I know she isn't coming back."

"Are you going to miss her?" Ann asked.

"Well, yes, but I was never that close to her, and I suppose her time was getting close. Even if her body was carrying on her brain was checking out. She wouldn't have wanted to linger, but she also wouldn't want to be poisoned – if that's what happened. I just don't know." John shook his head.

Ann reached out to hold his hand and said, "Maybe we'll get some answers tomorrow. I don't think either of us is in a fit state to talk to the police this evening. Why don't we go to the supermarket and buy some food. We'll need it for breakfast – unless you want to eat one of the frozen meals."

"You mean go back out there in the snow and sleet?"

"Yes, or eat freezer-burnt salty Salisbury steak for breakfast."

"Let's go."

They yawned, stood, which seemed to be taking more effort each time, and headed out of the house. They walked down the short pathway to the gate and turned left towards Morrison's supermarket.

Gareth had seen them arrive and now he watched as they walked past his car. He had a decision to make – should he follow them, or should he use the key he had to the back door and wait for them inside? He was parked fifty yards from the front gate in a road of houses built seventy years ago when private ownership of a vehicle in this neighborhood would have been unheard of. Now there were cars parked on both sides with a corridor down the middle only wide enough for one vehicle. He decided he was going to go for the house. He was about to step out of his car when a vehicle approached from the opposite direction. It was a police car and it stopped in the middle of the road blocking any potential traffic. A uniformed policeman got out of the car, walked up the path and knocked on the door. There was no reply. He knocked again with the same result. He walked back to the car and leaned in, talking to another occupant whom Gareth could not see because of the reflection of the sodium street lights off the windshield. The conversation ended, but instead of the policeman getting back inside the car he walked down the middle of the road towards Gareth. Gareth braced himself and reached inside his coat with one hand and placed his other on the door handle. The policeman walked passed a large, dilapidated Ford Transit van decorated with the fading logo of 'Williams and Son Construction of Pensarn'. Gareth moved his weight forward, but relaxed a little when the policeman abruptly turned to his right and rapped his knuckles on the back door of the van. He was two car lengths away. The back door of the van opened six inches. The policeman held a brief conversation with whoever was inside. The door closed, the policeman returned to his vehicle. Gareth sank as low as he could as the police car passed him and headed away.

That was a little too close. So, they were watching the house and presumably the police wanted to talk to Beaton. The watchers in the van may have told the police when Beaton and the woman arrived. They might want to speak to Beaton, but the setup suggested that they were more interested in something or someone else. That someone else might be Gareth. But the police hadn't talked to Beaton yet.

Gareth had to get to him first.

30

Assistant Chief Constable Clive Owen was not a happy man. He hadn't been happy for the last two days. Now he was getting a little pissed off and doing his best not to show it. The plan, which he'd reluctantly agreed to, had been for the watchers in the van to let the police know when the Beatons arrived at the house. That part of the plan had worked, but he, Detective Inspector Vince Jared who was the lead on Olwen Lewis's poisoning, and his driver Police Constable John Hughes arrived at the house only to find the Beatons had left a few minutes earlier. Why and where they were going wasn't known. Apparently, the watchers were more interested in catching, or trying to catch, someone they thought might be, but they weren't quite sure, could, well, may be an international terrorist. Didn't they think it would have been more useful if one of them had stayed in the van and the other had followed the Beatons? At least the Beatons hadn't taken their luggage, so they would be coming back, although even that was not a hundred percent guaranteed. But where had they gone? Where do most people who have been traveling all day across eight time zones and end up in North Wales in winter go? To bed, if they had any sense, and get some sleep – they would be needing it. Go for a walk? Well, maybe, so they could stay awake or enjoy the ambience of Colwyn Bay by sodium street lights in the tail end of winter? Go shopping? Most shops were already closed and the last to close, the supermarkets, had less than half an hour before they shut their doors too. Part of him wondered if he should just sit in the car, wrap up in a blanket and munch on an order of fish and chips while waiting for them to come back, but there was something going on here which was disturbing him. It was probably only his copper's instinct, but the people from London had seemed a little more tense than when he had dealings with their kind before. He knew he wasn't being told everything, for which he thought he might be grateful, but he wondered if he had been told enough. Then he thought again about fish and chips and how this had all started in his patch of Wales.

"Fish and chips," he said aloud.

"Sir?" asked Constable Hughes, and Detective Inspector Jared looked at the Assistant Chief quizzically.

Clive Owen hadn't considered that Hughes and Jared were not aware of the potential link between the fire in the fish and chip shop and the death of Olwen Lewis – he'd only found out himself today, and now was not the time to discuss it with them.

Owen covered his error and said, "Yes, fish and chips. Let's stop the car and think this one out. I was thinking of places where the Beatons could go, and what would be open at this time of night, and fish and chip shops came to mind, as well as supermarkets. Any other suggestions?"

"Well, sir, there's always the pubs." Constable Hughes said as he pulled the car to the side of the road and kept the engine running.

"I don't think it would be the pubs. What do you think, Jared?"

"I agree, sir. It wouldn't be the pubs. Pubs here are for locals. I also don't think it would be fish and chips. I went to Las Vegas last year, sir, and the last thing I wanted after flying back from there would have been fish and chips. On the other hand maybe they need some essentials for breakfast."

"So, do we agree they may have headed towards the supermarket then?"

"Yes."

"Yes."

"Morrison's is closest, don't you think? Let's head over there. Maybe we'll see them on the way."

Constable Hughes put the car into gear and headed towards Morrison's supermarket.

Chief Constable Clive Owen thought a little more explanation was necessary. It wasn't usual for police to pursue relatives of murder victims around Colwyn Bay, when it was most likely they would return to the house where they were supposed to be.

"I've been meeting with folks from the intelligence services last night, and today," he said, "and they are anxious for us to talk to the Beatons about the fish and chip shop murder. It's possible they may have some information about that. It's also possible someone else wants to talk to them. It's also possible that person could be dangerous."

Jared said, a little cynically, "Lots of possibilities, sir? Any probabilities? I wondered what the fuss was about. I mean it's not usual for you to come with us when we interview victims' relatives. And I am not quite sure who or why they are watching the Olwen Lewis house. So, we're not just meeting the Beatons and discussing her death?"

"That is correct. I'm sorry to say the intelligence services want my police to stay in the dark about this. I am sure they are not telling me everything either."

"It feels like they don't trust us, sir."

"I agree, but we have no alternative. People higher than us have been told to cooperate by the Home Office."

"Sir, if I am investigating the murder of Olwen Lewis and you, or they, have something I haven't been told then what am I supposed to think?" Jared sounded aggrieved.

"You can join me in feeling a little pissed off too. As I said, I only found out myself today, but basically they think the same person may be responsible for the fish and chip shop and the Olwen Lewis murders."

"Do they have any theory about why these murders would be connected?"

"They do."

"And is anyone going to tell me about it?" Jared asked his voice rising.

"After we've talked to the Beatons, Jared. For the time being the Beatons don't need to know there is any link. You just tell them that we have no leads on that so far."

"Is that fair to the Beatons?"

"Probably not, but it will have to do for the time being. After all it's early stages in the investigation. However, it's possible the Beatons will work it out for themselves."

Constable Hughes, who had not taken part in the conversation said, "Sirs, we are almost there. Which side are we going to park?"

"What side do you suggest?" asked Owen.

"The upper parking lot. It's better lit," replied Hughes.

Morrison's supermarket in Colwyn Bay is one of the "anchor" stores in the Bayview Shopping Centre. The Centre doesn't have a view of any bay, unless you stand on top of its roof when the bay, which gives Colwyn Bay its name, can be admired over the four or six lanes of the A55, and the London to Holyhead railway. However, you can tell you are near the sea by the evidence of the presence of lots of seagulls, which is one reason why you wouldn't want to stand on top of the roof of the Bayview Shopping Centre. The Shopping Centre also sits above a dismal, cavernous parking complex with concrete pillars big enough to grab the bumpers and paintwork on any size of car. If there was space, and there was at this time of day, most customers preferred the upper lot.

Gareth had also chosen to park in the upper lot. He had watched the Beatons enter the centre and had barely turned off his lights and engine when the police car pulled into a space outside Poundworld marked 'Parents with children only'. There were less than twenty cars in a lot which could hold eighty, and no vehicle between him and the police car which was idling less than fifty feet away.

He watched two men get out of the car and walk towards the entrance to the shopping centre. Both were about six feet tall. One was wearing the uniform of a senior police officer and the other wore jeans and a grey sport jacket. A third, uniformed policeman, the driver, turned off the engine and stepped out of the car, reached back for his hat, put it on his head, yawned and rested his back against the car.

Gareth got out of his car, pulled up the hood of his parka, bent his head, and shuffled towards the entrance to the centre giving an excellent impression of the gait of a disaffected teenager. The automatic doors to the centre opened and the policeman by the car ignored him.

Gareth increased his pace and closed the gap to Owen and Jared. By the time they reached the outside of Morrison's he was less than thirty feet away. The centre was almost empty – there were a handful of people leaving the shops, and further down the main concourse he could see someone in a green uniform pushing a wide broom across the floor.

Owen and Jared stopped outside the broad entrance to Morrison's. Gareth slowed and stopped behind them and looked intently in the window of Bevan's hardware store. Jared glanced over his shoulder at him briefly.

In the reflection of the window Gareth could see both men decide to stay together and walk into Morrison's. Gareth thought this was probably a logical decision since the store was shutting down. Only one checkout was open, customer service was unoccupied and the bare shelves of the produce section, near the entrance, were waiting to be replenished by the night crew. Owen and Jared concluded it should be easy to find the Beatons. It also made it easier for Gareth. He picked up a shopping basket and pushed through the turnstile into the supermarket.

John and Ann were having trouble with decision making. Should they buy the Weetabix or the Muesli? If they bought both would they have too much food left? In the end they threw caution to the wind, chose both and added a jar of lime marmalade, a small sliced loaf, a dozen eggs and then headed for the milk section.

They were mulling over the relative benefits of full-fat milk, reduced-fat milk, almond milk and soy milk when someone asked, "John Beaton? Dr. John Beaton? Ann Beaton?"

John and Ann looked up startled. For a brief moment John wondered why a former patient would be addressing him in a supermarket, near closing time, in Wales. Then he looked closer at the two men facing him and wondered for a little longer what he had done wrong. One was wearing a police uniform and the other a jacket and jeans. A third man was fifteen feet behind them bending over the butter section and putting a packet in his shopping basket.

The question was repeated by the man in uniform, "Dr. and Mrs. Beaton?"

"Yes," Ann and John replied simultaneously.

"I'm Assistant Chief Constable Clive Owen and this…"

He never finished his sentence. He registered the surprise on John's face as John watched Gareth, with a flesh colored surgical mask over his face, close the last ten feet, and he heard the sound of the shopping basket hit the floor. He half turned as Gareth's preferred weapon, the short oak baton hit him on the side of the head and he went down. Detective Jared had turned too. Gareth swung at Jared but missed his head and hit Jared's left shoulder. Jared reacted instinctively and aimed an uppercut with his right fist at Gareth's chin. But Gareth saw it coming and jerked his head back in time, but his mask slipped a little. Jared was no match for Gareth who recovered and hit him on the left side of his head. He fell instantly. Gareth looked down at both his victims and readjusted his mask. Owen was on his back with his eyes barely open, but not registering any comprehension, and Jared was lying on his side, unconscious and bleeding from his head wound. The whole attack had lasted less than five seconds.

John and Ann stood completely still and shocked by what they had just witnessed.

Gareth said, "You've seen what I can do. I'll do the same to both of you, and anyone else who gets in my way, unless you do exactly as I say. Understand?"

Both John and Ann nodded and said, "Yes."

"Put that basket on the floor and walk out of this supermarket. I will be right behind you. If you try to sound an alarm, call for help, or get anyone involved I will kill you and them too. Understand?"

"Yes."

"Start walking."

John and Ann started walking towards the supermarket exit. They had to walk through an idle till aisle. The single teller still working was serving probably the only shopper left in the store and ignored them. They turned right at the exit towards the car park. They were a hundred feet from the doors to the car park when they opened and Constable Hughes came running towards them with his police baton in his right hand. Automatically, the three of them moved to the side. Gareth moved behind and between them. Hughes ran past them focusing on reaching the supermarket.

"Get moving," whispered Gareth.

John and Ann continued towards the door with Gareth close behind.

"Hey, you! Stop. Police."

It was Constable Hughes. Gareth turned to face him. He took a step backwards and rapidly struck both John and Ann across the front of their thighs. He ignored their gasps of pain as they each clutched a leg, effectively immobilized, and he stepped forwards towards Constable Hughes.

With hindsight, the safest action for Hughes to have taken would have been to run away from Gareth as fast as he could, but that was not what he'd been trained to do. In some respects they were fairly matched. Both Gareth and Hughes were about the same height, weight and age, and both were right-handed and carrying batons. There the likeness ended. Gareth was used to wielding his baton to kill, Hughes hadn't used his in the last four years, but he was fast and today, when he needed to be, he was lucky. He saw John and Ann being hit and struck first. Gareth was a fraction of a second slow and reflexively blocked Hughes's baton with his left forearm. There was loud snap as Gareth's ulna broke but his momentum carried to his right arm. He swung and hit the unguarded left side of Hughes's head. Hughes crumpled to the ground unconscious. Gareth turned to John and Ann.

"Move it," he said and prodded both of them with the end of his baton. They limped ahead of him into the almost deserted parking lot and he directed them towards his car.

"You," he said, pointing at John. "You drive and no funny business." He moved his baton to his left hand and was in obvious pain as he gripped it. He reached into his pocket and handed the keys to John.

211

"We will sit in the back. Any funny stuff and she gets it. Understand?"

"Yes," John replied. It had been less than three minutes since they'd been worrying over milk selection in the supermarket. He'd been terrified and unable to do anything apart from obey Gareth's instructions, but he was beginning to think again. His medical training (keep calm in emergencies) was kicking in.

Gareth pushed Ann onto the back seat, moved in next to her, and sat behind the driver's seat.

"Where to?" John asked as he sat in the car.

"I'll tell you. Just drive."

John started the car, engaged first gear, circled the parking lot, and drove away from the supermarket.

31

"It's been two hours and there's been nothing," said Souza.

"He had plenty of time to get out of here. He's probably half way to London by now."

"Maybe, maybe not. The CCTV showed us he was injured, so that's going to limit him."

"All the more reason to get out of here."

"Agreed, but he may not have got what he came here for."

"Well, he has the Beatons. That's what we thought he was after, wasn't it? Maybe he just wanted them dead."

"If he'd just wanted the Beatons dead he could have killed them in the supermarket. I'm sure he's capable of that. I think he needs them now for a couple of reasons. He needs a driver because of his injury, and he also needs John Beaton because he thinks Beaton may have information for him. Don't forget the book that Jeremy Ellis gave him. He may want to get his hands on that, or at least find out what Beaton knows about the book."

"What if you're wrong?"

"Then it won't matter what we do. He gets away and the Beatons disappear. Come on – think about it. We're the only intact group here. The police are doing their best, but they're down three men."

William Burns was trying to be the voice of reason and authority to his junior colleagues. He was making them focus on their next moves, not on their anxieties about what had happened. He knew they would feel responsible, wondering what they could have done differently and beneath it all wondering how, in two months time, the committee of inquiry, with its perfect hindsight, would judge their actions. He cleared that thought from his mind too.

Burns was sitting with Souza and Tibbs in their surveillance van. Souza had driven it to the Bayview upper parking lot when they had concluded that monitoring Auntie Olly's house was no longer useful. The lot was a hive of activity as more and more police from nearby regions arrived and were assigned to their posts. Mukherjee walked rapidly towards them from the police control vehicle.

"I talked to the Chief Inspector." Mukherjee spoke rapidly. "He was in on the meetings we had today. He tells me one of the officers is still unconscious and is about to go into surgery, and the other two have come round. One of them, Clive Owen, the Assistant Chief Constable, apparently may have recognized his assailant."

"Really?"

"Yes. It seems he was quite agitated in the ambulance and wouldn't agree to any treatment until he could talk to a colleague. Apparently, he was talking to his brother – his brother's a cop in South Wales, and they were talking about someone they both knew from school. His brother texted a photo of him to him yesterday. The Chief Inspector has that photo now and texted the photo of him to me."

"So, you're saying we may have a photo of our Mr. X and we know who he is?" confirmed Burns.

"Yes."

"Well, text it to us too."

"Right."

The team members pulled out their cell phones and watched the image of Gareth appear.

"Do we know his name?"

"Gareth Williams, and he's from Abergavenny, or was at one time."

"Are we sure about this? From the CCTV he looks to have some sort of mask on."

"They don't know. Apparently, the Chief Constable was on the floor of the supermarket and the mask slipped and that's when he recognized him."

"That doesn't sound all that convincing. What do the police think?" asked Burns.

"They don't buy it completely, but it's a lead and they think they might as well run with it."

"Are they going to tell the media?"

"Er … they didn't say."

"Or, you didn't ask?"

"Yes. Sorry."

"Don't worry about it. This is not one of those times to pull rank with The Official Secrets Act. They want to find him as much, or more, than we do."

"What now?" asked Souza.

Burns hesitated before saying. "It's going to be a long night, and then maybe a long day. Let's be British and do what's expected of us. Tibbs, is there any chance of a cup of tea?"

Tibbs cautiously touched the kettle on the small propane stove in the van. "The water's still hot," he said.

"OK. Make tea for four please. The rest of us can take a toilet break and then be back here in five minutes. Tibbs, you can use the van's Porta-Potty, or some other way, if that's OK?"

The van was well-equipped for prolonged surveillance, but the unwritten rule was whoever used the Porta-Potty first had to empty and clean it.

"I'll find some other way," said an expressionless Tibbs.

Burns watched the others smile and felt the tension go down a notch or two.

The call was brief. The text read, "Gareth Williams identified." Again it went through France and to North Africa, but this time it was routed to Jones. Jones hesitated and thought through the options. In the end he decided to forward the text to Gareth. He made another call and then booked a flight out of Heathrow for the following day.

32

"Pull over behind that white mini," said Gareth.

John obeyed. He had no choice. Ann was held hostage in the seat behind him and Gareth had made it plain that he was capable of carrying out anything he threatened.

The car came to a stop.

"Turn off the engine."

Again, John obeyed.

"I have some questions for you. If you don't answer them, or don't do as I say, your wife here will suffer. Do you understand?" Gareth was still wearing a semi-transparent plastic mask. It muffled his voice but John thought he could identify a slight south Wales accent, but that was all he could make out – the gray, hooded sweat-shirtt hid any other features. He and Gareth were looking at each other in the rearview mirror.

"What did you do with the book?"asked Gareth.

"What book?"

There was a short cry from Ann as Gareth tapped his baton on the front of her thigh where he'd hit her ten minutes earlier.

"You don't have to do that," John shouted. "I don't understand. Just tell me what book?"

"Keep your voice down. I told you to tell me the truth," said Gareth softly. "A few weeks ago you were in a fish and chip shop here – right?"

"Well … yes?"John replied in a quieter voice.

"Tell me about it."

"Well … it was my last night here. I'd come over to look after my aunt and … it was snowing when I got out of the fish and chip shop."

"And?"

"I … I had fish and chips and I sat down at a table, and I talked to a man at the table. He, oh, yes! He gave me a book to read … is that what you mean?"

"Did he do anything with the book?

"Um … he wrote something in it and put it in a bag."

"What happened to the book?"

"I was going to take it with me on the plane, but I didn't. I remember. I left it in the house – Auntie Olly's house. I already had a book to read for the trip back."

"Are you sure?"

"Yes. I remember throwing it on the bed in the spare bedroom."

"I think you're lying. It wasn't there when I looked for it." John could see Gareth in the mirror raise his baton slowly.

"No, it's there. I'm not lying." John said quickly. "Don't hurt her. It's there. What? … You've been in her house?"

"Yes, and I didn't find any book."

"Look, I remember now. I threw it on the bed in the bedroom, but I threw it too hard and it slipped off the other side next to the wall. It was still in the plastic bag."

There was silence as Gareth considered this. It was unlikely that Beaton was lying – he was too concerned about his wife. Gareth had only taken about thirty minutes to search the house. It was possible that the book was still there – he hadn't looked where Beaton said it was. He made a decision.

"I want that book, and I want you to get it for me."

This seemed just as incomprehensible as anything else to John and Ann.

It was Ann who spoke this time. "What? We don't understand."

"You don't have to understand … neither of you. You just need to do what I say. Understand?"

"Yes," said Ann, and John nodded his head.

Both John and Ann realized, from Ann's simple statement, they were getting over the initial terror of their situation. They'd have to be careful to not show it.

"Start the car," said Gareth.

John obeyed.

"Pull out. No, wait!"

A police car passed in the opposite direction, its lights flashing.

"OK. Pull out and take the next left."

If John had any choice about driving a stick-shift on the "wrong" side of the road, at night, a few hours after getting off a ten hour flight he would have abandoned the car, but that option didn't even cross his mind. He drove where he was directed and realized they were getting closer to Auntie Olly's house. Gareth told him to stop at the end of the alley which ran behind the back yard of the house.

"Now, I want you to go to the house, get the book and bring it back here to me. You will not call anyone or talk to anyone. I will give you exactly five minutes to get there and back. If you are not back by five minutes I will break your wife's nose, not back by six I break her jaw, not back by seven … well, I'm sure you get the picture. Understand?"

"Yes," said John. The little confidence he had regained disappeared again.

"You will go in the back door, not the front. You will not put on any lights. You know the house so you can find your way to the bedroom and look around. Here is the key to the back door." With some difficulty, and avoiding using his left arm, Gareth pulled the key out of his inside jacket pocket and gave it to John.

"You have five minutes. Go."

For a second John looked at the key as if it could explain what he was doing in Wales, why Auntie Olly had died, why he and Ann had been kidnapped, and why he now found himself with the key to Olly's house in his hand. He felt like he had no choices, no will, but a little bit of him, somewhere deep inside, was getting to feel totally pissed off. He looked at his watch, nodded to Ann and walked down the alley.

He wasn't entirely sure which house was Olly's, especially since there was no street-lighting in the narrow lane, until he found the back gate he'd once tried to fix that led to the house's overgrown back yard. He walked slowly and cautiously to the house – he had no idea what underfoot hazards could have been lurking on the path, but he made it unscathed to the back door. He fumbled in the dark to try to find the keyhole. He had a moment of panic when he thought he couldn't locate the keyhole by touch, and then he found it and inserted the key.

219

Inside the house it was quiet. He reached, reflexively, for a light switch before he remembered Gareth's instructions. He edged along the corridor to the spare bedroom, lay prone on the bed and felt the floor furthest from the door for the book. He found it! He sat on the bed with the book in his hand and looked at his watch. He had taken just over two minutes. Despite Gareth's warning he thought about calling for help. He could have used Olly's phone, but he'd had that disconnected when he left last time. His cell phone was useless outside the US except for one thing – he turned on its flashlight app, pulled out the book from its bag and looked at the flyleaf.

"Jones. Goldsmiths. 2005. Arabic. J E. 0800 789 321," was written in a clear hand.

John had no idea what this meant. He looked at his watch. He had less than two minutes to get back to Ann.

He had one thought; if he was not supposed to turn on the lights it might be because Gareth knew the house was being watched. He couldn't risk being found in the house – by the time he explained what had happened Ann would be maimed or dead. He knew there was paper and a functional pencil by Olly's phone. Using the light from the cell phone he copied the note from the book, wrote the current date and time, his name and "Help, he has both of us." He put the note on the floor, placed his cell phone on top and glanced at his watch. He had less than a minute left.

He switched on the light in the front room for one second then turned it off for two. He repeated this three times then he fled.

With book in hand he ran out of Olly's back door, slamming it behind him, praying he wouldn't trip over any unseen obstacles he'd missed on the way in, and ran back up the alley to the car.

Gareth watched him coming and indicated John should get back in the driver's seat. John glanced at his watch as he sat and noted he had taken fifteen seconds over his time.

Gareth said, "That was close."

John nodded as he caught his breath. He looked in the mirror and could see the tension in Ann's face. She was unharmed and gave a hint of a smile back to him. John also realized that Gareth hadn't timed him. Gareth's watch was on his left wrist and he was doing his best not to move that arm. He hadn't needed to time John – the threat was enough. John also realized carrying out the threat would have been self-defeating. Had he not returned, Gareth would not have injured the only person with two good arms and a driving license.

"Give me the book," said Gareth.

John handed the book to Gareth who told Ann to take it out of the plastic bag. Using the illumination from a street light Gareth read the words on the flyleaf. They were vague and would mean nothing to most people. They were probably written in a hurry – well, he knew that. He tore the flyleaf out of the book, folded it with some difficulty and put it in his jacket pocket. Of course, he had to assume Beaton had read them, which was a pity. If he was to tidy up this loose end he'd have to get rid of both of them, but for the time being he needed Beaton, if only as his driver. Then his cell phone buzzed. He read the text and all his calculations changed.

"*You've been made, Gareth Williams*," was all it said.

Gareth leaned back in his seat and stared out of the side window. So, they knew who he was. He couldn't figure out how that had happened. He thought he'd been so careful. Was it the funeral? Was it one of the cops he'd hit? Had Beaton had time? He quickly decided that line of thought would get him nowhere. The message had come through Jones. They had an unwritten contract that if one of them was identified the other would have to immediately put in place the plans he had to disappear. Gareth knew for Jones that meant shuffling the assets in his offshore accounts, deleting computer files, wiping hard-drives clean and erasing any evidence of his ever existing in the UK. If he wasn't already on a flight out of London he, or rather someone who may have looked a little like him, but with a different passport, would be soon sipping Perrier in first class. As for Gareth, his exit plan required him to make it to London. It was less than two hundred miles away by road, but he might as well have been planning to get to Mars. He doubted he could drive that far with only one good arm and a manual gear shift. He needed an intermediate strategy. For the time being he realized that wearing the mask and the hoodie was no longer necessary. He pushed back the hood and took off the mask.

John watched him do this in the car mirror and inhaled sharply.

Gareth wiped the sweat of his face and looked directly into John's eyes. He knew the significance of his actions. He knew John and Ann would assume they were going to be killed, and in the past they would have been correct – leave no witnesses. Gareth could have told them that this was not necessarily so, but he hadn't decided yet if it was so. He'd wait – a little extra terror wouldn't do any harm, but they needed to move and he knew exactly where they should go.

33

Ten minutes later they were back in the van nursing the mugs of hot tea Tibbs had brewed. The short break had allowed them to settle and focus on their job.

"Now what?" Burns asked.

"Well, I was thinking that if you accept your premise that they are not already half way to London, then where would they be around here?" said Souza.

The other three looked at her.

Mukherjee asked, "And?"

"I think Williams wouldn't take the Beatons to a hotel, or motel, or wherever he was staying. It would be too visible."

"Couldn't he just have holed up in some quiet lane somewhere?"

"Maybe, but he is injured and needs to keep control of the situation."

"He could kill or dump the Beatons. Wouldn't that work for him?" asked Tibbs.

"Yes, but we already said he wants something from them, or more specifically from John Beaton. We assumed that Beaton was lured back here for a purpose and that was to find out what Beaton knows. Remember the book Ellis gave him? He wrote something in that book. That is maybe what Williams is after."

"So, what do you suggest?" asked Burns.

"We've been concentrating on getting to Williams. We should look at what Williams is after. It may be that Beaton has given him the information, or maybe he hasn't a clue what Williams is after, but Williams has gone to extreme lengths to get Beaton here. Of course, we are assuming the book has something important written in it. Maybe he took the book to the US with him, but if it's still here the only place it is likely to be is in the house. We need to go back to the house and get inside." Souza finished.

It took two seconds of silence before Burns said, "Tibbs, you drive."

Tibbs started the van, the others held onto their tea mugs and adjusted their seats to face forward. They edged out of the parking lot. A police sergeant approached the van. Tibbs rolled down the window and said, "We're going back to the house."

The sergeant waved them through. Tibbs couldn't quite determine if the sergeant was pleased to see them go, or if he wondered why they were even there in the first place. Tibbs accelerated while his passengers tried to prevent hot tea landing in their laps as he negotiated the bends and corners of Colwyn Bay's narrow streets.

The drive took less than five minutes. Souza jumped out of the van and removed the traffic cones from the parking place they had previously occupied. It being Britain, the cones could have probably saved the parking space for eternity, or until an angry neighbor's letter to the editor had been published in the North Wales Pioneer. Tibbs pulled into the space and Souza was about to climb back in the van when she glanced at Olly's house and saw the lights in the front room go on and off three times. The others saw it too.

"Tibbs, you and Souza take the front. Use the ram. Mukherjee come with me," said Burns. "Five minutes. You two come in the front. We'll wait at the back. Keep your weapons holstered. As far as we know no one is armed and we don't want any accidents."

Tibbs hoisted the ten pounds of the ram out of the van. It was light enough to carry in one hand but he found it awkward to walk fast, so he and Souza walked slowly towards Olly's house. A light drizzle had started to fall, but otherwise the street was asleep. No other traffic passed them and the yellow illumination from the sodium street lights was sufficient for them to approach the front door safely and quietly. All that was about to change, Tibbs thought. The good people of Colwyn Bay are going to be woken up with a bang. He checked his watch. With 15 seconds to go he and Souza picked up the ram, swung it backwards and just managed to stop in time as a light came on in the hallway and the door opened. Mukherjee appeared and said. "Back door was open. There's no one here. Get inside."

It looked like the good people of Colwyn Bay would be able to continue their slumbers after all.

Mukherjee closed the door after Tibbs and Souza slipped in.

"It looks like someone was here," said Mukherjee, "but not any more. We … what's this?" He bent down and picked up the note and cell phone John had left. He read it and passed it to Souza.

"So, you were right, Souza," he said.

"No, we were right. Let's get this to Burns," she said, and hurried to the back of the house.

"You came along the alley from that direction?" she pointed and asked Burns, after showing him the note.

He nodded in reply.

"Let's go the other way," she said to Mukherjee.

She let Mukherjee lead, since he had already negotiated Olly's back yard, and followed him to the opposite end of the alley. All was quiet. Anybody who had been waiting there had left. They walked to the other end of the alley and around the block but found nothing. They returned to Olly's house. Burns was on the phone.

"OK, so we'll sit tight here," Burns said. "I doubt they'll come back, but just in case we'll be here, and we'll be here if you need us too. We are armed … yes, I know … well, let's hope it doesn't come to that." He hung up and continued. "So, the police want us to stay here just in case anyone comes back. I told them that was unlikely, but we don't know that whoever came here, and it looks like Beaton may have written that note, got what they came for. So, we stay and we keep the house dark. It's better than sitting in that van. There are two bedrooms here. Let's see if we can find some hot chocolate first. Two of us can sleep, two can keep watch and let's make it two-hour shifts. We'll only get a few hours between us anyway. Tibbs, Souza, you take the first shift. OK?"

Everyone agreed. Five minutes later the house was dark again. Tibbs and Souza found seats, one in the front room, the other in the kitchen, and agreed to rotate their positions every fifteen minutes. Burns and Mukherjee stretched out on the beds.

All was quiet.

Burns felt the vibration of his phone against his leg. There was no one in the room with him – his door was closed and Mukherjee had taken the smaller bedroom. Without turning on any lights he looked at the text. It confirmed what he had been thinking. He lay back down for a few seconds and sighed – he was getting too old for this – it had better be over soon. The house was silent, and he couldn't risk a conversation which could be overheard by his colleagues. He summoned up his energy, sat up on the edge of the bed, pulled on his shoes and tied the laces firmly, slipped into his jacket and opened the door to the bedroom. He found Tibbs sitting in the dark in the front room.

"I've had a text from the police," he murmured. "They want me back at the shopping center. Something's come up. I'll take the van."

"Do you want me to come with you, sir?" Tibbs asked.

"No, I'm not sure what they want, but I'll call or come and get you if needed. You need to get some rest. I don't know how long I'm going to be. I suggest you talk it over with Souza and maybe just one of you can keep watch. OK?"

"Yes, sir."

"Do you have the van keys?"

"Yes … here they are."

Tibbs fished in the pocket of his jeans and handed over the keys.

"Thanks."

Burns opened the front door, stood outside for a few seconds, then walked across the road to the van.

The dome light was bright and he squinted against it for a second until he could close the door. He put the key in the ignition and paused.

This was it.

After this there would be no going back. Maybe there never was any going back. He'd known this day would come and he was as ready as he could ever be. He turned the key, the van started; he turned on the lights and pulled into the road.

34

Jones closed the front door, put the keys to his MINI on an entranceway table, and walked through to the dining room he had converted into a study and computer room. He put down his carry-on case, switched on the lights, checked the house's security readout for the time he had been away, made sure the perimeter locks and monitors were active and retreated to his kitchen. There he made a goat cheese and olive salad, accompanied by tomato soup and two slices of Italian bread. He sat at the kitchen table, ate his meal, and then heated water in the microwave to make a cup of ginseng tea. He sipped this and thought about his options.

He could, of course, retire. He had nearly fourteen million dollars to his name in various banks around the world. In that case all he had to do was to walk away now and he could live a life of luxury on some tropical island, or maybe in a hacienda somewhere in South America, surrounded by other retired, or exiled, European criminals.

The thought terrified him on many levels, but mainly because he knew no other life. Criminality was his life, his purpose. It provided everything he needed – money, entertainment, focus, and intellectual stimulation. He knew the risks, but it was like a video game – one he was good at and couldn't stop playing. He couldn't see why he needed to stop, but what addict does?

No, he would have to see this through, and it all depended on what happened with Gareth that evening in Colwyn Bay. He hadn't heard anything so far, and perhaps that was good news, but in the meantime he might as well get it all ready.

He took the remains of his tea to the study and opened the safe. He had current British, Irish, Italian and Lebanese passports – he might as well take them all. He put them in the carry-on he retrieved from the hallway, and added the twenty-thousand he had in Euros. He thought that would hold him for a couple of months, or until he could access his bank accounts in Zurich, or in

Italy. The harder part would be deciding which of his files he should take with him. He could upload duplicates to his Dropbox and other remote accounts, but he needed to take others with him on flash drives. He had five 32 GB drives – he hoped that would be enough. He got down to work.

He had been working for less than an hour when his phone beeped. He reached for it, looked at the screen and the three words – *Gareth Williams identified*.

That changed everything.

The message had originated in Colwyn bay and had come via the usual channels.

He thought he had prepared for this possibility, but now realized he hadn't. His heart rate increased, he stood and paced the room and he felt light-headed and anxious. "Damn, damn, damn," he said to himself repeatedly before sitting down and thinking through his next plans. He took a big breath and tried to calm himself. He steadied his hands to control their shaking, leaned back in his chair and thought through his options.

At least the message hadn't said that Gareth had been taken, so that meant there was still the possibility of whatever was happening in North Wales could work out, but he couldn't afford the risk of staying, waiting, and hoping for a favorable outcome. If it came to saving his own hide Jones knew he'd give up Gareth, and he had to assume Gareth would do the same. Basically, he had no choice but to get out of the country while he knew he still could. He returned to his computers and began to fill yet another flash drive, but then he paused. What should he do about Gareth? Of his few options he decided he would forward the message he had just received to Gareth, but he'd also call someone who owed him a favor and tell them their services might be needed in a hurry. It wasn't ideal, but it was one way of cutting his losses. He made the calls and returned to his task. He packed a change of clothes in his carry-on and made a flight reservation on British Airways.

It took him longer than he anticipated, but by 1:30 am he was ready. He wondered if he should change cars, but then had a better idea. He called a contact and arranged to have the vehicle 'stolen'. It would reappear in a few months with new paperwork in another British city. In return his contact would lend him a car. Jones told the contact where the car would be parked and hung up the phone. He walked outside to the MINI, opened the door and left the keys under the driver's car mat as instructed, closed the door and walked back to his house. He checked each room one more time just to make sure that he hadn't left anything that couldn't be replaced. He found nothing and overall thought that was good.

His last task, before heading out, was to set the incendiary device. It was quite simple to operate and when triggered it would cause no unnecessary deaths, at least he thought not, but it would obliterate any records or connections he had to this place.

Then he sat and waited for the call. It came an hour later – the car switch had taken place.

Jones could leave now.

He shouldered the bag containing his laptop, stepped down the two stairs from his front door, and walked through a cold drizzle to the new car, an older model, red, Volvo station wagon.

He opened the door and sat in the driver's seat. It was comfortable enough, and his contact told him it was mechanically sound, but it stank of cigarette smoke, cheap perfume, and sweat. He left his gloves on, started the engine and moved to adjust the rearview mirror, but it was loose and wouldn't stay in one position. He'd have to rely on his side mirrors which left him feeling a little uncomfortable – he was used to checking behind when he was driving. He hesitated a few seconds, took a deep breath and decided he might as well get moving – after all this was the beginning of a new life. He pulled away from the curb and took the left at the end of his street. He noticed no headlights following him.

The drive to the airport was uneventful. He'd taken the same route dozens of times before at this time in the morning and could almost drive it on auto-pilot, so he spent the time making sure, in his own mind, that he'd covered all his bases.

35

Ella took over at 1:00 and ran the engine for ten minutes. At 1:30 the door to the house opened. She decided to not wake the others in case Jones noticed their movement. She saw him go to his car. Her hand moved towards the keys in the ignition, but all he did was open the car door, reach into it briefly, and then go back in the house. She assumed he was retrieving something from his car. Nothing more happened.

At 2:00 she ran the engine for another ten minutes.

At 2:20 she couldn't fight it any longer and fell asleep.

At 2:32 a beeping sound woke her and the others. For a few seconds she couldn't recall where she was. She looked up, cleaned the condensation off the windshield and noticed there was still a light in Jones's hallway. She looked for the source of the beeping which was in George's hand.

He was holding the tracker monitor. "He's on the move. He turned left at the end of the street."

Ella started the engine, moved her seat to a more upright position, put the car in gear and followed George's directions to catch up with Jones's car. She noticed the empty parking space where Jones's car had been.

She apologized, "I must have fallen asleep. I'm sorry."

"It happens," said Marie.

"We don't have to follow too closely," said George. "This thing will pick him up at a couple of miles."

"It will?" Ella asked, suddenly wondering about the light in Jones's house.

"Yes."

"Then I can go around the block just one time to satisfy my curiosity."

She took a hard left and switched off the car lights before she turned the final corner back to Jones's street. She inched along until she found a parking spot and pulled in a hundred yards from Jones's house.

"We can't see a thing from this far away. George, walk up to his house and see if the light's still on. If it is try to get a glance through the door, or window, and then come back here ASAP. If all looks OK we'll have to get back to following his car with the tracker".

Ella kept the engine running and the inside of the car gradually began to warm and the condensation on the windshield started to clear.

It was less than a minute later that George ran back to the car.

"He's on the move," he said and slid into the passenger seat. "Good call, Ella. It's a red Volvo station wagon." He paused to catch his breath.

"It maybe a car that's been there all along, but I'm not sure. He may have had two vehicles. He came out of the house when I was about twenty-five meters away. He didn't see me. I hid behind a van. I could see it was him before he switched off the light."

As George related his tale Ella drove fast to the end of the street. She guessed Jones would turn left and she was rewarded by seeing his tail and brake lights as he slowed for an intersection. There were no other vehicles around.

"Do you think he was on to us?" Ella asked.

"I don't know," said George.

Marie leaned forward between the seats and said, "It's going to be much harder to keep up without him noticing."

"I know. Any suggestions?" Ella asked.

"I think all we can do is keep well back until we end up on a road with more traffic," said Marie.

And that's what they did. It was easier than they thought. It didn't take long for Jones to join a busier road heading towards central London, and then they closed the distance between them. They almost lost him on two occasions when they were stopped by traffic lights that he'd slipped through as they changed.

They were also hampered by not knowing where they were. They were familiar with the better known parts of London, but they followed Jones through Dulwich, Tulse Hill, Streatham and

232

Clapham Common – places they may have only seen on subway maps before. It wasn't until they crossed the Thames at Battersea Bridge and found themselves in Kensington that they had a better sense where they were.

Jones had been heading north, but now turned west along the A4.

"What's out this way?" Ella asked.

"Not sure," answered George looking down at the map on his phone.

"I think this is the way to Heathrow Airport," said Marie and, on cue, a road sign appeared indicating they were heading towards the M4, The West, and Heathrow Airport.

It had been forty-five minutes since they'd left Jones's house in south London, and from the road signs it would be another fifteen before they reached Heathrow.

They talked it over and came to the conclusion they needed help.

Ella handed her phone to Marie and asked her to call Stefan in Paris and to put the conversation on the loudspeaker.

"Where are you?" said Stefan.

"We're in a car on the way to Heathrow, and you're on speaker," warned Ella, just in case Stefan had any intentions of voicing thoughts on his mind she might prefer to hear in private.

Stefan heeded the warning and said, "How can I help you?"

"Marie will tell you," answered Ella."I'm driving."

Marie said, "We have been following this man and he seems to be on the way to Heathrow Airport. We assume he will get there and be in a terminal around 4:15. We know he is traveling light, so may not check in any bags, and so we assume, if indeed he is going to Heathrow, he will have a flight out at some time after 5:00."

"So you want a list of flights he could be on?" Stefan sounded doubtful.

"No, there are too many possibilities. We want you to stand by and as soon as we know which terminal he is using we want you to book a flight, any flight, leaving from that terminal. That

233

way we can get through security and passport check. Can you do that?"

"That should be no problem for European flights, but I don't know about ones to the USA, or further away."

"We'll have to take that risk," Marie said.

Stefan added, "And I suppose when you find out what flight he is taking you'll let me know. I'll get you ticketed and cancel the original tickets."

"That's the basic plan, but only Ella will need a ticket. He may remember George and me from Gatwick. He hasn't seen Ella yet. George and I will make our own way back to Paris."

"Good," Stefan hesitated. "All of you be careful.'

"We will," said Ella, surprising herself by fantasizing she was lying next to Stefan, but then, she thought, after trying to sleep in a cold, small car and peeing in the gutter somewhere in London, who wouldn't want to be with Stefan in Paris?

"There is one more thing which may help you relax a little," said Stefan. "Heathrow has a voluntary curfew on flights leaving overnight. Unless he's made some other arrangements he won't be on a flight before 6:00 am."

Marie said, "Thanks, we'll be in touch." She hung up and put the phone on the dashboard in front of her.

Ella had been concentrating on Jones's car – a hundred meters in front of her. She said, "He didn't take the exit for the M4. He's staying on the A4. Is that OK, George?"

George zoomed out on his phone and replied, "The A4 goes nearer to Heathrow than the M4."

"What's after Heathrow?" Ella asked?

"Well, all sorts of places. It seems to end up going to Bristol, and that's close to Wales."

"I hope he's not going that far"

"I doubt it. He'd be much better off on the M4. It avoids a lot of towns."

They drove the next five minutes in silence. There was more traffic and Ella drew closer to Jones. They could see they were approaching the airport by the number of hotels and businesses related to aviation that they passed. The sign to the slip road to

Heathrow appeared. Jones ignored it and carried on along the A4.

"There's one last possibility," said George, not looking up from his phone screen.

No one said a word – they all dreaded the possibility that Jones had ideas other than flying that day and they would have to try to follow him across the length and breadth of England and Wales.

The last chance came up. Jones put on his indicators and turned south on the A3044 and headed for Terminal 5.

They let out a collective sigh of relief. Marie picked up the phone and called Stefan.

"Marie here. He's heading for Terminal 5," she said.

"Good," said Stefan. "As far as I know that's exclusively British Airways. Let me have a look at the screen … yes, there are thirty or more flights leaving in the next couple of hours. I'll get back to you in a few minutes."

They followed Jones closer now. He passed the entrance to the long-term car park and took the entrance to the short-stay parking garage. There was only one car between them when he stopped at the ticket barrier.

Marie and George ducked down until Ella said it was clear. They decided to not follow Jones. It was safer to park the car and concentrate on its exits instead.

Stefan called back.

"You are all booked on a 8:14 to Paris. It's not the earliest flight to Paris, but if all else fails you can still take it and get back here. I'll text the boarding passes to your cell phones. OK?"

Ella replied, "Yes. We've just parked and are heading into the terminal."

The three split up and headed towards the terminal. In less than ten minutes they were inside the building, scanning the entrances.

But they didn't know if Jones had made it in five.

They tried to cover as many of the doorways into Terminal 5 as possible, but a half-hour later, at 4:45, it was obvious they had missed him.

Ella was frustrated – to have come so far and miss him at this point was so discouraging. She was exhausted, sweaty, dirty and would have loved to crawl into a corner and sleep, but she rallied and called the others.

"Let's get through security and take it from there. We should go through separately, but let's meet after outside the Harrod's store – it's on the way to the concourses." She didn't even want to consider that Jones may have taken the subway to another terminal.

George was the last to arrive at Harrod's and by then it was 5:10.

It was impossible to scan the faces of the hundreds of people passing by, so they gave up trying and walked into the store.

"We have to face the possibility that we may have lost him," said Ella, picking up a Paddington Bear soft toy and looking at the price on its tag. "There are probably thousands of people in this building now and we can't check them all out. There are three concourses here, numerous toilets, stores, so any suggestions?"

Marie shook her head, "We have to try something. I know it's a long shot but we could take a concourse each."

"I suppose so," said Ella. "George, any ideas?{"

"Well, I've been thinking. He left early for the airport – that might have been to get through security when the lines are still not too long, but crowds are his friends – somewhere he can hide. Now, when I've got up early and haven't eaten, I find a restaurant for breakfast. Why don't we check the restaurants first? It's almost an hour before any flights take off, and, if he's here, he's only been here a half-hour longer than us."

"Good idea," said Ella rekindling a little enthusiasm.

"Maybe. Let's hope so," replied George.

"Should we check all the food bars, restaurants, and fast food places?" asked Marie.

"No," said George. "Let's start with the up-market restaurants. You know, places where you can sit and maybe get some quiet. Places where they may have printed menus."

"Let's do it," said Ella with renewed energy.

They walked over to a map of the nearest airport map and searched for restaurants. They chose the nearest three to begin with.

Ella divided their tasks. "George, you go to 'The George' – it seems appropriate. Marie, you take 'Gordon Ramsay Plane Food' and I'll take 'Wagamama'. Keep in touch by phone and if we don't find him we'll meet back here. If you get stopped at the entrance to the restaurant tell them you are looking for your wife, or boss, or someone. That way you'll have a reason for looking around."

They all knew that if they didn't find him soon the chances of ever seeing Jones again were minimal, and for Ella that also meant never confronting the man who may have arranged her brother's killing. She approached the "Please Wait to be Seated" sign, told the greeter of her problem – she was meeting her boss and needed to get some papers to him and with a wave was allowed into the restaurant.

She walked slowly, but confidently, along the aisles between the tables apparently looking for her boss. She caught the eye of more than one male but didn't return their stares.

And then she saw him. She controlled herself and resisted the urge to double check, but there was no doubt it was Jones. He was sitting by himself at a table for two. He was studying a newspaper, had a cup of coffee in his right hand and was wearing a dull, grey jacket and a polo shirt. A waiter was clearing away the remains of his breakfast. He didn't look up as Ella walked by, not changing her pace, and she returned to the restaurant entrance. She told the greeter she hadn't found her boss, but would be back. She called the others on her cell phone as she walked back to their rendezvous point.

"I noticed two exits from the restaurant. One I used and the other is the stairs at the back down to level two. I don't think there are any more. Based on his activities since we've been following him I think he'll take the stairs. George, you watch the stairs. Marie, you take the front entrance. I'll stay out of the way. He should be on the move in less than ten minutes"

237

Ella was right. George called to let them know that at 5:25 Jones had taken the back stairs to level two and he was following him to the passage that led to A gates, 18-23. Ella and Marie followed George. Jones used the toilets opposite the 'Pilots Bar and Kitchen' restaurant and George waited across the concourse before Jones emerged and continued to his gate. He watched as Jones selected a seat at gate 19. He glanced at the sign above the gate which indicated, 'Berlin 6:19' and walked by.

He called Ella and Marie. "He's sitting outside gate 19 and waiting for the 6:19 to Berlin, which appears to be on time."

"OK, I'll call Stefan and get on the same flight," Ella replied.

Three minutes after the call her cell phone buzzed. She checked and noted she was booked on the flight to Berlin. It was now 5:40 and boarding was set to begin in ten minutes.

She called George and Marie and they met outside Harrod's again.

"I'll go and sit at the gate," she began. "There's another forty minutes till the gate closes, so I will stay there and fly to Berlin. I don't know what will happen when I get there. I talked to Stefan briefly. He said he will try to get people in place, but he wasn't sure. So, why don't you go and get some breakfast and … oh, yes … could one of you take the car back to the rental company?" She fished in her bag for the key, found it and gave it to Marie. "And thank you both for everything. We couldn't have done it without you. Dinner is on me when we get back to Paris."

They hugged and parted.

Ella walked to gate 19, stood to the side of the concourse, looked at the gate, checked her watch and walked by. She hoped to give the impression of someone who had other business, or maybe just wanted an extra stroll, before sitting on a two-hour flight. She spotted Jones – he was close to a window at the periphery of the sitting area. She walked to the end of the concourse, turned around and returned to the gate. She noticed some passengers were beginning to stand and line up for boarding, but Jones had continued sitting. She chose a seat behind and as close to him as she felt she could without being too obvious, but she didn't want her vision to be obstructed by standing passengers. Jones answered a call on his phone, wrote down details, and then made a call lasting only two minutes when he seemed to be relaying the same message. This was followed by another short call he made, again referring to the notes he'd made from the first cal.

'Pre-boarding' was announced and a handful of passengers with obvious disabilities and parents with young children, baby carriers, and soft toys made their way down the jet-way. Next call was for first class and those with credentials which placed them ahead of the masses. About twenty passengers, mostly men, lined up with their ties and briefcases and disappeared into the boarding tunnel. Then the order came for the remaining lower caste people to line up according to their seat number.

Still, Jones didn't move.

Ella was getting worried. Soon it would be just she and Jones sitting in the boarding area.

The last passenger in the line disappeared down the tunnel. An obese middle-aged man ran up, brief-cased with a jacket and tie, short of breath and red-faced. He showed his boarding pass and was allowed into the tunnel. The boarding attendant moved back to her desk and scanned her computer screen.

Ella had no choice but to stand and walk towards the gate. She slowed down as much as possible, without making it too obvious what she was doing, and fumbled in her bag for her passport and cell phone.

"Paging Mr. Ephraim Smith, Mr. Ephraim Smith to gate 20. The boarding gate to the 6:14 flight to Paris is about to close."

Ella paid little attention to the announcement coming from the boarding area across the concourse, but Jones stood, shouldered his carry-on, walked the thirty meters to gate 20, showed his boarding pass and disappeared into the tunnel. He was on his way to Paris. The door closed behind him.

Ella swore out loud, "Merde!" but there was nothing she could do.

She collected herself, explained to the gate 19 attendant that she felt unwell, did not intend to fly to Berlin that day and that she had no checked bags. Then, she called Stefan.

"That means he'll be getting to CDG by about 8:30 our time. That doesn't give me much time. I have to get moving," said Stefan.

"But it's so frustrating and I don't think he even knew we were following him. He's not an easy one to follow too. And, by the way, he's travelling under the name of Ephraim Smith."

"Thanks. It's up to us here from now on. I hadn't cancelled the 8:14 flight so why don't you take that and I'll check in with you when I can."

"Thank you, and guess what?"

"What?" asked Stefan.

"I miss you."

"You do?"

"Yes."

"Oh, good … but now I won't be able to concentrate on anything until I see you again."

"I don't believe you."

"You should. I must go. Love you." He hung up.

Ella was left wondering where that conversation had come from – maybe it was just lack of sleep. Maybe it was …? She decided she should probably rest her brain before exploring those emotions. All the tension of the last 24 hours drained out of her. She was tempted to lie down on the floor in the gate area and sleep, but she felt she had already attracted enough attention, and then she remembered Terminal 5's Aspire Lounge. She called George and Marie who had returned the car and just managed to get through security again and told them what had happened. She invited them to accompany her to the lounge.

There was one more thing Ella had to do before she could relax. She called Georgina Southport, who was having breakfast with some of her team at a motorway café somewhere in the middle of England. They spoke for ten minutes.

George, Marie and Ella enjoyed the peace of the lounge, the hot showers and the 'Hearty Hot Breakfast', followed by the hour's sleep they managed on the 8:14 to Paris. By noon Ella was back in the SIGNAK office and wondering what had happened to Stefan.

36

Jones was confident the problem in North Wales would be sorted out in the next hour or two. He was even a little surprised how easy it had been.

When the device in his house was triggered there would be no fingerprint or DNA evidence of his ever living there, and the car he was driving now was destined to be picked up an hour after he parked at Heathrow. Overall, he'd covered his exit pretty well. He was traveling with a British passport he'd used before; maybe he'd switch to Irish after Paris. At some point he would have to appear in Zurich, but in the meantime he would take up the offer from an Italian contact he'd helped before. He would consolidate his resources and then, well, he'd figure that out later.

He parked the car on the level and in the area he'd been advised to, left the keys in the glove box, and five minutes later was at the entrance to Terminal 5. He chose to enter through the busiest door and made his way, indirectly, to security. He noticed nothing to arouse his suspicions.

He'd used this passport before, so expected no trouble, and had none.

He headed for Wagamama and breakfast. He tried to eat at a different restaurant each time he breakfasted at Heathrow so he wouldn't establish a pattern, but he wondered if anyone would have recognized him as a repeat customer if he'd eaten there every day. He was just another anonymous face passing by in a huge airport.

He had one phone call from North Wales during his breakfast and all seemed to continue to be going as planned. The only mildly disconcerting event was just as he was finishing his meal a woman walked by he thought he half recognized. She was attractive with a middle-east complexion. He wasn't sure why, or from where, he knew her, but he had a feeling of unease and experience had taught him not to ignore these signs.

He paid the bill, picked up his carry-on and took the back stairs down one level. In retrospect he realized this was not a good move since there were now hundreds of passengers moving through the terminal. He couldn't make out anyone in the crowd, but standing on the stairs he could be seen by anyone.

He made his way to his gate, pausing only at the restroom. He could make out no one following him or watching him.

He always traveled first class, and he always waited at the edge of the boarding area, or in an adjacent area. He never boarded with the other first class passengers. What was the point of sitting down first only to have every other passenger cough on you, stare jealously at where you were sitting, or accidentally maim you with swings of their lethal carry-on items? No, it was better to sit, read, and attend to business until the last moment. Today, that was going to be easier since he noticed a Berlin flight was leaving about the same time as his flight to Paris from the opposite side of the concourse.

He took a seat in the waiting area and opened his book.

There she was again.

It was the woman he'd noticed in the restaurant. Out of the corner of his eye he watched her stop at the gate, check her watch, and then move on. He lost sight of her as she walked further down the concourse. He returned to his book, but ten minutes later, when he looked around she was sitting in the same waiting area. He returned to his book, but couldn't concentrate. He realized she was probably just another traveler and he was just being paranoid. After all, events in North Wales would not have caught up with him here yet. It's just that he couldn't shake the feeling he had seen her somewhere before. And, if he had seen her before – so what? She wasn't likely to be the police or any other government authority.

His phone buzzed and he was distracted. It was Gareth. He talked to him and then made a couple more calls. By the time he'd dealt with those he noticed the flight to Berlin was boarding, and across the concourse passengers were crowding the gate for the flight to Paris. He remained seated and so did the woman.

There were very few seated travelers left on either side of the concourse. Jones knew he would have to make a move soon, but why was the woman still seated?

A fat man ran up to gate 19, showed his boarding pass and walked hurriedly onto the jetway. Finally, the woman started to move towards gate 19. She was slow and was apparently looking for documentation in her carry-on. Gate 20 called him by name and announced the flight to Paris was leaving.

Jones stood, walked across the concourse, stopped briefly at the check-in, did not look back and walked to his seat in first class. Thirty seconds later the plane's door closed and he was on his way to Paris. He relaxed a little and that's when he remembered when he thought he'd seen her. Wasn't she the driver of the car that was behind him when he was driving from Gatwick yesterday? He had this vague memory of seeing her, or someone like her, in his rearview mirror when they both stopped for a traffic light somewhere in south London.

But then he thought it through again. There was no agency, governmental or private, he knew of which would have a reason, and the resources, to keep him under surveillance. He was becoming too suspicious for his own good. As soon as he got to Paris he would unwind and enjoy being free. He closed his eyes, took a deep breath, and enjoyed the rest of the flight.

37

Robert Holte left the security chain across the six-inch gap when he answered the knock on the door.

"Who is it?" he asked. He looked around the edge of the door at three people illuminated by his porch light.

"Police. Detective Sergeant Walcott," said a man he didn't recognize, standing at the back of the trio, holding some form of identification in front of his face. "We need to ask you a few more questions about the time you were in the fish and chip shop. There have been new developments."

"At this time of night?" Holte asked.

"Sorry about that, but it's urgent."

Holte hesitated for a second or two. He wasn't wearing his glasses and he couldn't quite reconcile the expressions on the faces of the other two people with the urgency of the request, but he was tired and it was urgent, and it was the police … he opened the door and let in John and Ann, followed by Gareth.

It took him less than a second to realize his mistake.

With his good arm Gareth pushed Ann and John forcefully from behind, making them stumble into the narrow hallway. Instinctively, they tried to shield their bodies from a fall by reaching out to find some means of protecting themselves. Finding none, Ann tried to steady herself on Holte's shoulder but just ended up pushing him sideways and she fell, pressing him into the wall. Then John, unable to avoid Ann's legs, tripped, and tumbled over her onto the carpeted floor. Gareth kicked the front door closed behind him, and said "Stay down" to Ann and John. He pushed a frightened Holte against the wall and held him there with his stick across Holte's throat.

"Who are you? You're not the police, are you?" Holte said, flattening himself against the wall of his hallway. It looked like he was trying to melt into the floral wallpaper as he pushed back from Gareth. He was wearing faded green-striped cotton pajamas, a couple of sizes too small for his 44-inch pink-skinned belly which bulged through the gaps between the buttons.

"No, I'm not the police," said Gareth. "The police are nowhere around. I am here. You do what I say – understand?"

Holte nodded his head, opened his mouth, but before he could say anything a door opened onto the hallway and his wife appeared. "Bobby, what's ha …?" She took one step forward and stopped when she saw her husband held against the wall and a man and a woman lying on her carpet. She was wearing a pink, semi-transparent full-length, shapeless nightgown, and instinctively crossed her arms over her breasts in an attempt to protect her modesty.

"Where's your dining room?" Gareth asked her.

No one spoke.

"Where's your dining room?" he asked again, making Holte gag by putting pressure on his throat.

"There." His wife pointed a shaking hand towards a door at the end of the hallway.

"Go in there, turn on the light, and sit down at the table," ordered Gareth.

For a couple of seconds she didn't move, not seeming to understand Gareth, but then she scuttled across the few feet to the dining room door, opened it, switched on the light, and disappeared through the doorway.

"Get up," Gareth said to John and Ann. "Follow her and sit down at the table."

John and Ann did what they were told. They had no choice – they knew what damage Gareth was capable of inflicting.

Gareth followed them in to the dining room pushing Holte in front of him.

Just like thousands of houses, bungalows and castles across the length and breadth of the United Kingdom the dining room was at the back of the house. The room at the front of the house was the sitting room, reception room, lounge, or parlor depending on which generation was describing it, or listing it for sale. It contained the ergonomically challenging, low-seated, plastic-covered sofas and chairs, the brass and ceramic souvenirs

248

from holidays spent in Spain or Cornwall, and the big-screen television. Its windows faced the street.

Gareth knew his houses. Dining rooms did not face the street and were more suited to his purposes – this was no exception. There were four wooden ladder-back chairs placed around a four-foot square, oak-laminate table. There were two more similar chairs on either side of a low sideboard, the top of which was covered by a floral cloth of exactly the same pattern as the wallpaper. On the opposite side of the room a glass and laminate hutch displayed shelves stuffed with rose and tulip patterned crockery. The room was glaringly lit by a four-foot long fluorescent light-fitting clinging to the ceiling. The heavy, floral-patterned curtains were closed.

Gareth indicated for everyone to stay sitting by holding his baton in front of him and pointing it at everyone in turn.

"Where's your son?" Gareth asked Holte.

Startled by the question Holte answered, "E's in bed, asleep."

"Go and get him."

"E's asleep. E'e won't wake up, and e's got school tomorrow."

"I said go and get him. You have one minute. If you don't bring him back in one minute I will break your wife's nose with this." He held the baton in front of his wife's face. "If you ask any more questions I may do it anyway. Understand?"

"Yes. I'll … I'll go and get 'im. It's all right, Margaret," Holte said to his wife and rushed out of the room. He was back in less than a minute, pushing his bleary-eyed son in front of him.

The boy blinked and looked around the faces in the room. He glanced at John, looked at everyone else, and then returned to John.

"I think I know you," he said. "You were in the fish and chip shop. You're that American."

John nodded in reply.

Gareth moved in front of the boy, looked down on him, and said quietly, "I'm in charge here. What's your name?"

"Billy," the boy replied glancing up. He turned to his father, "Dad, what's goin' on?" he asked.

"Do what 'e says, Billy," said Holte hurriedly.

249

"Your Dad is right, Billy. Do what I say and everyone will be fine. Your Dad is going to sit at the table and then I have something I want you to do."

Holte moved around the table and sat down, clearly reluctant to leave Gareth with his son. "Don't 'arm 'im, please. E's all we 'ave," he begged Gareth.

"He will come to no harm unless one of you makes me harm him," Gareth said looking again into each of the strained faces around the table. He turned back to Billy.

"Billy, do you have to wear a tie to school? I used to have to and I hated it," he said cheerfully.

"Yes, I 'ave to wear one, but I don't really mind it."

"How many ties do you have, Billy?"

"I 'ave two for school and I 'ave two others for best."

"Does your Dad have any ties?"

"Oh, yes. 'E has a lot." He looked at his father for reassurance. Holte managed a nod and a half-smile.

"Do you know where they are?" asked Gareth.

"Yes."

"Could you go and get your ties and your Dad's ties for me, please."

"I dunno. I'm not supposed to go in 'is bedroom." He looked again at his mother and father for support.

Gareth said, "I'm sure your parents won't mind, just this once, if you go in their bedroom." He looked at the parents and asked, "Isn't that right?"

They both nodded.

"See, Billy, it's OK. You go and get your father's ties and yours, and by the way, if you find any belts we could use those too. Off you go now."

Billy looked once more at his father who nodded and tried a smile. Billy turned and left the room.

No one spoke. The house was quiet, but they could hear the occasional noise from Billy as he collected the items Gareth wanted.

John watched Gareth sit in the chair next to the sideboard. From here Gareth could see the door in to the room and the four adults seated at the table, although Ann had half her back to him. Gareth rested his baton on the sideboard close to his right hand. He used his right hand to help his injured left arm on to his lap.

John thought Gareth was hiding the pain well, but he could see it was beginning to weaken him. He was moving a little more slowly and his face was showing the strain. He glanced around the table – they were all showing the strain. He wondered if he should offer to help splint Gareth's injured arm, but he chose to remain quiet. Maybe it was better to not show anything but dread, and wait to see if any opportunity arose to overcome Gareth. John's eyes were gritty, he'd slept for three hours in the last two days, he was hungry, thirsty and was feeling exhausted. He wasn't sure, if a chance arose, if he would be able to notice it or take it.

Billy returned to the room carrying ties and belts.

"Put those on the table, Billy," ordered Gareth.

Billy obeyed.

"How many ties are there, Billy?"

Billy counted and said, "Twenty-one."

"How many belts?"

"Five."

"Thank you, Billy. Now please go and sit in that chair." Gareth pointed, with his baton, to the chair at the opposite end of the sideboard from him.

Billy edged behind John and his father and sat in the chair.

Ann started in surprise when Gareth stood and tapped his baton on her left shoulder.

"You. You take these," he pointed to the ties. "Leave the belts and tie up their legs. Tie them one to each leg of their chairs and tie them just below the knee. Do it, and don't make them too tight or too loose."

Ann hesitated for a second while she processed what was being asked of her. She rose stiffly, picked up the ties and, starting with Holte, tied the legs of the three other people sitting at the table.

251

"Now tie their wrists to the side uprights of the chairs. One tie to each side, wrap the wrists twice then tie the knot," Gareth said.

Again, she obeyed. She finished with Holte, moved to John, and gave him a quick squeeze with her hand before she tied his wrists. He hoped his face didn't show any reaction, but her touch revived his spirits. Not that he could do anything about it. He couldn't move his arms and he couldn't stand. Even if he tilted his chair back his legs would still be attached to the chair.

Ann finished her task.

"Now, tie up the boy too," Gareth instructed.

Again, she obeyed. She smiled briefly at Billy while she fixed him in the chair, and was surprised he smiled back. She wondered how he was handling this. He seemed a little concerned, as he looked at the faces around the room, but said nothing while she finished her task.

"Now, sit and tie your own legs with the belts," said Gareth. "When you have finished that tie your right wrist to the chair."

Ann managed to immobilize her legs, but it was harder to fix her wrist to the chair. She was concerned about antagonizing Gareth and could feel her anxiety increasing knowing that he was behind her and was completely in control. Eventually, she managed to close the buckle and leaned back with a quiet sigh of relief. She could feel sweat beading on her upper lip and forehead.

Gareth picked up one of the remaining belts and using his one good hand tied Ann's wrist to the chair.

Satisfied his captives were all secured he allowed himself a moment of relaxation. Then, he said, "You may talk to me if I talk to you first; you may not talk to each other. If you do talk to each other I will have to gag you. If you try to escape I will kill you." He paused. "I will be back."

With that he left the room.

If she looked to her left, Margaret, Holte's wife, could see into the hallway, but she was frozen, tears rolling down her face as she stared across the table at her husband. Ann had the next best view, but her face could also be seen by Gareth from the hallway.

John risked looking around a little. To his right was the door. The hinged gap between the door and the door frame was obscured by the glass-fronted crockery hutch. At least that meant if Gareth wanted to see all the occupants of the dining room he had to come completely into the room. John looked ahead again, directly at Ann. If he was hoping for a smile he didn't get one. Instead she widened her eyes very slightly and Gareth stepped back in to the room.

The carpeted hallway and dining room had muffled any sounds of his appearance. He looked around the room again. He was satisfied that they all knew he could appear at any time without any warning. Again, he left the room. He turned off the porch light, and the one in the hallway, knowing this would imply to any outside observer that the household was safe and sleeping. It also made any appearances he chose to make in the dining room that much harder to anticipate. He made one more visit to the dining room and stood for a minute swinging his baton in a slow pendulum motion looking at each of his captives in turn. He wanted to give the impression he was trying to make a decision. He wasn't. He knew exactly what he was going to do, but a little more fear in his captives wouldn't do him any harm. He returned to the kitchen and made the call.

38

Jones cell phone rang. He looked at the caller ID, lifted the phone and said, "Hello."

"I need your help," Gareth said.

There was a slight pause on the line before Jones answered.

"How can I help you?"

"It's all gone to hell up here. I got the book that man wrote in. It didn't say much, but it would have been enough to finger you. Before that I was a little slow and had my left arm broken. It's between the elbow and the wrist, and it'll need fixing up, but I can live with it for a while."

"Where are you now?" Jones asked.

Gareth was sitting in a chair in the kitchen. He could hear airport announcements in the background. "I'm safe for the time being. It sounds like you're at an airport."

"I am. I'm at Gatwick. I have a flight out of here to Berlin in about an hour." He was at Heathrow and his flight to Paris was in four hours, but Gareth didn't need to know that. "So, how can I help?" Jones asked again.

"I need a car with a full tank of petrol and I need it to be an automatic. I am going to have difficulty changing gears with this arm."

"When do you want it by?"

"As soon as possible. I'll need it as soon as it gets light."

"That's not much time. That only gives me about four hours."

"I know, but it's all the time I've got."

"Where's your car now?"

"It's off the road and hidden."

"OK, let me think. This car you want. It'll have to come from Manchester. I haven't got anyone closer, so that will take a couple of hours to get to you anyway, but I'll see what I can do. Where do you want it delivered?"

"There may be road blocks on some of the roads out of here, so whoever delivers it should probably avoid coming into Colwyn Bay, especially if they want to leave undetected. If I take the smaller streets I can get out of here – maybe south of town. I think I could drive my car a short distance, or maybe I can get one of my hostages to drive me."

"Hostages!" Jones raised his voice. He checked around and no one in the airport seemed to have reacted to his surprised comment. They were all engrossed in their cell phones or were dozing.

"Yeah, but I have them under control."

"Where do you have them?"

"Tied up. There are five of them. They aren't going to cause me any bother."

"I hope you know what the hell you're doing."

"I do, but I need to get out of here. We both need to keep our heads down for a while. I may have to stay away from Wales forever and so may you. I don't think we'll be missed."

There were a few moments of silence before Jones spoke. "Well, it was good while it lasted. I need to make some calls for you. Good luck. Thanks for everything. I'll probably be in Berlin before I can call you back with details. Bye, Gareth."

"Bye."

The conversation had left Gareth feeling a little uneasy. Clearly, any relationship he'd had with Jones was now over. If they ever crossed paths in that mythical bar in Cairo in ten years' time they would probably ignore each other. But Gareth's current concern was whether or not he could trust Jones. If he waited until dawn, and there had been no news from Jones, would he have thrown away a chance to escape? Gareth assumed Jones wouldn't want him to be captured since he knew knowledge of their association was one of the few bargaining chips Gareth possessed. But Gareth knew he'd have to wait. He had no choice, but on the other hand there was no reason he couldn't work on alternative plans. In the meantime this was Wales, he was tired, hungry and thirsty, so he put on the kettle to make himself a cup of tea. He found a slab of Cheshire cheese in the refrigerator and with lettuce and tomatoes made himself a sandwich while he waited for the kettle to boil. He also needed to check his hostages.

39

They could hear the murmurings of Gareth's phone call to Jones, but couldn't make out what he was saying.

John had tried pushing against his bonds, and although he could move his feet, and he could slide his arms up the chair rails, there was no way he could free himself. He looked at the others. Margaret, Holte's wife, was still quietly sobbing with her head now bowed. Holte had a defeated expression on his face and occasionally glanced at Billy, his son. Ann, who was opposite John, was trying to loosen the ties around her arms and legs with as little success as John.

John looked at Billy and winked at him.

Billy responded by a wink and then looked at the bottom sideboard drawer behind Ann, then back at John again. He repeated this several times. John gave a quiet cough to get Ann's attention. She looked at him, and then at Billy. By leaning over towards him as much as she could, and with him leaning towards her, she could hear him whisper, "There's a knife in the bottom drawer."

Ann turned as much as she could and looked at the drawer behind her, then back at Billy. He nodded.

She was about twelve inches from the drawer.

She could still hear Gareth's conversation with Jones, so she was safe for a short time, but if she moved too far back there would be an obvious gap when Gareth next checked the room. She tried inching her chair back a little. It wasn't easy to move the chair over the carpet. She had to lean forward to take the weight off the back legs of her chair. She moved about three inches, then stopped. She could still hear Gareth's voice. She leaned forward again and stretched her hands back as much as possible, but was still too far from the drawer. She moved the chair another couple of inches, but was concerned about the space which had now opened between her and the table. She was about to try to move the chair again when she noticed she could not hear Gareth's voice. She slid her body forward across the seat of the chair and slumped her head forwards as if she were trying to sleep.

Gareth stepped silently in to the room. The boy and the two men noticed him and moved their heads slowly towards him, their faces fatigued and blank, but both women seemed to be out of it. Good. He left them alone and went back to the kitchen.

A minute later Ann could hear the clattering sounds of Gareth making a cup of tea in the kitchen. She indicated as best she could for John to push the table towards her. Eventually, he understood what she wanted. He edged his chair forward and using his chest pushed as hard as he could. He moved the table one inch and then another, but it was difficult finding enough stability and leverage. He had moved it only three inches when Ann shook her head. He stopped, sat back in his seat and listened. There was silence from the kitchen. His pulse was racing, but Gareth did not appear, and then the sounds from the kitchen started again. He took a big breath and pushed the table one more inch. Ann indicated he should stop and then pushed herself back another couple of inches. If she pushed the chair onto its back legs she could reach the handle of the drawer. She opened the drawer and risked a look to her right.

There it was – a serrated edge, stainless steel, carving knife. It was about a foot long and she could reach the handle with her right hand. She checked for noises from the kitchen. She could hear an occasional sound. Again, she pushed back the chair and using her right hand reached back and lifted the knife out of the drawer. She found herself shaking more than she thought, her heart was racing, but she managed to slip the blade between the wooden seat of the chair and her body. She pushed the drawer closed and slumped forward again to give herself time to recompose her body. Her heart rate started to settle, the sweat on her forehead didn't form into beads, and she controlled her breathing.

Ten seconds later Gareth walked into the room. Ann could see him out of the corner of her peripheral vision, but she remained with her head bent over the table. Gareth turned and left. One minute later he reappeared for another minute. He said nothing. He didn't feel he needed to.

Ann assumed he wouldn't be back for at least another minute and carefully, using as little extraneous body movement as she could, turned the knife 180 degrees so the blade was sticking out and she was sitting on the handle. She moved the belt holding her right wrist close to the blade and started to saw. This was going to take some time. She concentrated on trying to make her upper body seem motionless while she sawed at the leather.

40

Gareth knew it could be risky to develop a pattern. Next time he looked in on his hostages, he decided he'd recheck twice. Unpredictability was good, but for now he needed to attend to his arm.

A door off the hallway led to the garage. It was small and occupied by a single Ford Escort which looked like it dated back to the 80's. Its hood was up and various parts of its insides were piled at the edge of a minute work bench. Any thoughts Gareth had of being able to use Holte's car disappeared. He was stuck with his rental car. If his arm hadn't been damaged, and if he hadn't any hostages to watch over, he could have possibly swapped number plates.

He could get rid of the hostages easily enough, but that wouldn't help him. The only way he could have swapped the plates would have been for him to hand a screwdriver to one of them. They might seem passive now, but he couldn't guarantee what any of them would do in those circumstances. That would also demonstrate the reality of showing how weak and disabled he was with his broken arm – one of them might get desperate.

He looked around the garage for something he could use as a temporary splint for his arm. Among the extension cords, oil cans, power tools, gasoline cans and usual detritus of a suburban garage he found what he wanted – a cardboard box which had once held a 42 inch Chinese-made television. It wasn't easy, but he managed to cut it with a utility knife and then wrap a roll of black insulating tape around a four-foot length of the stiff cardboard which he bent around his forearm. It extended from the top of his left fingers around his elbow to the palm of his hand.

He stopped at one time to check on his hostages. Nothing had changed except the men were also leaning forward and there was a distinct smell of vomit in the room – the fat woman had vomited and yellow liquid dribbling from her chin down her front and onto her lap. That was just fine. He hadn't planned to let them up to use the toilet either – making them sit in their own urine and feces was a great way to minimize any resistance.

He checked on them twice more before returning to the garage. Nothing had changed.

Back at the bench he fashioned a short length of tape and cardboard which he attached to the splint from above his forefinger to above his left thumb. He had created a loop which, with his forefinger and thumb, made a circle that would fit over the gear-change in his car. This way he wouldn't have to reach over with his right arm to change gears. He tested it with his baton. It was still painful to push the lever away, but pulling it towards him was almost painless. It wasn't ideal. He didn't want to rely on it to get him to London, but in a pinch it would work. He'd give Jones another two hours to call. In the meantime he knew he would have to have all his wits about him to get away from Colwyn Bay. He needed food and he needed sleep. There was plenty of food in the kitchen and there were beds to sleep in, but could he sleep soundly with his hostages still alive? The answer to that was obvious. He'd deal with it, but first things first – he would eat.

41

Ann found cutting the leather of the strap that encircled her right wrist difficult and slow. If she didn't sit on the knife in just the right position it wouldn't stay still when she moved her wrist against the serrated edge. She tried to get the blade between the strap and her skin, but she couldn't maneuver her wrist through the ninety degrees needed to line up the blade without leaning back, and making it obvious what she was doing. The only way she could use the knife was to hold it in her right hand so the last couple of inches of the blade just reached the bindings around her left hand. She could look down at the leather, but if Gareth saw her doing this, or making a sawing movement, she had no doubt he would carry out his threat. His appearances were unpredictable. Sometimes it would be fifteen minutes between his checks, at others only one or two minutes. She sat slumped forward, head a little to the right, so when he reappeared she had some warning in her peripheral vision.

Holte's wife, Margaret, vomited. She retched once or twice before the vomit reached her mouth then it slid down her front – its odor pervading the room. Ann thought Gareth would have heard the retching, but he didn't appear. Ann hoped this meant wherever he was he was out of earshot of his hostages. She allowed herself to saw a little more vigorously at her ties. She almost gave it away and for a split second was sawing when Gareth reappeared, but he noticed the stench and the vomit and had looked at Margaret before scanning the room and withdrawing.

Ann knew she'd have to be more careful and only saw when she could hear other sounds in the house. Although this wasn't ideal it was safer, and she needed to rest her right arm. She also did not want to drop the knife – it was their only chance they had of getting out alive. She didn't think about what she was going to do when she got her left hand free – she'd worry about that when she got there.

One thing she did realize is that Gareth did not need five hostages. She had no idea what his plans were, but they certainly didn't include taking more than one or two with him when he left.

Holte and his son Billy appeared to be asleep with their heads slumped forward. Holte had tried to stay awake between intermittent snoozing, but now seemed in deep slumber. Billy had remained watchful for a while, but had eventually succumbed. He was asleep when his mother, Margaret, had vomited. She was still quietly sobbing and had slumped forward too.

John looked across at Ann, but she had her head bowed. After Gareth's last check they had briefly made eye contact before Ann had leaned forward and resumed her sawing. Occasionally, she would hit part of the chair with the knife blade. John would wince and hold his breath; Ann would stop and wait to see if Gareth had heard. He never appeared and she resumed the sawing after thirty seconds. Her luck might not hold out forever, but there was nothing John could do to help her. He had tried to loosen the bonds around his wrists and legs, but there was no movement. He wondered if Ann had tied him like this so he would be unable to take the risk of escaping.

The night dragged on.

42

Gareth checked his hostages one more time. Perhaps he could relax a little – they were sufficiently scared and submissive to not cause any problems for him, but he couldn't be too sure. He'd stick to his plan and eat first. There wasn't much he liked about Welsh cooking, but he did appreciate a mixed grill and it looked like Holte's refrigerator had been stocked with this in mind. He heated a little vegetable oil in the large Teflon-coated frying pan on top of the stove, and turned on the upper burner in the gas oven. To the pan he added bacon. It was good bacon too – Holte, or his wife, knew their bacon. It had minimal fat and curled appreciatively as he added a few mushrooms. To a tray in the oven he added a small cut of sirloin, three large sausages, and a slice of gammon – in his opinion you couldn't have too much animal protein. He sliced a couple of tomatoes in half and added these to the grill. The bacon and mushrooms were done first and he pushed them out onto a plate warming in the bottom of the oven. He added a couple of eggs and a slice of bread to soak up the fat in the pan. He couldn't find any black pudding, but he found Cheshire cheese and melted a few slices on to the bread.

Ten minutes later his meal was ready. He took an oven mitt and piled all the food from the pan and the oven onto one plate, then sat at the small table in the kitchen to enjoy the fruits of his labors. The one item he couldn't risk, and which would have completed the experience for him, was a bottle of IPA from a local brewery in Conwy. There were six nestled in the door of the refrigerator, but he reminded himself he needed to be as alert as possible for the next few hours.

He also needed that hour's sleep he'd promised himself, and for that he had to deal with the hostages. Thinking about his problem he wondered about keeping the boy alive. What was his name? Oh, yes, Billy. Children could make good hostages because the police might take risks with an adult they wouldn't with a child – they would make sure no harm came to the boy. But it wasn't that simple – children wouldn't make good shields.

They were too short and too small, and would give police marksmen too big a target for even them to miss. No, he was probably better off without a hostage. In some ways a lot better off. The authorities knew he had at least two hostages and as long as they didn't know what had happened to them it could work to his advantage. He munched his way through the food. He was hampered by not being able to use his left arm, but found that cutting his meat using his right hand made for a slower, but more enjoyable meal. He wondered if this would be his last mixed grill for a while – his escape plans didn't include ending up in countries where he could easily find this food.

He scraped the last of the egg yolk off the plate using a half slice of bread and picked up his baton. He looked at its polished wood. "Why not?" he thought. It had served him well so far. The easiest way to do it would be to take out the fat woman first, then the American woman, then Beaton. The boy would be last. He stood, stretched, put his baton down briefly, placed the dirty dishes in the sink, because that's what he always did, picked up the baton, and started for the dining room.

His phone rang.

43

Ann could hear Gareth preparing his meal in the kitchen. She tried to use the time to be more aggressive with sawing at the leather, but her right hand was becoming more fatigued and she had to stop every minute for at least thirty seconds to regain some strength. She also found that if she waited too long before a rest she would end up clumsily nicking her skin. Each nick was only small, but together they caused a rivulet of blood to run from her wrist to her chair and drip on to the carpet. She risked a glance at the belt. She estimated she had sawn through three-quarters of its width. She tried moving to see if the remainder would break, but it held tight.

She kept on sawing.

The sounds from the kitchen faded. She stopped sawing. After about a minute she could still make out some noises – she assumed that Gareth had finished cooking and was now eating his meal. She resumed sawing. She wondered what was going to happen when he finished his meal – she had a bad feeling about it. Did he still need any of them? He might need John to drive his car, but she'd noticed the splint he'd fashioned for his arm and hand and realized it could be used to change gears in a car. What was he planning to do? Would he check to make sure his hostages were still securely restrained? Maybe he wouldn't bother, but she couldn't be sure. Maybe he'd ... she preferred not to think about that. She closed her eyes and focused on the sawing. If she concentrated she thought she could cut through the belt in another ten minutes – and then what? She kept sawing.

The sounds from the kitchen changed. It sounded like he'd finished his meal and was putting a dish in the sink. Ann stopped sawing and listened. She couldn't hear anything for a few seconds. Then, a phone rang.

44

Gareth put his baton back on the table, pulled his phone out of his jacket pocket and answered the call.

"I've got you a car." It was Jones.

"Good, thanks. That's earlier than you said."

"I know. I didn't have to go as far as Manchester. I couldn't get an automatic, but I've gone one better. I've got you a car with a driver."

Gareth said nothing.

Jones continued, "I know you like to work alone, but this driver needs to disappear too. He's worked for us for a long time, and he has his own plans, so he needs to get to London. Are you OK with this?"

"Do I have a choice?"

"Probably not. I suppose you could drive whatever vehicle you have to London, but I give the chances of your making it about one in ten. This way I give the chance of not making it one in ten. Agree?"

"Maybe. Tell me more."

"I am not sure where you are in Colwyn Bay, but I have arranged a vehicle and driver to be at Bryn-y-Maen when you get there. He will be there in fifteen minutes from now and will wait a maximum of another fifteen minutes before he takes off. Do you know where Bryn-y-Maen is?"

"I'm not sure."

"Do you know the Llanwrst road?"

"Yes. I'm not too far from it now."

"Well, it's on the Llanwrst road and about one or two miles south of town."

"OK."

"But don't drive there directly. There's a road block at the edge of town. You can get around it by taking a narrow country lane down towards Mochdre and taking a left back up the hill to Bryn-y-Maen. You'll have to check it out on your phone."

"OK."

"A couple of hundred yards south of Bryn-y-Maen, on the right-hand side, there's a widening of the road and enough space for a couple of vehicles to pull over. That is where your ride will be waiting for you. It will probably be a van, and the driver will have instructions to change that vehicle for another. It's all been set up. Got it?"

"Yeah."

"Well, the driver won't have all the details of where the next vehicle will be. You'll have that."

"OK?"

"After you meet him you'll carry on towards Llanwrst. Before you get there you will turn right on the A548 which will take you through the town. Follow the signs to Betws-y-Coed. When you get there continue on the A5. About a mile out of town there is a pub, the Horse and Crown, and in the parking lot at the back of the pub there will be a car with a note under the wiper. The note will have your name written on it. Keys will be on top of the rear tire, driver's side. Got it?"

"Yeah. Get to Betws-y-Coed. Horse and Crown on the right."

"Good. I have a little further to travel today to cover my tracks, and then … well, who knows? Bye."

He hung up.

Gareth stayed sitting. He wondered if he had a choice, or if he could trust Jones. By now his face and his car would be known to every cop from Colwyn Bay to London, and probably every cop in Wales too. He could risk trying the ferry from Holyhead to Dublin, but his escape plan involved documents and plans still in his apartment in Battersea. And, say he got to Dublin, where was he going to go from there?

No, it had to be London, but he didn't like the idea of the other driver. The other driver probably didn't relish it either. At least Jones had given him a little edge by telling him where the next car would be. It still seemed like a set-up, but Gareth brought up Google Maps on his phone and worked out how he would get to the meeting spot. It was as simple as Jones had said. The only problem he could foresee would be on those narrow one-car-width roads. There probably wouldn't be any traffic on them at this time of night, but if he had to back up to a passing area he might have difficulty with only one useful hand. He wondered what he could do to improve the odds of at least getting to the meeting. He smiled to himself – maybe he could create a diversion and deal with his hostages at the same time. Colwyn Bay had seen it once before – maybe they would get to see it again

45

Ann thought she heard noises from the garage and maybe the sound of a car starting and driving off, but she couldn't be certain. She rested her arms. She found she was now only able to saw about ten seconds before she had to take a break for a minute or two. She let her head fall forwards and she closed her eyes.

John had done his best to keep awake, but as the night drew on, he found his head falling forwards more often and his eyelids closing. He'd tried to encourage Ann and he knew she was working on cutting the leather straps, but he knew she couldn't afford to be seen to be communicating with him. The first face Gareth saw every time he came in the room was Ann's, and she had to appear to be subdued and beaten.

He must have dozed off because he suddenly jerked his head up.

Something had changed. He looked around.

Ann was leaning forward just as before, but was completely still. Holte on his left was snoring, Billy was asleep and Margaret seemed to be sleeping too. The lights were on, the door to his right was open. He looked up – thick black smoke was creeping across the ceiling and into the room.

For a couple of seconds he hesitated, not wanting to incur Gareth's wrath for speaking, then realized it didn't matter.

"Ann," he said.

She looked up, surprised, and saw the danger. As they looked the smoke increased and thickened. They could hear noises from the kitchen now – or maybe it was the garage – but they didn't sound human. They sounded like the crackling of a fire growing and taking over the house.

Ann redoubled her efforts and with one last pull the belt holding her wrist separated and her left arm was free. She began to untie her other belts.

John watched the smoke now billowing into the room. He began to cough. Holte, Margaret and Billy had woken and were coughing too. Ann might escape by herself, but the smoke would suffocate the rest of them unless … there was one thing which might work. He managed to free his feet just enough that he could rock the chair from left to right, and with a final push of his left foot he, and the chair, fell to his right. The falling chair hit the door and it closed. John was now on his side on the floor and more helpless than before. Smoke was still coming in around the edges of the door, but he'd stopped most of it. However, he knew it wouldn't last long. He also knew more people died from smoke inhalation than burns in a house fire, and the flimsy door might hold smoke back for a while, but when the fire arrived on the other side the door it would only last for seconds. He could hear the crackling of the fire had turned to a roar.

He was coughing and his eyes were streaming when Ann reached him and slashed at the ties around his arms and feet. He stood and found himself free. In the haze he could see that the rest of the Holte family was still tied to their chairs. Ann gave him the knife and shouted at him to free them.

John cut away Margaret's bonds first. She started towards the closed door, as if to escape that way, but John stopped her and pushed her around the top of the table where Ann had sat.

Ann had gone behind Holte and pulled back the drapes to reveal a narrow patio door. It was locked. For a second she panicked, then realized the key was in the lock. She turned it, pushed the door handle down and the door opened letting in fresher air. She pulled Margaret through the door and looked back into the room.

John had freed Holte's wrists and was cutting the ties around Holte's legs, but he could feel the heat of the fire coming through the wall behind him. Through the haze he could see the surface of the door beginning to buckle and smoke. He only had a few seconds left. Holte was free. John pushed him towards the patio door, grabbed Billy and his chair and pulled both after him through the patio. He kept going until he was twenty yards away, when he was stopped by a garden fence. He looked back at the house in time to see the fire explode into the dining room and engulf everything. The glass in the windows shattered and the fire billowed onto the patio and licked at the eaves.

The roar of the fire made any conversation impossible, but at only twenty yards away they still weren't safe – it was going to get hotter. John could see the wooden fence beside him beginning to steam and looked around. They were all still coughing uncontrollably. Billy was still tied in his chair and was staring at the fire. His parents were doing the same, apparently mesmerized by what they were witnessing. Ann had backed up to the fence and in the bright light and heat from the fire looked for a way to get further from the house. She found it. There was a gate in the fence which led to the back yard of the neighbor's house. She opened it and let John through – he was still pulling Billy in his chair – and then she pulled Holte and Margaret through the door too. In the shelter of the fence John freed Billy from his chair. They all moved away from the fire.

46

Gareth thought about starting the fire in the kitchen, but he couldn't be certain that it would get noticed soon enough. If a diversion was going to be effective it would have to be quick, sudden and happen soon. It needed to be spectacular too. The object was to divert attention from him while he drove to the meeting place. It needed to be at the front of the house, not in the kitchen, which was too far back. It had to start in the garage.

He already knew there were cans of paint, white spirits, kerosene, acetone, engine oil and gasoline in the garage. It was also likely the gas tank of the car Holte had been working on still held fuel. There were canisters of propane and butane for camping stoves and there was plenty of plastic, cardboard and wood.

Using mainly his right arm Gareth made a small pile of wood and cardboard and topped it with a plastic sac full of rags to which he added several pints of kerosene and engine oil. He loosened the cap on the acetone and poured a little on the floor about six feet from the pile. He poured gasoline on the pile and then laid a trail of gasoline from there, out of the side door of the garage, and towards his car. He checked his watch. He had just over twenty minutes left. He sat in his car and struck one of the matches he had taken from the kitchen and dropped it on the gasoline.

He didn't wait to see what happened.

He didn't need to – he knew exactly what was going to happen.

He'd driven less than five minutes when he pulled over for a police car coming towards him with its blue lights flashing. The police ignored him completely. He wondered if the road-block was now unmanned. He checked his watch. He still had time if he avoided the road-block, and it was probably better he didn't tempt fate, so he took the narrow lanes Jones had suggested. It wasn't easy. Changing gears was hard and painful, even with the device he'd made, so he just kept the vehicle in a low gear. The engine screamed if he went over twenty-five, but it wasn't his car, and at that time in the morning there was no one around to complain. He reached the hamlet of Bryn-y-Maen, turned right and in a hundred yards had left the village behind him. A half-mile further and there it was, just like Jones had said – a van at the side of the road. He pulled up behind the van and checked his watch. He still had three minutes to go. He slipped his baton under the splint wrapping he had on his left arm. He got out of the car, pocketed the keys, walked forward to the passenger side and opened the door to the van.

"Give me one reason I should let you into this van," Burns said. He was holding a pistol directed at Gareth's head.

Gareth hesitated for a second before replying, and hauling himself into the van. "I know where our next vehicle is."

"Where is it?"

"In Betws-y-Coed."

"Where in Betws-y-Coed?"

"I'll tell you when we get there," said Gareth fastening his seatbelt. He looked at Burns and the gun then nodded towards the road. "I think we'd better get going, don't you?"

Burns said, "You weren't in my plans." He put the gun on his lap, started the van and moved onto the road.

"You weren't in mine either," said Gareth, "But I wasn't expecting a broken arm. Thank you for helping me out."

Burns said nothing and kept driving. The first signs of dawn were appearing with the hint of lightening of the grey sky in the east.

Gareth weighed the odds. He noticed the van had an automatic transmission, which would have made it easier for him to drive, but it also had some sort of logo on the side which would make it easy to identify, so even if he could change number plates he wouldn't achieve very much. He had to assume the van was being sought by the police, or soon would be. He didn't know what vehicle would be waiting at the Horse and Crown. He just hoped he would be able to drive it, because it was obvious to him that either he or Burns was going to make it to

London – one of them wouldn't. There was no advantage having two men in the car once they left Betws-y-Coed. He also had to assume Burns had made the same calculations. For the time being he might as well relax because nothing was going to happen until they reached the pub.

47

It had been a rush job. For anyone else he would have said "no", but he also knew this was someone he shouldn't say "no" to. He'd always been paid well by him and this time he was getting another five thousand because of the urgency. His only hesitation was because he was working on his native soil. He didn't mind carrying out his profession abroad, but it could be dangerous so close to home. The police here had access to CCTV, labs, and techniques those foreign countries had never heard of.

He'd got another five grand for obtaining the car. He'd had to give his brother-in-law, Richie, half of that, but Richie said the car was untraceable and legal. He pointed out it couldn't be both, but Richie had only shrugged and smiled. He got his wife to drive the car – it was an older model anonymous white Ford – while he drove his own car with the goods inside.

It wouldn't take him long to rig up the Ford. He'd invented his own device and had learned to set it up in less than five minutes in Afghanistan, and he still had a few of the Soviet F1's he'd acquired then. Most were safely stored in the Middle East, but a few had made it back to Wales after his deployment ended. For years he wondered why he had risked bringing them back here, but at least he would have two less to worry about now.

He was told to stay around and make sure the plan worked, which was no problem – he was a professional and always made sure. If it didn't work he was told to use alternative means to achieve the goal. He was tempted to ask, "What is it with the euphemisms?" but he decided to keep quiet. He was also told there would probably be only one of them – one with a slight limp – it was unlikely there would be two.

They were now less than ten minutes from the pub. He found a place to pull off the road and his wife stopped close behind him in the Ford. Using illumination from the parking lights of her car he changed the rear plates on his car in less than a minute. Next, using a small flashlight held in his mouth, he changed the front plates. Out of the trunk he took a package and laid it on the front passenger seat in the Ford. His wife took over driving of his car while he took the Ford. It had taken him less than three minutes and during this time no vehicle had passed them – this time he took the lead. They reached the Horse and Crown and continued past. The rear parking lot was dark. There were no security lights, which probably meant there was no CCTV either, but he had to make sure.

They turned and drove back past the pub and pulled over to the side of the road. He got out and walked back to his wife and asked her to meet him in the same spot in exactly fifteen minutes and every five minutes after that. She drove away. He walked along the edge of the road. There was no traffic, but that might change soon, the sky in the east was turning to grey from black and it felt like it was going to rain. He walked past the pub building, turned into the entranceway and followed it to the side of the pub. He stood at the corner of the stone building and glanced around the back. In the half light he could see there were security lights, but they were not switched on – he assumed that they were only active during opening hours. He couldn't see any cameras or any motion detector lights, and there were no lights on in the pub, but there was only one way to be sure.

He pulled a peaked cap out of his pocket, put it on his head, stepped into the driveway and walked directly across the parking lot with his head bowed and looking away from the building. Nothing happened – no lights came on and no dog barked. He reversed direction and walked back the same way.

Again, nothing happened.

He walked back to the Ford, started it, performed a U-turn and as quietly as possible drove it into the parking lot as far away from the pub building as he could. This was always the tricky bit. The Soviet F1 hand grenade was now obsolete, partly because it offered a choice of time fuses, and in the heat of combat a wrong fuse could be chosen. He'd always used the standard four second fuse. It was also a so-called "defensive" device. It was supposed to be used from cover because it could scatter shrapnel up to two hundred yards away.

It hadn't always worked. There'd been that time in Kandahar when … well, he didn't like to think of that. He concentrated on the task. Five minutes later he stood, carefully closed and locked the doors, placed the key where he had been told to, left the note he'd prepared under the wiper, and walked back across the parking lot to the road. He turned right and two minutes later his wife picked him up. For a few moments he looked at the map on his phone. He asked his wife to drive a few hundred yards and then take a right onto a narrow country lane. She did this and pulled into a widening of the road by a field gate. He got out of the car and leaned on the gate while his wife turned the car around.

Across the field, and an intervening hedge, he could just see the parking lot. It wasn't ideal, but it was far enough away from the blast. Now, all he had to do was wait.

It started to rain.

48

"Where now?" Burns asked.

"What?" Gareth said and sat upright.

"Where do we go now?"

"Sorry, must have dozed off," said Gareth, rubbing his eyes with his right hand. "Where are we?"

"Look."

Gareth saw a 'Welcome to Betws-y-Coed' sign drift past his window.

"Oh, we're here. Take the A5 south."

"Then what?"

"Tell me when we get to the A5." Gareth rested his head against the passenger door window and closed his eyes.

Maybe if the security services had spent a little less money on the eavesdropping equipment, and a little more on the comforts in the van, Burns would have had an even chance, but the bench seat was going to make it too easy for Gareth.

"We're on the A5 now," said Burns.

"Keep going until we get to a pub. It's called the Horse and Crown and it should be on your right. The parking lot is behind the pub." Gareth eased back in his seat and resumed his relaxed position. Burns drove into the parking lot. There was one other vehicle there – a white Ford. So much for making sure it was the right vehicle. Burns parked between the Ford and the pub. He put the vehicle in park and reached for his gun. He never made it. His face exploded in pain as Gareth's baton hit him across his nose. He turned away. Gareth's second blow hit him in his left temple and then it was over. He slumped forward. Gareth hit him once more across the back of his neck, but he knew it hadn't been necessary. He replaced the baton in his splint and picked up the pistol. It was a 9mm Browning – maybe it would come in handy – he stuck it in his jacket pocket. He reached over to the key and turned off the engine.

He stepped down from the van and looked around. The sky was struggling to get lighter and a few drops of rain were falling.

It looked like one of those times when it was going to rain all day. He walked over to the Ford and slowly walked around it. He was reluctant to change to this vehicle when he had a perfectly good one with automatic transmission already, but he knew he had little choice. He tried the doors, but they were locked so he reached under the wheel arch and found the keys where Jones said they would be. He opened the driver's door and looked in. It was an automatic. Maybe Jones had come through for him after all.

He pulled himself into the car and sat in the driving seat. That was when he heard the pop and the fizz.

He knew what it was.

"You bastard, Jones," was the last thing Gareth said.

From his vantage point the man at the gate watched Gareth get into the car and sit down. He started to count, but only got to three when the first grenade exploded. The second grenade, the gas tanks in the Ford and the van blew up moments later.

He got back in the car next to his wife and they drove back to their home, and breakfast, in Wrexham.

49

Tibbs watched Burns leave, unobserved behind the net curtains and darkness of Auntie Olly's front room. He picked up his phone and texted, then turned to walk back and wake the others. He didn't have to – Souza and Mukherjee were standing in the hallway outside the kitchen in the darkness.

"I thought I heard the front door," said Souza.

"You did," Tibbs replied. "I don't know where he's gone. The car will be here in a minute. Let's get outside."

A few spots of rain were falling when the Jaguar pulled into the kerb. Georgina Southport, the 'Witch", rolled down the passenger window and said, "Get in".

Tibbs, Souza and Mukherjee obeyed and slid into the rear seats.

"He's headed south," she said, when they were all seated, and indicated to her driver to carry on. She swiveled in her seat to face the others. "I'm afraid this is what I suspected. On the other hand I'm not sure what I thought would happen, but it wasn't this. We are still not sure what's going on, but we are following Burns. We have a tracer in the van and our other car is following him closer." She paused when her cell phone beeped. She looked at the screen.

"He's about a mile south on the Llanwrst road." She looked at the vehicle's GPS display. "That's down here? Got it?" she asked her driver and pointed to the screen. He nodded. It was Jack who had been with her in London the previous day. She turned to the back seat again, but before she could say anything her phone beeped again.

"He's stopped. We'd better pull over before we get too much closer. Apparently, he's just south of a place called Bryn-y-Maen." Again she looked at the GPS screen.

Jack pulled off the narrow road into the space in front of a farm house. They waited, saying nothing and hearing nothing apart from the distant wails of emergency vehicle sirens. Souza, who was seated on the left noticed a glow in the sky to the east, but kept quiet. They were all focused, and despite their lack of sleep, were all alert.

After five minutes The Witch's phone beeped. "He's on the move again. Let's go."

They passed through the hamlet of Bryn-y-Maen encountering no other traffic. A quarter-mile further on they came across a single car pulled off at the side of the road. Southport ordered the car to slow. She made a note of the vehicle's number plate, checked it with her colleagues and said. "That's the car the police have been looking for – the one Williams was driving. Souza, jump out and check it. Tibbs, call the police and tell them where it is. I'm looking at the GPS and you can tell them it's on the Llanwrst road, just south of Bryn-y-Maen. "

"Yes, Ma'm," answered Tibbs and Souza simultaneously.

She continued, "And it probably means that Burns now has a passenger. I am not sure what that means, or if it's Williams, but Burns must know we can track him, so at some point he's going to have to switch vehicles or at least get rid of the van. We've been following him for fifteen minutes now, so he's going to have to make the switch soon."

Souza returned to the Jaguar and said. "Doors unlocked, no one inside, nothing in boot to interest us."

"OK, get back in. Let's catch up. I want us two minutes behind our car, and they have to be two minutes behind Burns."

As soon as Souza closed her door Jack accelerated and pushed the powerful Jaguar through the bends and small villages, paying no attention to posted speed limits, and rapidly closed the time between them and the van Burns was driving.

They followed Burns as he drove through the sleeping town of Llanwrst and took the turn to Betws-y-Coed.

Southport's cell phone rang.

"Yes?" she answered. "Oh … drive past at the speed limit and make sure you're out of sight before you turn around and close up on him. Where has he stopped? OK. The parking area behind The Horse and Crown. And what did you see? OK. I understand."

She hung up and said, "Jack, slow down, lights off and we'll wait. We are about a quarter mile away. I want us 100 yards away and on this road. It seems he pulled into the Horse and Crown and our other car got a glimpse of the van and another vehicle there. Any vehicles leave the parking lot … we stop them."

They waited. In the darkness they could make out the swinging Horse and Crown pub sign. A few more drops of rain fell on the windshield, otherwise it was quiet.

The first grenade exploded.

Both security vehicles were shielded from the secondary blasts of the fuel tanks by the pub's buildings, but not from the surprise, the flash, the noise and the falling debris.

Southport took a few seconds to react. "Oh, my God. Go and check, but just look around the edge of the building into the parking area. I don't want any casualties, then come back here.'

Tibbs, Souza and Mukherjee left the vehicle.

She called their other car, "Are you all right? Good … I don't know. I assume it was a bomb of some sort. Can you see the others from where you are? Good. Hold on."

A couple of minutes later the rear doors of the car opened and the three shaken security officers took their seats in the car.

Tibbs spoke for them all, "It's a mess Ma'am. There were probably two vehicles which are still burning. At this distance we couldn't tell, but there seemed to be a body in the van. There is debris all over the place. Most of the windows of the pub have gone. A few lights have come on in the pub. It's impossible to say if there are any other injured."

"OK. Thanks, all of you. It's worse than I thought. I didn't for one moment expect this. Tibbs, make the 999 call, but then we have to be out of here."

"Ma'am?" Tibbs asked.

She turned and could see the questions in their eyes. She said, "I can see you would like to help, and I really appreciate that, but the best thing you can do is call 999." She nodded at Tibbs, who reached for his phone. She added, "We have to think of the best way of handling this, both in the short term and the long term. We are going to get together and talk about this before we get

289

back to London, and I am sure we'll be talking this over for the next few weeks."

She called her other car. "Let's take off. We'll wait till you pass us then we'll follow you back to London. We can stop for breakfast on the M6."

She turned to Jack and said, "Give us a few minutes then we can head back." Their other car passed them. Jack kept his lights off, turned the car around and parked at the side of the road. The light from the burning vehicles in the pub's courtyard illuminated the road behind them.

"Now, there's something unusual Ma'm," he said, looking ahead.

A car turned out of a lane a two-hundred yards away and headed away from them. They watched its tail lights receding.

Jack added, "I don't think your average British motorist could completely ignore a fire in a pub parking lot and drive away like that."

"Good point, Jack. Wait until he's out of sight then get going," said Southport.

"Do you want me to close on him?"

"Not yet. He's going to get suspicious if we suddenly appear on his tail – after all why didn't we stop for a pub fire? I think it would be better if we call our other car, ask them to stop at the roadside, and make a note of his number plate as he drives past. What do you think?"

Jack nodded. Southport made the call and five minutes later they caught up with their other team at a roadside parking area. She confirmed with them that there was only one car between them and took the number plate details. They decided on a venue for breakfast and headed off south and east into the rain and towards London.

50

The ambulance had taken Holte and his family away. John and Ann had refused the ride to the hospital, but accepted the space blankets the fireman had offered them, and the cups of tea a neighbor magically produced. They were coughing less, exhaustion was overcoming them, but they hadn't been able to tear themselves away from the spectacle. They were standing a hundred yards from the fire and even at that distance could still feel the heat, but it was becoming less intense and the flames were being rapidly controlled by the hoses. Holte's house had been destroyed and the adjoining houses damaged. The neighborhood would have something to talk about and some healing to do. Property values would be temporarily lower until the scars of the fire had healed, but it could have been worse. John thought how lucky they had been and how close they had come to being killed. He put his arm around Ann's waist and found himself crying with tears running down his smoke-blackened cheeks.

Ann, hugged him back, kissed his cheek and said, "I love you."

"I love you more than ever."

They both sobbed and held each other close.

It had only been thirty minutes since they had knocked on the neighbor's door, but by then the fire had been called in and the fire trucks were on their way.

A uniformed policeman approached them.

"John Beaton? Ann Beaton?" he asked.

"Yes."

"I'm Sergeant Llewellyn. I'm in charge of controlling this site. Could you come with me, please?" It was said more as an order than a request, but John and Ann followed him to a dark blue police van where he introduced them to another man who was standing at the back between the open doors. He was wearing blue jeans, and a thick waterproof jacket. He looked weary as he showed them his ID.

"I'm Detective Inspector Joel Johnson. I am based in Chester and wouldn't normally be here, but, as you might know, the police force here is overwhelmed and we are helping out. I would like you to answer a few questions."

Both John and Ann nodded. It seemed easier than speaking.

Johnson continued, "I've seen the recordings from the supermarket and the shopping centre. It looks like you drove away with Gareth Williams."

"Who's Gareth Williams?" asked John.

"The man whose car you drove away in."

"Oh, that's his name. We didn't know. He never told us."

"So, why did you drive away?"

"He gave me no choice. We'd seen what he could do with that stick of his. He hit those policemen hard – by the way, are they OK?"

"Who?"

"The policemen he hit in the supermarket and the one who tried to stop him."

"I can't tell you."

"Yes, you can," John said, louder than he wanted, surprising himself and noticing he was a little irritable.

Johnson hesitated, "I can say that two are going to be OK and the third had surgery, but I don't know any more than that."

"I hope they are all going to be OK," said Ann.

John added, in a more even voice, "The reason I ended up driving is the policeman who tackled him, broke his left arm, and he told me unless I drove he was going to take the stick to my wife's face."

"Thank you. We figured as much, but we couldn't be certain. Then what happened?"

"He made us drive up here."

"Do you know why?"

"Not to begin with, but he'd met the family who lived here before. It turned out I had met them too."

"When?"

John replied, "I was here a few weeks ago and the night before I left I went to a fish and chip shop in Colwyn Bay. The family was there. I think the shop was burned down that night. Do you know what happened?"

"Well, not really. As I said, I'm from Chester. The detective who had been investigating that was injured in the supermarket, so I'm playing catch-up. I did read about it in the newspapers, and I have talked to some of my colleagues here about it."

"Well, I can't be certain but I think he was involved in that too. He seemed to know the family."

"So, you drove straight up here?"

"Yes, no, sorry, no. We went to Auntie Olly's house first."

"Auntie Olly?"

"She's my aunt. Well, she was my aunt. That's what I'm here for – to find out what happened, and then ... don't you know about that?"

"No."

"I'm not sure what happened to her. We are staying at her house ... look, couldn't this wait until later? We need to get some rest and clean up. We haven't slept since ... well, I don't know."

"OK. One last question and I'll have an officer drive you to where you are staying. What happened to Gareth Williams? Is he in that house?" Johnson asked looking at the fire.

"No, I don't think so."

John and Ann turned to look too.

"I parked his car on this side of the house and I can't see anything of it now."

"Thank you."

"You know he set the fire."

"No."

John opened his mouth to say a lot more, but all he could say is, "Let's talk later."

51

The restaurant on the M6 motorway was nearly empty. It was a rainy Saturday in early spring and no one who had any alternative would stop there for breakfast. It smelled of disinfectant and urine. It was inhabited by the bleary-eyed on their way home after dissipated Friday nights, truck drivers who had to be there, and the group of seven security team members who sat quietly around a couple of tables they had pushed together. They'd tried to get some sleep during the two hour drive from Betwys-y-Coed, but mostly they had sat quietly with their own thoughts.

Georgina Southport took aside the two men who had been driving the other car and talked to them for five minutes. Shortly afterwards, they finished their breakfasts, said their goodbyes, and headed off to London. Southport returned to the main group.

She had already decided what to do, or at least what she hoped the security services would do – the final decision would be made by some committee somewhere in the corridors of power in Whitehall. She needed to convince those sitting around the table with her now of the value of her approach.

"William Burns was a good friend of mine and a valuable member of my team," she started. She pulled out a chair and sat down. "But sometime in the last five years something changed. At first I didn't notice – I was just too busy, but other colleagues mentioned he was withdrawn, and distracted. I talked to him and he denied any problems, and maybe I could have stopped thinking about it there. As far as I knew he was single, lived alone, and he was nearing retirement. He was good at his job and had worked mainly in the Middle East section. He was fluent in Arabic. He's not the first late middle-aged male to wonder if his life choices had been good ones and I thought that was all it was.

"But then we started noticing some leaks of what was to us superficially minor information. Some tip-offs from reliable sources didn't pan out, some information we shared with Special

Branch and The Metropolitan Police got into the wrong hands. A contact in Syria was murdered, one in Lebanon disappeared. It seemed unfocused and unrelated. It wasn't like a specific foreign power could benefit from this information, but then who could? And then, for some reason, the Americans seemed to find out that we were having a problem. They are particularly sensitive about that because of our problems back in the 50's and 60's. So, I had to do something about it. If nothing else, someone was distracting us from our mission.

"You three," she nodded to Tibbs, Souza and Mukherjee. "And you, Jack, were ruled out early on in my checking. You either didn't have access to the information contained in the leaks, or you came to the service after the leaks started. Eventually, it came down to about five people who could have had access to the information. I won't tell you who the others were, but I talked to Burns, told him about the leaks and asked him to investigate. I also asked him to continue, or increase, his demonstration of his dissatisfaction with his job.

"He did a good job of that, but then he told me he was suspicious of Tibbs." She looked at Tibbs who gave a small nod of acknowledgement. "I gave him the benefit of the doubt and re-evaluated the security information I had on Tibbs, but I had Burns watched more closely. Then, one day he used a cell phone which he threw away in a bin in London. We got hold of it, analyzed it, and realized its significance, although it still didn't give us any information about the bigger picture.

"Then, we all ended up in Colwyn Bay." She paused. "It's going to take us longer to figure everything out, but in the meantime we are going to have to figure out a response we all agree on.

"I propose we develop the narrative that we are not entirely certain what happened, but it seems like Burns was acting on a tip, for some reason did not follow protocols, and was kidnapped and killed in the line of duty. It's a lie, I know, but it's probably a simpler story than having to admit he was a 'rogue' agent and we don't know why, and it'll still give us time to try to figure out what motivated Burns." She stopped.

"So, he died a hero, or that is what the public will be told?" asked Souza.

"Basically, yes."

No one spoke for thirty seconds as they considered the ramifications.

Souza said, "I can live with that, assuming the physical evidence doesn't contradict it. It spares the Service the embarrassment of the truth." She looked around the others. Mukherjee nodded his head in affirmation and said "OK", and finally Tibbs said, "OK."

Jack said, "I really haven't been involved, so I have no opinion, but I'll go along with it."

Souza added, "I assume there will be internal enquiries and maybe we'll all have to give statements, and be interrogated. If that happens I don't want to lie. You aren't asking us to do that are you?"

Southport replied, "No, that wouldn't be fair. I am only asking that if the Service decides to go along with this scenario that you will too. Internally, the Service needs to know the truth, but that may not be what we tell the public."

Southport looked at the others. None seemed particularly happy with what was being asked of them. She hoped in the long run they would appreciate keeping this out of the public eye.

She took a sip from her coffee. Her cell phone rang. She looked at the caller ID, stood, moved to a nearby table, and answered.

"Georgina Southport."

"Hi, it's Ella. How are you this morning?"

"Tired. I don't think I got any sleep last night."

"Well, I'm not sure I got any either. That car we rented was cold and painful the longer we stayed in it. I wanted to update you on what happened yesterday."

"OK."

"Basically, we followed the unknown man to an address in London. That you already know. I'll text you the address. We watched him and sometime in the early hours he decided to leave his house and we followed him. He didn't make it easy, and

297

we thought we'd lost him a couple of times, but we were lucky. He's not an easy man to follow – I think he naturally tries to cover his tracks and do the unexpected. I don't think he knew we were on to him, but I can't be sure. Eventually, he took an early morning flight to Paris, and he should be arriving there soon. I'm hoping our French associates will follow him from there. I'm flying there myself in a couple of hours."

"Did he do anything else?"

"He had breakfast and he made a few phone calls, but otherwise he was just another passenger waiting for a plane."

"So, he looks completely ordinary."

"Maybe, but he changed cars to get to the airport, he sat in the waiting area of another flight until the last moment, and then there was his behavior leaving Gatwick. I don't know what he has to do with the Hand of Hamsa, but something smells here."

Southport hesitated. She wasn't sure how much she should divulge. She said, "I spent the last twenty-four hours chasing around North Wales, or that's what it felt like. After I left you … and that was just, yes it was just yesterday … I went to Wales. Unfortunately, I lost one of my men. He was killed by what was probably a bomb, but it may also turn out that another man was killed in the explosion, and that man may have been involved in Hamsa too."

"Oh, dear. I'm sorry. That makes my complaints about sleeping in a car seem so petty," said Ella.

"It's OK. I don't remember my days of waiting around in cars with any fondness. You should get your employees to do that for you."

"I did. They shared the pain with me, and I was glad to have them with me – it took all three of us to get this far. I hope my colleagues in Paris can keep up with him."

"I hope so too. Look, I have to get back to my team. There's a lot to organize. Why don't we talk again at the beginning of next week. I'll call you."

"OK. I'll let you know what's happening at that end too. Au revoir."

Southport returned to the rest of her team. She was pleased to see they were talking more. She was about to comment when her phone gave a single beep. She looked at the screen. It was the message Ella had promised – the address Jones was using in London.

"Before my brain shuts down completely," she started. "I want to make some housekeeping arrangements. It occurred to me on our way down here that some of you may have had belongings in the van we lost."

"I had a bag in there – change of clothes, book, nothing much," said Tibbs.

"You need to claim it anyway. You can put that in next week – don't forget."

"Yes, Ma'am," replied Tibbs.

"What about you two?" she asked Souza and Mukherjee.

"Our stuff is still in a motel room in Colwyn Bay," answered Mukherjee.

"Well, I want you and Souza both back up there this evening." It was clear Mukherjee and Souza were not enthusiastic about this, but both kept silent. "I want you to liaise between us and the police. One of you will have to take Colwyn Bay and the other the bomb site. I will call you and discuss what we planned to say about Burns after I've arranged a meeting with some of my superiors – that should be today. I don't want to leave you naked up there. And for you, Tibbs," she faced her other colleague. "I will text you this address," she tapped her phone, "and you are going there this afternoon to check it out. We'll try to get the search warrant this morning. I'm not sure how important it will be, but don't go alone. Get some help from the local police. I don't think it'll be dangerous, but it will be better to assume it might be. Any questions we have we can discuss further in the car. We've still got another couple of hours before we get to London."

52

John and Ann sat in the back of the police car for the ten minutes it took to get to Auntie Olly's house. By the time they arrived there the rain, which had started out as a few drops on the car's windshield, was settling in for the day.

The grey dawn was light enough to allow them to see the lock, fumble with the keys, and open the door.

John let himself in first and switched on the lights for Ann. He looked at the floor, expecting to see the note he had left in the short hallway, but it wasn't there. He asked Ann to stay by the door while he looked around.

He checked the rooms, and found no one. He tried the back door and found it was closed with the key in the lock on the inside, and he found drying cutlery and china on the draining board next to the kitchen sink. He didn't know what to make of it, but at that moment he didn't care. He told Ann about what he had found, but all they were really concerned about was the outside doors were locked, the bathwater was hot, and a bed was waiting for them.

Four hours was not enough sleep, but it helped. The ravages of jet-lag, full bladders and feeling almost alert at the wrong time of day prevented John and Ann from sleeping any longer. They got up, dressed, brewed a cup of tea and ate a meal which could have been breakfast had it not been the wrong time of day. It was almost noon on Saturday, or 4:00 am back in Washington State, and they realized they had to face the authorities sooner or later, so they decided to get it over with. It was still raining outside, or they would have walked, so John called for a Hall's taxi and six pounds and ten minutes later they were dropped off at the headquarters of the North Wales Police.

Ten minutes later, for the second time in less than twenty-four hours, they found themselves facing Assistant Chief Constable Clive Owen. He smiled as they were ushered into his office by a constable, stood, shook their hands and invited them to sit. John noticed Owen looked tired and drawn, and wondered if he didn't look the same. Owen also had a dressing over a wound in his scalp, presumably the one caused by Gareth. Owen sat down slowly in his own chair.

"Thank you for coming in. I had planned last night to talk to you, but obviously that didn't happen. I am sorry you had to go through all that's happened to you, and I don't know how we could have prevented it." He hesitated, seemed to gather his thoughts and then began again. "I apologize if I seem a little slow. The doc told me to go home and rest, but there's a lot to do here. I'm expecting some relief in a couple of hours though."

John said, "The doctor's right. You had a concussion from that blow to your head. You need to go home and rest your body and your brain or you won't be good for anything or anyone. Go home and don't turn on the television, don't answer the phone, and don't read the newspapers."

Owen smiled, "Spoken like a doctor. Thank you. I appreciate it and I will go home as soon as I can." He pushed a button on the intercom and said. "Please could you ask DI Johnson to join us."

A minute later the door to Owen's office opened and Detective Inspector Johnson joined them and sat down.

"I believe you met briefly this morning. DI Johnson is taking over the investigation from Detective Jared who was injured yesterday."

Ann nodded and asked, "Was Jared the the policeman with you in the supermarket?"

"Yes."

"How is he doing?"

Owen hesitated for a second. "He's still unconscious. He underwent surgery last night for a blood clot on his brain. We are told he is likely to make a full recovery, but we don't know yet."

"What about the younger constable? The one who broke, oh … what's his name? Gareth? Yes, Gareth Williams's arm?"

"Constable … Constable Hughes. He's fine. He's like me – has a bad headache and is at home resting his body and brain, but he'll be OK."

"Good," said Ann.

Owen said, "I am going to let ... Johnson here take over most of the questioning and we are going to record this interview. Is that OK?"

Both John and Ann nodded. Owen seemed a little slow and if he wouldn't go home John thought the next best thing Owen could do would be to let someone else run the interview.

Johnson started by stating who was present, asked John and Ann for their full names, addresses and dates of birth. He then asked them to relate what had led to their coming to North Wales and the events of the last twenty-four hours.

For the most part Johnson let John and Ann relate the story with only a little prompting. He scribbled occasional notes on the pad in front of him. It was only when he got to the time when John had gone in to Olly's house to retrieve the book that he needed more details.

"So, you got the book and took it to Gareth Williams who was sitting in the back of the car?"

"Yes."

"What did he do with the book?"

"He looked at what had been written on the flyleaf, tore that page out and put it in his pocket."

"What did he do with the rest of the book?"

"I'm not sure. I think he put it on the seat next to him."

"And this was the book that was given to you in the fish and chip shop?"

"Yes."

"What was the title of the book?"

"I think it was Reamde."

"Reamde?"

"Yes."

"Did you read the message?"

"Yes."

"When?"

"In the house, before I took it to Gareth?"

"Do you recall what it said?"

"Some of it, not all. It said something like, 'Jones, 2005 I believe, Goldsmiths, Arabic'. Then there was a telephone number which I don't remember."

Johnson wrote this down and then asked, "Did it mean anything to you?"

"No, not really. I know Goldsmiths is a college in London, but that's about it."

Johnson paused for a few seconds to consider this then asked John and Ann to continue. It took about another half-hour before they came to the point, after the fire, when they first met Johnson. Johnson looked at his notes for a minute, thanked John and Ann for their help and terminated the recording.

"Now, we have a few questions," Ann said. "We don't have to record your answers, but we would like to know a few things."

"That's fair enough," answered Johnson, "but there may be a few things I cannot tell you about, and there are some things I still don't know anything about."

"Well, the first question I have is; are we safe? Where is Gareth Williams and can he still harm us?"

"That's one of the things I am not entirely certain about. First of all, from what you have told us, and from other evidence, we think he was acting alone here in Wales. There may be other players, whom we are trying to identify, but we doubt those are local. We also think it's highly likely he's dead. There was an explosion in Betws-y-Coed early this morning which it looks like killed two people – we think one is him, but we are going to have to rely on dental records, if we can get hold of them, and maybe DNA to make sure. We also found the book you gave to Gareth in the car you drove for him. I didn't really understand its significance until just now. The car was abandoned just south of here. So, yes, I believe you are safe."

"That's good," said John, but then he asked the question to which he thought he knew the answer but didn't really want to. "Why was Auntie Olly killed?"

"I don't know," said Johnson.

"I might know," said Owen, who had hardly participated in the interview. "You remember eating in the fish and chip shop?"

304

"Yes."

"And there you were given that book."

"Yes."

"The man who gave it to you worked for the security services. The message in the book was written for the security services. It's a pity he wasn't more direct when he gave it to you."

"He seemed in pain and injured at the time."

"Well, he was, and we think he was killed in the fish and chip shop by Gareth and an accomplice after you left."

John thought about that for a few seconds before asking, "But what has that got to do with Auntie Olly?"

"There is really only one reason why your Auntie Olly was killed and you may have worked it out. Have you?"

"I think so, but I'd really rather hear it from you."

"I believe, and so do the security services and the investigating officer, that Olwen Lewis was killed to get you back to Colwyn Bay. Is that what you were thinking?"

"Yes. I was afraid of that," said John.

"I'm sorry."

"But, who killed her? I understand it was likely digoxin poisoning. Is that correct?"

"That's correct, and it's likely that Gareth Williams was the one who gave it to her. Again, we're not completely certain."

"Oh." John couldn't think of anything else to say. He looked away and his eyes moistened.

"I have a couple of photos, and a short video of the person whom we think was Gareth William's accomplice. We got them a few hours ago. Have you ever seen this man before?" Johnson fished in his briefcase and pulled out a cell phone and a couple of photos and laid them on the desk in front of him. John and Ann leaned forward and looked at the photos of Jones, and at a brief video of him walking in an airport. Ella had sent them to London earlier in the day. John shook his head and remained silent.

Ann stated, "I've never seen him before," and then wondered. "What happens now?"

Owen replied, "The post-mortem, autopsy I believe you call it, was done yesterday. I don't have all the results, but it's likely the

305

body will be released to an undertaker next week. So, you can start to make funeral arrangements now. Sometime in the next month, maybe two, there will be an inquest. You don't have to be here for that."

"Thank you. We'll work on that now," said Ann. "Do you need us for any more questioning?" she asked Johnson.

"No, I believe we have it all. Why do you ask?"

"Well, one of the reasons for coming here was to spend some time with our family. We have a daughter in Italy who has asked us to visit her. We'd like to go there for a week or two. We'll check in here when we get back."

"I have no reason to ask you to stay around. Please let us know how we can contact you – just in case, and here's my card if you have to contact me." Ann took the card. "Do you have any objection to these arrangements?" he asked Owen.

"No." The reply was a little late coming. Owen was still not tracking appropriately.

Ann said, "We'll be staying at Il Villino hotel in a place called Santarcangelo." She wrote the names on a slip of paper and handed it across the desk. "I think you can find it on the internet. It's close to San Marino."

Johnson accepted the note and added, "However, I would like to ask you not to talk to the press about this. They might make both our lives a little difficult."

"We have no problem with that. It might even help if we were in Italy, but won't they be talking to others?"

"Oh, I am sure they will have a story, and we have no trouble with letting them know the truth eventually, but we are still pursuing the possibility of Gareth having an accomplice, and we don't want any information out about that just yet. Also, in particular, I believe Mr. Holte regrets talking to the press last time. By the way, he and his family are now on their way to stay at his sister's in Birmingham."

Johnson stood, indicating the end of the interview. He shook their hands, leaned over the intercom and asked, "Please arrange for someone to take Mr. and Mrs. Beaton home, and to take Assistant Chief Constable Owen home."

Owen opened his mouth to object, but said nothing.
John did not have to play doctor again.

53

"There's no alley at the back of the house, but we have a couple of constables watching the back from a house almost behind this one and they say it's all clear. I think we can go, Mr. Tibbs."

"Thank you, Sergeant. Let's go before it gets any darker."

It was 5:45 pm on the same afternoon that Tibbs and his colleagues had been taken back to London after their exploits in Wales and Tibbs was exhausted. He just wanted to get home, shower and sleep, but instead he was following up on Southport's instructions to search a house in south London. He was standing outside in the chilling rain, and the only saving grace was that when this task was eventually tied up his own flat was less than a fifteen minute drive away.

He followed the sergeant and a constable up the few steps to the front of the house which Jones had left just over twelve hours previously. Both policemen were wearing Kevlar jackets and helmets and carried a hand battering ram. Tibbs had a brief déjà-vu moment when he remembered he had been carrying a ram, intent on a similar purpose, less than a day earlier in Colwyn Bay. He stayed back and to the side while the policemen carried out their task.

The sergeant rapped on the door with his police baton and said in a commanding voice. "Mr. Jones, this is the police. I am Sergeant Thomas Underdown of the Metropolitan Police. I have a warrant to search this house. Please open the door."

There was no reply. He waited ten seconds and repeated the request.

Again there was no reply.

"Mr. Jones. If you do not open this door in the next thirty seconds I will be obliged to force an entry."

Tibbs was wondering why it couldn't be five seconds and he could get out of the rain, but he was also a government employee and he knew protocols were protocols, sometimes for a good reason.

The thirty seconds expired, the policemen swung back the ram and the door splintered and opened with the first blow. They put down the ram at the side of the entryway and walked into the house. Tibbs followed. All was quiet inside the house, then they heard a voice.

"Eight – seven – six – five…"

"Get out!" Tibbs shouted, but by then both policemen had turned and raced into the street with him. They hurtled across the road and all three crouched behind the police vehicle.

They couldn't hear the rest of the countdown, and there was no blast from an explosion, but there were several low thumps and when they risked a look flames had already filled the hallway where they'd been standing, and intensely bright fires could be seen in both upper and lower rooms of the house. The glass in the windows of the lower room shattered.

"Shit," said Sergeant Underdown. He took charge, "Constable, take the house on the left. Get people out. I'll take the one on the right. Tibbs, call for fire and help."

Underdown and his colleague ran across the road and started banging on doors. Tibbs dialed 999 for emergency services. Was that the second or third time he'd called them today? He didn't want this to become a habit, nor did he want to make a habit of being nearly blown up or fried. The fire was becoming more intense, so he moved a little further along the road away from the heat.

The two other policemen who had been watching the house the rear ran up. Underdown told them to move the cars, block off the street, and continue knocking on doors. People started coming out of nearby houses. Some were dressed only in bedroom slippers and shirtsleeves, but others were fully prepared with umbrellas, boots and coats. Uniformly, they stood and stared, reluctant to move away from the disaster revealing itself before them, but like all Londoners they moved when the police herded them away from the fire. Tibbs heard sirens and another police car arrived, then another. Barriers across the street were erected and the first fire engine arrived. Hoses were uncoiled, hydrants located and in less than five minutes the first jet of water leapt through the window of the upper storey of what had been Jones's house.

Tibbs looked at the remains of Jones's house and knew that they would be very lucky to find anything remaining which would help the security services pin down who Jones was, or what he had been up to.

For the second time that day he turned his back on a disaster. He now understood better why Southport had left the scene in North Wales. He walked around the corner to his car, started it and drove away. He called Southport on the way and left a brief message on her answering system.

Less than an hour later he was asleep in his own bed.

54

The signal never reached Jones. If it had he might have been surprised that the authorities had so quickly got on his trail. The system he had installed in his house gave him thirty seconds to shut down its auto-destruct application. If it received no return signal from him in those thirty seconds, the count-down recording played for ten seconds, and then the incendiary devices were triggered. Within five minutes all evidence of the activities surrounding Jones's existence in London would be destroyed.

The signal could have reached the cell phone Jones had been using, but by Saturday afternoon the phone was no more. He'd taken it on the plane with him when he left Heathrow earlier that day, but he was aware that a review of the calls he'd made on that phone would link him to the events in North Wales he was trying to distance himself from. He'd resolved to get rid of the phone as soon as he could after he arrived in Paris.

And then there had been that fuss at customs when the flight arrived in Paris. It had taken an extra thirty minutes to get through the disgruntled line of delayed travelers. He'd had no problem with passport control, but it seemed that everyone from the flight was having their carry-on baggage rescreened. It looked like one poor sucker had been caught with contraband in his briefcase – he was certainly protesting his innocence enough. Jones's bag had been examined too, but he always played it safe. The extra currency he was carrying was distributed between his pockets and the lining of his cabin baggage – not completely risk-free, but almost.

He took a cab into Paris and his hotel, the Aligre, near the Gare de Lyon. He'd never stayed there before, and on his many trips to Paris had never stayed in any hotel more than once. He usually chose slightly run-down, three-star hotels in quiet streets and had hundreds to pick from. He was feeling tired, but strangely energized. He'd got out of London and England with most of his business assets still active. He could carry on where he'd left off and could probably function anywhere in the world, but for the time being he had decided to stick to European countries. He liked predictability and most European countries ran predictably. The trains were usually on time, the police mainly behaved appropriately, you knew what you would find in a hotel, and the public health systems ensured that restaurant dishes were unlikely to give you cholera. Most middle-east countries could fulfill some of these criteria part of the time, but not as consistently.

So, he'd decided on Italy. He'd buy his ticket tomorrow and take up the offer of a contact to use a house in Emilio-Romagna for a couple of months. It was close to San Marino and he had assets there. In the meantime he might as well enjoy Paris. He was always cautious and left most of his valuables in the room safe at the hotel. Then, carrying only a light bag and an umbrella, he ventured out onto the rainy streets of Paris.

His immediate goal was to destroy and dispose of the cell phone. He'd done this before and had found that nothing worked so well as a car tire. Well, salt water was better, but that required a little more time and he was miles from a quiet beach or pier. For five minutes he looked at the pedestrian and traffic flow around an intersection. The pedestrians crossed in groups of about twenty when the lights were in their favor, but less than a second after the last pedestrian reached the safety of the opposite sidewalk the vehicular traffic accelerated through the empty crosswalk.

Jones timed it perfectly. The phone slid down his leg on the inside of his trousers and he stepped onto the sidewalk. He heard the slight bump as the first vehicle squashed the cell phone. He walked on a few meters before looking behind and noting with satisfaction the continuing obliteration of the phone by the Parisian traffic.

He stopped for coffee and a pastry at a corner café. This was not his usual diet, but he was enjoying a feeling of freedom, almost elation, which for him was highly unusual. He strolled on and headed towards the River Seine, took the Austerlitz Bridge to the Botanical Gardens, which were not at their best at this time of year, but he didn't care – he'd escaped and was feeling pleased with himself . He walked north, crossed the river again at the Pont de Sully, and meandered back to his hotel. He'd have an early dinner and tomorrow he'd go to the Gare de Lyon, buy a ticket to Turin, stay there a couple of days and then head to his destination – the small town near the Adriatic coast where he could hole-up for a few months. Overall, things were looking up.

55

"We tried, and maybe someone else would be more successful, but we couldn't get any information from it," Stefan said. He walked into the room and placed a clear plastic bag on the table. It contained the remains of a cell phone – Jones's cell phone. "It looks like he dropped it on purpose so that it would be destroyed by traffic running over it. It also looks like he was successful." He placed the bag on the table in front of Ella and sat down across from her.

"I thought there were all sorts of ways of retrieving information from phones and computers," she said looking at the offering.

"There may be, but SIGNAK doesn't have that sort of technology."

"Who does?" She looked up.

"The police in some countries, including France: some universities; tech giants I suppose, but basically no one with whom we have a relationship at present. We need to work on that."

"I agree," said Ella, "But I might have an idea. It's probably a British cell-phone?"

"Yes."

"Then perhaps the British would like it back. Why don't I get hold of my contact in their security services and ask her if they would like it. It's no use to us and they would owe us."

"Why not? It might be of some use to them."

"I'll call, but I'd like to give them an update on what is happening to our Mr. Ephraim Smith, or whatever his name is."

"OK. You can tell them we followed him from CDG airport to a hotel in Paris. It's near the Gare de Lyon, but we don't know if that is significant or not. After he checked in he took a stroll around Paris and, again, we followed him at a discreet distance. He tried to dispose of the cell phone in this bag." He pointed at the table. "As far as we know he has settled in for the night. We will be watching him all night and tomorrow too. I suggest you don't have to tell them about the tracer we managed to slip into his luggage at the airport – that can remain a trade secret. It cost me a 500 euro note, and I hope it'll be worth it. Now, what about you? You still exhausted?"

"Not too bad." Ella smiled at Stefan. "I got a couple of hours sleep when I got back here. How long will the tracer signal last?"

"About a week, but I hope we have an opportunity to replace it with another in a few days."

"So, what are you going to do?"

"I'm going to follow him, or rather, the team will follow him."

"Until?"

"Until he goes to ground."

"Will he go to ground?"

"Probably. It's a reasonable supposition. I'm also assuming he has assets, which are unknown to the British government, in any one of several countries. Historically, that means a numbered account in a Swiss bank, but he could have multiple accounts elsewhere – maybe some are legitimate. At some point he will have to access them. Also, he has very little clothing with him and some time he is going to have to buy more. I'm assuming he will do this when he's reached his goal. He may be following an escape plan. We'll just have to keep up and see what happens."

"You seem to have it covered."

"As you've found out watching someone can be extremely boring. I've had plenty of time to consider his options and think about what I'd do in his place."

"I've been thinking about this too and I suppose I didn't think we'd get this close so soon. What do you think I should do when he does go to ground?"

"Do you want to talk to him?"

"I think so. I want to know who ordered my brother to be killed, but I'm not sure if I confront him if it will help me. What happens if he denies everything? I can't make him talk."

"I agree. So, let's cross that bridge when we get to it. I need to get back to the surveillance team in the morning, maybe sooner.

If our Mr. Smith makes a move we will be following him and I will have to go too. This could be my last night in Paris for years!"

Ella smiled at the exaggeration and reached across the table to briefly hold Stefan's hand.

"When Napoleon allows you leave you know I'll be here waiting for you," she tossed her head and smiled coquettishly.

It was Stefan's turn to smile.

"In the meantime how about dinner?" he asked.

"Great idea. Why don't you go across the road, get some food from our restaurant and bring it back here. I will make the call to London, lay the table and open the red wine to let it breathe."

Stefan leaned over, kissed Ella's hand and muttered, "Magnifique," before leaving on his mission.

He returned after thirty minutes with dinner in a brown paper bag.

"When Monsieur le Chef found I was not eating there the menu choices became markedly reduced," Stefan said emptying the bag.

"Oh, I know. He can be like that at times. On the other hand he is a great cook and I would hate to have to replace him. What did he permit you to take out?"

"Soup, or shrimp bisque to be more precise." Stefan took the lid off the small pot and Ella leaned forward to catch some of the aroma. He continued emptying the bag, "Bread, of course, a spinach salad, and green beans, potatoes and fillet of sole with his own sauce. And, finally, two slices of his chocolate torte."

"I'm surprised he let you out with the sole."

"So am I. I think he'd over-ordered the fish, or it wasn't as popular this evening."

"Well, I'm glad he can temper his idealism with a little practicality," Ella said and ladled soup into bowls. "Let's work on this and I'll tell you about the call to London."

Stefan poured two glasses of wine. "Once again the senior staff at SIGNAK are expanding their frontiers of experience. We are having red wine with fish. I believe that's not done."

319

"We'll have to keep it to ourselves. Our little secret," said Ella. She tasted the soup, accompanied it with a sip of wine and said, "The combination seems fine to me."

Stefan nodded his approval too.

Ella said, "I called my contact in London and told them we had a damaged cell phone which had once been owned by our friend, Ephraim Smith. They were very interested and will be sending a courier to collect and take it back to London. He'll probably fly over and take the train back. They are going to tell me when to expect him. They were also interested in our surveillance of Mr. Smith. Apparently, his real name is Jones, or at least that was another name he was using. He left incendiary devices in the house we were watching in London which went off when the police entered the building. Apparently, no one was hurt but they think they won't be able to get much information from the blaze. So, we are it, and they have asked us to keep following him until they get their act together."

"And when is that likely to happen?"

"They thought they would be able to get a team over here in the next few days. Apparently, they don't have quite enough evidence to go ahead and arrest him, and we are stuck since we have no authority to arrest him. After all, it's just us, SIGNAK, and they can't arrest him based on what we have given them so far. If there's anything they can glean from the phone it may change that."

"So there's no one coming to help, and they're just sending this courier, but they still want us to monitor him?"

"Yes."

"And they will pay us for this?" asked Stefan.

"They didn't mention that."

"Hmm. I didn't think they would. What government agency ever does?"

Ella shrugged and nodded in agreement. She picked up a fork and began to tackle the fish.

"This sole and the sauce are up to standard. He really does a good job." She savored the taste of the fish for a minute and then added. "All this we're doing is not really part of what SIGNAK is about, and I am not particularly comfortable with it."

"What do you mean?"

"Well, some of it is work we have done before, but we're acting like a police department, or maybe private investigators. I wouldn't want SIGNAK to move towards more of this work."

"I can see that, but it's encouraging to know we are doing a good job of it, or at least I think we are."

"We are, and I agree we are doing a good job, and I got us into this so I have no complaints. But it's been a stressful few days, well weeks really, and I want to make sure I am doing the right thing for SIGNAK and myself."

"I wonder…" began Stefan, but was interrupted by his phone ringing. He looked at the screen to see who was calling him. "I have to take this," he said.

The call was brief; Stefan hung up, shrugged and said, "I should go. We'll have to continue this conversation at another time. I'll take my dessert with me and pretend I'm with you instead of Jean Paul when I'm eating it."

He stood. Ella looked around, found a napkin and a paper plate onto which she scooped a slice of the torte, and presented it to Stefan. He put the plate down, walked over to her and gave her a hug which she reciprocated.

"Thank you, Stefan," she said. "Thank you for always being here for me. I really appreciate it." She squeezed him a little harder. They broke apart. He kissed her briefly on the cheek, looked closely into her eyes, smiled and said, "I'll always be here for you, but I suppose I'd better go or I, or maybe we, might do something we'd regret."

Ella smiled and said, "Of course I have no idea what you are talking about, but whatever it might be I don't think I know if I would regret it … now, you'd better go."

"I'll keep in touch."

56

The Ryanair flight from Manchester, England, arrived on time at Bologna airport and by noon John and Ann had cleared customs and passport control and were enjoying the welcoming hugs and handshakes of their daughter, Laura, and her boyfriend, Davide.

Laura and Davide had taken a few days away from their academic responsibilities and had arranged for John and Ann to accompany them to a small town near Rimini.

There, John and Ann were hoping to relax, establish and reestablish relationships, and put the events in Wales behind them.

John thought Davide was very brave or very naïve, but both he and Ann had welcomed the chance to get away and thanked Davide for arranging the accommodation in Italy.

They had spent part of the previous three days walking around Colwyn Bay dodging rain showers. The rest of the time they relaxed, as much as they could, in Auntie Olly's house. They tried to concentrate on reading books, sleeping off jet-lag and letting the bruises on their legs heal, while attempting to not let the memory of the encounter with Gareth dominate their lives. For the most part they succeeded and each day seemed a little easier than the last.

They decided to preempt arrangements for Auntie Olly's funeral and discussed these with a local undertaker, T. Conchar and Sons, who promised they would handle all the details. Auntie Olly had indicated she wanted cremation, no dismal hymns or boring preachers at her funeral, and above all it was to be the cheapest possible way of putting her in the ground. The undertakers said they would arrange what they could, but asked John and Ann to work on the service with the minister. The minister of the church Olly had attended in more lucid times was anything but boring and she said she could comply with Olly's wishes. Tentatively, she arranged for a service a couple of days before John and Ann's flight back to the USA.

John sat in the back of the Lancia Ypsilon, happy to let Davide do the driving. He'd never driven in Italy and was content to sit back and look at the country, or at least the part of Italy he could see from the autostrada, flash by his window. He found looking out of the side windows was less scary than looking ahead. The speed limit was posted at 130 kilometers per hour, but it seemed that many Italians took this as a challenge and treated it as the minimum speed instead.

Davide and Laura had been chatting in Italian, occasionally including John and Ann in English, but after about an hour Laura turned and asked, "Dad, we just crossed the Rubicon. You know what that means?"

John hesitated for a second then dredged up a memory from his high school history class and replied, "Isn't that something Caesar crossed?"

"Very good. In fact he probably crossed it about two kilometers west of here, on the Via Emilia. Davide has his own theory about it though." She looked at Davide who shrugged and said.

"Well, Caesar, 'e was an Italian and was probably riding his horse too quick and 'is army was behind 'im. 'E couldn't stop quick enough when 'e got to the Rubicon and not could his army, so they end up crossing the Rubicon. For this 'e was probably given a speeding ticket. Being Italian 'e had to object. Well, one thing led to another and before you know eet there's a civil war – over a speeding ticket. Eet's so Italian eet has to be true."

John and Ann laughed.

Davide took the Rimini Nord exit off the autostrada, insisted on not having any help paying the tolls, and fifteen minutes later dropped John and Ann off at the gate of their hotel, Il Villino, and into the care of the owner, Giovanni, a friend of Davide's. Laura said the building dated from the fifteenth century and meant "The Little Villa" when translated. They agreed to meet in two hours.

John and Ann opened the doors to the garden, allowed the early spring breeze to blow into their hotel room, and took the opportunity to get over the last of their travels and jet-lag with a forty minute nap. They awoke, refreshed, read silently for a short time, and were at the door to the hotel when Laura and Davide returned.

Laura and Davide had told Ann and John they were staying at a miniature apartment owned by Davide's family, who only used it occasionally. Unfortunately, it was just big enough for two people at the best of times. John was more than happy to stay at the hotel, where his total lack of Italian was rarely challenged, and reminded himself he had been young once. He, too, had loved his parents and, like all children, found that what his parents didn't know wouldn't hurt them; a little separation of the generations was always good.

They walked down the path towards the town center and John realized he was hungry. He hadn't had much of an appetite since his encounter with Gareth, but overall thought being hungry was a good thing.

Laura pointed out a gate set into the base of the old city walls on their right. "There are tours of the tunnels which use that gate. I think they happen every day. Apparently, there are all sorts of tunnels under the city and I don't think they are all mapped. A few have collapsed but some houses have private entrances from their basements, and the restaurant we are going to has an entrance, but it's gated off."

"What were they used for?" Ann asked.

"I think they were used for wine storage."

"That's interesting. I wonder if they were ever used for protection."

"Maybe; I know there was a major battle near Rimini in the Second World War, so I suppose they could have provided shelter then."

"One more thing I have to look up," commented John. "Fortunately, my cell phone doesn't work here, so I can't look it up right now. I'll just have to enjoy the walk with you instead." He put his arm around Laura and gave her a paternal squeeze.

"It's good to have you both here, Dad."

"It's very good to be here. We've had a trying few weeks, so I am just pleased to be here and away from it all."

"Perhaps you don't want to talk about it, but what happened to Auntie Olly?" she asked.

"Well, you have a right to know, and I don't mind talking about it. In fact it may help me to get over it if I talk about it, but let's wait until after dinner. What do you think, Ann?"

"Maybe after dinner, or perhaps tomorrow," she replied. "I'm looking forward to some of your famous Italian cooking."

Davide said, "I promise you have come to the right place."

They turned right into the Piazza Balacchi and Davide led them to his favorite restaurant, Monte Giove, on the north side of the square. They paused to discuss whether it was warm enough to sit outside and collectively decided it wasn't. Davide led them inside and introduced them to the proprietor. They sat, and spent the next two-and-a-half hours sipping wine, sampling antipasto and other epicurean delights ordered by Davide.

John had been relieved to find that the conversation flowed easily, and he even practiced a little Italian which he hoped he would remember the following day. When it came time to leave Davide would not let anyone else pay – he insisted the meal was his treat. Before they left he showed John and Ann around the restaurant. The building had a narrow street front but was surprisingly deep and seemed to extend back to the mound on which the old city was built. At the back the restaurant was further lengthened by a low tunnel which was blocked after a meter by an iron railing gate; this was secured with a padlock and chain. Apparently, this was another entrance to the tunnels under the city.

John was no longer hungry when they left the restaurant. The delicious Italian cooking and his life-long responsibility to try everything on the plate (since you can never be sure when Armageddon will happen) left him feeling quite full, and he was glad of the walk back to their hotel. After hugs, thankyous, and goodbyes Laura and Davide left John and Ann at the lobby with the promise of meeting the next day for lunch and a visit to San Marino.

As the younger couple left John commented to Ann, "I'm glad she didn't ask any more about Aunt Olly. It would be easy to see how it could have ruined this evening."

"She'll ask again and we can tell her, but I agree; I'm glad too."

"Maybe we'll get the opportunity to talk about it tomorrow, but whenever we talk about it it's not going to brighten anyone's day."

"Auntie Olly was her family too."

"I'm not going to keep anything from her about what happened, but I think she doesn't need to know all we went through too."

"I agree. Let's sleep on that and enjoy our time with her and Davide. We need it."

"OK, I agree. Sleep. We'll need the energy for San Marino tomorrow."

57

Jones drove his rental car out of Bologna airport and, like hundreds of other drivers every day, had to take a second pass to find the exit on the roundabout that led to Autostrada A14. He continued south, getting used to the pacing of Italian traffic, and left the freeway shortly before his destination – Santarcangelo di Romagna. It took him a couple of tries before he found the correct cobbled access road to the middle of the old walled city and the house his contact in Turin had arranged. As instructed, he parked about 50 meters away and walked the remaining distance carrying his few bags along the narrow street. He let himself in using the number code and looked around; he was pleased with what he found.

The north-facing outside walls of the building next to the street measured at least a meter deep. Inset into the walls were a few narrow windows which allowed in very little light, but they were complemented by a large skylight providing good illumination to the interior of the house. He looked around and it was much as he'd expected – the fittings were modern and comfortable and the bedroom was set back from the front of the house.

He reviewed the security system and noted, to his satisfaction, that there were two cameras monitoring the road outside. He looked around, found the second exit and thought that it would serve his needs perfectly. He hoped he wouldn't need it, since it involved parking his car outside the city walls, but he could live with that.

His knowledge of the Italian language was good. He knew he would be rusty with a few phrases and words, but that would improve with a few weeks of practice, and he thought he might as well stay here until the dust had settled in London. He'd caught up with British news in Turin and was surprised how soon someone, and he had to assume it was the police, had located his house in the London suburb. He couldn't figure that one out, but from the aerial photos it looked like the building, and the ones on either side, had been completely destroyed by the incendiary devices he had planted. He was pleased with that. He had no plans to return to London in the immediate future and would be quite happy to never go back there. He wondered if Italy would be a good base for him to set up his business activities again – he'd always liked it here.

However, his current plan was to accomplish the more mundane task of buying groceries. From the directions he found on a brochure in the house he walked the quickest way to the tourist office on Via Cesare Battisti. Here he picked up maps of the city, the area, and directions to the nearest supermarket. Apparently, there were two, and also a popular street market on Fridays where, he was told, he would find an excellent selection of local cheeses. He chose to walk to the Co-op supermarket where he picked up some essentials and walked back to the house along the Via Porte Cervese. He was enjoying himself; the feeling that had begun in Paris, of being free, alive, and ready to begin again was still with him.

The next day he planned to go to San Marino.

58

In some ways their visit to The Republic of San Marino was just as John expected. The guidebook said it was an autonomous country, perched on a rock and completely surrounded by Italy that had more or less maintained its independence over the centuries. It had survived two world wars and, per head of population, was one of the wealthiest countries in Europe. Tourism was one of its main industries and John was not disappointed.

Davide had business to attend to, so Laura had driven them the half-hour from Santarcangelo to the top of the rock. John wandered the streets with Ann and Laura. The town on the top of the rock was clean, clearly successful, and a pleasant tourist trap. The shops sold upscale trinkets, souvenirs, post-cards and alcohol. Their window boxes were full of early spring blooms, and it was sunny and not too full of visitors – in another month or so they would be there in full force. It was pleasant and relaxing walking as a family along the city walls where they could look down on the surrounding Italian countryside, and to the east could see the Adriatic Sea beyond the city of Rimini. They walked through the Palazzo Pubblico and briefly slowed to look at the distinctive red and green uniforms of the Guard of the Rock. As a matter of principle they took few photos, preferring the here and now to picture shows later, but sight-seeing can be exhausting and they found welcome relief over coffee and pastries sitting outside at a quiet café in the warm sunlight. It was there that Laura asked about Auntie Olly.

They told her as much as they knew. They didn't mention all the details of their kidnapping – that could wait until later, or never, but for fifteen minutes they both related the story of what had happened to Auntie Olly. Laura only interrupted once to ask, "You mean they killed her to get you to come back to Wales?"

"Yes, that's how it seems," John replied.

Laura shook her head and wiped away a couple of tears.

John continued, "The police think one of the people responsible for her death is also dead, but he didn't act alone."

"But it's so awful. Why do people do things like that?" Laura sobbed. She glanced up for a second when a man stopped near them, but then looked at her father again when the man moved on.

John wanted to say the obvious, "For money," but instead leaned forward and put his arm around her.

They finished their snack, headed back to the elevator to their parking lot, and found their way out of San Marino.

The atmosphere in the car on the way back to Santarcangelo was subdued – Laura was still affected by the news of how Auntie Olly died . She gave both John and Ann prolonged hugs and left them at their hotel – they had previously agreed that they would meet again in early evening to go to dinner – the Osteria del Campanone near the clock tower in the middle of the old city had been recommended. They planned to get there early; it was popular.

59

Jones was having a good day. He'd never been to San Marino before which may seem strange for anyone, like him, who had a perfectly legal and transparent bank account there. San Marino was not a 'numbered bank account' or Grand Cayman 'offshore account' type of country, but from here he could send money anywhere in the world, and with a little laundering and tidying he could also send money from anywhere in the world to San Marino. It had worked well for him over the years and he now had an investment portfolio, managed by Banca San Leo, in excess of five million euros. Of course, not all his money was secreted away there, but he saw no reason to mention this to anyone.

He had debated whether or not he should arrange the transfer of most of his money remotely, or visit the bank in person. Since he also had a safe-deposit box there, and he was enjoying Italy, he thought the trip to San Marino would be worthwhile.

He met with one of the bank's officers, who had been appropriately courteous. He thanked them for their service over the years, and discussed the plans he had for his money. A brief hint of disappointment passed the officer's face when he heard of these plans, but it was quickly replaced by the classic bankers' expression of equanimity. Jones asked to see the safe-deposit box in private and chose to remove five of the two-carat diamonds he'd asked Gareth to deposit five years previously. So far he hadn't missed Gareth, and maybe he never would. In fact he'd probably be better off without him. He may even be better off without the Hand of Hamsa, but he could decide that later.

He'd have to keep some money in his accounts to maintain the safe-deposit box, but it was better not to keep his clean money all in one place. He had transferred all his money out of England the night before he flew to Paris.

He strolled back towards his car, but thought he could enjoy staying in San Marino a little longer and wondered about getting a coffee. He hoped he could buy decaf here – there was no harm in asking. He slowed his pace a little near a restaurant where only a few tables were occupied, and would have stopped, but as he approached the establishment he overheard parts of a conversation in English coming from one of the closer tables. There seemed to be some bad news being discussed. He hesitated, one of the participants glanced up and he looked into the tear-stained face of a young woman. She looked away and Jones walked on.

60

The Osteria del Campanone was popular because of its piadina. This is a regional specialty. Essentially, it is a flatbread, about the size of a tortilla, but thicker, filled with cheeses, meat, vegetables and sauces. It goes well with regional wines and beer.

Davide had rejoined them for the evening. He told them Laura had discussed Auntie Olly's death with him and this may have helped lift her mood because the conversation flowed naturally; there was joking, laughter and plenty of food.

John looked up to catch the waiter's eye, and that's when he saw him.

For a couple of seconds he couldn't remember when he had seen the face of the man who was paying his bill. Then for a few seconds more he thought it couldn't be him – the man whose face they had been shown at the police station in North Wales.

John nudged Ann who looked at John and then in the same direction he was looking. She gave a little grunt.

"Is it him?" John asked Ann.

"I don't know. It looks like it could be him, but what's his name? Oh, he's walking out."

"I don't remember his name. I think it was … Jones? What should we do?"

"It can't be him. It couldn't be."

"I'll have to follow him."

"Be careful."

John stood and tried to make his way to the restaurant door, but was obstructed by a waiter serving the next table their piadina. Eventually, he made it past, moved as quickly as he could to the door and then ran outside. The man was nowhere to be seen. There were a dozen people standing in line to get into the restaurant and another dozen in the small square, but no man. Two cars drove away, but he couldn't see who was driving. He didn't think anyone could have made it to their vehicle and driven away in the 20-30 seconds it had taken to get out of the restaurant, but he couldn't be sure. He ran around the other side of the clock tower, but there was no sight of the man. He stood and looked around. He could feel his heart beat slowing. He waited another minute, circled the clock tower again and then returned to his seat in the restaurant.

"He wasn't there. I couldn't find him," said John, shaking his head.

"Who couldn't you find? You just rushed off," asked Laura.

John hesitated, glanced at Ann and then answered, "I thought I saw someone whose photograph I was shown in the Colwyn Bay police station. It was someone who may have been involved in Auntie Olly's death, but I'm not sure. I mean … what would he be doing here?"

The question was aimed at Ann who said, "I thought it could be him, but we only had photographs to go by and a short video. He sort of moved like the person in the video, but I'm not sure. What do you think we should do?"

"I'm not sure," replied John.

"Well, could it have been him, even remotely?" asked Laura.

"Yes," John answered, and Ann added, "Yes, it could be."

"Well, shouldn't you let someone know?"

"Who?"

"The police," said Laura.

"I don't know. The story seems a little far-fetched and I don't think the Italian police can do anything about it," said John. "I suppose we could call Johnson in Colwyn Bay. What do you think, Ann?"

"I think we should call someone and why not him?"

"OK. But my phone doesn't work here. I could call from the hotel when we get back there … maybe?"

Laura reached into her bag, pulled out her cell phone and thrust it at John.

"Here, Dad, this one works to reach England, maybe even to Wales. It's new technology but maybe Americans haven't heard of it?" she smiled.

John said, "I am sure it exists in America, but I believe it also would cost me $10 per day and I kind of like not having to worry about calls when I'm in Europe. Besides, all you have to do is direct me to the nearest telegraph office and I could send a telegram. There is one around here isn't there?"

John and Laura smiled and she gave up the phone.

"Before you call, let me try something," said Davide. He stood and went over to a woman at the desk where Jones had paid. He came back a minute later.

"She is my cousin's daughter, so I knew 'er and I ask 'er if the man, by 'imself, who just paid 'as been 'ere before, and she said she 'adn't seen 'im before. But, she said 'e 'ad an accent. His Italian was quite good, but she noticed the accent. She thought it might be English."

"Thank you, Davide. That helps a lot."

Ann presented John with the calling card Johnson had given her and John made the call. He got straight through to the detective and explained what had happened. He found himself downplaying the sighting, but did explain that both he and Ann were convinced the man looked the same, or was very similar to the photos they had been shown of Jones. The conversation lasted five minutes and then John hung up and returned the phone to Laura who asked.

"Well, we only got half the conversation, but what did he say?"

"He said he would look into it, discuss it with a few contacts he has and maybe get back to me."

"That sounds suitably vague."

"It is, but … well, he didn't sound too incredulous, but he also said he couldn't contact the Italian authorities just yet, and before he did that he would definitely have to discuss it with his senior officers."

"So, for the moment it seems like a brush off?"

"I suppose so, but what else could he do? What else can we do?" John replied.

No one answered.

Finally, Davide said, "All we can do is 'ope we see 'im again," and shrugged his shoulders.

"I think you're right, Davide," agreed John. "If we see him we could at least follow him and try to see where he's staying, and if

337

the British police think it's worthwhile we could let them know and hope they tell the Italian police. I don't think we want to approach him ourselves. I don't know what I'd say. I can't say 'Did you kill Auntie Olly?' I don't think it would help. Any other suggestions?"

None was forthcoming.

The spotting of the man they thought was Jones had put a damper on the evening. For those who knew her it was hard not to think of Auntie Olly, how unfair things seemed, and how getting justice seemed to be so difficult. But they did their best. The evening was still a success and while sipping their limoncello liqueurs both John and Laura could almost put aside the intrusive thoughts of the circumstances of Auntie Olly's death. But as all four walked back to the hotel, down steep steps and along cobblestone streets, John found himself looking more closely at other men they passed – just in case. They said goodbye at the lobby and planned to meet the following evening. Ann and John could have the day to themselves. It was market day and they had no other plans, but the weather forecast said it would be a good day for a long walk and about the right temperature for an evening in Rimini.

61

Ella answered her phone. "Where are you?" she asked.

"Bologna," Stefan answered. "And I have some bad news – we lost him."

"Oh, no; when did this happen?"

"About an hour ago … here in Bologna."

Stefan and his team had followed Jones, who had taken the train from Gare de Lyon. Jones had stopped briefly in Turin and had taken another train that morning to Bologna.

Stefan continued, "We were on him the whole way. He took a bus from the train station to the airport, so we thought he might be flying somewhere. We were ready for that. However, he rented a car in the airport and we were ready for that too. What we weren't ready for was the Bologna garage where he rented his car. He was renting from Budget while we were filling out the paperwork at Hertz. The rental garage is noisy, crowded, dark and the lanes are narrow. We were only five minutes behind him and we had a new tracker on him, so we weren't worried, but one of the lanes was blocked with another two cars. Then there was a hold up when we were leaving and by the time we got out of the place we lost his signal. We had to make a guess and took the road we thought he might be on, but it was the wrong one, and ten minutes later we knew we'd lost him. He's somewhere in Italy, but I don't know where. It's so frustrating to have come this far and lose him."

"There's no way we can catch up with him?"

"None I can think of. I'm sorry; I know how much this has meant to you."

"There's nothing else you could have done. There was always a chance we'd lose him. How about the rest of your team? How are they taking it?" asked Ella, doing her best to hide her disappointment.

"Oh, they're pretty upset about it."

"Well, please tell them they did their best."

"I have and I will."

"So, what are you going to do now?"

"We are going to be tourists."

"Tourists?"

"Yes. None of us has been to Bologna before, and it's been a tense few days with not much sleep ... I even wonder if that isn't one of the reasons he got away ..."

"Don't beat yourself up about it," Ella interjected.

"I won't. I just have to get it out of my system then I'll be OK. So, I understand Bologna has some interesting architecture and several good restaurants, so we are going to wander around the town, I'll buy dinner for everyone somewhere nice, we'll spend the night in a decent hotel and head back to Paris tomorrow. Oh, and just in case we are extremely lucky I will be leaving the tracker monitor on. Who knows? He might still be in the Bologna area."

"I'll look forward to seeing you tomorrow then."

"Not as much as I am looking forward to seeing you."

"Oh yeah?"

"Yes. You'll be surprised. See you tomorrow." He hung up before she had time to think of an answer.

Ella sighed and once again questioned where her relationship with Stefan was headed. She hoped she knew, and thought she was ready for it, but part of her was still uncertain. She was also disappointed to know that all the effort and energy which had been put into following Jones had come to nothing. There was nothing else to do. She had been standing by the window looking down on the restaurant opposite which was enjoying a quiet afternoon; one of the waiters was wrapped in his coat, relaxing with a book and a coffee, and only a couple of the other tables were occupied. She wondered why her life couldn't be so simple. She moved back into the room and remembered one obligation she had left. She called London and was put through to Georgina Southport.

"How are you doing, Ella?" asked Georgina in her business voice.

"I'm OK, but I have some bad news; we lost him – we lost Jones."

"Oh, dear. What happened?"

"We followed him as far as Bologna Airport where he hired a car, but by the time my people had extricated themselves from the airport there was no signal. They gambled on going one way on the autostrada, but he must have gone another and they didn't pick up his signal. I assume he's somewhere in Italy, but I don't know where. I'm sorry."

"You don't have to be. Even with all the staff at my disposal here we can lose someone. It's much easier for someone who suspects they are under surveillance to disappear than it is for us to watch them 24/7. However, we've had a little more luck with the phone you found and got to us. We lifted some complete numbers from the phone for the time you watched him at Heathrow airport. He called one number a few times. We have tried to follow those through, but I doubt they will lead anywhere; there is no way of finding the owner of that phone – it was apparently a "burner" phone, but there were a couple of other calls that night between the phone you found and someone whom the security services have been concerned about for a while. He lives in North Wales and he may be involved in this."

"In what way?"

"He may have been involved in the bombing which killed my colleague."

Georgina had hesitated for a second before answering, and Ella reminded herself that as far as London was concerned she was just a civilian and any information given to her was at the whim of the security services.

"Oh, yes. I can see how important that must be. I'm sure you have your hands full, but could this person help us get hold of the man called Jones?" Ella asked.

"Maybe. I'll let you know. In the meantime I have a meeting tomorrow where one of the items which will now be on the agenda is what we do with the information that Jones is in Italy. Like it or not, the best thing may be to do nothing until we have more information about his whereabouts. At this stage, if we try to let all of Italy know that he is a 'person of interest', nothing will happen. There must be thousands of 'persons of interest' in every country. We need to see if we can narrow down his whereabouts."

"Well, please let me know if I can be of any help. I do have resources."

"I know. As you know; I've looked you up. SIGNAK has done well. I will let you know. Bye." She hung up.

SIGNAK may have done well, thought Ella, but it didn't make it any the less frustrating to have failed to keep up with Jones. She realized she was feeling sorry for herself and that wouldn't help. She tried to concentrate on her work but was feeling restless

It was a late afternoon in early spring in Paris. There was a light breeze, the sun was still shining, and hordes of tourists wouldn't begin blocking sidewalks and restaurants for another month, so she put on a light jacket and went for a walk. Of all the places she had lived Paris was as close to any she could call home and where she could feel comfortable, but sometimes she felt she wasn't taking advantage of the city around her. Today, was different. The city was busy, but not crowded, and there were others, like her, enjoying being alive in Paris.

As she walked her mood lifted. She walked towards the River Seine, past Les Halles and turned right; she passed the Louvre and strolled on to the Jardins des Carrousel. The trees were almost fully leafed and daffodils and tulips were opening their petals to the world. She was feeling happy but as she turned into the Tuileries her phone rang. She was tempted to ignore it, which she realized was not like her, but the responsible part of her stopped, sat down on a park bench, and answered the call.

It was from Georgina Southport in London.

"Twice in a day," Georgina almost apologized. "I hope I haven't disturbed you?"

"Not at all. I was just out for a walk," Ella replied.

"This may be nothing at all, but Jones might be in a town in Italy near Rimini. It's a long shot, but I thought you should know."

"How did you get this information?"

"Very indirectly. Briefly, Jones and his partner were involved in the bombing in North Wales I mentioned before. However, it's also probable his partner killed another woman here. Her nephew also had an encounter with Jones's partner, but survived. During discussions with the nephew he and his wife were shown photos of Jones. They said they had never seen him before. The nephew and his wife have family in Italy so they left North Wales a few days ago to take some time out to relax and get over what happened to them here. Earlier this evening both the nephew and his wife think they saw Jones. They didn't follow him and there is no other confirmation. The nephew called a police colleague in Wales, who mentioned this to one of my team still in Wales and it was passed to me. Now, I am passing it to you."

"Thanks, but it sounds pretty unlikely."

"I know. I talked to the policeman who took the call. He knows the couple and says they are level-headed, and they really don't want any attention. Apparently, that is one reason they left for Italy.

So, I'm passing this on to you for what it's worth."

"Thank you. What's the name of the town?"

"Santarcangelo. It's a small town near Rimini and is not that far from Bologna."

Ella pulled a pen and paper out of her shoulder bag.

"Let me write that down … OK. And what is the name of the nephew, and do you know where he's staying?"

"He is John Beaton. B-E-A-T-O-N. His wife is Ann and they are staying at Il Villino hotel."

"Thanks. I've got that." Ella read the details back to Georgina who confirmed them.

"Would you like me to contact John Beaton?" asked Georgina.

"Not yet. Let me contact my people in Italy and then I'll get back to you."

"Right, thanks." She hung up.

Ella sat for a few minutes enjoying the last of the sunshine and considered what she should do next. It was certainly a long shot, but it was the only shot. It was possible, but not probable, that Jones had been identified and located. It was not the sort of odds by which she had developed a successful international company,

343

but if there was any way of finally confronting Jones she had to take it.

She stood and called Stefan as she walked briskly back to the office. She told him her plans.

"I checked," she said. "There's a plane leaving for Bologna in two hours. I'll be on it. Please meet me and make reservations at Il Villino. We can drive down there over night."

62

John and Ann slept badly. Alone in their room the previous evening they'd discussed whether or not the man they had spotted could have been the one involved in Olly's death. The more they thought about it logically, the less likely it seemed he could be the same man.

However, it wasn't logic which kept them awake; it was the unsettling emotions associated with the surprise of the encounter, and the reminder of how close they had come to being killed less than a week previously.

After only a few hours sleep they were both quiet the next morning and hoping that breakfast would revive them. It was going to be a day for an afternoon nap if they hoped to accomplish a long morning walk and be fit and alert for dinner in Rimini.

John was contemplating the dilemma of drinking another coffee – it might revive him a little now, but where would he be when its diuretic effect kicked in later? He decided to go for the coffee anyway, stood and made his way to the coffee urn. He paid little attention to the person on his right until she asked, "Mr. John Beaton?"

John was startled out of his inter-coffee reverie, turned and automatically answered, "Yes."

He looked into the face of a woman he had never met before. She was in her mid-thirties, with dark hair, brown eyes, and a smile. She was a couple of inches shorter than he, but behind her was a man of about John's height. He was about the same age as the woman, and also had dark hair, brown eyes and a slightly darker complexion. She spoke again with an accent he couldn't quite place, "We'd like to sit with you, please." Before John could answer she carried her own coffee and moved towards the tables. She pulled out a chair and sat across from a surprised Ann. Her companion sat next to her. John sat last.

"Let me introduce myself," she continued. "My name is Ella and my associate here is Stefan. I believe you are Ann and John."

She offered her hand which Ann, then John, shook. Stefan offered his hand, nodded and smiled.

With the formalities over she said, "No doubt you are wondering what this is about and why complete strangers like us are sitting down with you."

Ann and John nodded and mumbled, "Yes."

Ella said, "The simple answer is we were contacted by the British authorities last night and we drove here from Bologna. I think we got here around 2:00 am, so we are not at our most alert this morning – I suspect you may be the same?"

Ann said, "We didn't sleep well last night. You're right there."

John added, "But why did you think we might be tired too?"

Ella pulled a notebook out of a purse, consulted it briefly and said, "I believe you called an Inspector Johnson last night. You saw someone whom you thought might be of interest to him."

"Yes, that's right," replied John, suddenly more alert. "So, you're the British police?"

"No, not exactly," Ella glanced at Stefan. "We are working with them."

Stefan spoke for the first time. His voice was quiet with a hint of a French accent. "We are not the police, and we are not Interpol or any governmental organization. We represent a private company that is also involved in tracking down the man you saw last night."

"So, the British authorities are working with you? They are … what … contracting with you?" asked Ann.

Ella hesitated before replying, "Yes and no. Yes, the British are working with us, but unofficially, and no, we don't have a contract with them. I have a contact in the British Security Service who I am liaising with. The company we represent works on security so we have some experience with surveillance and protection, but that is not why we are involved." She stopped and looked at Stefan again.

He nodded and said, "I think you could tell them why we are involved."

"Stefan and I discussed how much we should tell you. We haven't told you any lies but the simple reason for our interest in the man you saw – his name is Jones by the way – is that he is probably responsible for the death of my brother."

John looked closer at Ella's face and saw the slight moistening and blinking of her eyes.

Ella cleared her throat and continued, "He was killed in Istanbul earlier this year and we have been working to identify his killer ever since. It turns out the British authorities are also interested in getting hold of this man. He is probably responsible for the death of one of their own in Wales and, I believe from what they told me, may have had a role in killing your aunt."

No one said anything for several seconds, but Stefan laid a comforting hand on Ella's shoulder and they exchanged brief glances.

John, who was wondering if the Istanbul link explained Ella's accent, spoke first, "My aunt was killed in Wales just a week or so ago and the police showed us photos and a video of the man they were interested in. They said his name was Jones."

Ella said, "They may be the shots and the short video we took of him. I have them here on my phone." She replaced her notebook, pulled out her phone, brought up the photos she had of Jones and showed them to John and Ann.

They looked at them carefully.

"Some of these seem to be the ones Johnson showed us," confirmed John.

Ann added, "And they are of the man we saw last night." She looked at John, "Do you agree?"

"Yes, that's him, and I am pretty sure we saw him last night."

"Can you be certain?" asked Ella.

"Well, at dinner last night we were certain, but when we discussed it later it didn't seem possible, or maybe it was slightly possible, but highly improbable."

Stefan asked, "What is the name of the restaurant and what happened yesterday?"

"It was the … Osteria del Campanone … yes, that's the name," said Ann. "It's in the middle of the walled city, near the clock tower." John nodded in agreement and they both related the events surrounding their spotting the man they thought was Jones.

When they finished Stefan stated, "So, you think it's possible this man is Jones, but no one can be sure just yet?"

Ann and John nodded in agreement.

Stefan said, "John, do you think he could have driven one of the cars you saw leaving?"

"It's possible, but he would have had to move very fast to do that."

"Where is the toilet, the restroom, in the restaurant?"

"I used it once. It's near the entrance door."

"Do you think he could have been in there and you missed him?"

"I suppose so. I didn't think of that at the time."

"So, I have to ask you the question," Stefan said. "What would you have done if you had caught up with him?"

"I'm not sure. In the heat of the moment I might have tried to stop him and confront him, but I suppose I'm glad I didn't. Now, I think all I could do is follow him and let the authorities know where he might be staying."

"I agree it's better you didn't confront him. At best it would mean he would be long gone from Santarcangelo; at worst he may have killed you."

John was startled and said, "You think he's dangerous? He doesn't look it."

"Maybe," Stefan shrugged. "I agree he doesn't look dangerous, or at least physically dangerous, and I don't think he is, but if cornered who knows what he would do? I think you should play it safe. Even following him could be difficult. We have both followed him at times and he is what you might call a 'slippery customer'. We followed him from London as far as Bologna, but lost him there."

"So, what do you suggest?" asked Ann.

"We have to try to find him and we have one way of helping do that. We planted a tracking device on his luggage a few days ago. If he has not located it yet it should still be working. I doubt he's located it because if he had he would still be on the move. It will work for a couple more days, maybe three. The signal can be detected up to a kilometer away by direct line of sight. If it is not direct it can be as little as a hundred meters. If it has to go through walls like these," he pointed to the ancient thick walls of the hotel dining room, "then we might be lucky if it could be detected at twenty meters."

"So, you are going to walk around the town and see if you can pick up a signal?" John asked.

"Basically, yes. We are going to walk and drive around the town. We'll also keep our eyes open in the hope of identifying him," replied Stefan.

Ella added, "He may recognize me so I hope we don't literally bump into him. I'll have to think about disguising myself as much as possible. The problem we have is the tracker is attached to his luggage, not to him, and during the day it's likely he and the tracker won't be in the same place. We also have to assume he is not staying in the countryside around here and is still somewhere in this town, and that this man is, indeed, Jones."

John asked, "And what will you do if you find him? From what you're telling me you have no more authority than we have to detain him."

"That's correct," Ella replied. "If we grab him we are undoubtedly committing a crime in Italy and he probably knows that. We have some ideas about what we can do if we locate him."

"Are you going to tell the British authorities about this meeting?"

Ella and Stefan looked at each other before Ella replied, "No, not yet. If we find it is Jones then we may need to contact them, but the wheels of bureaucracy turn slowly in London, and in Paris, so we may have an alternative plan we can work on. It is likely Jones has been involved in many deaths and many other crimes over the years. We are not the only ones who have suffered from his activities."

Stefan added, "We are not a vigilante group, and we work within the law. If we locate Jones we can discuss our next moves." He stood and extended his hand across the table to both Ann and John.

"So, what happens now?" John asked.

"We are going to find a map of the town and wander around. I think we'll visit the market first. Maybe we'll have lunch somewhere in town. It's market day and the town will be busy in the morning and early afternoon, so we might as well be tourists for the time being."

Ann asked, "Is there anything we can do?"

"What had you planned to do today?"

"Walk, lunch, nap and dinner in Rimini," John replied, looking at Ann for confirmation.

"Sounds good," said Stefan. "We may end up doing the same, although we may also drive around and see if we pick up a signal."

"Please let us know if you find him. We want to help if we can."

Stefan hesitated briefly before saying, "Of course. How can we reach you?"

It was John's turn to hesitate; this was one more reason why he wished he had paid for a European phone. "You can leave a note at the front desk for us, and if you give us your number we can get in touch with you through my daughter's phone." He shrugged and added, "That's probably the best we can do at the moment. We are meeting my daughter for the meal in Rimini this evening."

Stefan said, "Enjoy your day," and held out his card to John who put it in the top pocket of his shirt.

John and Ann had remained seated and waited as Stefan and Ella left the dining room.

"What do you make of that?" John asked.

"I'm not sure. Do you think they believed us?"

"I'm not sure either. Do you think they will ask us to help if necessary?"

"I don't know. I'm not sure what we can do to help."

"So, what should we do?"

"Follow their advice, I suppose. We should carry on as if we hadn't seen this man, Jones, and go for the walk we planned," said Ann.

"Oh. Okay."

"Do you want to wander through the market on the way?"

"Might as well," John replied, still feeling a little perplexed by the situation. He considered pouring himself another cup of coffee to try to realign his thoughts but realized a walk was a better alternative. They stood and made their way to their room.

63

Ella and Stefan left the hotel lobby and took a flight of stone stairs down to the market.

She considered wearing a headscarf and sunglasses to minimize the chance of being recognized, but thought she would see what the current fashion was at the market first. If she was the only one dressed like that she would attract the attention she didn't want. At present she was just enjoying the warm morning and Stefan's company.

She asked him, "Are you going to ask them to help if necessary?"

"I would prefer not to, but we may have to."

"Yes, I picked up on your hesitation there. They may have done as well."

"Part of the problem is no one is really sure if Jones is here or not, and so it's hard to commit resources and energy to what might turn out to be nothing."

"And if it turns out to be something?"

"Then," Stefan acknowledged, "We'll probably need all the help we can get for at least 48 hours."

There were few sets of sunglasses, and even fewer headscarves to be seen at the market, though hundreds of Italians were enjoying the atmosphere, both in the congested square, and where stalls had spilled over onto the side roads. Ella considered that she and Stefan blended in anonymously in their current clothing, and no one paid them undue attention.

She could get by speaking Italian, but Stefan's grasp of the language was better, so he bought the quarter-kilo of local cheese, a loaf of bread, and fruit for their lunch. They retreated from the market to a quiet restaurant and took an outside table for coffee and a mid-morning pastry which they shared.

Stefan asked, "How do you think we should go about this?"

"You mean eating this delicious food and drinking the coffee?"

"No," Stefan smiled.

"Then you must mean locating Jones?"

Stefan nodded.

Ella continued, "I was trying to be a good Buddhist and live in the moment – I've enjoyed this morning – but you're right, we have to make a plan. However, knowing you I suspect you already have some ideas. Am I right?"

"Yes and no. There is no point in trying to start driving around until the market is over and the streets cleaned up; I suspect that will be by mid-afternoon, but after that I haven't any definite plans."

"So, we have a few hours to ourselves. No one should be calling us – I made arrangements before I left Paris to have the office covered. I think we should go back to the market, buy a couple of those second-hand books – I think there were some in English, and in French, read, eat our lunch in the hotel garden, go back to our rooms, have a nap, and around 4:00 pm start driving around the town. When do we ever have five hours of time away from work?"

"If we had five hours together what would we do?" rejoined Stefan, looking directly at Ella.

She looked away for a couple of seconds, then leaned closer to Stefan, gave him a sisterly peck on the cheek, and replied, "We need to work on that, but for the time being we have separate rooms for a reason. Maybe it's to protect my honor from you, but could it be to protect your honor from me?"

"And I just thought it was to keep tongues from wagging when we put in claims to our accountants back in Paris," Stefan replied with a straight face.

Ella smiled, leaned back, hesitated and said, "Typical male. Well, what do you think of my plan for the next few hours?"

"Sounds almost perfect." He accented the 'almost'. "Let's buy those books, go back to the hotel, eat our lunch, go to our rooms and make sure to double-lock our doors."

He stood, held out his hand to Ella, who graciously accepted it and they strolled hand-in-hand back to the market.

354

64

Ella drove while Stefan navigated their path through the narrow streets of Santarcangelo. It was shortly after 3:00 pm and they had limited their initial search to the part of town south of the Via Emilia. It wasn't easy – there were multiple one-way and dead-end streets, often lined with parked cars, which restricted their access and progress. After an hour they had covered less than a sixth of the town and they needed to refuel their rental car.

Ella had been told at the hotel that the location of the best gelateria in town was at the junction of the Via Emilia and the Viale Giuseppe Mazzini.

She and Stefan agreed the gelato was definitely worth the short drive from their search area. She wondered where, in Paris, she could find as good an ice cream, but then thought it might be better, for the sake of her waistline, if she never knew.

They headed back out, filled up with gas, and took the Via Daniele Felici back towards their search. They had only covered about a hundred meters of the street when the detector started with a low whine that rapidly turned to a loud screech. Both Ella and Stefan were jolted out of their post ice cream daze.

"Oh, my God," said Ella.

"What the ..." added Stefan. He looked at the device on his lap, "Keep driving."

As she drove the detector tone returned to a low whine then disappeared completely, she reached the end of the street, turned in to the small piazza and stopped the vehicle.

"He's here after all," she said. "I think I must have been trying to not get my hopes up just in case this was a wild goose hunt."

"Me too. I was going through the motions, but that was about it."

"Now what?"

Stefan looked at the device. "The signal is coming from that street we just turned off. I can't see where in the street it might be coming from though. You stay here; I'll go and take a look."

"Be careful."

"All I'm going to do is walk up and down the street once. I'll be back in ten minutes."

Stefan closed the door and Ella parked the car. He was back in seven minutes.

"The signal is coming from a parked Fiat 500 about 200 meters from here. There is a small logo on the back window for 'Europcar', so it's probably a rental. I couldn't see the bag we'd put the tracker in, so it's probably in the back. I risked feeling the hood of the car and it was cold. The car hasn't been driven in the last hour or two, maybe longer."

"So, what do we do now? Do we watch the car?"

"That could be difficult. There are narrow sidewalks each side of the road. A lot of the houses have front doors which open directly onto the sidewalks, and both sides of the road are lined with parked cars, so it's not easy to see and not be seen. There are a few parking spaces further down the road, but they may be taken any time by the local residents."

"But, we have to try don't we?"

"You're right. We do. Let's go back there and see what we can do."

Ella backed out, negotiated the one-way system, and five minutes later grabbed one of the few parking spaces available. They parked thirty meters from the unremarkable, white, Fiat 500 which Stefan had identified – it was one of nine or ten they had passed along the street.

Ten minutes later Ella said, "This is not going to work."

"I agree."

"We're too exposed." Ella voiced her frustration. "He could spot us if he walks up behind us and we would never know. Someone from one of these houses could call in a suspicious couple sitting in a car, and we can't sit here forever either. He may be hiding out in one of these houses and this way he's going to spot us before we spot him."

"I agree. We'll have to move from here, although I don't know what we should do after that. I think I could get another tracker, one that I can attach to his car, in about four hours. I could pick it up at Bologna Airport. It probably has a range of five kilometers, but it's only useful if he moves the car. It may mean we can monitor the car's movement out of sight, but he could still come and go and we would not be any the wiser."

"Could we disable the car?"

"Maybe. We could give him a flat, but it would be difficult to do any more than that."

"I think we should risk it, or we'll just have to accept that there is no way to slow him down, or stop him over the next four hours."

"Okay. I'll be back."

Stefan returned in less than five minutes.

"Mission accomplished," he said. "Let's get out of here."

Ella started the car, moved into the street and headed back to their hotel. As she drove Stefan made a couple of phone calls and by the time they reached the hotel he had arranged to pick up a tracking device in Bologna. She was parking the car when she noticed John and Ann walk out of the hotel with a younger couple. They sat in a car and Ella watched it leave the parking lot.

"I suppose they're going to dinner with their daughter in Rimini. Should we tell them?" asked Ella.

"Let's let them enjoy their dinner. They should get back here about the same time I get back from Bologna, then we can all meet."

"I'll leave them a note in the lobby. You want a bite of food to take with you?"

Stefan replied, "No, not after pastry and gelato today. I think I'll grab something at Bologna airport, but I want to go to my room first."

They both stepped out of the car and walked into the hotel.

"I'll call London and, if necessary, put our other plan into operation," said Ella.

"Good. Let me know what happens."

Ella waited for Stefan in the lobby and when he reappeared gave him a hug and a kiss on the cheek. He responded by pulling her closer, looking into her eyes, and giving her a lingering kiss on her lips. She put her arms around him and pulled herself towards

357

him for a few seconds, and then slowly broke away. She whispered, "Drive safely. I'll see you in a few hours," and turned away.

65

Jones hadn't managed to get to the market until mid afternoon. He'd been forced to go to his bank in San Marino again that morning and had not returned to Santarcangelo until nearly 3:30 pm. By then most of the market stalls had closed, so he'd had to postpone some of his shopping for a later trip to a supermarket. He'd managed some shopping, put the little he had bought in his car, and then found a nearby restaurant for a late lunch. It had been a frustrating day, but at least the food in the restaurant was good.

He lifted the rear door and opened the bag he had left in the back of the car. He carefully wrapped the few vegetables he'd managed to buy in a plastic bag, then added them to the paperwork he'd taken on his trip to San Marino, hefted the shoulder bag out of the car, and headed towards the walled city. After an aggravating day he thought the walk would do him good.

He didn't notice he had one flat tire.

66

"I am not sure I can help you," said Georgina Southport. She had been in a meeting with the heads of departments at the security services in London, had answered the call from Ella and listened to her tale of catching up with Jones.

"You can't help?" a surprised Ella asked.

"I would love to help, but my hands are tied. You pulled me out of a meeting with some of my colleagues. I explained what you'd been doing, and how useful you had been getting hold of the cell phone in Paris. However, they are highly skeptical. They see no reason to support the unauthorized surveillance you have been carrying out, and they are not sure how you know you have the right man. They always work on the hypothesis that something will go wrong, and they don't want to be caught holding the baby. However, the main reason is they consider this a job for the police now, not the security services, and they have tied my hands because of that. Now, you tell me you have traced the car of the person you have been following to Santarcangelo, but have not found out the whereabouts of this person?"

"Yes."

"Then acting now is going to be a hard sell to the police here, and then it's going to be a hard sell for them to contact the Italian police and get their cooperation. From their perspective they would be asking the Italian police to take a lot on faith. I don't necessarily agree, but, as I said, my hands are tied and I wish they weren't."

Ella asked, "What could we do to help you, or make you get involved?"

Georgina hesitated before replying, "I am not sure you could do anything. One of the problems is if we could bring him back here we have limited evidence to charge him. We are still working on that, and I am hopeful we can unearth more evidence, but it could take time."

"How much time?"

"Days optimistically. Weeks realistically."

"Oh, so we just let him go?"

"No. Can you keep monitoring him?"

"How long?"

"For a few days – well, until we can get a police team in place to take over from you. We'll have to get permission from the Italians. I am working on that."

"So a few days are likely to be three to five?"

"That's probably realistic."

"Well, there's no way we can do it. We don't have enough resources." Ella sighed, discouraged by the conversation. "I suppose, in that case, we'll have to go to plan B."

"What's Plan B?" Georgina asked.

"It's the … it's probably better you don't know," Ella answered.

"You're not going to – "

"No," interrupted Ella. "We are not going to do anything illegal, and certainly not lethal, if that was what you were wondering about."

"Well … good … um … take care. Should I wish you good luck?" Georgina asked.

"I hope we don't need it, but thank you." Ella terminated the call.

She thought of a few unkind words about London bureaucracy, and wondered how the British had once ruled half the globe, but then thought – maybe that's why they don't anymore.

She picked up the phone, dialed a number, and put plan B into operation.

67

John and Ann said their goodbyes to Laura and Davide and walked up the short flight of stairs to the door of their hotel. They'd enjoyed the evening. The walk along the Rimini waterfront, followed by the seafood dinner, had been refreshing. In the morning they had strolled through the countryside surrounding Santarcangelo, had taken a long nap to recover from the sleepless night, and were feeling good about the world. They entered the lobby where Ann was presented with a note from Ella. It read, 'Please come to my room, 212, when you get back'.

Ann sighed a little and showed the note to John. He closed his eyes, his shoulders slumped and he said,

"Back to reality, I suppose." They walked the stairs to Ella's room and knocked on the door.

Ella let them in. "Please come in and take a seat. Stefan will be here in about fifteen minutes. He's been to Bologna. Let me tell you what's happened."

John and Ann sat on the only two chairs available and Ella sat on her bed.

She briefly explained how she and Stefan had identified the car they assumed Jones had been using, and the limitations of observing the car for any length of time. She told them Stefan had partially immobilized the vehicle by giving it a flat, and she mentioned the reason he had gone to Bologna. She also told them of the conversation with Georgina Southport, her contact with the British Security Service.

"I can't believe they aren't going to help. I mean ... what do they expect us to do?" asked John.

"I think it's because we, and that includes you and us, have no history of credibility with the police, or any other authorities in Britain."

"So, we just let him go?"

"No, and it seems that London doesn't want us to let him go, but they seem to be in no particular hurry to catch him."

Ann said, "It's almost like they hope he'll get away."

Ella had a brief moment of insight and realized there could be other reasons for London's procrastination.

She started to speak, "I wonder ..." when there was a knock on the door. She stood and let Stefan into the room. He gave Ella a peck on the cheek and sat on the bed next to her and across from John and Ann.

Ella rapidly brought him up to speed and said she'd put plan B into operation.

"When does he think he'll be here?" Stefan asked.

"By tomorrow evening," Ella replied.

"That's quick."

"The man has contacts," said Ella, "and is using them."

"What's plan B?" asked John. "In the USA it's the term for emergency contraception, but I don't think that applies here."

"If only it were that simple," smiled Ella. "Stefan, why don't you explain."

Stefan collected his thoughts for a few moments. "The man we are after, Jones, has been operating an organization we have called The Hand of Hamsa. It's probably part of a criminal organization with a slight difference in that it organizes some criminals, and uses others on a contract basis. Well, that may sound like any criminal organization, but this one has been very successful and used resources sparingly and in a particularly focused manner. Many organizations have multiple layers of criminals – think of them as middle-men – the Mafia is supposedly organized this way. Well, The Hand worked with no middle-men, or maybe just single-use middle-men, and, as I said, has been remarkably successful.

"However, one of their criminal enterprises was organizing assassinations. I don't have all the details, but I suspect the Hand would be contacted and they would get hold of another organization – it could be military in some countries, a terrorist group in another, maybe the police – and an assassination would be arranged. All that was asked, apart from payment, would be to leave a metal hand at the kill site. Most of these assassinations have taken place in the middle-east, or in countries where the rule of law is weak or non-existent. By leaving the metal hand, like a calling card, its reputation was maintained. The Hand is probably also interested in other criminal activities, but we are not too concerned about those at the moment."

Stefan paused, poured himself a glass of water, and continued, "We have been in contact with another person who lost someone to the Hand. He will be here tomorrow night and when he gets here we will discuss what happens."

"What is likely to happen?" asked Ann.

"I'm not sure. There will be no violence as far as we are concerned, and this other gentleman agrees to that stipulation." He stood, stretched his back then sat again. "Any questions?"

"Yes, what now?" Ann asked. "We still don't know where he is."

"We know where his car is and I am going to fit the tracker I brought from Bologna to the car."

"We'd like to come with you," said Ann.

John, who was hoping for a quiet evening, opened his mouth to say something, but decided against it. Stefan and Ella also paused for a couple of seconds before Ella said, "Of course. We'd love to have you along."

68

The Aegean Airlines plane left Athens airport on time and just over two hours later landed at Split airport. The man they knew as Ali had been there before and used his Croatian kuna to buy a seat on the bus into the city. He went to his room in a hotel near the ferry terminal. He set the alarm on his cell phone, and then called reception to ensure he would have a default morning call at 7:00 am. By 9:00 am he would be on the Jadrolinija ferry to Ancona, Italy. He anticipated reaching the first rendezvous eight hours later.

The second man had just begun appreciating driving the rented VW microbus around Italy. He'd been told to stay within four hours of Ancona, but that gave him a lot of leeway. He'd never been to a western country before and was enjoying himself. He wasn't as certain if his wife was enjoying it though. She had been told to not wear any headscarves or outfits which would identify her as coming from a middle-eastern country. After twenty-five years of wearing such clothing she had found the first few days stressful. He hoped she was becoming used to it.

After he received the message he checked the map and calculated he was less than 150 kilometers from Ancona. First, he'd have to drop off his wife at the hotel he'd chosen, but then he would have nearly all day to get to the meeting place.

The third man read the text and then consulted his charts and GPS. He had enough fuel on board. He'd call ahead to make a reservation for a slip in the Darsena di Rimini marina. He'd ask for one away from the restaurants and lights, and only for a night or two. He changed course, set the autohelm and calculated he would be there in time for lunch the next day.

69

Ann and John sat in the back of Stefan's Alfa Romeo and they drove the short distance to the Via Daniele Felici where Jones had left his car. All the parking spaces, and a few other gaps, had been taken in the usual imaginative Italian-parking manner. They drove on, past Jones's vehicle, and found the nearest parking space was around the corner in the piazza where Ella had waited earlier. Stefan left his car and walked back to Jones's vehicle. Without breaking his pace he stooped slightly and attached the transmitter under the passenger-side rear fender. He walked on, crossed the road and made his way back to the piazza.

Back in the car he pulled out the tracking receiver, inserted four AA batteries, and turned it on. The device responded by emitting a tone, a map display lit up and a flashing red spot indicated the transmitter's position on Jones's car.

"That's working well, "said Stefan. "It gives a stronger signal – I think it's up to five kilometers – and I should be able to pick it up from the hotel."

"Will it interfere with the other transmitter?" asked Ella.

"No, they are different frequencies. I'll show you." He reached into the glove compartment for the other receiver and turned it on. It lit up, but was otherwise silent.

"That's strange," he said. He got out of the car and walked towards the corner, then disappeared in the direction of Jones's car. He was back in five minutes.

"Bad news. It looks like the transmitter is no longer in his car," he said, looking at Ella.

"Oh, no. Not after all this work." She closed her eyes, sighed, and put her head back.

"I'm afraid so."

"Could the batteries have just gone flat?" she asked.

"Unlikely. The signal was good just four hours ago."

John asked, "What was the transmitter attached to?"

"His bag … well, it was attached under a protective stud on the bottom of the bag."

"Could he have found it?" wondered John.

"Maybe, but I think he'd have put as much distance between Santarcangelo, and wherever he is now, as quickly as possible if he'd found it. That would probably have meant using his car. It would take him less than fifteen minutes to change tires."

Ann said, "Perhaps he took the bag out of the car. Maybe he was using it for something else. After all, it was market day today."

"That's possible," said Stefan. "In which case it's likely he's living around here. Why don't we drive some of these streets and see if we pick up a signal. Ella, what do you think?"

Ella was clearly disheartened, "Well … yes, let's try it. It may work."

Stefan started the engine and for the next fifteen minutes they drove around the streets which were within 200 meters of Jones's car and then returned to the piazza.

They had picked up no signal.

"What now?" John asked, and then realized he had asked the same question earlier that day.

Stefan shook his head and replied, "I'm not sure. Before we found his car this afternoon we'd been driving other roads in the city. We thought we'd covered less than a quarter of them. I think we can go back and drive the other streets, but why would he leave his car here and live in another part of the city? There's plenty of parking around, especially in the suburbs."

"But what about inside the walled part?" asked Ann. She nodded towards the clock tower in the middle of the old city. "I don't understand all the Italian road signs, but the few times we've been in the old part of the city I've seen very restricted parking. This could be the closest street parking to the walled city."

Stefan looked at Ella who nodded and said, "What have we got to lose? Let's try it."

There was restricted access by road to the old city. There were no sidewalks, and the houses opened directly onto the smooth

370

cobble stones. Some roads were one-way and others had limited passing spaces. Stefan conceded it might be a reason to have a car nearby, but not in the old city, where it could be easily cornered and trapped in the narrow streets

It took them a half-hour of winding through the streets to make it to the far side of the city. And there, in the last street, Contrada del Signori, for only two seconds the receiver made the same noise it had made that afternoon on Via Daniele Felici.

Stefan exclaimed, "We have him!"

He drove along the narrow lane and parked as soon as he could, out of view of the house where they'd picked up the signal.

A collective sigh of relief came from all of them, followed by the realization that none of them really knew the answer to the "What now?" question on all their minds. For the umpteenth time that day Stefan left the car. This time he avoided walking back the same way, and the circuitous route took him fifteen minutes to return.

"It's the only house without flowers, or at least a flower basket outside," he reported. "There's a light on in the house. When I walked past I triggered a motion detector light and there are surveillance cameras pointing both ways up the street. The lock on the door seemed to be a basic Yale-type, but I didn't get a good look. The windows on to the street are small and deep, so he can't see out very far. That's about it."

"And we only have to keep an eye on him, make sure he doesn't skip town, for the next ..." Ella looked at her watch, "... twenty-one hours. After the chase he's led us on that should be a piece of cake, but I bet it won't be."

"I hope you're wrong," said Stefan. He swiveled in his seat to face Ann and John. "You asked if you could help. Are you still interested?"

"Of course," said Ann.

"But, what do you want us to do?" asked a more cautious John.

"Like Ella said we have to watch him until tomorrow evening and prevent him from leaving if we have to. Preventing him from

371

leaving is going to be the hard part. We may not be able to physically restrain him if he chooses to leave. All we can do is just make it difficult for him."

"Could you stop him using his car at all?" John asked. "Could we put sugar in his gas tank, or I heard a potato in the exhaust pipe can stop a car from starting?"

Stefan smiled and said, "I don't think either of those would work. It took me thirty seconds to give him a flat tire. Hanging around any longer to immobilize the car would look suspicious. We are stuck with that. All I want you to do is to watch his door and let us know if he moves."

"I suppose that sounds easy enough," said John.

"It is, except I want you to start doing it now."

"Now?"

"Yes, you and Ann can take the night shift. I think it's very unlikely he will leave his house until morning. I can't be certain, of course, because we don't know anything about his habits."

"But we can't even see his door from here. The curve of the street prevents that."

"I know. Let's find a better place."

Stefan left the car and walked over to where the city walls led down to the north-west side of the city. He looked down, beyond the city walls, and estimated he was about fifteen meters above a street with a few houses and several parked cars. He calculated the angles and thought it would suit his purposes.

Ella drove, they left the old city, and after only a few minutes Stefan asked her to pull over. He looked up and to his right and could see the house where Jones was staying. It was less than seventy-five meters away, but below the limited line of sight from the house windows. He asked Ella to move to a parking spot where his car was pointing at the house, and where his was not the only vehicle.

"Perfect," he announced. "I don't have any binoculars, but we're close enough we don't really need them. It shouldn't be too cold tonight. I'll bring you some blankets. I'll give you my cell phone and you can call Ella if he moves. Let me check the receiver..." He turned on the instrument, but it gave out no reassuring beeps or whines. "As I thought – the transmission barely gets through those thick walls. It could still be useful if he moves and takes his bag into the open, but it doesn't work even this distance away."

John asked, "Are you going to leave us here?"

"Yes, but I'm leaving the car too. I'll leave the keys in the ignition. I'll bring you some food and coffee with the blankets. Um ... turn off the dome lights, so if you have to get out of the car the lights won't come on. Drink the coffee so you have to get out of the car. Leave the windows open a little to stop the windows from fogging up. If he moves, don't follow him. Call us, I'll keep the receiver, and we'll take it from there."

"It's mainly very boring," said Ella. "Keeping awake is the hard part. I suggest you take half-hour shifts. You can even spend the half-hour outside, as long as you don't look suspicious. It's very unlikely the police will bother you, but if they do I suggest you say you borrowed the car from Stefan, you pulled over to discuss your ... to discuss your love-life together and are just about to move on. If that happens you'll have to move on and we'll have to work on a plan C. Any questions?"

"No," Ann said. "I am sure we'll be fine. We'll just have to look at it like it's an adventure."

"Correct," said Ella. "Although, to be honest, it may be hard to hold on to that idea at 3:00 am."

"We'll get through it."

"Right," Stefan said. "I'll be back in less than an hour. You may as well sit in the front." He and Ella vacated the front seats of the car, left the doors open and started to walk back along the Via Puzzo Longo towards their hotel.

Ann and John moved forward, closed the doors quietly, said nothing for a minute, then John commented, "I'm thinking of Laurel and Hardy."

"Oh, yes?"

"Yes. 'Well, another nice mess you've gotten me into, Stanley'. Remember that?"

373

"Of course, but they always figured it out and were back the next time ready for more adventures. You're not being a curmudgeon are you? It's really not like you."

"I am feeling distinctly curmudgeon-like. What I would really like is to be back home in Port Orchard, Washington State, in my own bed cuddling you. In fact, when we do get back there I want to travel no further than the nearest supermarket for the next month. I want nothing to happen to us. I want a totally bland, uneventful life from here on."

"You'd get bored."

"I'd love to be bored."

"I think you will have the opportunity to be bored tonight"

"You're probably right," agreed John.

They were both silent for a minute.

"Well, since we're here, aren't we supposed to follow Ella's suggestion and discuss our love-life?" asked Ann.

"So, if the police come along our alibis will be air-tight?"

"Yes."

"So, three times a day is not enough? What more do you want?"

Ann laughed, "That's more like you!"

"Well, if it is supposed to be three times a day we'll have a lot of catching up to do when we get home."

"Yes, it's hard to get enthusiastic with all that's been going on. On the other hand," she looked around and pointed at the back seat, "We've never had a car date like this before."

"That's because we didn't get together when we were teenagers. We didn't have to have liaisons in the back seats of cars – we could go straight to motels."

"We didn't go to motels either."

"That would have been far too expensive at three times per day," agreed John. "And, we had perfectly good beds of our own."

Ann smiled and asked, "Did you have liaisons in the back seat of cars when you were a teenager?"

"You're kidding. I think it is physically impossible to have sex in the back seat of any vehicle made in Britain in the fifties and

374

sixties. Besides, it was also too cold. I remember one of the first vehicles my family had – it was a Morris Minor and the heater was optional. Imagine that – in Britain too."

"You poor boy," said Ann and gave him a pat on the knee.

"I'm not going to ask what you got up to. I know every American car from the fifties and sixties was specifically designed so you could have parties, or even orgies, in the back seat. I've seen 'Grease'. I know what it was all about."

"Oh, yes, 'Grease'. I found that interesting. The moral seemed to be if you stuck to your principles you didn't get your man. If you wore skin-tight leather clothing, you did. Anyway, that's irrelevant – I saved myself for you."

"You did?"Asked John.

"Of course."

"Fifty years of celibacy until I came along?

"Yes."

"What about your daughter?"

"Virgin birth," said Ann, nodding sagely.

"Wow. Is that why you're making up for it now?"

"You've figured it out."

They were both quiet for a few minutes.

"We haven't had any moments like that in a while," said John. "You know – when we can talk and joke, just be ourselves and just be a couple. I hope we get back to our lives again. I was looking forward to our time in Italy and then … this."

"I agree. We have to help them out though."

"I know, and I agree, but it seems that every time I plan one thing, another gets in the way. I was just looking forward to the bed in the hotel, and not the front seat of an Italian car."

"I was looking forward to the bed too. What are we going to tell Laura and Davide? We have plans for lunch tomorrow."

"Lunch should be OK. We shouldn't be sitting here then, but it looks like we'll need another afternoon nap."

There was another pause.

Ann asked, "What do you think their plan B is?"

"I'm not entirely sure. They were a little vague about it. I was wondering if they weren't entirely sure either, or they didn't want to give us any more details.

"That's the impression I got too."

"I was also wondering why the British Security Service seems reluctant to help. Of course we only have Ella's word for that, but I think she was telling the truth."

70

The walk back to the hotel was mainly through the old city.

"So, how do you think they'll do?" asked Stefan.

"I think they'll do as well as anyone else," said Ella. "Around 3:00 am they might find themselves napping, but that's about as good as I would do." She paused as she stepped over a gutter. "I suppose you asked them to monitor him overnight so we could get some sleep?"

"Yes, he's not likely to move at night, and we need to be as alert as possible by tomorrow evening. I should have checked what the arrangements were with John's daughter. I'll ask when I take them the blankets."

"And what are the arrangements for tomorrow evening? Do we really know what's happening with plan B?"

"No. I'm surprised he can make it at such short notice, and bring some help along too."

"When I talked with him he said he had faith that we would succeed, so he already had part of his plan in place."

Stefan said, "I think he was impressed by you, and probably by SIGNAK's reputation."

"Well, let's hope this all doesn't go to hell and ruin my reputation and SIGNAK's."

"I'll look after SIGNAK's, and I think he'll make sure you don't come to any harm."

"I thought it was you who was supposed to guard my reputation," teased Ella.

Stefan waited a minute before asking, "What do you want Ella? I keep getting mixed signals. I think you know how I feel about you."

Ella hesitated at the top of a flight of stairs. "I am not sure what I want. I haven't felt centered for a while and then, after my brother was killed, and I nearly joined him, I have found it hard to be focused. In terms of SIGNAK – it's been my life for so long, maybe too long, and I think it's time for a change and I need to figure it all out. I'm getting there, but it's taking longer than I thought." She paused. "Then, there's you. I've been thinking a lot about you and I apologize. I think I've been leading you on."

Stefan nodded.

Ella continued, "I'm sorry I've done that. I've been hot and cold with you and it's because I don't want to hurt you, or myself. You are my best friend and I don't want to lose you. You don't know how much I would love to just let you hold me again. I remember how it was before, and I'd love to spend hours naked lying in bed with you again, but I'm terrified of losing myself."

"Maybe you'd find another self?" suggested Stefan.

Ella smiled and said, "Would I have to let the old one go?"

"I don't think so. I got on pretty well with her."

"Thank you." She continued walking down the steps. "For the time being, and until this thing with the Hand of Hamsah and my brother's death is played out, let's stick to single rooms. Please give me a little more time. I think I need more time."

Stefan stopped at the bottom of the stairs, gave Ella a brief hug and said, "I'll give you anything you want."

They reached the hotel. The lobby desk was closed so they agreed to take blankets from their own rooms back to John and Ann.

Stefan was folding a blanket and stuffing it into a large plastic bag. There was a tap on the door and he let Ella in. She handed him her blanket, turned around, closed and locked the door.

"I've had enough time," she said.

Stefan was nearly an hour late getting back to John and Ann.

378

71

The night passed slowly, very slowly. John and Ann tried using the radio to keep themselves awake, but all the stations were in Italian and after a while the background drone seemed to make them sleepier. Eventually, they found the best way to maintain their vigil was for one of them to stay outside, walk around, flap their arms, practice swing dance moves and silly walks while the other slept. They had to duck down out of sight if a vehicle came along, but very few appeared, and they managed to give each other an hour of unbroken sleep at a time.

However, by 7:00 am they were exhausted, thirsty, disheveled, sore, and overjoyed to see Stefan. They returned his cell phone and retraced the path he had taken back to their hotel. They enjoyed a silent breakfast, a hot shower, put the 'Do not disturb' sign on their door, inserted ear plugs, and by 9:00 am were fast asleep. Unfortunately, their circadian rhythm woke them a couple of hours later, but by then they were feeling relatively refreshed.

They had decided to not tell Laura and Davide about locating Jones and about their nocturnal activities. They thought it best to not involve them any further. Lunch passed uneventfully and they promised to meet the next day for a trip to Ravenna. It was to be the last full day they could have together – their flight back to Manchester was the following day. They were returning to the hotel when they met Ella coming out through the lobby door. She walked past them and without breaking her stride or turning her head she murmured, "Come to my room in fifteen minutes."

John had an immediate sense of impending doom, but said nothing and followed Ann to their room. He tried reading for a few minutes, but couldn't concentrate and fifteen minutes later they were let into Ella's room. She closed the door and once again sat on the bed across from them.

"I have a couple of updates for you. The first is Jones left the house this morning, went to the supermarket, bought some provisions and returned to his house. He used his shoulder bag to carry the items and Stefan was able to track him there and back. I coordinated with Stefan, but stayed way back in case he recognized me. So, it doesn't look like Jones has any plans to move in the immediate future. That's good." She paused. "The other update is a little bit concerning. I received a phone call this morning from Georgina Southport. She is the person with British security services I talked to yesterday. I didn't recognize the number, almost didn't answer it, but it turned out she was calling on a single-use mobile phone. I think they call it a burner phone. Anyway, she told me our conversation the other day was not private and she had been directed what to say to me. She had been told to tell me there would be no help coming, but there may be if they could work it out in London. She did a good job – that was the impression she gave me. However, with today's call she basically told me to be careful, and she thinks London may have already sent someone here."

"To help?" asked John.

"Maybe, but … to help themselves would be more like it," Ella replied.

"I don't understand."

"I'm not entirely sure I understand. Georgina is still loyal to the security service so she didn't come out and say anything directly, but from my previous conversations with her I inferred that Jones may have had a link to someone in the service. So, the questions are: was their more than one link, and/or are they interested in making sure Jones doesn't talk to anyone? Or, it could just be they would prefer to make sure Jones gets away and thereby avoid any embarrassment to them?"

"So, what you are saying is …?" asked John.

Ann added, "You are saying they might be interested in Jones disappearing, one way or another?"

"Exactly, and the only people who know his location are the three of us and Stefan."

"Do they know we've found him, or just his car?" asked Ann.

"They don't know we've identified where he is living, but they do know we've found his car, and that is one of the points. They may want us to tell them, or let them know, where he's living."

"So, we do what?" asked Ann.

"The only person they may not be able to recognize is Stefan, so he has to stay away from us. London knows you're here and may assume you know where Jones's car is. I haven't told them that you know, but it is a reasonable assumption. If asked, and I am not sure who is going to ask, we are saying we are monitoring his car only with the tracking device. If he moves we think we have enough time to get on his trail. I don't think we have that time, but as far as they are concerned we're amateurs and don't really know what we're doing. Let's not convince them otherwise."

"Where's the tracking receiver now?" asked John.

"Here," Ella pointed to the power cord leading into a bedside table drawer. "It's set to signal if the car moves."

"And where do we say Stefan is?"

"Let's just say he has gone to Bologna for supplies."

"How long are we going to keep this up?" asked Ann.

"Only for a few more hours."

"You mean plan B?"

"Yes."

"I think you should tell us a little more about plan B," suggested Ann and John nodded in agreement.

"Well, I suppose you are entitled to know since you are involved. My brother was shot and killed earlier this year in Turkey. Nothing appeared in the press, and there was no investigation, but I was there when he was killed." She paused for a few seconds as the memory replayed itself in her mind. "Stefan and I found out what we could, and our investigations led us to a man who called himself Ali. He, too, had lost someone to The Hand of Hamsa. Since then we've kept in touch with him, and by a bizarre twist of fate, it turns out he had dealings with Jones in the past. He has resources we do not have, and he's bringing some of his assistants with him, and should be here by

7:00pm this evening. As soon as it's dark they intend to confront Jones."

"And then what?" asked John.

"I think they plan to take him to Turkey to answer for his crimes. He probably won't go willingly."

"You mean ... well, isn't that kidnapping?"

"Yes, but it's the only way he can be brought to justice. Most of the killings by The Hand have taken place in the Middle East. It's not ideal, and I'm not entirely happy with it, but in the circumstances it's the best solution. All of the alternatives, and there aren't many, are unacceptable. We can't let him go to carry on with his criminal activity. For all we know we could be next on his list, but we cannot kill him either."

"We'll have to think about that," said Ann.

"You won't be involved any more than you have been. Stefan and I discussed this and you've done enough."

"Well, thank you ... I think," said John.

"We'll have to think it over, but what are we supposed to do now?" asked Ann.

"I suggest a gelato. We need to be seen for the next few hours. I hope it'll keep the attention off Stefan. I'll bring the receiver with me."

John smiled, "That sounds like a great idea, and then I can tell you the story of my life."

Ella looked a little confused.

"Don't worry," said Ann. "It only lasts five minutes."

72

They strolled slowly to the gelateria Ella and Stefan had visited the previous day, and opted for the three-for-ten-Euros deal. John tried the Arcangelo flavor, wasn't entirely sure what it was, but regretted his body couldn't risk asking for seconds. Ella proved to be an excellent companion and they enjoyed the stroll back to their hotel. The goods in the shops were much more expensive than in the USA, but there were multiple small shops, with a wide range of items, that had not yet succumbed to competition from online purchasing. However, the main reason they walked slowly and window-shopped was to use the reflections in the windows to see if they were being observed. Ella thought they were in the clear, but told them she couldn't be sure.

Back at the hotel they collected their books and met in the garden. They picked a sheltered arbor which held a table and reclining chairs and captured the late afternoon sun. None of them had had a full night's sleep and they dozed between reading their novels and guides. Ella left the receiver on a table in plain sight.

The sun moved on and evening approached.

"I'm not sure why no one has contacted us," murmured Ella as they collected their books. "It could be because London hasn't got anyone here yet, or it could be because we, and the receiver, are being observed. It could be good or bad. Either way, it's time for dinner."

"More food!" groaned John.

"Yes," said Ann. "Another couple of days and we'll be heading back to the frozen north. You might as well enjoy it while you can."

"I'll remind you that you said that when we get back home and you step on the bathroom scale and it complains," said John. "I think I'll stick to a salad this evening."

Ella added, "I agree. Salads all round."

73

At 7:30, dusk, they were just finishing their dinner.

At the same time Stefan was waiting at the rendezvous.

He didn't have to wait long. The white Volkswagen van pulled in behind him and flashed its lights.

Stefan stepped out of his car and walked back to meet Ali who opened the passenger door. They both shook hands.

"Thank you for coming," said Stefan.

"It is I who should be thanking you," Ali replied with a slight bow. "I have everything we should need and what we agreed on."

"Good. I have been watching him today and he's still here," said Stefan.

"Who is watching him now?"

"Me. I've been in this street for most of the last twelve hours." Stefan turned and pointed to the house where Jones was staying. "It's the one without the flowers."

Ali looked up and asked, "Can't he see us from there?"

"No, the windows are too small and set back in the wall, but just in case he steps out we'd be better off sitting in your vehicle."

Ali opened the van door and motioned to Stefan to sit inside. The two other men in the van shook his hand.

"You may remember my companions from our last encounter."

Stefan looked them over and said, "Well, I see you've all shaved and had hair-cuts."

Ali grinned and translated Stefan's comments into Arabic.

"It was time to shed our jihadist look. We are Greek tourists enjoying our time in Italy. Besides, if we hadn't changed we would have attracted more attention. I can't speak for my colleagues, but I prefer this look. No one pays us any attention here and that's how I want it."

Stefan again wondered what Ali's true nationality was, but thought it inappropriate to ask. Today, at least, he was Greek.

"I think the best time to carry out our plan will be around 11:00pm," said Stefan. "That's later than I thought, but most of the town will have settled in by then. Is there any problem with that?"

Ali asked one of the men, the one who had brought the boat to Rimini, if the delay would cause any problems and translated his reply to Stefan.

"He says there should be no problem. And, by the way," continued Ali, "where is your colleague?"

"She's around, and keeping her distance. She has a contact in London who was concerned that we might not be the only ones with an interest in our man. Also, he's probably called Jones."

"That's the name I know him by."

"Well," continued Stefan, "it seemed preferable to not lead anyone else to Jones, and so we have not had any contact for the last four hours. As soon as we move, at 11:00, I'll let her know."

"That's a pity. I would like to meet her again."

"If you do it may be that things have gone wrong. If the plan works she, and a couple of other people who helped direct us here, will keep well away from us."

"So, we have a few more hours," said Ali. He turned to the driver and asked him something in Arabic, waited for the reply, and then turned to Stefan. "Would you like a cup of tea? Apparently, this van can make cups of tea."

"I'd love a cup of tea."

"Good, and we'll all join you."

74

Jones wasn't sure what was bothering him. He'd been feeling unsettled for the last couple of days. It wasn't like him to feel this way. He'd tried analyzing his feelings and now found himself second-guessing his plans. He was wondering if he'd stopped too soon, and if he'd been followed in his flight from England. He thought he should be feeling secure by now, but he wasn't. Much of the elated feeling of being free during those first few days in Paris and Italy had disappeared and he was even feeling a little lonely. He'd rationalized away some of his feelings, but had realized he was missing the stability of his life in England, and he even wondered if it would ever be safe for him to return there.

Then there was this house. He couldn't stay here forever and he wasn't sure how long he should stay. The owner owed him a favor, but Jones knew the reality of the 'No honor among thieves' aphorism, and what better way to wipe out the obligation of one favor than by tipping off the authorities?

No, the only way to be certain he was free and clear was to enter a third-world country overland, or by sea, and avoid points of entry like airports and train stations. There, he could remain anonymous and eventually re-emerge with another identity. It was going to be harder than he'd thought, but not impossible.

He'd begun reestablishing his network with mild success. In the last few days he'd concentrated his activities and had been rewarded with the job of making a banker in Lebanon disappear. He had contacts in Syria who might welcome part of the task, and he would personally make sure the banker's absence would be accompanied by the disappearance of half-a-million dollars from the bank's accounts. That way the police efforts might be concentrated on looking for someone who they thought was still alive. The best part was he could arrange all this without setting foot in Lebanon or Syria.

He smiled at that thought and put the remaining papers in his shoulder bag. He was packed, and tomorrow he would move on. He stood, checked the time – it was nearly 11:00 pm – and stretched. He glanced at the live feed from the security cameras aimed at the road outside, and was surprised to see a white van approach and slow as it got near. It stopped.

Jones stared at a man who stepped out of the van. He was holding something about the size of a teacup, he placed it on the roof of the van and it started flashing. He couldn't see what color it was on the monochrome screen, but at the same time three other men left the van – two were dressed in the uniform of the carabinieri. This didn't seem right, and then Jones looked again at the first man who was approaching one of the cameras. Jones hesitated for two more seconds, then he realized who the man was.

He fled.

75

Ali said the hardest part about making a replica of the carabinieri uniform from outside the country was acquiring police hats. In the end it was ridiculously easy and the driver had picked up a couple at a second-hand store in Alcona. The white web belts, the diagonal cross-chest belts and the blue shirts were generic enough to be found in most countries. Ali had obtained the LED flashing blue light from a child's toy and added a magnet so it would stick to the van's roof.

Ali knocked on the door while Stefan confirmed the presence of the transmitter in the house. The other two men played at policemen and stationed themselves in the road on either side of the house.

There was no response to the knocking.

Ali tried the handle. It was locked. He got to work – it took him ninety seconds to get the door open, another fifteen to snap the security chain, and another fifteen to check the rooms.

There was no one there.

Stefan checked the receiver. There was no signal.

"How could he …?" he asked, bewildered.

Ali shook his head.

"How did he get away?" Stefan asked again.

They started looking around the house. They moved rugs, they checked for other doors, and then they checked the closets. Ali opened one tall wardrobe set against the back wall and hesitated, Stefan joined him.

"That's strange," Ali said. "For a few seconds when I opened this it seemed cooler inside."

They both looked inside the closet, which was full of clothing hanging on a rack. This was odd – the other closets were empty. The clothes looked a little dusty. Stefan leaned in and pulled out handfuls of clothes and dropped them on the floor so he could see the back wall of the wardrobe. In the middle he noticed the rear left half was set back a little. He moved to the left corner, searched with his hands and found a handle. He moved it sideways and it opened to reveal the entrance to a tunnel almost six feet high.

"He's going for his car," said Stefan. He pulled out his cell phone and ran back to the van.

76

Ann was reading Terry Pratchett's 'Small Gods' with her feet resting on the bed, John had his feet on the floor and was thumbing through the Ravenna section of their Italian guide, and Ella was lying on the bed immersed in 'Elle' magazine.

They all became alert as Ella put Stefan's call on speaker.

"He's got away. There was a tunnel at the back of the house. One of us will follow through the tunnel. I guess he's headed for his car. We're going there now." He hung up.

John was up and at the door first, but then he hesitated and turned to the others who were putting on their footwear. "Why would he go for his car? If we know where he lives why wouldn't we know where his car is?'

Ella asked, reaching for a shoe, "So, what do you think he'll do?"

"I don't know – maybe steal a car. But he's got to get out of the tunnel first."

John opened the door and ran.

He ran down the stairs, dashed across the lobby and then he was in the open. It was slightly downhill and less than two hundred yards. He made it in a little over thirty seconds – not good for a high school athlete, but amazing for a sexagenarian who had been surviving on pasta and gelato for the last week.

Jones beat him by three seconds.

"Stop," yelled John to the figure emerging from the gate to the Santarcangelo tunnels tourist entrance.

It was Jones. He turned to face a panting John. He was still holding the set of bolt-cutters he'd just used to cut the chain securing the gate. Jones couldn't afford to be delayed, but there was only one person trying to stop him and he had to deal with that. He vaguely recognized him, but was not sure from where. He advanced towards John holding the bolt-cutters in his right hand.

John realized the danger when Jones was less than six feet away. Jones swung, aiming for John's head, but John moved back just in time to feel the air from the swing pass his forehead. John was not as lucky with the back swing which caught him a glancing blow on the upper part of his right arm. He also realized this could only end one way unless ... Jones drew his arm back for another swing and John leaped at him, pinned both his arms and head-butted Jones on the nose. He was rewarded with an instant gush of blood, but Jones moved back, twisted and pulled away from John's grasp. He hesitated briefly and looked over John's shoulder.

Suddenly, there was someone else in the fight. A man appeared to John's right and squirted an aerosol into Jones's face. Jones immediately dropped the bolt-cutters and put his hands over his eyes. John looked to see who was there and received the same blinding, painful spray in both his eyes. He could barely open his eyes to see what was going on – it was so painful. Someone pushed him and he fell awkwardly. He tried to get up, but stumbled and fell again.

Through the haze and the pain he watched the man punch Jones in the stomach and the back of the neck, then catch him as he fell. He lifted the unconscious Jones in a fireman's lift and slowly carried him towards the steep stone stairs leading to the town center.

John tried to get up to stop the man, but a second later Ann was at his side. "Stay down, John," she said. "Ella will handle it."

Ella picked up the bolt-cutters and ran at the back of the man who was carrying Jones. Holding only one handle she swung the tool and hit the man across the side of his right shin. Immediately, he cried out in pain, buckled, almost fell, and dropped Jones. He turned to face Ella who swung again and hit him on the left knee, but when she swung again, he caught the other handle, pulled it out of Ella's grasp and threw it away. Ella had slowed him, he couldn't move as quickly, but he still came at her. He was stocky and powerful but she was lighter on her feet and easily moved away out of his reach. She moved in and tried a roundhouse kick to his head, but he saw it coming and ducked in time. He reached in his pocket and brought up the pepper spray he had used on Jones and John, but Ella moved back and ducked so the jet passed her harmlessly.

And then Stefan was there. He grabbed the arm holding the pepper spray and used his heel to kick the man in the testes. He wrenched the arm back, immobilizing his shoulder. The man's head snapped back as Stefan elbowed him under the chin and he went down. He lay motionless on the ground. Stefan picked up the spray, gave the man a short burst in his face and then threw the device away.

"Are you OK?" he asked Ella.

"Yes, I'm fine. A little short of breath, but I'm fine. Who is he?" she asked.

"I don't know." He bent down and rifled through the man's pockets. Apart from a few personal items the man was carrying no form of identification.

Stefan added, "The fact that he has no identification should tell us something. Let's hope he was working alone. From what I saw he seemed to be carrying Jones over to the steps. I assume he was going to throw him down them."

Ali walked up from one direction and Ann from the other.

"Is John all right?" Stefan asked Ann.

"Yes, he's got a few more bruises, and his eyes are making him miserable, so I need to get him to a wash room as soon as possible." She turned and headed back to John.

Stefan, Ella, and Ali looked at the two unconscious bodies on the ground.

"I think you should put on your blue-flashing light again and get your policemen to help move Jones into your vehicle. So far we seem to have been lucky that no one has passed us. Maybe the blue light will reassure people that all is under control."

"I still have one man, my boat captain, in the tunnels."

"Then, I hope he finds his way out soon."

Ali returned to his van, the blue-flashes started again and the van drove onto the sidewalk next to Jones. Jones was trying to sit up.

Ali pushed on his shoulder to prevent him standing and whispered in his ear. "You are coming with us. We just saved

393

your life, but if you don't cooperate I won't hesitate to kill you, or maybe I'll think of something worse. Think about it." He spoke to his driver in Arabic, which he knew Jones understood, and together they hoisted an unresisting Jones into the back of the van. He tied Jones into a seatbelt then reached into a cooler from where he withdrew a syringe. He plunged the needle into Jones's thigh and emptied the syringe. He then took a similar syringe and injected the contents into the other man's thigh. If they had any more thoughts of resistance the shots took them away.

The other man in Ali's trio, the boat captain, appeared at the gate and made his way towards the van. On the way he noticed a bag, the one Jones had been carrying. He stooped, picked it up and offered it to Stefan who shook his head and indicated Ali should take it.

Ali turned to Ella and said, "I wish we could have had more time together. I saw the way you fought and you were magnificent. Maybe you and I can work together again sometime. I would invite you to join my harem, but I don't have one."

Ella smiled, "Well, then I could invite you to join my harem, but …" She shrugged.

Ali laughed, picked up Ella's right hand, gave it a kiss and said, "Until next time?"

"Until next time," said Ella with a slight bow of her head.

They watched Ali take the light off the top of the van. He jumped in and the vehicle made its way out of town along the cobbled street.

"I think we'd better get out of here," said Ella, "before any more blue-flashing lights turn up."

"I agree," said Stefan. "What shall we do about him?" He indicated the man still lying prone on the ground.

Ella kneeled next to the man. He was breathing normally and his pulse was slow and regular. He was not obviously injured in any way apart from swelling around his eyes. She pulled out a phone and took a photograph of the man's face.

"I suppose we are assuming he has something to do with London, so he could be dangerous yet?" she asked Stefan.

"Yes, I suppose so too. I don't know what was in that shot that Ali gave him; I probably don't want to know."

Ella stood and joined Stefan. "Where was Ali taking Jones?" she asked.

"I didn't ask. What I don't know won't hurt me, but how about this? I've an idea. Let's see if any of these trash cans contains a wine bottle, preferably one with a little wine still in it."

Two minutes later they had found two bottles and one was still a quarter-full. They turned the man onto his side, poured the remaining wine onto his face and clothing, and a little into his mouth. They left the empty bottles next to him and walked back to their hotel. They had almost passed out of sight of the area when something caught their eye. They looked back and saw flashing lights approach the unconscious man.

77

The Darsena di Rimini marina was quiet at 2:00 am. No one noticed a couple of policeman aiding an intoxicated mariner back to his boat, and if they had they would have appreciated the flexibility and help shown by the police. They may have found it odd that neither policeman returned to their vehicle, and that the boat left the marina twenty minutes later, but by then they would have probably gone back to sleep.

The man stayed in hospital until afternoon of the next day. His name was entered as the Italian equivalent of John Doe, and at 4:00 pm he walked out. No one noticed his absence for an hour. He returned to his vehicle and wondered about retrieving the listening devices, but his head and shoulder were killing him, his thinking not quite straight, his face was puffy and bruised, and he thought it better to put as much distance between Santarcangelo and himself. He didn't really want to be interviewed or finger-printed by the police – he knew what they'd find. Five hours later he was resting at his cousin's house in Porcari, on the other side of Italy. He'd get someone to check his shoulder when he got home to Livorno the next day.

Next time he'd let the Brits deal with it themselves. He'd insisted, as before, on payment up front, so that wasn't a problem, but in future, he said to himself, he wouldn't work for them.

Of course, that's what he said last time.

78

John's eyes were almost back to normal the next morning. There was still a pink tinge to the conjunctiva, and a little swelling of the lids, but Ann had done a good job of flushing the worst of the pepper spray off his eyes and face. They went down to breakfast and found Ella and Stefan already there.

They filled their plates at the buffet, balanced tea and coffee cups on their trays and accepted the invitation to join the couple.

"Sleep well?" asked Ella.

"I slept surprisingly well," answered John. "In fact better than I have for a while. My eyes were sore for a while but that passed, and I think I fell asleep soon after that. I'm not sure it was the lack of sleep catching up with me, or I needed to get into a fight, but whatever it was I feel pretty alert this morning. I seem to have a few new bumps and bruises, and my legs ache," he patted his thighs, "but not too bad really."

"Your quads probably ache," said Ann, "because you haven't run that far, that fast, in months."

"Oh, yes, I hadn't thought about that, and my right arm is bruised a little, but … well … what happened last night? Ann has filled me in on some of the details, but she was helping me and didn't see it all."

Ella looked at Stefan who smiled and said, "I believe you saved the day. When we found his escape tunnel we thought he would be headed for his car and started in that direction, but then Ella called me back and told me where she thought you'd gone. She followed Ann out of the door, but apparently you were hard to catch up with."

"Who sprayed that stuff into my face?"

"We don't know. I suspect he was hired by someone to get to Jones and silence him, but we managed to prevent that. We left him unconscious, but it looked like an ambulance, or police car, was going to deal with him."

"And what happened to Jones?"

Ella answered this time. "Plan B worked, although for a few seconds there I was worried. But then, Stefan showed up."

"Plan B involved a sort of kidnapping didn't it?" John asked in a lowered voice.

"Yes, and Ali took him away per the plan. In fact, we probably saved Jones's life, but I doubt he will thank us for that."

"Who is Ali?" asked John.

Stefan said, "Well, we aren't sure. I've made a few enquiries and didn't get too far. He certainly has money and resources, and in the Middle East that often means oil, but I can't be certain. He did say he'd worked with Jones, but didn't elaborate in what way. He also hinted, when we first met him, that he might not be welcome in the UK. So, at one extreme he may be an international criminal, and at the other a sort of unrecognized Arabian Robin Hood or super hero." He shrugged his shoulders and didn't seem convinced by his own argument.

John and Ann looked skeptical.

Stefan continued, "I have to say I am not completely happy with letting him have Jones. I think I mentioned before that he promised not to kill him, and he then said he would make sure justice was done, but I'm not sure how he intends to accomplish that. For what it's worth I spent a couple of hours with him last night while we were waiting, and I think he'll stick to what he said he'd do."

"But, that seems to mean he made no promises," said Ann.

"I agree. We'll have to see what happens. We have no control now. However, I will make a promise to you – I promise I will let you know Jones's fate whether it's good or bad. I hope that will do."

Ann and John looked at each other for a few seconds.

"Thank you," said Ann. "I think that will be sufficient. John?"

"I agree," said John.

"Good," said Ella. "There is one other thing we need to deal with. We need to have the same story if anyone asks us what happened. I suggest we say we located Jones's car and then found out where he lived by following him. We decided we couldn't watch him all the time and we would confront him and try to hold him in his house for the authorities. Unfortunately, when Stefan and I tried this it took us longer to get into his house than we thought and he escaped through the tunnel. We asked you to help. John confronted him at the lower end of the tunnel, they fought briefly and then another man intervened. It seemed like Jones had help and John was disabled with pepper spray. Stefan and I turned up and tried to get to Jones, but the other man kept us away. Eventually, we managed to overcome the man, but in the meantime Jones got away. Does that sound good?"

"Yes," said John, looking at Ann who nodded. "I think we should add that Jones must have had access to some other form of transportation because you went to his car and it was still there."

Ella nodded.

Ann added, "I will say I didn't see much of what went on. I was more interested in getting the spray washed off John's face."

"What about the man who sprayed us? What should we say about him?" asked John.

"I think we say he was down on the ground, but we waited at a safe distance until an ambulance came to pick him up," suggested Ella. "However, you were not there when that happened. You were under Ann's care back at this hotel."

"So, the story is plan B didn't work?" asked John.

"Correct, but it almost did," said Ella.

"But, who's going to be asking us about what happened?" wondered John.

Stefan said, "I hope no one is going to ask you in detail. Ella is going to call her contact in London this morning and tell her this story, but when you get back to the UK you may be questioned. Ella will have to say she is disappointed, but you may have to both say it and show it. You may even want to practice what you are going to say."

"I don't quite get it," said John. "We haven't done anything wrong … have we?"

Ella interrupted, "We think the most we could be accused of is attempting to take the law into our own hands by restraining

401

Jones. We tried, it didn't work out, but we thought it the best plan at the time. We'll be in Paris and the British police are not going to bother with us there. The US police are not going to bother you, but in the interim, until you leave the UK, you may be questioned."

John frowned, was about to say something, but Ann got in first and said, "I think we get it. We'll be OK."

"Good," said Ella. "We're checking out this morning and will be back in Paris in a few days time. Do you have any plans?"

"Ravenna today," said Ann, "and then fly back to the UK tomorrow."

"I think you'll find the mosaics in Ravenna quite fascinating," said Stefan. He reached into a pocket, handed Ann a card and pencil and asked her to write down a contact number and address for him. While she was writing Stefan handed another card to John with his own contact information.

Ella and Stefan rose, said their goodbyes, and promised to keep in touch.

Ann and John watched them leave. They seemed to be walking a little closer than before, and Stefan's guiding hand was a little lower when he steered Ella through the door from the dining room.

Ann and John finished their breakfast.

"What do you think of them?" Ann asked John.

"Who?"

"Ella and Stefan of course!"

"Well, they seem like nice people."

"Is that all you can say?"

"Yes," said John, a little puzzled by the question.

"No more?"

"No."

"Are you sure?"

"Oh, you mean did I notice that their relationship seemed to have changed in the last day? Instead of professional colleagues they are behaving more like young lovers. Is that what you mean?"

"Well, yes."

"Ann, surely you realize I am too much of a gentleman to mention, or even consider, such an observation."

"John," Ann replied, leaning forward. "Don't you know you are playing with fire? How do you know that I am not too much of a lady to empty this cup of coffee into your lap?"

"Ah, well, if you put it like that it's got nothing to do with being a lady. If you did pour that hot cup of coffee onto me in that particular place I'd have to go upstairs, change, wash my clothes, leave them hanging up to dry all day, apply burn cream, and then contact my attorney. It wouldn't be worth it ... on the other hand why don't we go upstairs and get ready for Ravenna?"

"What a great suggestion."

They stood, and John guided Ann through the exit door with his hand on her waist. Ann stopped, smiled at John, grabbed his hand and moved it a little lower.

79

"I'm afraid he got away," said Ella.

"I'm sorry," said Georgina Southport in London. "You must be very disappointed."

"Frustrated is more like it. We were so close to catching him. He had help, which is why he escaped. We tried to pick up his trail but we couldn't."

"What happened?"

Ella related the version of the previous evening's events she had discussed over breakfast with Ann and John.

"I'm so sorry. No one hurt though?" said Georgina.

"No, but I'm not sure about the man helping Jones."

"So, what are you doing now?"

"Ah …" Ella was tempted to answer literally, but instead said, "In the short term I am taking a few days off here in Italy. I'll be back in Paris after that, and if any leads come in I'll follow them up."

"I have a few days off next week. I was thinking of going to Paris. Perhaps we could meet up?"

"That sounds like an excellent idea. Let me know when you're coming and we can meet for lunch. I believe it'll be my treat. I'll look forward to seeing you."

"Bye."

"Bye."

Ella hung up and wondered what that was about. It was a totally bland conversation. Georgina gave nothing away, which was probably the point of the conversation. Maybe she couldn't risk giving anything away, maybe others were listening, maybe …?

She turned to look at Stefan lying beside her and said, "You know what? I'll worry about it, or not, when I get back to Paris. In the meantime I have other priorities." She smiled.

80

As Stefan had said, the mosaics in Ravenna were quite unusual and John managed them with little discomfort. It wasn't until he had to climb stairs in the last building that he listened to the complaints from his thighs and decided sitting down on a bench for twenty minutes was the appropriate response. He was also in danger of renaissance overload – this condition, he'd described to Ann, was when you have seen so many works of art, dark churches, and museums that your mind blends them into one bland cultural blob.

But he relaxed sitting on the bench. He was not entirely happy with how the Jones problem had been solved, but the more he thought about it the more he began to accept it. The fact it had been solved seemed to relieve him of some vague sense of responsibility. He also thought Auntie Olly would be pleased to know her killers had not escaped justice.

He'd been concerned that he had not spent enough time with his daughter, Laura, and her boyfriend Davide, but when he apologized to her for this it seemed that Laura thought they had struck the right balance between too much togetherness, and too much independence. He told her about finding out where Jones lived and the subsequent events of trying to confront him, but he confined it to the version Ella had outlined at breakfast. Laura still had a black-and-white approach to life and lies, and John didn't want her to change. She was in love, content, and there was no point in altering that.

They all enjoyed dinner in Ravenna.

The next day John and Ann flew back to Manchester.

81

Auntie Olly's memorial service at Bryn-y-Maen church was attended by about thirty people. She had lasted long enough to attend the funerals and memorials of her friends, and there were few left who had known her in her better years. The rest of the congregation was made up of John's cousins, their spouses and children, and Olly's distant family.

John had woken that morning to a world covered by a thin coating of late snow that had melted before the service. The grey clouds had been replaced by a clear blue sky, but a cold wind persisted, moaning through the stone walls surrounding the graveyard, challenging the few brave daffodils and crocuses that were reaching out of the grass patches around the church.

John placed the small urn containing Olly's ashes into the shallow grave. He retrieved a bar of Cadbury's chocolate (Olly's favorite) from his pocket and placed it on the urn, picked up a trowel and dropped a little soil on top. The other mourners followed suit and filled in the hole.

John looked around to the mountains of Snowdonia, where the snow had yet to melt, and to the glimpse of the Irish Sea he could see to the west. He could hear the bleating of ewes on the hillside and the response from their spring lambs, and wondered if he'd ever be back. Wales had been part of his life, but there was little left to draw him here now. Ann came up to him and put her arm around his waist.

He walked with her to the church-yard gate and shook the hands of people he didn't know, and of those he did. He reminded them of the refreshments he had organized at the nearby Pen-y-Bryn pub.

For a few seconds he didn't recognize the last person to leave who approached him and shook his hand.

"Detective Inspector Johnson! I didn't know you'd be here," said John.

"I saw the notice in the newspaper and I thought this might be the best place to talk to you. I wasn't sure I could catch you otherwise."

"Well, it's good to see you here."

Johnson was mildly apologetic and said, "I don't usually attend these services. Sometimes the police presence isn't welcome."

"No, it's good to see you," said Ann and John nodded.

"I thought I would update you on what has been happening here. We are sure the man who poisoned your Aunt was the man who was killed in the explosion at the pub near Betwys-y-Coed. It looks like he was also responsible for other murders. There will be an inquest on your Aunt's death, but that may take another month before it happens. You don't have to be there."

"Thanks for the information," said John. "What happened to the policemen who were injured by that man?"

"I think they'll all be OK. Detective Inspector Jared is out of intensive care and may be out of commission for a few weeks. I just hope he'll be able to return to police work. The Assistant Chief, Owen, has tried to come back, but has been ordered to stay away for another couple of weeks, so things are basically returning to normal."

"That's good to hear," said John, involuntarily shivering wondering how long the conversation would last in the cold wind.

Johnson picked up on this and said, "I don't want to keep you. It's cold, but can you tell me what happened in Italy? I have tried to get information from our security services, but they seem unwilling to let me know what went on."

John had prepared himself for this question and as briefly as possible related the tale he'd agreed on with Stefan and Ella. Johnson had heard nothing since he had passed on John's message and asked a little more about Stefan and Ella.

John said, "They told me they operated a personal security business out of Paris. They were interested in Jones because Ella's brother had been killed in Istanbul and they thought he was responsible."

"What was the name of their company?" asked Johnson.

410

John looked at Ann for help and she replied, "I think it was SIGNAK."

"S-I-G-N-A-K?"

"I believe so."

"So, you must have been disappointed he got away?"

"We were, and so were Stefan and Ella."

"So, what are your plans now?" asked Johnson.

"In the short term we are going to the Pen-y-Bryn pub to have a bite to eat. You are very welcome to join us," said John.

"I'd love to but I'm on duty today and have paperwork which is waiting for me."

"I understand that," said John. "And tomorrow we'll tidy up Auntie Olly's house, put it on the market and we leave here in three days time."

"Back to America?"

"Yes, and no more travelling for a while. We plan on staying close to home for the rest of the year."

"Well, thank you for your help with this. I hope you have a pleasant flight back to the US."

Johnson shook their hands and walked briskly to a red Ford Focus.

Ann and John waved briefly as he drove by then hurried to their own car, started it, turned up the heat and drove away,

82

John held his umbrella against the wind and rain, slipped the letters and packet into the pocket of his anorak, closed the mailbox and walked back to the house.

It was December 1st. It had been raining for the last week, and windy for the last two. It was Port Orchard, Washington State, in winter, and if not exactly loving it, John was accepting it.

Since they'd returned to the USA in March they'd made the most of a Pacific North West summer. They'd climbed peaks in the Olympic Mountains, kayaked on Hood Canal, wandered the Seattle Art Museum and improved their Pickle-ball skills to the point where they even won an occasional game. They'd slimmed down, flattened up, tightened up, and had physically recovered from the abuse they'd suffered earlier in the year at the hands of Gareth. Mentally, they still had short flashbacks and dreams of their captivity, but these were fading and overall they were content – they had each other.

John took off his shoes, hung up his wet clothing and sat down at the kitchen table. Ann placed a cup of coffee in front of him and returned to chopping vegetables. He reached for a kitchen knife and opened the first envelope. It was post-marked from Italy and it was from Laura, his daughter.

He scanned it quickly and announced to Ann, "It's from Laura. She says she and Davide getting engaged and we can see the details on Facebook. What details would that be?"

"I don't know. It's probably a photo of a hand with a ring. Why didn't she just email us or call us?"

"I don't know either. Let me read it a little more."

There was silence as John finished the letter and said, "She says she wrote me a letter because she felt it was a formal way of letting me know, and she wasn't going to post it on Facebook for…" he looked at his watch for the date, "… one more day. Didn't she know that her fiancé was supposed to call me and ask my permission?"

"You didn't call my father."

"I would have done … if he hadn't been dead."

"Huh! Just be lucky she told you in the first place."

"I suppose so. I'll call her tomorrow. It's already 11:00 pm there."

"What else have you got?" Ann asked, pointing with her knife at the pile.

"Mostly junk," he sorted through the pile, "and this."

He held up a thick packet and looked at the stamp and customs sticker which stated 'travel guide'. "Another international communication. This one's from France."

He opened the packet. Inside was a book wrapped in plastic, and a letter. He ignored the book and opened the letter.

"It's from Ella," he said, surprised.

"Oh, good. Why don't you read it to me."

"OK."

November 22nd.

Dear Ann and John,

When we last met I promised I would keep you up to date on any news of Jones, and until last week we had none, but a package arrived exactly a week ago and we are now acting on it.

The package was sent from Germany and contained a letter from Ali.

In the letter he said he took Jones to a place where he could keep him for a while and ask him questions. He doesn't say so, but that could be his place in Turkey.

Ali also found out about his finances. He said he didn't have to use any coercion or 'enhanced interrogation techniques' like Americans would (his words, not mine) and so he was able to identify the relatives of twelve victims of the Hand of Hamsa. You, the security service man who was killed in the restaurant, and I, are three of them.

Ali was surprised to find how much money was in the accounts and how easy it was to get hold of. He thought reparations should be made to each victim's relatives. He has divided it this way:

Each victim's family will receive 1% of the money
For expenses SIGNAK and Ali will receive another 1%.
30% of the money will go to funding for girls' education in a
refugee camp in Jordan and the rest will go to causes Ali is
interested in supporting. I hope this is something like the World
Wildlife Fund, but I have no idea what he means by that. He said
he plans to name the school in the refugee camp after me, so I
am pleased I have a name which is so common that I hope no one
will associate it with me.

He also said no harm will come to Jones who will be left with
1% too, if, or when, he gets out of prison. I couldn't understand
that, but there was an oblique reference to watching the British
newspapers in the next few weeks, and he says Jones will only get
the money if he is released, and if he says he has no knowledge of
the identity of his captors.
I hope you enjoy the enclosed book.

Ella

PS. On a more personal note I am working less and painting
more. I have been taking art classes and they're fun. Stefan and I
are enjoying life together and I have a goal to get him to work a
little less. Please don't imagine I am pregnant and knitting baby
clothes – that isn't me, but who knows?
I hope to see you for dinner next time you are in Paris.

John finished the letter and picked up the book.
"Should I open it?" he asked Ann?
"Why not?"
John unwrapped the book and opened it.
There was no text. The middle of the book had been carved
out and replaced with hundred-Euro notes. By the time John had
counted them his coffee was cold.
"I make it five hundred," he said.

"What? That's fifty thousand dollars! Oh,no, Euros," said Ann. "That's more like … fifty-five thousand dollars!"

"Wow!"

"And that's 1% so that means the total is … five million!"

"Crime must pay."

"What are we going to do with it?"

"Well, it would buy a lot of gelatos," said John.

"But, it's blood money really, isn't it?" asked Ann.

"Well, I suppose it is."

They both looked at the money.

"I never thought receiving a pile of money could be so difficult," said John.

"I know. What are we going to do with it?"

"Well, it is a form of compensation for Auntie Olly's death, but we don't really need the money. On the other hand it would be nice to spend a little on ourselves."

"And give the rest away?" asked Ann.

"Yes, but I'm not sure who we could give it to, especially since it's in Euros."

"We'll have to think that one through."

They stared at the money and wondered what to do with it. John put his coffee in the microwave to re-heat and then decided to place the money back in the book. He took the book to the bedroom, hid it at the back of his sock drawer and returned to the kitchen.

"Where did you put it?"

"I can't tell you."

"At the back of your sock drawer?"

"Damn! You've seen through me, and I thought I was being so clever."

"You were. No self-respecting thief would look there – it's far too obvious."

"I think we should just get on with our lives and think about it over the next month or two. It's winter and we're not going anywhere for a while."

Ann agreed, "That sounds reasonable. What are you going to do the rest of the day?"

"I think I'll write back to Ella and thank her for forwarding the gift. She may have ideas of how to spend the money. Maybe I could write it in French." He wandered off to his computer.

Ann looked skeptical, but kept her thoughts to herself.

83

It was also raining in London where Georgina Southport was chairing a meeting.

She said, in a quiet voice, "I want your resignation letter on my desk by the time I get back from lunch, and I want you gone too. If I find you in the building after that time I will have you arrested and you can suffer the consequences."

"You can't do this to me," the man sneered. "You have no proof."

"You did this to yourself, not us, and we can get rid of you. We are not going to use the methods you like to use, and you will go," Georgina emphasized.

The man looked at the three-person panel facing him and seemed to make a decision.

He snarled, "I want my pension and the severance package."

"If it were up to me," another of the panel spoke, "you would get neither. You will get the pension, but no severance."

The man opened his mouth to object, but thought better of it. He stood, strode to the door and slammed it as he left.

Georgina turned to her right and to her left and thanked her colleagues.

"Georgina, I have to ask. Do we have enough evidence to get rid of him like this?" asked the man on her left.

"I'm not sure. I was hoping he wouldn't resist too much, but he doesn't know how much we know. I'm still not sure of the level of his interactions with the man we now know as Jones. I hope Jones was just a contact who could arrange things for him, but he was running his own little hit squad, in the name of queen and country, with none of us knowing. You just can't do that. I hope Jones was not blackmailing him. We have no proof he was, but I wonder if he was the one who arranged for whoever helped Jones to get away in Italy. He certainly did his best to obstruct my efforts to help there."

"Any chance of finding Jones?" asked the other colleague.

"There hasn't been any sight of sign of him since he was last seen in Italy."

"So, he got clean away?"

"Apparently, but we can always hope he'll turn up some day and we can ask him a few questions."

"That would be nice," said the colleague. "I'd like to find out what really happened in … where was it?"

"Santarcangelo," said Georgina. "As you say, that would be nice."

Georgina knew exactly what had happened in Santarcangelo. She had talked to Ella in a quiet Paris restaurant over six months ago. There she'd been told plan B had been successful.

However, it had taken her this long to get rid of a senior colleague who had acted as though he was living in a Cold War, James Bond novel. As far as she could ascertain the senior colleague and Burns had been working independently, with no knowledge of the other's involvement.

But she was tired – maybe she'd think about retiring next year, or maybe the year after.

Of course, if Jones did turn up they might learn a lot more, but that seemed unlikely.

The British Coast Guard had been watching the small boat for the previous hour. They'd received an anonymous tip that it contained illegal immigrants and since it was approaching the English shore, just off the town of Brighton, they had notified the police. A reporter from the Brighton and Hove Independent was waiting on the promenade, and was a little surprised to see he was accompanied by one of his colleagues from a national newspaper, The Guardian, as well as a film crew from the local BBC station.

The boat was about eighteen feet long and looked to be an old, less-than-immaculate, cabin cruiser. There was no one visible at the helm and the boat was making slow progress directly towards the beach. A handful of onlookers watched it continue straight onto the beach where it was stopped by sand

and gravel. An enterprising youth hauled himself onto the boat and stopped the outboard motor which had been churning the water and sand behind the boat. He was shooed off by the police who kept the growing crowd back.

A police constable climbed aboard, opened the door to the cabin and disappeared inside.

At the press conference that evening the Chief Constable for the county of Surrey said they had only found one person inside and he appeared to be a British citizen. He didn't mention the passports from other countries which were on board – all bearing a likeness to the single passenger.

He also stated that accompanying the man were approximately twenty kilos of a substance which were still being tested. It was marijuana, but the Chief Constable thought it better if he withheld some details.

The man on board had been evaluated at a local hospital and released. The Chief Constable didn't mention that the man had been restrained by two sets of handcuffs attached to the boat's grab rails, and had seemed intoxicated when first found. He did mention the outstanding warrant for his arrest, on a charge of arson, issued by the Metropolitan Police.

He didn't say that papers accompanying the man had been seconded by the security services. He stone-walled any further questions and left the podium.

The next day the story made national news and the BBC aired a short video of the man being removed from the boat and posted it on their news website. They'd used a drone for more dramatic coverage, and at one point they zoomed in for a close-up of the passenger.

It wasn't easy to see his face, but to John, browsing on his computer five thousand miles away in Washington State, there was no mistaking who it was.

Jones had made it back to England.

421

SILLY JOKE BOOK

The first silly book Stoo Hample wrote and illustrated was called *The Silly Book*. Since then he has written and drawn many more books for children, including *Children's Letters to God*. Stoo Hample also writes plays, and is the artist of 'Inside Woody Allen', a syndicated comic strip based on the famous film director, writer, and actor Woody Allen. Mr. Hample lives in New York City with his wife and their infant son.

Stoo Hample

SILLY JOKE BOOK

Scholastic

Scholastic Publications Ltd
in association with Pan Books Ltd

this one is for
Martha and for Zachary

First published 1978 by Delacorte Press
This edition published 1980 by Pan Books Ltd,
Cavaye Place, London SW10 9PG
9 8 7
Scholastic Publications edition first published 1980
© Naomi-Stuart 1978
ISBN 0 330 26054 5
Printed and bound in Great Britain by
Richard Clay (The Chaucer Press) Ltd, Bungay, Suffolk

SILLY QUESTION
Why do elephants have trunks?

SILLY ANSWER
Because they would look
silly carrying suitcases.

6

A boy with an elephant on his head
went to see a doctor.

The doctor said,
"Wow! You really need help."

"You said it," the elephant cried,
"get this kid out from under me!"

7

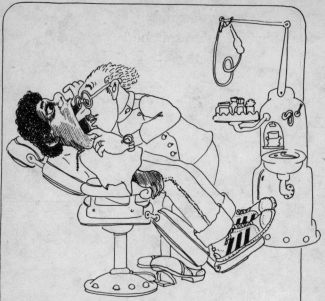

A boy went to see the dentist.

"My word," cried the dentist,
"you have the biggest cavity
I've ever seen! Ever seen! Ever seen!"

"Well," said the boy,
"you don't have to repeat yourself!"

"I didn't," the dentist replied.
"That was the echo!"

9

A dentist's phone rang.
The lady on the other end was very angry.
"You charged £40 to take out
my little boy's tooth,"
she cried. "Isn't it £10 anymore?"
"Yes," said the dentist,
"but your son screamed so loud, he scared
three patients out of my waiting room!"

Janie's mother saw her snooping around in the kitchen. "What are you looking for, dear?"

Janie jumped with surprise. "Um...*nothing*," she replied.

"Good," said her mother. "You'll find it in the jar where the cookies were."

THE SILLY PHOTOGRAPHER

Did you hear about the photographer who was so silly he saved burnt-out light bulbs to use in his darkroom?

"How do you like my new swimming pool?"
a man asked the girl next door.
"Very nice," the girl replied,
"but why isn't there any water in it?"
"Because," said the man,
"I don't know how to swim."

15

A woman came running
out of her house.
"Am I too late
for the garbage?"
she cried.

16

"No, lady,"
said the driver,
"jump right in!"

17

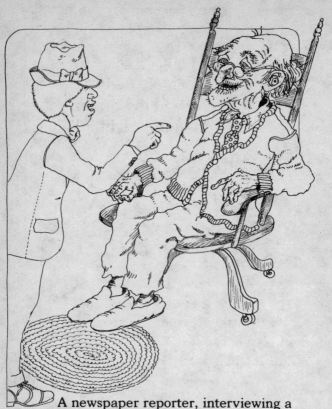

A newspaper reporter, interviewing a man who had reached his 99th birthday, said, "I certainly hope I can return next year and help you celebrate your 100th birthday."

"Can't see why not, young feller," the old-timer replied. "You look healthy enough to me!"

"I beg your pardon,"
said the man when he returned
to his seat in the theatre,
"but did I step on your toe when I
left?"

"You certainly did!"
the woman in the next seat
replied angrily.
"Good," said the man.
"That means I'm in the right row!"

19

20

21

"I had a scary dream last night.
I dreamed I was standing in
New York harbour holding a torch."

"What's so scary about that?"

"I'll tell you what's scary about it,
people were looking out
through the windows in my head."

23

I have a canary at home
who can do something I can't.
Who knows what?

Take a bath
in a teacup?

27

Molly, how does it happen,
do you suppose,
that you have exactly
the same answers as Katie
on the math test?

We used
the same
pencil.

David,
you missed school yesterday,
didn't you?

No,
Mrs. Lowry,
not a bit.

30

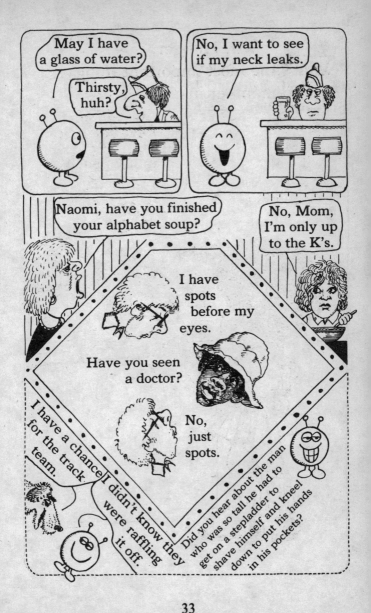

33

34

35

An angry woman went into a bake shop. "I sent my son to your store this morning to buy two pounds of cookies," she said. "When he brought them home and I weighed them, I found that they weighed only one pound.

"I suggest you check your scale!"

"Madam," said the baker, "I suggest you weigh your son!"

Zachary and Naomi were leaving the restaurant. They went up to the cashier and Zachary paid his bill.

But Naomi took out a pad and pencil, wrote the number I004I80 on a page, tore it out and handed it to the cashier.

She looked at the number and let Naomi pass without having to pay.

Why didn't the cashier ask Naomi for any money?

ANSWER

The number Naomi wrote — I004I80 — was in code and meant, "I owe nothing, for I ate nothing."

37

Alex went into a candy store with a friend. He asked for ten pence worth of green jelly beans.

The storekeeper climbed a tall ladder and had a very hard time finding the jar of green jelly beans.

When he finally balanced on the ladder and found the jar, he asked the friend, "Do you want the same thing?"

"No," said the friend.

38

The storekeeper climbed down the ladder with great difficulty, holding Alex's order of green jelly beans.

When he got to the bottom, he said to the second boy, "Now, what do *you* want?"

The boy said, "I only want *three* pence worth of green jelly beans!"

39

41

A small boy went into a country store and put a large jug on the counter.

"May I please have 50 pence worth of molasses?" he asked the storekeeper.

When the jug was filled, the boy picked it up and started out the door.

"Haven't you forgotten something?" said the storekeeper. "I don't think so," replied the boy.

42

"Where is the money to pay for the molasses?" called the storekeeper.

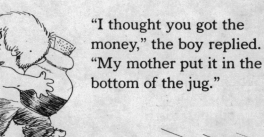

"I thought you got the money," the boy replied. "My mother put it in the bottom of the jug."

A boy walked into a pet store
and asked for some birdseed.

"What kind of birds do you have?"
asked the clerk.

"I don't have any,"
the boy replied,
"but I want to grow some."

A motorcycle cop caught up with a man who was driving the wrong way on a one-way street. "Where do you think you're going?" he demanded.

"I'm not sure," said the wrong-way driver, "but I must be late – everybody is coming back!"

48

49

The door to a pony express office
swung open. A cowboy rushed out,
took a running jump,
and landed in the street.

"What's the matter with you, pardner?"
asked a bystander.
"Did they kick you out,
or are you just plain crazy?"

"Neither," answered the cowboy,
"but I shore would like t'git my hands
on the guy who moved my horse!"

52

SILLY RIDDLE

A lady was sitting in a diner having lunch when a man came in and ordered apple pie with peach ice cream and a lime soda. The lady knew at once that he was a sailor. How did she know?

ANSWER

He was wearing a sailor suit.

Egg White. Get the yolk?

Then there was the guy who got on his tractor backward and unplowed four acres of land!

BOB: "Did you hear about the guy who met the girl in the revolving door?" JANE: "No, what happened?" BOB: "He's been going around with her ever since!"

I don't know.

Who was Snow White's brother?

Bet you ten pence I can stay under water for five minutes.

Bet you can't.

53

Hey, waiter,
how much longer
do I have to
go on waiting?

You're just
sitting there.
I'm waiting!

Waiter, how do you serve shrimps here?

We bend down.

57

Waiter, this food
isn't fit for a pig!

All right.

I'll go get you
some that is.

Waiter, do you have frogs' legs?

Yes.

Good, then hop into the kitchen and get me a bologna sandwich.

Waiter, I'll have a pepperburger medium rare on toasted sesame raisin bread with peanut butter and grapes, a boiled potato out of the skin and topped with two pickles and a cherry, a side order of artichoke without the heart, and a chocolate-covered fried egg.

Do you have all that?

Rosie, gimme a number 8!

Waiter, there's an ant in my pudding!

Quiet... everybody will want one.

What happened
to the other claw
on this lobster?

He lost it
in a fight.

Then take this back
and bring me the *winner*!

MORE SILLY RIDDLES

What's green and squishy and lives under the sea?

An avocado with an Aqualung.

How many feet in a yard?

It depends on how many people are standing in it.

What has antlers and eats cheese?

Mickey Moose.

A SILLY DEFINITION

Mushroom—The place where they keep the food for the school cafeteria.

65

67

69

How is a chicken like a grape?

I don't know.

They're both purple.
Except for the chicken.

Why don't you ever see chickens in the zoo?

Because they can't afford the admission?

73

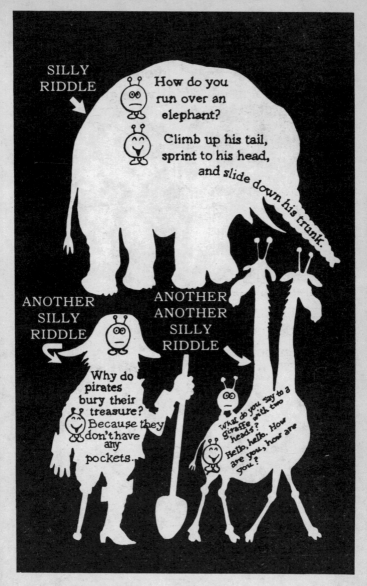

You've been locked in the dungeon under the castle of the evil king, Charles the Rotten.

There are two doors by which you could escape. One leads to safety. The other leads directly to the king's den of monsters!

There are also two royal parrots in the dungeon. One always tells the truth, and the other always lies.

You don't know which door leads to safety. Or which parrot tells the truth. You can only ask one parrot one question.

What is the question you should ask?

ANSWER

Ask either parrot which door the other parrot would tell you to go out. Since one parrot tells the truth and the other lies, they would both give the same answer: "the monster den." Go out the *other* door.

79

The safari guide came
running out of the jungle
to the hunter's tent. "I just
spotted a leopard," he cried. "You
can't fool me," replied the hunter,
"they're born that way."

"How did you get this skillet so clean?"
asked the scoutmaster.

"Easy," said the scout,
"I just scrubbed it with an extra
hamburger left over from dinner."

Once there was a man who was holding a frog in his hands. A lady said to him, "Where are you going with that frog?" The man said, "I'm taking him to the zoo."

The next day the lady saw the man still holding the frog. "I thought you took the frog to the zoo," she said. "I did take him to the zoo yesterday," the man replied. "Today I'm taking him to the movies!"

TWO SILLY JOKES ABOUT BRICKS
(One with two bricks and one with one brick)

How come you're carrying only two bricks while the other guys are carrying four?

I guess they're too lazy to make two trips!

How is an elephant like a brick?

brick

elephant

ANSWER
Neither one can climb trees.

SILLY QUESTION

What's tan on the inside and
red and gold on the outside?

SILLY ANSWER

No, ma'am,
only once.

SILLY RIDDLE

What seven letters did the little girl
say when she opened the refrigerator
and found there was nothing in it?

SILLY ANSWER

O, ICURMT.

92

93

LAST SILLY QUESTION

How do you know
when you've finished a book?

LAST SILLY ANSWER

When every page is read.